Please return/renew this item by the
last date shown to avoid a charge.
Books may also be renewed by phone
and Internet. May not be renewed if
required by another reader.

www.libraries.barnet.gov.uk

TO WALK ALONE
IN THE CROWD

A NOTE ABOUT THE TRANSLATOR
Guillermo Bleichmar holds a BA in English literature from Columbia University and a PhD in comparative literature from Harvard University. He teaches liberal arts at St. John's College in Santa Fe, New Mexico.

TO WALK ALONE IN THE CROWD

ANTONIO MUÑOZ MOLINA

Translated from the Spanish by Guillermo Bleichmar

TUSKAR ROCK PRESS

First published in Great Britain in 2021 by
Tuskar Rock Press,
an imprint of Profile Books Ltd
29 Cloth Fair
London
EC1A 7JQ

www.serpentstail.com

Originally published in Spanish in 2018 by Editorial Planeta, Spain,
as *Un andar solitario entre la gente*
First published in English the United States of America by Farrar, Straus and Giroux

Designed by Gretchen Achilles

1 3 5 7 9 10 8 6 4 2

Printed and bound in Great Britain by
Clays Ltd, Elcograf S.p.A.

A CIP catalogue record for this book is available from the British Library.

ISBN 978 1 78816 194 7
eISBN 978 1 78283 521 9

Um andar solitário entre a gente.

—LUÍS DE CAMÕES

Un andar solitario entre la gente.

—FRANCISCO DE QUEVEDO

A book should not be planned out beforehand, but as one writes it will form itself, subject to the constant emotional promptings of one's personality.

—JAMES JOYCE

I.

OFFICE OF
LOST MOMENTS

LISTEN TO THE SOUNDS OF LIFE. I am all ears. I listen with my eyes. I hear what I see on advertisements, headlines, posters, signs. I move through a city of voices and words. Voices that set the air in motion and pass through my inner ear to reach the brain transformed into electrical pulses; words that I hear in passing, perhaps if someone stands beside me talking on their phone, or that I read no matter where I turn, on every surface, every screen. Printed words reach me like spoken sounds, like the notes on a musical score; sometimes it is hard to unscramble words that are spoken simultaneously, or to infer those I can't quite hear because they're whisked away or lost in a louder noise. The varied shapes of letters give rise to a ceaseless visual polyphony. I am a tape recorder, switched on and hidden away inside the futuristic phone of a 1960s spy, the iPhone in my pocket. I am the camera that Christopher Isherwood wanted to be in Berlin, a gaze that must not be distracted by even the merest blink. The woods have ears, reads the title of a drawing by Bosch. The fields have eyes. Inside a dark, hollow tree glow the yellow eyes of an owl. A pair of large ears dangle from a burly tree as from an elephant, nearly grazing the ground. One of Carmen Calvo's sculptures is an old wooden door studded with glass eyes. The doors have eyes. The walls have ears. Electrical outlets can hear what we say, according to Ramón Gómez de la Serna.

PERFECTION MAY BE CLOSER THAN YOU THINK. I go out as soon as it gets dark. It's the late dusk of the first night of summer. I hear the rustle of trees and ivy from neighborhood gardens. I hear the voices of people I can't see, eating outdoors on the other side of fences topped with creeping vine or mock orange, sheltered from the street by thick cypress hedges. The sky is dark blue at the top and light blue on the horizon where the rooftops and chimneys stand in silhouette as on a garish diorama. I don't want to know anything about the world, I only want to be aware of what reaches my eyes and ears at this very moment, nothing else. The street is so quiet that I can hear my footsteps. The rumble of traffic is far away. In the soft breeze I can hear the rustle of leaves on a fig tree and the slow, swaying sound of the high crown of a sycamore, like the sound of the sea. I hear the whistling of swallows flitting through the air in acrobatic flight. One of them, swooping to catch an insect, touched the surface of a garden pond so pristinely that it didn't cause the slightest ripple. I hear the clicking of bats finding their way through the air by echolocation. Many more vibrations than my crude human ears can detect are rippling simultaneously through the air at this very moment, a thick web of radio signals spreading everywhere, carrying all the cell phone conversations taking place right now across the city. I want to be all eyes and ears, like Argos in the ancient myth, a human body covered in bulging eyeballs and blinking eyelids, or perhaps in the bare, lidless eyes on Carmen Calvo's door. I could be a Marvel superhero, the Eye-Man, or a monster in a 1950s science-fiction film. I could be a random stranger or the Invisible Man, preferably the one in the James Whale movie rather than in the novel by H. G. Wells. It is the film, more than the book, that really attains the height of poetry.

TECHNOLOGY APPLIED TO LIFE. I read every word that meets my eyes as I walk by. Fire Department Only. Premises Under Video Surveillance. We Pay Cash for Your Car. There is a kind of beauty, an effortless fruition in the gradual approach of night. The word *Libre*, lit in bright green on the windshield of a taxi, floats above the darkened street as if clipped and pasted on a black background or a page in a photo album. A glaring, empty bus rushes from the mouth of a tunnel like a ghostly galleon in the high seas. Its entire side is taken up by a large ad for gazpacho. Enjoy the taste of summer now. Words fall into a rhythmic sequence. We buy silver. We buy gold. We buy silver and gold. Donate blood. We buy gold. At every bus stop there is a glowing panel advertising a new film. *Gods of Egypt: The Battle for Eternity Begins. Teenage Mutant Ninja Turtles: Out of the Shadows.* There are invitations, commands, prohibitions that I never noticed when I walked down this street before. Do not leave plastic containers outside the trash bin. No pedestrian traffic. Enjoy our cocktails. Celebrate your event with us. Long before you walk past the sidewalk tables outside a bar you are met by a murmuring choir of voices, tinkling glasses, the sound of silverware and china. I go through the thicket of voices and smells without stopping. Roast meat, animal fat, fried fumes, shrimp-shells, cigarette smoke. Try our specialties, lamb cutlets, grilled meats. Try our lobster rice. The lavish verbal succulence of the lettering on the signs is not unlike the splendor of a Dutch still life. Croquettes. T-BONE STEAK. *Gambas al ajillo. Callos a la madrileña.* CHEESES. Eggplant and gazpacho. Grilled sea bass. Tuna fritters. Paella. Entrecôte. On a June night, the sidewalks of Madrid have a languorous seaside calm like a beach filled with families on holiday. As I drift along, I realize this is the last night I will live in this neighborhood where I have spent so many years. A man and a woman, white-haired but youthful, press their faces together and smile in the window of a store that sells hearing aids. Old people in advertisements smile with a certain optimism. Young people laugh and laugh, opening their mouths wide and showing their gums and tongues. I never noticed this particular sign before, its invitation or command, the white letters on a blue background, the joy of retirees wearing invisible earbuds: Be All Ears. Hear the genuine sounds of life.

GO AS FAR AS YOU CHOOSE. I close my eyes so that the sounds can reach me more clearly. On the Metro I sit down and close my eyes as if I'd fallen asleep. I try to keep them shut all the way from one station to the next. I notice the weight of my eyelids, the faint quivering touch of my eyelashes. When I finally give up and look around, the faces around me are even stranger. There's a book in my satchel but I don't read it. I only read the signs I come across, each in turn, from the moment I hurry down the stairs and push open the swinging door. So many things that I never noticed or that I read without paying conscious attention. Entrance. Shorn of articles and verbs, the phrases become crude robotic indications. *Estación Cobertura Móvil.* Some subway official believes in bilingualism and in literal translations: Station Coverage Mobile. No smoking anywhere on the subway system. Insert ticket. This is a Public Announcement from the Metro de Madrid. Don't forget to take your ticket. A group of grinning, multiethnic, multinational youths in an advertisement. Join the largest design network in the world. One of them is Asian. He's wearing glasses and looks at the camera. Another is Black, with a pierced nose and his arm around the shoulders of a girl who is clearly Spanish. Turn this summer into something unforgettable. Use it or lose it. Exclusive opportunities for those who act quickly. Going down the escalator I close my eyes though not completely. For your own safety, hold the handrail. An emergency intercom addresses me with an almost intimate suggestion: Use me when you need me. The city speaks the language of desire. Instead of instantly turning to my phone while I wait on the platform, or searching for something else to read, I stay on my feet and squint at nothing for a few moments. "Use Me" was the title of a song I used to like many years ago. You are being filmed. Over a thousand cameras are watching over your safety. At each step there's a new instruction or command. Break only in case of emergency. Don't be afraid to use me, the song said. Commanding voices join the written injunctions. Next train approaching the station. The lack of an article or even a verb heightens the sense of imminence. This is a public announcement. The ground shakes a little as the train approaches. Do not enter or exit subway cars after the signal sounds. I look at people's faces and listen to their voices. I am all ears. I move closer to a man who is talking on his phone. Nearly every person in the subway car is absorbed in a cell phone screen. A tall, serious girl is reading a Paulo Coelho book. Her choice in literature is a discredit to her beauty. "I'll tell you everything," someone says, right behind me. He leans his head against the glass and lowers his voice, so I can no longer hear him over the automated message that begins to announce the next station. "All right, perfect, okay, all right. See you soon."

PARROT COULD BE KEY WITNESS IN MURDER CASE. Wearily, a woman turns the pages of a free newspaper. Beyoncé unveils outfits for upcoming tour. The train is moving more slowly and more quietly and I am better able to hear the male voice talking on the phone behind me. He's so close to me that I have no idea what he looks like, this man who now begins to laugh. "His mother is eighty-seven and she just went to the dentist to get braces." I have Montaigne in my backpack but I don't take the book out; I don't even look for a seat. I am alert, waiting for whatever new instructions will be addressed to me in an imperious or enticing tone. Let passion be your guide. This seat reserved for people with disabilities. Beneath the noise of the train there is a murmur of voices, almost all of them talking on the phone. "You have no idea how many years I've lived in England." The voices of people I'm not able to see seem especially near. "Neither you nor your siblings should sign anything until you're sure." A screen hangs from the ceiling. A young man with a shaved head and a black beard moves his lips and the words appear below. I am Gay. Then another man, younger, beardless, wearing eyeliner and also moving his lips. I am Trans. The face of the man with the shaved head appears again. They flicker back and forth so quickly that their features superimpose. I am me. And then a third face. I could be you. Live your difference. Then a purple screen. Another invitation. Another command. Someone must have measured the minimum time required for the faces not to become indistinguishable. A woman is speaking softly, very close to my ear, in a tone of warning or censure. "He says he's changed, that he wants to come back. But it'll all depend on how he behaves." I try to inscribe in my memory the phrases I hear, the bits and pieces of conversation. Words flow together, blurring and disappearing as soon as I hear them. Forget-It-Fast, says an ad, though I'm not sure what it's selling. Words are drowned by the noise of the train or by announcements on the intercom. "We'll see if he's really changed. I don't even believe twenty percent of what he says." Emergency hammer. I read everything, even the headlines on the pages of the free newspaper that the first woman holds right up to my face.

POLICE WILL KNOW WHEN YOU USE YOUR CELL PHONE EVEN WHEN THEY CAN'T SEE YOU. Salamanca man beheaded by eighteen-year-old son. Emergency exit. The great arctic adventure. I barely notice the faces, just the voices and the printed words. A ringtone. The sharp trill of a text message. Everyone is connected to something or someone who is somewhere else. "I'm on the subway. Just in case we get cut off." When the train comes to a stop, the doors open in front of an advertisement that reaches up to the curved ceiling of the station. The best family holidays ever. First-time ocean dives. Find a new landscape at every turn. A group of young people is jumping off a cliff joyfully into the sea. Some are about to plunge fearlessly and others are already floating against a deep blue. The fun of summer can be yours. Click for incredible prices. Some reservations can't wait. Book now. Find out more. Find out now. Buy it now. Try it now. All the different messages seem to come from the same voice, the same source, and to be addressed to the same person: me, you. It's me, but it could be you. You, yes, you, says a lottery ad, as if pointing a finger to single you out in the crowd, a face that can see you and has chosen you from a TV monitor. You can be a millionaire. Master the elements with your fingertips. Find the perfect class for you. The woman who was reading the newspaper left it on the seat when she got off the subway, a mess of crumpled sheets. Join the leading brand in hybrid technology.

TRACK YOUR DNA. Get there sooner. Let nothing stop you. Don't wait until you're down. In just a few years, printed newspapers have lost all their material dignity. Madrid sets a world record in the hunt for Pokémon. They crumple and fall apart immediately, squalid and superfluous, especially now, in summer. An entire page can be scanned as quickly as a screen. Enjoy a fabulous gourmet experience by the sea. I close my eyes again to hear more clearly as I let myself be carried along by the train's motion. The city makes a thousand simultaneous promises. Choose everything. Enjoy it whenever and wherever you like. One need not choose a particular thing anymore and forego what was not chosen. Save while you spend. No regrets. Lose weight by eating. Create your custom trip today. I have an old, irresistible addiction to cheap newsprint and the smell of ink. Cannibalistic fight between hammerhead and tiger shark videotaped at sea by tuna fishermen. We move heaven and earth to bring you the best.

TAKE A BIT OF OUR TASTE WITH YOU. First, all of a sudden, it was that word, REMEMBER, up on a traffic sign on a street I used to walk down every day, but now detached from its context by a chance shift in my attention which up until the prior instant had been busy with other things—not the things around me but the things within me—like a sleepwalker suddenly awakened by that visual knell, RECUERDE, forcing me to open my eyes and ears even though I had seen the sign many times before and though it is in fact quite common, a metal triangle with a pair of simple black silhouettes alerting drivers to a pedestrian crossing outside a school. Remember *what*, I suddenly wonder. Who is asking or ordering me to remember; what inaudible, printed voice is forcing me to look at something I have seen all my life but that I now perceive as if for the first time, on this sidewalk, this corner, this crossing, the triangle high up on a metal post with its powerful and simple color combination: red along the edge, white on the inside, black for the silhouettes and for the single word in large block letters. Two children holding hands and carrying satchels, a pair of antique children without backpacks, a boy and a girl who seem in a hurry, as if they were about to break into a run. I look more closely and they are indeed running. The satchels in their hands are nearly flying behind them. Children out of a fairytale, brother and sister, abandoned by their parents and lost in the woods; or children fleeing an airstrike on their way home from school in Aleppo.

ISN'T DISCOVERING NEW THINGS WHAT KEEPS YOU ALIVE? You can tell it's an old-fashioned sign because it employs the polite form of address, *recuerde*, in a city where every other voice addresses you informally.

In saying "*recuerde*," it also brings to mind the first word of the first verse of Jorge Manrique's *Coplas* on his father's death: "*recuerde el alma dormida*," let the sleeping soul recall, which is in fact an appeal to the soul to awaken rather than to remember. My eyes felt suddenly as though they'd opened wider, my ears too, as when they pop from a change in pressure, "*avive el seso y despierte*." And I began to notice other things as well, momentarily forgetting the path I was on and the darkness seething in my brain: I saw a handwritten sign taped to a lamppost, "Reliable person available for house-work and eldercare"; I saw a picture of a tanned blonde in a white swimsuit in the window of a drugstore, "This summer, lose weight when you eat"; I saw a chalkboard sign outside a bar listing the day's specials, "squid, lentil stew, octopus salad," with a steaming plate of stew skillfully drawn in several colors. A young woman went by just then, talking on the phone, waving her free hand so that a loud jingle of bracelets accompanied the imperious staccato of her steps. A woman transfixed by anger, who had no qualms about speaking loudly. "Mom, she's your daughter. Are you listening, Mom? What do you care what her husband says? There's no reason for you to pay for your daughter's gym. Are you listening, Mom? When have you ever paid for anything for me?"

WHERE YOUR FANTASIES COME TRUE. Ever since that day I've been on a secret mission when I walk down the street. I used to do it intermittently, if I happened to think of it on the way to some other task. Now those other tasks are disappearing. They are just an excuse to go out on the street. I don't choose the quickest routes but those that are likely to be more fruitful. I almost never ride a bicycle and I never take a taxi. I either walk or I ride the subway. All my worries and obsessions are dissolved in ceaseless observation. I am no longer my own thoughts, the things that I imagine or remember, just what meets my eyes and ears, a spy on a secret mission to record and collect it all. I used to check my phone for messages every few minutes. I used to lower my head and scrunch my shoulders, caught in a toxic bubble of gloom, traversing an endless tunnel of mid-morning anxiety. Anxiety was my shadow, my guardian, and my double. It kept up with me no matter how fast I walked. It stood beside me as I went down an escalator, whispering into my ear. It turned the mild dizziness I got from my medication into vertigo and nausea. There was a morbid magnetism to the muzzle of the train when it came from the depths of the tunnel into the station. There was a voice in my ear, inside my head, far back at the nape of the neck, and in my throbbing temples. Now there's no longer one voice but many, a flood of voices, coming always from the outside and as immediate as the things I see, the people going by, the noise of traffic. "*Niña*, two pairs of stockings for three euros, *niña*, look, two pairs, three euros." Expert tailoring alterations and repairs. So that your business can run full speed. How can I have walked down this street so many times without noticing the river of spoken and printed words I was traversing, the racket, the crowds, the clothes in the window of a dingy store. Wool slippers, orthopedic footwear, shoes for sick children. Orthopedic shoes in the window of a store selling prosthetic supplies. Crab, shrimp, huge lobsters in a restaurant's refrigerated display, Gran Cafetería los Crustáceos, and rows of silver fish with toothed, gaping jaws and glassy eyes. Try Our Lobster Rice, twelve euros per person. The nauseating smell of fish at ten in the morning blending with the nauseating smell of tobacco.

WHY GO SOMEWHERE ELSE WHEN EVERYTHING IS HERE. If you listen carefully you can distinguish between the steps of women wearing sandals and those wearing heels. Come to a Gin Masterclass. Your beauty center. Car insurance for just thirty-two euros a month. A gin masterclass sounds like an Intro to Alcoholism. Offers, gifts, proposals, overtures, all of it spreading before you on either side as you walk down the street. Find a new reason to keep smiling. A slim brunette stands on a beach in a bikini, looking off toward the sunset in a man's arms. If you like the Dead Sea, wait till you see what else is here. Come in for a free consultation. Ask us about health insurance. Smoking causes cancer. Insure the future. Come in and discover the ingredients of life. At each step there is a voice, a door that opens into radiant discoveries and revelations. Come in. Find out. Come in and ask. Come in and see how technology is changing sports. I am holding a cell phone, like everyone else around me, but not to my ear. I hold it near my mouth instead so that I can repeat what I read or what I hear, mumbling as I walk, pretending to be busy with some urgent task, perhaps giving someone instructions over the phone or telling them I am coming to the office, to a meeting, while in fact relaying all the secrets I observe. Trust, reliability, peace of mind. NeoLife Age Medicine. NeoLife could be the name of one of those apocalyptic technological foundations dreamed up by Don DeLillo. All safety regulations are mandatory. Welcome to the secret world inside your cell phone.

REDISCOVER ALL THAT A PHONE CAN DO. I switch on the voice recorder to repeat something I've read. I press stop but a moment later I have to switch it on again. Give blood. We buy gold. The signs along the sidewalk gradually fall into a cadence. We buy silver and gold. Give life. An automated chirp at the corner lets you know that it's okay to cross. Through the sound of footsteps, now that the cars have stopped, I can hear the tapping and scraping of a blind person's cane behind me. In the movie *M*, a blind man follows the child murderer at night through the streets of a stage-set city. Oriental massage 24 hours. Asian girls. Fifteen minutes 30€. Twenty minutes 45€. One hour 70€. Complimentary drink. A digital stopwatch is running silently on a nightstand in a room where an Asian girl lies naked. Her heavily made-up eyes glance sideways at the clock in an artificial half-light of clandestine lust. Beautiful and discreet. There's heavy breathing on her face and neck, and in the background she can hear the morning sounds of traffic, the same siren that I hear approaching and that will be recorded by my phone. I'm just an app away. Where time doesn't matter. Discover the pleasures of tantric massage. Take a bit of our taste with you. You make me melt, says an ad for ice cream with a tongue and a pair of red lips licking a chocolate cone. Giovanni Bojanini Skin-Care Clinic. Change anything you want. Centaur Security. There's a painting by Velázquez where a centaur in the background seems to be calmly chatting with St. Anthony in a field next to a river, like neighbors who have just run into each other. Attend a special tasting. As unique as you. Want to eliminate the toxins that build up in your digestive tract? Centaurs and security guards, plastic surgeons and young Asian prostitutes, rows of silver fish and orthopedic shoes and white canes and locksmiths. The voyage is you. Who are they taking away in that ambulance that just went by, the sound of its siren drilling into my ears before it got stuck in traffic up ahead? Internal cleanses from fifteen euros a month. Stop & Go. The city speaks in polyglot voices. Cream and Coffee. More apartments than ever. Shop online. Wedding and reception rentals. Argonaut. The word *Argonaut* is a spark of poetry, like *siren* or *centaur*. Café Prensa Pizza open 24 hours. Luxury apartment for rent, newly renovated. By removing the prepositions they speed up the tempo of language. Magic House Riddles and Mysteries. March to Abolish Zoos and Aquariums. We Love Churros con Chocolate. We catch shooting stars.

EVERYTHING YOU NEED TO ENJOY THE SUMMER. It was the summer of short, light dresses like tunics on a Greek frieze, of shorts cinched at the top of the thigh and flat sandals with thin leather straps and toenails painted in bright colors, red primarily, though also green, blue, or yellow. Your skin, your city. A destination that will reach your heart. Night begins when you decide. It was the summer of bare shoulders and bare legs and a glowing sense of change and newness, as when miniskirts first appeared in the sixties. An overflow, an excess of youth and beauty during those first days of mild weather following a long winter. Choose your next adventure. Young girls walked down the street in straw hats that they wore tilted back on their heads. They talked on the phone or gazed at their screens, completely absorbed, typing swiftly with long, wavering fingers and painted fingernails that pecked on the glass like birds. To help us enjoy the good times.

WHEREVER YOU GO THIS SUMMER. The sharp edges of the present were softened and veiled as if by the sudden retrospective distance of the past. Show your best smile. No sooner did something happen than it seemed to have taken place long ago, as if instantly deprived of its immediacy by a dizzying combination of trivial and terrifying incidents. The sunny days are back. Now is the moment to enjoy the moment. It was the summer of long, straight hair cascading down a tanned back. This is us. Anxiety and nostalgia were twin poles between which I oscillated at every moment. The novelty of the latest fashions seemed to announce their own anachronism in advance. Groups of young people in ads for banks or cell phone companies glowed with the unanimous joy of a cadre of red guards or of peasants and

15

proletarians in the posters of the Chinese Cultural Revolution. *Quiero ser happy.* The midnight air in Madrid was as thick as syrup and all through July the cicadas buzzed into the evening as if it were still the heat of day. The French army was declaring war on Pokémon. The brother of a Pakistani model murdered in an honor killing said he felt no remorse or shame at taking her life. The present tense slipped into the past at the very moment something was written down or said in conversation. Summer, at its height, seemed lit by the glow of the final summer at the end of an era, the one that people would remember soon after with an exaggerated sense of distance, the last summer before a war, an epidemic, or a great disaster. Spain was the seventh most wasteful country in the world in food consumption. Every day the papers said that a new temperature record had been set, that larger swaths of ice were melting in the North Pole and Antarctica. Blue or emerald cliffs crumbled into the sea as solemnly as ancient temples brought down by earthquakes. Don't miss the chance you were waiting for. Fall in love with our bargains before summer is out.

NO MATTER WHAT YOU THIRST FOR. Ocean currents were going to cause huge storms all over the world. Full-page ads, color brochures, and digital screens in the windows of travel agencies offered lavish, adventurous cruises to tropical paradises. The place you were dreaming of is real. This summer, take your best selfies. Many coastal cities to be under water in a hundred years. *Star Wars* characters make an appearance at the Brussels airport. A woman was dying after being attacked by several tigers at a Beijing zoo. It was the summer of Pokémon Go and of suicide attacks. A fashion student in London used a tuft of Alexander McQueen's hair to develop a type of human leather honoring the dead designer. Go as far as you want to. In Kabul, a radical Islamist set off a suicide vest in a crowd, killing ninety people. Pope Francis was urging cloistered nuns not to use the internet to escape the life of contemplation. Mick Jagger was expecting the arrival of his eighth son at age seventy-three. The Unquenchable Fire of Rock-and-Roll's Most Sexually Active Great-Grandfather. Reduced to fewer and fewer pages, and printed on the cheapest possible paper, newspapers literally began to fall apart in their readers' invariably aged hands. They ran opinion pieces on politics and terrorism, or devoted entire pages to horoscopes and Egyptian tarot readings. In Nice, the driver of a truck prayed to God, took a selfie and posted it on Facebook before unleashing terror and mayhem. Ask the Oracle of Ammon whatever you want to know. A German climbed the outside of the tallest building in Barcelona to catch a Pokémon. Your past is buried inside the Great Pyramid. Horror and idiocy flooded the headlines in equal measure. A Dutch man was hospitalized after spending ten days in a Chinese airport waiting for a woman he had met on Facebook.

INVASIVE SPECIES STRIKE BACK. The trivial and the apocalyptic appeared in such close proximity that they sometimes seemed to turn into each other. Porn actress Carla Mai dies after falling from a window at a party where cocaine was being consumed. Man's head found in waste treatment plant. The stories in the paper were like disaster movies, and the movie trailers seemed to be about calamities and horrors that were really taking place. The Zombie Apocalypse hits Mexico City once again. The world unites to save the Earth from an alien invasion and the total extinction of the human race. Cleveland pays five million dollars in compensation for the death of a Black boy shot dead by police while playing with a toy gun. It was the summer that I was without a permanent address for several months. We moved from hotels to borrowed houses or to other cities, carrying backpacks with our laptops and notebooks and dragging behind us a massive suitcase, a whale of a bag that got heavier and took up more space with each passing day. Five hoodlums between the ages of fifteen and twenty-two terrorize moviegoers at a shopping mall in Fuenlabrada.

ONCE NIGHT FALLS YOU'RE NO LONGER SAFE. I was reading Baudelaire, Thomas De Quincey, Lorca, Fernando Pessoa, and Walter Benjamin as if I was twenty and had never read them before. The pranksters put on masks and went into a theater that was screening *Ride Along 2*. Shouting "Allah is great," they threw firecrackers and backpacks into the crowd, panicking terrorized patrons who had gone to see a lighthearted comedy and now thought they were in the midst of a full-fledged terrorist attack. Four hundred stranded whales were dying on a beach in New Zealand. I was looking for a music of words, one that belonged simultaneously to poetry and to everyday speech—advertisements, headlines, fashion magazines, erotic classifieds, horoscopes: an inconspicuous music that you could simply breathe in like the air, but that no one had ever imagined or heard before. Go where you didn't know you wanted to go. E-cigarette explodes in a man's pocket in California. Humans and robots may become indistinguishable in the future. I felt as free of everything I'd ever done as of the house we'd left behind, the furniture, the closets full of clothes, the books for which I no longer felt the slightest need. I was never without my notebook anymore, or without the dwindling pencil I had bought in Paris at the start of summer. Elephant populations were being decimated by an ivory rush. The largest species of gorilla in the world was about to go extinct. Dutch police were training birds of prey to hunt down drones suspected of carrying explosives.

TIMELESS LITERATURE IS BACK LIKE NEVER BEFORE. I took notes in bars and restaurants, on a bench in El Retiro, lurching along on a bus on the outskirts of Madrid. By 2025 the oceans will contain more tons of plastic than fish. Video of an eighteen-year-old Irish girl practicing serial fellatio on a score of drunken young men in exchange for a drink at a Mallorca nightclub goes viral all over the world. Choose your own adventure. Go where your dreams take you. In Germany, a Syrian refugee attacked a pregnant woman on a train with a machete. Break the mold. An idiot in a Zorro costume caused a panic inside LAX. Young woman dies after being struck by a car on a pedestrian crossing on Goya Street. Crimes and hoaxes caused the same amount of fear. Panic on Platja d'Aro as a prank is taken for a terrorist attack. On the promenade, in Nice, people thought the first shots fired by police against the terrorist truck driver were firecrackers from a pyrotechnic show that had just ended. Chinese mining villages were buried in landslides that blocked the course of rivers. New York was gripped by fear following a bomb explosion. Everything you desire is so much easier now.

CREEPY CLOWNS TERRORIZE GREAT BRITAIN. *A student started a panic at Brunel University in London this week by running through campus dressed as a killer clown wielding a chainsaw. A clown frightened people in Leicestershire when he was seen wandering through a cemetery near a school. A blurry picture posted on Facebook showed the clown carrying an ax in one hand. Two clowns in a black van drove up to a pair of girls on their way to school in Essex and asked if they wanted to come to a birthday party. In response, the school board of Clacton County ordered students to remain inside school buildings during lunch. The epidemic of creepy clowns seems to have spread to England from the United States, where novelist Stephen King recently warned on Twitter to "cool the clown hysteria." Dozens of similar incidents were reported across Great Britain in the last few days according to the police. A clown jumped out of a hedge in a park. Another one walked up to a car at a stop light, opened the door, and sat next to the driver before running away. Anti-clown patrols have formed in some areas. Professor Mark Griffiths, a psychologist at the University of Birmingham who specializes in addictive behaviors, said that several children who were traumatized by clown sightings had to be kept home from school. The sudden rise of creepy clowns has caused alarm in Australia as well. Last Tuesday, police arrested a clown carrying an ax in Victoria, in the country's southwest, after it accosted a woman in her car. On Sunday, the Thames Valley police said they had received fourteen calls reporting frightening clowns in a twenty-four-hour period. Professor Griffiths says that coulrophobia, or fear of clowns and jesters, is a well-documented syndrome that can cause panic attacks, cold sweats, and difficulty breathing.*

IT'S NOT SUMMER UNLESS YOU HAVE A STORY TO TELL. "My mother was a very good swimmer, but she never got her hair wet," he says. I am all ears. I listen with my ears and with my eyes. I notice the moment when an ordinary conversation changes course and begins to turn into a confession, as unexpected for the person making it as for the one receiving it. You hear yourself speak with a feeling of disbelief, of gratitude and reprieve, a witness to your own telling. It was the way he said his mother's hair never got wet that warned me. I did not ask any questions, I just waited. I saw the expression on his face change along with the tone of his voice. Suddenly he is more present than before, yet also much farther away, a time traveler. These things are never planned, they only happen by chance. The person telling the story didn't know a few minutes earlier that he was about to do so. He didn't even remember the story. It was the circumstances, a moment of distraction, something unexpected and a little awkward. The two of us are alone because we arrived at the restaurant early. We have known each other for years but have never been alone until today. We arrived before anyone else, each of us separately, at midday, on a Sunday in summer. The neighborhood is as empty as the restaurant. There are flags and paper lanterns from a recent feast day, Manila shawls are still draped over some balconies. We sit facing each other at a table for six. Being alone is pleasant and strange. We both know we are fond of each other, but we have never shown it beyond the ordinary pleasantries of a family gathering. Now that no one else is present—his wife, my wife, the rest of the family—I can see him as an individual, freed of all generic attributions. He is no longer my niece's husband, one more among the many youthful faces that once belonged to children who are now grown-up, even if we continue to see in them a mirage or a persistence of that earlier age; as if their childhood selves were still their true identity, and everything that followed, all of *this*, were simply an addition, meaningful, perhaps, but only insofar as it confirms their congenital dispositions, childish features that have simply surfaced more distinctly with the passing years.

DISCOVER THE STORY BEHIND THE STORY. I want to listen to him and no one else. I want to see him on his own, outside any group portrait, those generational pictures like the ones in the cell phone ads. It's easier now because we are alone. Our mutual affection prevails over the ordinary masculine reserve. "We always went to the same beach during the holidays," he says, "to the same hotel that you and your family go to." He is quite young, but there is silver in his hair around the temples and in front, over his forehead. He has a deep voice, perhaps slightly put-on from the habitual need to command respect at work, but his eyes are extraordinarily frank and his cheeks are ruddy with a healthy, childlike glow. The expression on his face is at once indelibly forlorn and full of gratitude and pure joy at being alive. When the waiter brought us two glasses of beer he drank half of his in a single thirsty gulp, happy in the midday heat, wiping the froth from his lips. These are the gifts of Madrid. He says there's nothing he enjoys more in life than drinking a cold beer while he makes lunch on Sundays listening to the radio. He finds it amusing and endearing that his wife, my niece, doesn't know how to cook even a fried egg or some broth from a bouillon cube. They were married two years ago in a ceremony that seemed a bit inspired by some American film, on the grassy lawn of a country house outside Madrid in an area surrounded by shopping malls, highways, and parched fields. They got married and he is happy with his wife and with her family, her mother and sister, her uncles, all of us, some of whom, six to be precise, agreed to meet today at a late Spanish hour that he and I wanted to abridge. That is why we arrived before anyone else and why we find ourselves here, at a table for six, in our summer shirts and our sneakers and shorts, joined by a camaraderie that at least on my part is somewhat of a misunderstanding. As the years go by, our perception of our age grows disconnected from reality. Our true age keeps rising but our perception of it stops, not in the prime of youth, since then it could be easily refuted, but later, in our early forties. He must be around thirty, yet to me we do not seem so far apart: he could be a somewhat younger friend, surely not someone so young as to belong to another era, another world. Our summer shirts and sneakers and the easy flow of conversation make it possible, at least for me, to feel a closeness that is in fact illusory. I am not a somewhat older friend. I could be his father.

LIVE YOUR DAY WITHOUT LIMITS. In fact he has no father or mother, despite being young. He is a lawyer with significant credentials, and holds a position of considerable responsibility at a legal publishing house. Our perception of our age may be an illusion, but that does not eliminate the risk of condescension. In a little while the others will arrive and our conversation will be forgotten. It will even be as if it had never happened. But right now he is speaking and I am listening. The supreme authority of pain does away with the privilege that my years might have conferred on me.

NOW YOU MUST LEARN EVERYTHING. "I was thirteen," he says. "We'd gone to Mallorca on vacation, my parents, my siblings, and I. We boarded our car into a ferry in Valencia and spent the night at sea. I kept leaning over the handrail, it all felt like a movie. That day my brother and I were playing on the beach, away from our parents and our older siblings. My mother was a very good swimmer, but she never got her hair wet, never let her head dip in the water. That was how women swam back then. She didn't like to get her hair wet. My younger brother and I were making sand castles and tunnels and stomping them with our feet. We never got tired of it. Then we saw people running on the beach and gathering into a large group at a little distance. They said someone had drowned, or had nearly drowned but had been rescued by the lifeguard. People speak with such authority of things they know nothing about. I saw my father in the group of people. He was always easy to spot because he was so tall, even if it can be hard to recognize people at the beach. My brother and I left our ruined castles and our pretend fighting and broke into a run. People were standing in a semicircle around a drowned woman. I couldn't quite believe it was my mother, because at first I did not recognize her. Not because her face was a different color, but because I'd never seen her hair wet."

THE WAY YOU MOVE REFLECTS WHO YOU ARE. That silhouette coming down Oxford Street now that all the windows are dark, and the stores are shut, and no one is out—no carts, no carriages or horses on the road—is Thomas De Quincey. From a distance he looks like a child, one of the many children roaming the streets, begging, then huddling together against the cold at night under the eaves of buildings. He is small and stunted and he has a creased and childish face that is also the face of an old man. When he walked endlessly through these same streets in his early youth he already seemed aged and shriveled by misery. As he grows older, his features, his gestures, and his always rather alarming figure become at once childish and decrepit. As a boy there was a gleam of ancient malice in his eyes. As an old man, the wicked, canny glint that lingers in his glance produces an incongruous air of mischief that is heightened by his crazy clothes: old hats that come down to his eyebrows, outsize coats that drag along the ground, outfits that could equally belong to a beggar or to an eccentric old man.

A FIREFLY IN THE FOG. He walks in place, as on a moving walkway, while at his back the city is projected on a screen like a still from one of those old films that were shot entirely inside a studio. He walks at a steady pace that never seems to flag. The pictures change behind him, compressing time and space in a series of juxtaposed shots. An early-morning light begins to spread behind him as he walks, a din of open shops, of vendors' cries and people hurrying by, of carts and carriages and horses, a rising, endless racket. The light begins to change, from morning to afternoon, and the street is different too. Greek Street, Oxford Street, a wide avenue, an alleyway, then Soho Square. It begins to grow dark and the lamplighters lift their poles to the oil lamps. The far reaches of Oxford Street, out beyond the last lamp on the last corner, are nothing but dark fields. Time is compressed by the walk and the projected image of the city into a single sequence. Sometimes De Quincey is accompanied by a female figure who is slightly taller than him. It's hard to tell if it's a girl, a teenager, or a grown woman who is already quite run-down. Her appearance alters in the changing light or as she steps in and out of the shadows. She is fifteen or sixteen, a prostitute. There are many in the neighborhood, heavily made-up, brazen, dressed in rags, their tangled hair infested with lice.

YOU'RE SO MUCH MORE THAN ANYONE EXPECTS. The projected image changes, now De Quincey is alone and it is no longer the buildings of London but the masts of Liverpool that rise behind him. De Quincey moves very frequently from city to city. Sometimes he is not sure anymore where he is, or whether he's awake or dreaming, or if the city around him is really there or just a memory or a fantasy implanted in his starving, sleepless brain by a dose of opium. He walks in order to stay awake but falls asleep even as he continues to put one foot in front of the other. He takes shelter at night in the hollow of a doorway or outside a church but hunger and cold will not let him sleep. He and the girl huddle together for warmth, covered in rags. They are young and pale, like those homeless kids begging on the freezing sidewalks of New York, trying to stay warm in their sleeping bags and whatever old clothes they can find in the trash, their fingers and their blackened, broken fingernails poking out of frayed woolen gloves. Some of them read tattered books that they must have also picked up while rummaging about. Some write in spiral notebooks or on mangled pads, urgently, with a pencil stub, or gnawing at the cracked end of a ballpoint pen. In the fall and winter of 1803, De Quincey was seventeen and living on the streets of London, always near the same places, Oxford Street, Soho Square. London is the largest, most populous city in the world and De Quincey doesn't know a single soul in it except for Ann, a teenage prostitute who keeps him company and gives him a little warmth at night. Sometimes he finds shelter in a big, empty house whose only other occupant is a ten-year-old girl that has no name.

Either she doesn't know it or she forgot it or she never had one. They sleep on the bare floorboards covered by an old blanket they found in the attic. The girl clings to him and trembles thinking that the house is full of ghosts. When they grow still they can hear the scurrying and squeaking of rats.

LIKE WALKING DOWN A DREAM. By the summer of 1804 De Quincey has managed to earn a little money and finds himself in Liverpool. He goes on endless walks and keeps a diary, making quick notes about his activities, what he sees, what he reads. The diary seems written at the pace of a hectic walk. He is in ceaseless motion, standing on a moving platform from which he never gets off. Liverpool is pulsing with international commerce and the vast wealth it extracts from pillage and the slave trade. Cotton, tea, coffee, sugar, whale oil for lighting homes and streets, big factories working through the night, coal to feed the steam engines, opium to put children to sleep and to soothe the pain, the melancholy and the brutal fatigue of all those men and women trapped in workhouses and coalmines. De Quincey writes everything down in his diary. He seems to be simultaneously writing and living what he recounts. He writes about the taverns and the coffee houses, what he eats and drinks, the various kinds of people from all over the world that he encounters on the narrow streets near the harbor, the bookstores that he visits, the books he buys. He sleeps with a prostitute and instantly records the price he paid, the services rendered, their quality, and his degree of satisfaction. He has not seen his friend Ann again. He said goodbye to her when he had to leave London for a few days in the hope of finding some relief from his misery. They planned to see each other when he returned, agreeing to meet at a certain corner, by a clock tower, at a given time of day. If one of them failed to appear the other would come back to their meeting place the next day and continue to wait. It took a few more days than he expected to get back to London. He went immediately to the place they agreed upon and waited for hours. He went back the next day and the one after, but Ann never came. He wanted to look for her but realized he didn't know her last name. He left for Liverpool shortly after.

DRIVE TOWARD THE UNEXPECTED. The silhouette is still walking at the same urgent pace. It seems to draw near but in fact remains at the same distance, outlined in black against the screen behind it. De Quincey is always moving from place to place. He arrives as quickly as he can with the sole intention of leaving as soon as possible. From London he goes to Liverpool. He settles down in Edinburgh, but soon after is living in Glasgow. The city in the background changes at every moment. In a village in the north of England, his wife and his young children are waiting for him. He is gone for months at a time and they have no idea where he is, nor do they receive any money to live or to pay off the debts he left behind. He reads and writes, hoarding books and newspapers as well as tall piles of his own manuscripts, all those pages written in tiny rooms where he works until there's no more space to move around, even for him who is so small. When the chaos of those jumbled piles reaches a certain point De Quincey leaves it all behind and takes up somewhere else. Sometimes he comes back after a while or after a few years. Some rooms he never returns to, and so escapes being hounded for past rent. He stays up writing late into the night but gets distracted and his hair is singed when his head gets too close to the candle. Sometimes his papers catch fire. He pours water on the burning pages or he throws them on the floor and stomps on them, which makes the whole disaster even worse.

BENEATH THE SKIN YOU SEE. The walking figure can be seen more clearly now because the background is much brighter. It emerges from what he calls London's powerful labyrinths. It is night, and the rows of lights on Oxford Street are now much brighter, no longer weak oil-burning lamps scattered through vast areas of darkness, but gaslights. In the autumn of 1821 De Quincey spends his days writing in a garret over a gloomy courtyard and his nights wandering down the same streets that he roamed in the fall of 1803. He has come back to London on his own, leaving his wife and children in the rural house in the north of England. Solitude contributes to the trancelike state in which he writes during the day and walks by night, unable at times to tell the two activities apart, just as when he wandered through those streets as a young man without quite knowing if he was awake or dreaming. Memories gain an even greater hold on him because writing fosters remembrance, and also because the things that come back to him occurred in the same places he now wanders through.

REGRESSIONS TO PAST LIVES. Suddenly, no time has passed. Time and space distend as in an opium dream. Fantastical views of oriental cities spread before him as he walks, floating domes and minarets that sometimes shift and turn into a claustrophobic maze of battlements and crypts and pyramids. The dreadful thought occurs to him that nothing can truly be forgotten: the pictures that he gazed at as a child in a volume of *The Thousand and One Nights*, the plates by Piranesi that he glimpsed one afternoon at an antiquarian's shop come back to him now as visions in the spell of opium. Darkness and exhaustion make the city grow and swell around him, lit by the technological wonder of gaslight. What began as an essay of reasonable length on opium eating begins to spill and overflow onto the page, turning into an immoral confession. Matter encroaches upon form and transforms it into itself. His account of the pleasures of opium and of its torments and hallucinations acquires the very texture of delirium. De Quincey is thirty-six, but looking at the faces he meets in the crowd he sometimes thinks that he can see himself among the wandering children and teenagers of Oxford Street. He dreams the city even as he walks through its streets or as he writes about walking. He gazes at the strange new glow of gaslight in the houses and shops. When he walks past the house on Greek Street where he sometimes slept in the arms of a nameless little girl, all the windows are lit. He looks into a parlor and sees a joyful family gathering. In every woman's face he searches for Ann's unforgotten features. He thinks he sees her, walking up ahead, and rushes to catch up with her so he can look at her face. The thousands of strange faces he has seen in London, Liverpool, and Edinburgh appear again in his hallucinations, floating side by side with eyes wide open, swaying in dark ocean waves. De Quincey takes opium in the form of laudanum, a tincture dissolved in cognac or wine. Laudanum has a bittersweet taste and is the color of rubies. He sees something on the street with extraordinary precision and there is a slight change, a ripple that makes him realize he is no longer walking through reality but within a dream. In these visions he searches for Ann as obstinately as in his waking life. One day he finally sees her approach and it makes him tremble with a wondrous, weakening feeling. A moment later he realizes, with bewilderment, with grief, that if he can see her it must be because he's dreaming.

IT MAY LOOK LIKE GARBAGE TO YOU. Anyone paying attention to him will notice that he picks things up off the street as he walks. He moves like a dignified pauper, furtive and alert, looking around for a moment before rummaging through a garbage can or peering into a trash container. He bends down quickly to pick something up off the ground, something he examines before putting it away in one of the loose, baggy pockets of his trousers or his jacket, which are always stuffed; or perhaps, instead, in one of those leather satchels that people used to carry before there were backpacks, the kind of briefcase a professor or a lawyer might own, but so battered and worn as to dispel any suggestion of affluence or even of practical sense despite its many buckles, side pockets, bottomless compartments that open and shut like the bellows of an accordion. He looks closely at the flyers placed under windshield wipers by people you never see. Colorful cards offering erotic encounters, leaflets for moving services or African fortune-tellers who can cure the evil eye or bring back a lost love, ads for cars, for silver and gold, for fast food or dental treatments. He always looks around him as he leans over the hood of the car, perhaps fearing that the owner will turn up and take him for a thief. He studies carefully each printed, xeroxed, or neatly handwritten sign that people tape at eye level on lampposts and streetlights. He notices the tiny stickers for locksmiths pasted all over the intercom panels on apartment buildings. But he also picks up the empty cigarette packs that lie crushed on the ground, and keeps them too, once he has looked at the horrible pictures of tumors and agonizing maladies and at the printed warnings and deterrents by which no one seems deterred: SMOKING KILLS, in big black letters on a white background, as in an old funeral notice.

THE PERFECT IMAGE AWAITS YOU. He seems to be searching for something he lost, or to be constantly finding unexpected things, or to suffer from some sort of mania, one of those disorders that afflict lonely people in big cities when they reach a certain age: a normal-looking, respectable man with that businesslike satchel under one arm, picking things up off the ground or taking eagerly, almost politely, the flyers being offered everywhere by dismal people no one else notices, stuffing his pockets for some reason with those printed or xeroxed cards that usually peddle erotic massages or some other kind of pleasure dispensed by sweet-faced Asian girls or by large Caribbean women in plunging leotards that show off their big asses and bulging breasts. Maybe at some point he'll take out his wallet to pay for something at a store and all those compromising leaflets offering erotic services or cash payments for gold will flutter to the ground. When he gets home, or to the tiny office that he rents somewhere on the outskirts of the city so that he can spend hours undisturbed by visitors or by the ringing of the telephone, he empties his pockets one by one, his many pockets, and he also opens the accordion folds of the satchel to dump their contents on the table.

COME AND START LIVING. The gray metal table is made by the Roneo office supply company and so is the gray filing cabinet by the window, both salvaged from some decommissioned government building. Once he has emptied his pockets, still on his feet and perhaps, depending on the time of year, still wearing his raincoat, he stares at the table as if baffled or overwhelmed by such catastrophic abundance. He takes off his raincoat and puts it on a hanger. He sits on a reclining chair that belongs to an era of office furniture several decades older than that of the table and the filing cabinet. He rubs his hands gently, an ingrained habit that is entirely unnecessary since they tend to stay quite warm, which means he wears gloves only on the harshest days of a northern winter. Then he gets to work, taking out of a drawer a three-ring binder with clear sheet protectors of the kind that were common in the equally vanished era of photo albums. From a second drawer he brings out a pair of sharp pointed scissors, some notebooks, some used envelopes bearing labels that he made himself, cutting and gluing them over the bank or company letterhead. Each label consists of a word or a short phrase that he found and cut out somewhere or other—an ad, a headline, a brochure for hearing aids or plastic surgery—and that he chose and affixed to the envelope entirely at random, just as he fills his blue binders at random with clippings, flyers, business cards, pieces of paper, drug names cut out of the boxes they came in, subway tickets, restaurant bills, a napkin from a bar or a café. If anyone were to stand outside the office door, pressing an ear to the panel of frosted glass, he or she would hear the sound of scissors carefully slicing through paper with a quick, efficacious, rhythmic sound. One might even hear, if equipped with a highly sensitive instrument, the rustle of a pencil moving ceaselessly over the stiff wide pages of a notebook.

FORGET EVERYTHING YOU KNOW. Maybe now and then there is a different sound that may at first be hard to identify, the sound of a pencil turning in the hollow of a metal sharpener. A dark blotch appears and dissolves across the translucent pane of glass, which lets shadows through but not volumes or clear outlines. He must have gotten up to stretch his legs, gripped by the instinctive urge to walk that is always in him, and taken a few turns around the table in the cloudy light of a window that probably opens into an inner courtyard. Then he goes back to his task, leaning over the table and rubbing his hands together one more time, as absorbed in his work as a tailor, one of those tailors with a measuring tape draped over their shoulders like a liturgical vestment and a worn piece of chalk behind the ear or as a watchmaker peering through his loupe, enthralled by tiny escapements and miniature wheels that come together as meticulously as the words that he cuts out with his scissors, the ads, the pictures, the slogans and lurid headlines, all jumbled together like a set of dominos, forming connections that are as wondrous and unforeseen as chemical reactions.

SECRETS THAT DO NOT PERMIT THEMSELVES TO BE TOLD. The cities that Edgar Allan Poe knows well do not appear in his stories. He writes in Baltimore, New York, Richmond, and Philadelphia, but his stories take place in the vague landscapes of a gothic novel or in a European city like Paris or London. There is no literature for Poe in his immediate surroundings. His imagination is as out of place in his native country as his disastrously unstable life. As a child he had once been to London, which he chose for the setting of "The Man of the Crowd." That ancient memory can hardly have helped him write the story, which nevertheless seems as literal as a firsthand account pieced together from direct experience of the streets of London. The city through which a nameless narrator follows a stranger without pause for twenty-four hours—in the crowd, down empty streets, in the glow of gaslight, past storefronts, through vast open markets, down dark alleys—is the London of De Quincey's *Confessions*; the same city that shines darkly in Dickens and Wilkie Collins and in the adventures of Sherlock Holmes. Forty years later, the sinister, withered stranger in Poe's tale will become Stevenson's Edward Hyde. Even the gas lamps remain, although in Stevenson's time there were many more of them lighting up the larger streets. Their glow shines against the darkness of the poorer, narrow streets and alleyways. "The street shone . . . like a fire in the forest," Stevenson says. He greatly admired De Quincey. As a young man he had often crossed paths with that strange errant figure in the streets of Edinburgh. His description of Mr. Hyde exactly matches every testimony we have of De Quincey's appearance in his old age: "Mr. Hyde was pale and dwarfish, he gave an impression of deformity without any nameable malformation."

WE CAN'T CHANGE YOUR PAST. "The Man of the Crowd" is a story without a plot. It could be a prose poem, anticipating the ones that Baudelaire would write years later under Poe's direct influence. It has a beginning and a guiding mystery but not a clear ending or an explanation. Poe, who so often drew up elaborately sinister plots, now allowed himself a remarkable narrative freedom. "The tale is garbled, the sorrow clear," as Machado says in one of his poems. There are no proper names. Freed from the trammels and the obligations of plot, the story flows like life itself or with the musical movement of poetry. We do not know the narrator's identity, his profession, where he comes from, or why he is in London. We are told that he is convalescing but not from what illness. The state of convalescence is crucial: he takes pleasure merely in breathing, and feels, he says, "a calm but inquisitive interest in every thing." He is an immobile spectator, a figure in a photograph, sitting by a bow window at a café inside a hotel with a cigar and an open newspaper on his lap, in perfect idleness. Occasionally, he says, he glances at an advertisement in the paper or he lifts his eyes to look at the other customers in the café. Newspaper ads were still a recent commercial invention when Poe was writing his story. Many more people could read, and technical advances had made cheap mass printing possible. Baudelaire's poems and prose pieces appeared in Parisian newspapers, lost in large pages crammed with tiny print. The few of Emily Dickinson's poems that were published during her lifetime are nearly impossible to find in the crowded columns of a local paper, anonymous and so concise as to be almost entirely clandestine. In the pages of the *New York Sun*, a penny sheet, Poe published an extensive and entirely spurious account of a manned balloon flight across the Atlantic that had supposedly reached the United States in just three days. Thousands of copies had sold by the time people realized it was a hoax.

WE UNDERSTAND WHY YOU WOULDN'T WANT TO LOOK THROUGH THAT WINDOW. Now and then the narrator looks out the window. The day is waning, the streets are filled with people leaving work and coming out of shops. The gas lamps are being lit as dusk begins to fall, bodies and faces stand out in unnatural relief beneath the yellow glare as in a parade of figures drawn by Daumier. All classes of people, all characters, occupations, and types of dress mingle confusedly as night descends and the gaslight grows brighter. "The rays of the gas-lamps . . . threw over every thing a fitful and garish luster. All was dark yet splendid." The intensity of Poe's writing arises in part from the strain to which language had to be subjected to depict new sights. The faces of the crowd spread and multiply in the gaslight as hideously as in De Quincey's hallucinations. One particular face among them, for no clear reason, awakens in the narrator the urge to go out on the street and begin a pursuit. It belongs to a little old man, a figure who once again seems strikingly like the ghost or double of De Quincey: "a decrepit old man, some sixty-five or seventy years of age," "short in stature, very thin, and apparently very feeble," "in filthy, ragged clothes." Something in the stranger suggests "the ideas of vast mental power, of caution, of penuriousness, of avarice, of coolness, of malice, of blood-thirstiness, of triumph, of merriment, of excessive terror, of intense—of supreme despair."

WE'RE WAITING FOR YOU. There is a pressing urge to keep the stranger in view, to know more about him, about the wild history "written within that bosom." For twenty-four hours the Man of the Crowd and his pursuer devote themselves to an episode in the ceaseless wandering motion that defines their century: "roaming far and wide until a late hour, seeking, amid the wild lights and shadows of the populous city, that infinity of mental excitement which quiet observation can afford." For an instant the narrator catches a glimpse "both of a diamond and of a dagger" in the dark folds of the man's old coat. But nothing more is said, no answer is given at the end of the search, and they shine on as pure, inscrutable mysteries. Just the flash of a dagger, the glint of a diamond in the gaslight.

AN ÉMINENCE GRISE. Poe's other city is Paris. As a young man he liked to recount trips he had never taken. He claimed to have been to St. Petersburg and China. He had never been to Paris but he read about its crime-ridden slums in cheap French feuilletons that were translated and pirated in American newspapers. He was familiar as well with De Quincey's ghoulish narratives, attempting on occasion and with little success to imitate the gallows humor of "On Murder Considered as One of the Fine Arts." Newspapers are a cheap mass product for quick consumption, without the least concern for the truth. They print lavishly illustrated stories about gruesome crimes, premature burials, resurrections by electric current, balloon flights to the moon, mesmeric trances carried out on agonizing men who continue to speak at the hypnotist's command when they are already dead. American publishers are not interested in books by American authors because they can earn much more by pirating popular English novels. A writer must make a living. Poe will never stop writing and he will never come out of poverty. A girl named Mary Rogers had been murdered and thrown into the Hudson from the New Jersey shore, probably to erase all traces of a failed abortion. For Poe, remoteness is a necessary ingredient of literature. He writes a story in which Mary Rogers becomes Marie Rogêt, substituting Paris for Jersey City and the Seine for the Hudson. The murder of Marie Rogêt will be investigated by amateur detective C. Auguste Dupin, who also solved the murders of the Rue Morgue.

THE ALLURE OF YOUR AGE. For as long as I have known her she has always been the right age for me. Now I can hardly believe that when we first held each other she was twenty-eight and I was thirty-four. Neither one of us realized how young we were. As the years passed she went through new stages of her beauty, like phases of the moon that were never exactly alike. She remained youthful but she attained new forms of plenitude that only time could bring. Life continued to shape her to my taste. She shaped herself, carefully attentive to her person, an exact observer without the least self-indulgence. She changed and she became someone else by remaining herself. She was and she was not the same person she had been a day, or two months, or two years before. One could witness these changes in photographs. She got a short haircut once that gave an adolescent glow to her smile. She thought of dyeing her hair a platinum blond but never did. She would put her hair up in a bun, which made her seem taller and emphasized the flowing grace of her walk. For a while she had two identical linen dresses, simple, short, tight-fitting, one red and one yellow. The bright colors and the cut gave her a sixties air, like the bun in her hair. She would ask me to hold her lipstick when we went out so she didn't have to carry a bag or anything else. She liked to go out entirely unburdened, and could do so, in that time prior to cell phones. She would not say *pintalabios*, lipstick, just *pinta*. That clipped word held for me all the excitement of the way people talked in Madrid and of the new life we were sharing together.

EXPRESS YOUR STYLE FREELY. She used to wear a pair of very graceful shoes that I had given her, black and white, with a leopard print and heels that were not too high. She would glance sideways at her reflection in a shop window in a way that was both coquettish and critically discerning. Since she and I are always moving through time together, we barely notice its passing, just as someone drifting in a balloon in a faint current of air will be unaware of its motion. When she was forty I was turned on by the fact that she was so attractive as to look ten years younger. I look at her past fifty and I can't imagine anyone more desirable. All the more so because of her age. She is enriched by the treasure of time. Her skin is so soft that the slightest brush is a caress. Time has shaped us separately and it has shaped us together in our ceaseless contact. We are who we were when we were born, and when we met, and as we have become in being together. We are the air that the other one breathes. When she is gone I like to open her closet and breathe her presence in her clothes. When I sleep alone I never take her side of the bed. I remember her reading me some lines by Donald Hall about his wife, Jane Kenyon, who is herself a wonderful poet: "She came into her beauty like into an inheritance."

MADE TO FIT YOUR HAND. He found an interesting sheet of paper in a box full of old typewritten forms that someone left by the side of a garbage bin. It has the dimensions of a shoebox lid and it is thick, though not stiff, and spotless white despite lying among old papers and all kinds of waste. He wishes, as so many times before, that he had the least bit of talent for drawing. The piece of paper is of the right size and shape to draw something precise and austere, like a Juan Gris sketch for a still life or one of Giacometti's lonely human figures. He tucks it away in his great omnivorous satchel without first looking around to see if anyone is watching. As he walks down the street he is aware of the beautiful and secret possibility that he carries with him. He enters a drab café that is quite crowded. The empty tables are littered with trays and leftovers that those who just had breakfast didn't bother to remove. But there is one table, just one, that is clean, and it happens to be by the window, a miracle that he must take advantage of before it disappears. He sits down at the table without ordering anything and pulls out the sheet of paper. For a moment he searches his pockets uneasily for a pencil, worried that he might have lost it. The smaller a pencil stub gets, the more cleverly it will conceal itself. A fold in his clothing or the depth of a pocket provides it with a perfect burrow. Just as he suspected, the sheet of paper has the perfect texture, smooth enough to write on swiftly without being slick. He licks the sharpened tip of the pencil, and only when it touches the paper do the words begin to emerge.

BE READY FOR WHATEVER COMES YOUR WAY. "All artistic work," he writes, "however literary or speculative it may be, must in part be a physical task, involving effort and labor and requiring the use of one's hands.

Emily Dickinson would make a clean copy of her poems when she was done writing them and stitch them into little notebooks in which she sometimes also pasted the leaves of trees. Or she would carefully fold the sheet of paper and place inside a pressed flower that often has some relation to the poem. Her room was a comfortable cell for contemplation but she never stayed inside for too many hours at a time. She walked in her garden, tending to it with a farmer's vitality and skill. The same quick hands that wrote her poems wielded the hoe and the pruning hook, put seeds in the ground and crushed clumps of black earth. Dickinson took part in all domestic chores and was an assiduous cook. Confined to her house by her own volition, she displayed a practical activism similar to St. Teresa of Avila's though fortunately free of any asceticism, or even of any desire for transcendence. Paradise is here, just like the family house, its garden, its cupboards, the view of the fields from a window and the natural life of plants, birds, insects, and farm animals, the entire world, a roofless Noah's ark. The human brain becomes deformed and atrophied when the mind is too exclusively concerned with work requiring no physical activity, manual skill, or strong sensory stimuli. To make a drawing you need the resistance of the sheet of paper as well as your determination to overcome the clumsiness of your hand. This encounter with materiality produces setbacks and chance revelations that are more fruitful to the future work than any prior intentions. Words have no material substance but their resistance is just as stubborn as that of wood, clay, or stone. One can force their fixed sounds and meanings only to a certain point. Syntax offers as powerful a resistance as gravity or as the physical composition of matter. Besides, words are used up, mistreated, spoiled by toxic residues just as the bodies of marine animals are poisoned by chemical spills or by the antibiotics and antidepressants that people expel in their urine or simply flush down the toilet."

THREE DAYS OF QUANTUM ACTIVISM. "The nobility of the folk artist has always consisted in working with whatever happens to be at hand; cheap, accessible materials, wood if there was wood, stone if one could find it, clay if there was neither wood nor stone. In Africa there is a man who turns the plastic canisters in which the poor carry their water and gasoline into sculptures that resemble masks or idols. Emily Dickinson stitched together her books of poems with the same needle and thread that she employed for her domestic sewing. She also made her verses out of the simple rhythms and monotonous stanzas of the hymns they sang in church. As a teenager, she made an album containing every species of herb and flower in her garden and in nearby fields. She had studied chemistry and natural history. She pressed plant specimens with great care, making sure that their characteristic features were fully and clearly preserved, affixing the stem to a sheet of pasteboard with tiny strips of paper or fabric and writing the name underneath. Gary Snyder has written poems all his life and never stopped working with his hands, primarily with wood, and doing construction. When he was very young he wrote a poem about stoneworkers carving out steps on the side of a mountain: each verse was as solid and deliberate as a hewn step, tier upon tier to make the path firm. Manual work produces a healthy absorption, you focus on the task at hand and at the same time you forget yourself, your history, your identity, things float weightlessly around you like objects set free from gravity inside a space station. The task has a practical and verifiable aim, yet it produces at the same time a self-sufficing pleasure. The finished piece, whatever it may be, exists in a fully objective manner even if bound inseparably to the particular life and character of its maker. It seems anonymous, impersonal, standing squarely on its base and occupying a precise amount of space: a jug, a chair, a painting, a wooden box or one made out of cardboard. It was born from someone's labor yet it has an emancipated existence. It can last for a few days or it can last for centuries or millennia. It can become as elemental as the enduring forms of nature, shaped and altered by time or by the hands of those who use it, like stone steps that are gradually smoothed and worn away by those who tread on them. The head of an Egyptian queen or goddess carved in basalt, its upper half gone. The radiant splendor of its ruin, a chin, half the oval of a face with a broken smile that is all the more beautiful because there are no eyes; halfway between a sculpture and a piece of rubble, between sensuous beauty and a sacred shudder." A brusque voice makes him look up but it takes him a moment to realize it is addressing him. "You can't sit here unless you order something." He nods politely, puts away the sheet of paper in his satchel, slips his pencil in the inner pocket of his jacket so as not to lose it. But its sharp tip is already beginning to poke a little hole in the lining.

FILL YOUR LIFE WITH FLAVOR. He is a restless archeologist of the present, of the moment when what is valuable or pristine turns into debris, when
the words and pictures of an advertisement pass from ubiquity to nonexistence. He is a scrupulous collector, asking for and gratefully receiving leaflets that everyone else immediately discards, taking them from overflowing
garbage cans or from unemployed middle-aged men handing them out by
the entrance to a shopping mall. Big Sale, Customize Your Mattress, Final
Days, Tourist Menu Spanish Paella. Samantha Reincarnated Priestess and
Sorceress of Love. He is an archivist, trying to rescue just a few things from
the ceaseless flood of all that comes into existence only to be stuffed into the
trash, a supermarket flyer with special offers, still smelling of fresh ink but
already lying on the sidewalk. Things that belong to the present but are also
premature relics that future archeologists will barely manage to recover, since
nearly everything will have decayed, or vanished, or will lie buried away. He
picks up the empty packs of cigarettes that people crush and throw away, like
an envoy from the future or a foreign power sent to gather indiscriminate
materials for other experts to classify and study. He collects the gruesome
pictures of cancerous lungs, ravaged mouths, and dead men just as he collects
the pictures of Asian and Latin girls offering massages with a happy ending.
He thinks with a touch of commiseration about the person at the ad agency
responsible for setting up the photo shoots, the white hospital lighting, the
pale children who grew up sick because their parents were addicted to smoking. He thinks even more about the anonymous writer in charge of drafting
the health warnings, sitting at a table looking at photographs that, instead of
young people leaping joyfully into the air, show the gangrened feet, mouths,
and bodies of dead smokers. Maybe he will even light a cigarette before beginning to write. For inspiration, like writers do in the movies.

GET YOUR SMILE BACK WITH A 3D-PRINTED JAW. Smoking affects sperm health and can reduce fertility. Smoking causes fatal cancer of the lungs. Smoking causes heart attacks. Smoking during pregnancy stunts fetal growth. Tobacco is highly addictive. Tobacco smoke contains over seventy carcinogens. Smoking clogs your arteries. Smoking can cause erectile dysfunction. Your smoke is harmful to your family and friends. Smoking causes heart disease and stroke. Smoking ages your skin. Smoking reduces blood circulation and is a cause of impotence. Smoking takes away years of your life. *Fumar mata.* Smoking kills.

AROUND THE CORNER, AROUND THE WORLD.

"You want to live in a bubble? Is that what you want? And what should the rest of us do?"

"I can't go back there, I'd just be too afraid."

"I know I'm a bad influence on you."

"Everything was going so badly and suddenly my life is totally fine."

WHERE HAVE I HEARD THAT VOICE BEFORE?

"They're putting her in the pain clinic because she's a total wreck."

"Tell Cristina to get on the phone. Tell her. Tell her to get on the phone right now."

"They must be at the doctor's already. They arrived early."

SO THAT YOU AND YOURS CAN ALWAYS STAY CONNECTED.

"You've got bags under your eyes."

"Of course I do, what do you expect?"

"Nerea, what do *you* think?"

"Fuck their dead, that's what I think."

"They're fake, girls, the flowers are fake."

"I consider myself a brave woman."

"You *have* to be brave to do what you're doing."

"That's how it goes, you tried your best but you couldn't manage, now we have to leave it to the experts. I'm not just saying that because I'm your mother."

THE MOMENT YOU FIND OUT WHAT YOU WERE MISSING.

"Have you ever been to the Ice Palace?"

"Spare change, spare change for something to eat?"

"I have to come here every fucking day to see you?"

"Like I always say, they've suffered a lot, but what are *we* supposed to do about it? They're not like us."

"No, he's not up yet. He just woke up. He's opening his eyes."

"I'm willing to give him something, but not everything he wants, of course."

"When he was thirteen his father died of a heart attack, hunting pheasants in Cortina."

"It has to be by night."

"No, better by day."

"A little help, please. Please, a little help."

I'VE GOT THE IPHONE I WANT.

"Spare change, sir. Please, a little help."

"A lot of people say it's all witchcraft."

ALL YOU HAVE TO DO IS CALL US. Writing with a pencil is like speaking quietly to myself. If a word is wrong or if I want to take it back I can rub it away with the dark eraser on the other end. Adding an eraser to a pencil was a bit of poetic practical genius, like adding wheels to a suitcase or like the time Joan Brossa nailed a playing card to a skull. The whisper of the pencil is like the sound of words flowing in the mind, words that have a kind of sound even when they're never spoken, only murmured through barely parted lips. With a pencil I am closer to the silence I seek. The words seem to emerge neither from my will nor from my mind but from the lead tip, the black lode of graphite where they lie like the mineral itself in galleries beneath the ground. I am not making a confession as I write, nor do I affirm any opinion, belief, or purpose whatsoever. I just disperse, letting myself go. I follow the rich subterranean vein, the flow of words. I write by ear. When I sharpen the pencil, the outline of the words becomes too clear. There is an excess of precision, a frail tautness that could very well snap the thread of my writing along with the tip of the pencil. But after a few lines it all softens. Without realizing it I come a little closer to one of the things I envy most, the craft of drawing.

YOU MAY NOT SEE US, BUT WE'RE HERE. Wherever you go, wherever you are, the city speaks to you in a voice or in a series of changing voices directed precisely at you. Like this, in the second person, the second person singular, like a love song or a poem. Sometimes the voice will identify itself, sometimes not. It gives you directions or it offers or suggests things you may like. It states universal principles or laws. The voice assures you that nothing you could possibly desire or imagine is out of reach. You could win a VIP experience in Vegas. Night doesn't have to mean the day is over. You don't need much to have it all. Over three thousand experts to look after your dental health. Five thousand cars at your disposal. The voice communicates thoughts of great philosophical and poetic depth. To find new oceans you must go far from the shore. Often the voice is plural: a *we*, an *us*. A generous, festive, cheerful us that understands you, that offers everything you want, knowing how to hear your desires or guess what they are before you know it yourself, before you say it, or do not dare to say it. An us that speaks with the bland though somehow threatening affability of an evangelical preacher, pressing and ubiquitous, allowing no escape. We're always near you, even if you don't notice. Our greatest gift is knowing you. We make it easier for you to shop. We see incredible things in your future. Get our newsletter. We want to read your book. We deliver your groceries to your home. We make your dreams a reality. We stock your fridge. Do you miss your old car? We can lend you a new one. It is an invisible us, pervasive, caring, always near, benevolent without being condescending, protective without being oppressive, all-knowing, all-encompassing. We are working for your safety. We bring you food at any time of day. We want to improve your experience. Discover the world with us. Join our team. We'll be back very soon to surprise you. We know just what you need, even before you do.

BREAKING NEWS, ALL THE TIME. I like literature that has the disruptive and intoxicating effect of wine or music, making me forget myself, forcing me to read it aloud and to give in to its contagion, explaining the world to me while setting me at war with it, giving me shelter even as it reveals the horror of everything around me as vividly as its beauty. I like literature that gives me a lucid high without derangement, a sense of calm in which there is no coldness or indifference, compelling me to be fully who I am yet someone else as well, or no one, a nonentity, Don Nadie, Monsieur Personne, Mr. Nobody, gazing at the radiance of things no longer as a witness but as if it could be seen when there is no one there to see it. Garry Winogrand said that when taking pictures he would go fully outside himself: as close as you can get to not existing. By poetry I understand a drunken rapture, a height of expressive intensity that can be found in any art form, any memorable image or object in the world around us. What it resembles most is the supreme transport of a love that keeps its eyes wide open. It leaps down into the unknown. It vanishes without a trace.

ENJOY THE SPELL OF EVERY DESTINATION. I have always tried to live in "the moment of true feeling" (Peter Handke), the utmost presence and power of what is magically concrete. Having a kind of gift for despair, I have it for joy as well, especially the kind of joy that lives within us even when it is experienced in the company of others: the demure joy of sharing a conversation with a friend, a pleasant meal, freed from all feelings of reserve or any sense of looking on from the outside. As a child, I often experienced secret moments of fulfillment. I spent much of my time alone but solitude was not a sadness or a burden. I lived in a time outside of time, beyond the hours

49

and minutes on the face of the clock. Everything vanished in my complete devotion to whatever I was doing. Playing, reading, listening to the radio; looking at the fire in the kitchen; going from one relative's house to another pretending I was on a galloping horse; going to the movies in the summertime. I liked the ones that were set in ancient Rome, with battles, chariot races, gladiator fights, women in low-cut dresses with a slit on the side that revealed a long leg and a foot in a braided sandal. Walking back from school in the afternoon I rejoiced at the thought of the newly purchased comic book I would read when I got home, a pristine treasure waiting for me. There were songs on the radio that made me shudder inwardly with something I was incapable of naming, something in the voice, the wavering melody, even if I hardly ever understood the meaning of the words, which always had to do with love and jealousy.

A tu vera
siempre a la verita tuya
hasta el día en que me muera.

By your side,
always by your side,
until the day I die.

EXCLUSIVE BENEFITS JUST FOR YOU. I used to wait from the start of the song for that exact moment, that effusion of feeling that never failed. I never mentioned it to anyone. Not from shyness or reserve, but because I didn't think those feelings could be expressed in words or needed to be shared. I felt no need to do so. My father and mother were kind and comforting figures who lived for the most part in a separate world that was exclusively their own, just as I lived in mine, or a cat lives in its cat world. I collected color stickers from the movie of *The Ten Commandments*. They came in packs and they were bright and glossy and you had to carefully align each one in the right space in the album. The slick surface was as pleasant to a child's fingers as the slightly narcotic scent of ink and glue was pleasant to his sense of smell. Since we had no nativity figures at home, I would draw them on thick paper and then cut them out and glue them to a cardboard base. At night, in the dark, before falling asleep, I would go over the plots of movies I had seen or make up elaborate stories that I never told anyone. I would bury myself under the covers as in the hollow of a cave in a fairy tale. I fantasized about an older brother who was studying abroad and one day would come back and look after me, teach me games, tell me all the things that he had seen, take me on a trip.

NOTHING IS AS BEAUTIFUL TO US AS A CHILD'S SMILE. I was happy just to look at certain toys. It didn't make me sad that I couldn't have them. The possibility never occurred to me. Now I realize that I enjoyed looking at them on a shelf the same way I have admired, many years later, an ancient Greek vase, a painting in a museum, a valuable primitive mask kept behind glass at an antiquities dealer. Who needs to own what can be gazed upon at leisure? I remember a boat with a blue-and-white hull and a lateen sail. I remember an electric train moving through a model landscape, vanishing into the mouth of a tunnel and reappearing on a metal bridge beneath a cardboard sky. I was almost never unhappy during the first eleven years of my life. I would walk down the street or down a path in the countryside and always keep my eyes on the ground to see if I happened to find something interesting: a marble, a coin, a toy cowboy or Indian.

THIS AMAZING GIFT COULD BE YOURS RIGHT NOW. Walter Benjamin collected toys and children's books. He bought them for his son, Stefan, but he enjoyed them as much as the boy and he continued to purchase them when Stefan was grown and they no longer lived together. As an adult, years after his father died, Stefan Benjamin became an antiquarian book dealer in England. In his Moscow diary Benjamin recounts long and difficult journeys through the snowbound city to visit the Toy Museum or the street markets on the outskirts of town that sold used toys and children's books. It's the winter of 1926 and Benjamin seems caught in a dark fog of misfortune. He is destitute, life in Moscow is full of hardship, his love for Asja Lācis has ended in disappointment. The crude colors of those wooden blocks and of the pictures in the children's books must have seemed brighter still during those gray days without sunlight or hope.

IF YOUR DREAMS HAVE NO LIMITS. Joaquín Torres-García made use of old wooden blocks in the toys he made for his children. Unlike most avant-garde artists and writers of his time, Torres-García was a faithful and devoted family man. His wife and children were always with him as he traveled to yet another city, as he searched for a house or an apartment thinking that he'd finally found his place in the world when in fact it would not be long before their poverty forced them to move again: Barcelona, New York, Paris, Rome. In New York he partnered with a businessman to start a factory that would manufacture his toys. All the materials were lost in a warehouse fire before production started. Men who lead destitute, wandering lives without any practical sense will suddenly dream up projects to try to earn the money they are unable to make through their art. James

Joyce traveled back to Dublin in 1917 determined to launch the first chain of movie theaters in Ireland with the support of a few senseless investors in Trieste. Torres-García's toys have all the heft of a piece of wood and all the whimsical beauty of a picture in a tale or a fable. He would pick up bits of wood on the street, scraps from a woodshop. Each of his toys contains the spark of his imagination and the skilled work of his hands. So, too, do the books he wrote and illustrated entirely by hand, from the title page and the picture on the cover to the drawings inside, whole pages covered in tidy hieroglyphs and words traced in a neatly uniform script. Each book is entirely unique, each page bears witness to the immense labor that went into it, a silent devotion like that of a medieval copyist or an Egyptian scribe, hours, days, weeks bent over a task that was essential to him yet entirely superfluous, even ruinous, since he could have spent that time doing something that produced some kind of income; since no one ever bought those books, and if he did manage to sell one, whatever amount he was paid could not have compensated him for an iota of all the talent and work that had gone into them.

FEEL LIKE A CHILD AGAIN. When he was teaching at the Bauhaus, Paul Klee made hand puppets and wooden figures for his son to play with. A sophisticated yet childish or primitive aesthetic unifies the great non-egomaniacal artists of the twentieth century: Klee, Torres-García, Alexander Calder with his miniature circus; Ravel with his scores for music boxes and windup toys; Béla Bartók's piano pieces for children; Federico García Lorca and Manuel de Falla bringing together all that was best in their individual talents to stage puppet shows at a friend's house. Helen Levitt took photographs of children at play in Spanish Harlem and of the chalk drawings they made on sidewalks and buildings. Lorca's ballads sway with the simple and mysterious cadence of the songs that young girls sang on the playground or while skipping rope.

> *El lagarto está llorando.*
> *El lagarto está llorando.*
> *El lagarto y la lagarta*
> *con delantalitos blancos.*

The lizard is crying.
The lizard is crying.
The Mr. and the Mrs.,
all dressed up in white.

Of all the things that Walter Benjamin collected so avidly only to lose them just as quickly not long after acquiring them, just one survives: a Paul Klee drawing that looks like a picture for a tale, *Angelus Novus*. The things that artists made with their hands from cheap materials and bits of junk, the things they cared for and preserved through lives of poverty and grief are now trophies for billionaire investors, gleaming like gold ingots in crypts of bulletproof glass.

OUR EXPERTS WILL ANALYZE YOUR NEEDS. This is a list of the objects found in the room in Portbou where Benjamin took his life: a black satchel, a watch, a pipe, six photographs, an X-ray plate, a few letters, some newspapers, a few coins, a handwritten note that said, "It is in a little village in the Pyrenees where nobody knows me that my life will end." No one ever learned what was inside the satchel, or what became of it.

WHISPER IN MY EAR. No one can fully recognize their own voice. Almost no one can hear it on a recording without a certain feeling of distaste. For a few seconds you see or hear the stranger that others see and hear in you, as when you unexpectedly catch sight of yourself in a shop window and are surprised by it. This is not the same person you see in the mirror. In the mirror you prepare instinctively, like an actor right before he or she goes onstage. In the mirror you see what you're prepared to see, as when you think you've read a word in its entirety when in fact you inferred it from the first few letters. The mirror you look into as you go about the day does not reflect the passage of time. This notebook is being written by a stranger.

CAPTURE THE FAINTEST SOUNDS. I don't write because I have anything urgent to say. I write for the pleasure of filling the white pages of a notebook that lies open before me. A blank notebook is a book that's already been written in invisible ink. Without having made a conscious decision, I always use a pencil. Writing in pencil is like speaking softly. The movement of the pencil on the page is the very trace of the moment of inscription, the tiny groove incised with music for a diamond needle to play. The tip of the pencil is a seismic needle registering the trembling flow of words as they emerge. I write with a pencil and a pencil sharpener that I always keep by my side. I write with the feel of paper on my fingers, with a pair of scissors that I use to cut out phrases, headlines, random words that acquire in isolation a spark of beauty, a poetic quality that neither I nor anyone else had to invent because it arose from pure chance. The pencil glides across the page as stealthily as bare feet on a hardwood floor. A woman rises from her bed after making

love and on the way to the bathroom the soles of her feet slide on the polished wood with a rumor of silk.

YOU'LL WANT TO HOLD IT IN YOUR HANDS. The pencil is gradually
consumed between my fingers, growing shorter, though quite slowly in the
course of days and weeks, as the notebooks are filled and the task proceeds
without any need to know its direction. A pencil lasts as long as the ideal
cigarette in the mind of a contemplative smoker or as a glass is emptied
sip by sip, unhurriedly, by someone having a drink in a pleasant bar. My
fingers adapt easily to its dwindling length. They have to curve a bit more to
handle it now, exerting greater pressure so the letters will keep their shape.
As it shortens, the pencil becomes an increasingly intimate instrument,
better adapted to the small movements and the feel of writing; an append-
age as closely connected to my body as a pair of glasses; an extension of
the hand, just as glasses are an extension of the eye. Suddenly, I remember
that as children, from so much writing, we would grow a callus on the first
joint of the middle finger. My friend Ricardo Martín once told me that his
brother Paco, who for many years was a newspaper cartoonist, used each
pencil nearly to the very end, maniacally attached to it, with a complete
appreciation of its individual worth. Paralyzed many years ago in an accident that left him nearly incapable of moving or speaking, perhaps even of
knowing where he is or of remembering anything, Paco laboriously holds
the pencils they put in his hand and draws vague shapes, rough attempts at
pictures on a sheet of paper.

FOR YOUR INNER CHILD. Here and there you see many solitary people
writing by hand. Sometimes quite uncomfortably, on the subway, holding
a notebook on their lap and pressing down hard with a pencil or a pen to
counteract the swaying of the train. Some homeless people write while they
wait for spare change. They write on battered notebooks, pushing the tip
of a pencil stub on a ruled page. Their fingernails are dirty and cracked,
their fingers are black, red, purple with cold, wrapped in the shreds of an
old glove. They write out their appeals for help carefully in block letters

with a felt-tip marker on a piece of cardboard. In New York I saw one that said, "I killed my stepfather because he tried to abuse my sister." I saw mentally ill people writing furiously without pause on notebooks held together by a tangled spiral coil, swiftly covering each page with very large letters that they themselves would be unable to decipher later. I saw beautiful girls traveling alone who looked like a young Virginia Woolf, languid, elegant, eccentric, and enraptured, like Pre-Raphaelite hippies. When they get to a park or to a boardwalk by the sea they take off their backpacks and sit on some steps to write in a hardcover notebook where they also paste leaves, clippings, photographs, bits of poetry.

YOU ONLY HAVE TO CLOSE YOUR EYES. In the real city of Paris, Charles Baudelaire reads stories about an imaginary Paris invented by Edgar Allan Poe. He looks at a place he has known all his life with eyes that are warped and illumined by the imagination of a man who has never been there. In his youth, like all of his contemporaries, Baudelaire wanted to write novels set in distant lands, against lavish literary backdrops. He loved Delacroix's paintings because he saw in them an exotic and fantastic beauty, far nobler in his eyes and those of his contemporaries than the mediocre spectacle of a reality whose low materials were of use only to newspaper cartoonists and crime reporters. It is by reading De Quincey, who writes about London, and by reading Poe, who writes in New York about an imagined Paris, and then by taking on the immense and unlucrative task of translating them both, that Baudelaire begins to learn how to see Paris, to passionately perceive all the things that respectable art and literature never know (or want to know) how to see, everything that lies immediately before his eyes: the noise, the speed, the vulgarity, the sheer and overwhelming abundance of it all, the crowds, the voices, the mud and manure on the street, the shops lit up at night—that murky, urban night where artificial lighting and the smoke of factories have blotted out the constellations forever.

IT SHOWS YOU THE CITIES OF THE PAST. But it is all a series of misunderstandings. Baudelaire, who coined the word *modernity*, was posthumously enshrined as the prophet of the modern world when he in fact detested, with a spite as searing as his genius, everything our experts declare he wished to celebrate. Baudelaire hated photography, newspapers, gaslight, the perfectly straight boulevards they were building in Paris, the posters and handbills that covered the streets and appalled him. "*J'ai l'horreur des affiches.*" He said he couldn't open a newspaper without feeling nauseous. He hated democracy, industry, lithography, the omnibus. Walter Benjamin said that Baudelaire was a secret agent, a renegade from the bourgeois class to which he belonged by birth (when he was living in Brussels, a rumor spread that he was a spy for the French government). But he would have liked to be even more than that: a dissident, a saboteur of the same modern age that nourished his talent and originality by provoking a furious rejection. He articulated more explicitly what he intuited in the writings of his two masters and predecessors: that horror and fascination can be the same, like devotion and contempt or like taking pleasure in the very thing we want to destroy; that in the city we can see the real closeness between filth and gold, wonder and trash. He said he had written *The Flowers of Evil* with fury and patience. A friend came to visit once and noticed that he didn't have a desk. He composed his poems in his mind as he walked down the street. He had to find new metaphors to tell of things that had never existed before: the chaos of traffic and people, the new landscape of factories and of industrial gas tanks spreading to the horizon. "Those obelisks of industry, spewing forth their conglomerations of smoke into the firmament."

YOU WANTED TO COME BACK. He first read Poe in poor translations and loose adaptations that had somehow found their way into a French newspaper. It made him tremble with excitement and recognition. He would approach someone in a café and say, "Do you know Edgar Poe?" One day he heard that an American traveler passing through Paris had mentioned Poe or claimed that he was an acquaintance. He asked a friend to come along and went to call on the American at his hotel. The man agreed to see them, but was busy trying on different pairs of shoes. He told them absentmindedly that he did know Mr. Poe, having met him once or twice. Baudelaire and his friend waited anxiously to hear more while the traveler kept musing and comparing pairs of shoes, trying them on a second time, putting them aside, inspecting the stitching around the sole. He said that

Poe was a strange man, somewhat incoherent in his talk. He was surprised that someone would have heard of him in Paris. Baudelaire and his friend grew indignant and left the room, outraged, while the American traveler kept trying on boots that a shoemaker presented to him. "A Yankee," Baudelaire said disdainfully, putting on his hat as they left the hotel.

COME IN AND DISCOVER THE INGREDIENTS OF LIFE. One morning I was sitting in the Café Comercial on one of those red banquettes that share a backrest with the ones behind them. This allowed me to hear the conversations of people who were sitting very close to me but whom I couldn't see. I went often to the Comercial and usually sat at one of the tables facing the street and looking out on the roundabout of the Glorieta de Bilbao, with its elegant newsstand that seems to belong to an earlier era, the still recent but utterly abolished golden age of print. Though the café has closed, and though newspapers are vanishing before the very eyes of the few people who still buy them, the newsstand remains and even prospers by selling used DVDs. I used to sit on a banquette at a marble-top table, looking out the window at people on the sidewalk or coming up in droves from the subway station. I had a good view as well of the large and bustling interior of the café, where there were always couples, and groups of people sitting at tables that had been pushed together, and solitary customers absorbed in their newspaper, sometimes with a propped elbow on the table as if to hold between raised fingers the cigarette they were no longer allowed to smoke. The vanished cigarette of their longing.

IT GREETS YOU WITH A WELCOMING LIGHT. The café was one of those increasingly rare places where people of many ages and diverse types can mingle naturally. There were older men playing dominos and chewing pensively on toothpicks, but also pale hipsters with shaved heads and the bushy beards of Taliban warriors. There were high school students with colorful binders and cell phones next to prim old ladies having a midmorning breakfast of *churros y chocolate*. I liked the bustle of the café: no ambient music, just a big space where all you could hear was the sound of voices in conversation and the clink of dishes, glasses, coffee spoons. Sometimes, if I had a notebook, I wrote down for no particular reason the scattered phrases I overheard, fragments of conversations that often turned out to be the monologue of someone talking on the phone. But this was before the fever and obsession came over me in earnest, before I started going out for the sole purpose of spying on people's voices. That was later. Perhaps that morning at the café was partly when it began. Suddenly, against the background noise, I distinctly heard a sentence spoken behind me, quite close, in the deep voice of a man who spoke softly but clearly, with a vague accent that might have been foreign or just old-fashioned, dignified, unemphatic, hardly Spanish. There was a slight lilt to it, as if he were reciting something to a companion sitting very close to him. The voice said: "The great poem of this century can only be written with refuse."

GO ONLINE ONLY IF YOU NEED TO. That disconnected sentence was all that I was able to hear, in part because a group of high school kids at a nearby table had burst into laughter. I turned around on the banquette, pretending to look for a waiter who could take my order, but the man who had spoken was directly behind me and I was unable to see him. I couldn't tell if he was sitting with someone or talking on the phone. I heard the voice again, speaking even more softly now, unless perhaps the café was getting louder as people started coming in for lunch. I got up to go to the bathroom thinking I'd be able to see my neighbor on the other side of the banquette when I came back. The restrooms were on the far side of the café. When I returned, there was no one in the seat behind mine. Out on the street, through the plate-glass window, I saw a blurred, well-dressed figure in a coat, carrying a large black satchel in one hand and peering into the café, in my direction. He seemed to be looking at me, but at that time of day the café was sunk in a gray half-light that did not allow me to distinguish his features or any details of his clothing, just a vague sense that someone was there. A shadow, more than a solid figure.

CREEPY CLOWN STABBED BY TEENAGER IN BERLIN. *A man dressed up as a creepy clown was stabbed in Berlin this past Monday by a teenager he tried to scare, requiring emergency medical treatment to save his life. The attack was part of a spate of incidents in Germany where people dress up as creepy clowns to frighten or threaten passersby, sometimes even with chainsaws, axes, and knives. Incidents involving creepy clowns are increasingly common in Germany, and have spread in recent weeks to other parts of northern Europe including Austria, Sweden, Norway, and Denmark.*

LISTEN TO MY VOICE INSIDE YOUR HEAD. It's me. Whispering in your ear. Of all the voices in the city, mine is closest to you. Always near. I don't hide behind a corporate or conspiratorial *us*. I don't erase my tracks with impersonal statements or invitations that pretend to be disinterested. It's me. I'm speaking directly to you. I'm here to make you happy. I'm so close to you that my words will be like warm breath on your skin. I'm just an app away. When I speak I nearly touch you with my lips, a prelude, an anticipation. My words are meant for you and only you. I am the pure voice of desire. You make me melt. I can be whoever and whatever you want, whenever you want it, all you have to do is ask. Whatever you wish, whatever you dream, even if you can't bring yourself to say it, or even know that you desire it. Every morning I fall in love with you. I show you my beauty from every angle. I'm a man, a woman, a Latin girl, a volcano in bed, a naughty boy, a transvestite with a big package. I'm also a phone, a bank account, a car, an island, an ATM, an ice cream cone. When you insert your card to make a withdrawal, I am there to greet you like an unexpected friend. Hi, I'm your new ATM. I'll buy your car if you need to sell it. If you're in a tight spot I'll buy your gold and jewelry. Come see me for a professional and personalized appraisal. I speak to you as wine speaks to the drunkard in Baudelaire's poem. *Je suis l'espoir du dimanche.* I like to hear you talk. Just the two of us. I'm real. Say you love me. I'm waiting for you naked. Just dial my number. Click here. I'm not a robot. Come in now. Whisper in my ear.

COME AS MANY TIMES AS YOU LIKE. You can't see my pixelated face on the flyer you found this morning on the windshield of your car, in the gray light of a Monday, but you can see my prone and pliant body on all fours, like a cat, posing with my haunches up in the air in high heels and fishnet stockings. I bring you the brightest colors. I am a camera, a curved-screen TV, a Caribbean resort. I am a handbag in the window of a high-end store and I speak to you in French. *Je suis un sac en cuir.* You look through the glass and I beg you to caress me like a half-naked woman in a window display in Amsterdam. Touch Me & Feel. Let me take you for a ride. Discover pleasure. Try a free session. I am waiting for you in an air-conditioned room in an apartment. Fanny, Latin Girl. A minute away. Whatever you need. Fifteen minutes, twenty euros. Little morning fucks. Pleasure Fun Serious Discreet. Complimentary drink. One hour sixty euros. Far from prying eyes. Twenty euros fifteen minutes. Total comfort and discretion.

I'D LIKE TO DRINK YOU UP. I want your voice. Experience pleasure. Don't miss a thing. Tell me a secret. Beyond your wildest dreams. More than beauty. Your own private paradise. Anything you want. Let me blow your senses. Wild beauty. Follow your dreams. Catch the fever. Replenish your skin. Feel the flavor. Give yourself a gift. Live. Taste. See. I'll come meet you wherever you are. Home or hotel. Let me pamper you. Anytime. Anyplace. One in a million. Just like your dreams. Taxi fare included. Secret paths. Names like fire. I am the voice in the phone and the phone itself, so sensually adapted to your fingers and to the palm of your hand. Don't throw me out. You may need me one day. Enjoy your experience. Are you really going to miss out on something like this? Touch me. Have you seen me? Try me now. Revitalize your skin. You wanted to come back. I won't let you down. Should we go away together? Take me wherever you want. I'll show you things you'd never see without me. Cum with me.

THE GREAT CATACLYSM NOW IN 3D. Man arrested for threatening passersby while shouting "Allah is Great!" Hooded men desecrate a church in Chile. Armed police inspector barricades himself in a bar at Alcobendas. Arsonists cause the first large fire of the season. Looting of a supermarket filmed by security cameras in Venezuela. Madrid breaks world record for Pokémon hunts. Ivory rush decimates African elephants. Two French policemen stabbed to death by a jihadist. Nineteen species of Mediterranean butterflies at risk of extinction. *Star Wars* characters greet travelers at the Brussels airport. Lost cities found in the jungles of Cambodia. Man dressed up as Zorro causes panic at LAX. Scientists alarmed by the spread of blue lakes in Antarctica. Scientists search for the origins of life in planets made of diamond. A battered fashion model looks out from the cover of a celebrity magazine. Goats stare fixedly at human beings. Animals have perfect teeth. Scenes of panic at a subway station. Growing likelihood of attacks inspired by Islamic State. Man mummifies his dead cat and turns it into a drone. Top motorcycle racer destroys the window of his Porsche with a hammer. Amazing virtual reality tours of Mars. Largest gorilla on Earth is near extinction. Seeds of life in the heart of the galaxy. Ancient beetles crawl beneath the streets. Horror film written by artificial intelligence goes into production. Orlando suspect's wife knew about his plans. Samsung recalls Galaxy Note 7 after several devices burst into flames. Students faint at school while observing Ramadan. Attacker swore allegiance to ISIS while negotiating with the police. Neanderthals may have made us less fertile. First fragment found of the asteroid that changed life on Earth. Former NASA engineer reveals the truth about UFOs. A hundred and sixty bags with millions of dollars found stashed away in a convent. Man's head found in waste treatment plant. Quantum computer defeated by the human brain. Scientists investigate strange signal detected by Russian telescope. Teenage suicide bomber kills fifty people at Kurdish wedding. Truman Capote's ashes auctioned off in Los Angeles. Twelve-foot crocodile terrorizes cattle in Australia. Police inspector barricaded in a Chinese restaurant at Alcobendas commits suicide by shooting himself in the mouth. A little silence is increasingly important.

YOUR LOW-COST URBAN OASIS. I put on earbuds and listen to the recordings on my phone with an open notebook and a pencil in my hand. I transcribe quickly what I hear but I fall behind and have to stop and rewind to the moment I left off writing. Some phrases and bits of conversation I remember well, and can recall exactly where I was when I first heard them. At other times it is all unrecognizable. Or the noise of traffic is so loud that it drowns out my voice and I'm unable to understand what I said, no matter how many times I replay it. My voice sounds very strange, deeper than I would expect and a little weak or faltering. It is only on the recording that I become aware of the full volume and intensity of the endless noise that I failed to notice even as it was drowning out my voice and everything else around me. I thought I was capturing every little sound as I walked down the street when in fact I could barely hear the loudest sound of all, the one that never ends, like the roaring of the sea, growing worse if a truck or a bus happens to pass by or if there's a clamor of engines, a clatter of machines and clanging metal plates laid over potholes, of bulldozers and pneumatic drills tearing up the asphalt and digging into the sandy soil beneath. Over the monstrous bass of the city's traffic you can hear the beeping sound of a crossing signal, the long wail of a siren or an ambulance.

WE HELP YOU DISCOVER WHAT'S INSIDE YOU. I hear quick bursts of conversation of which I can only distinguish a few words. I hear the age-old singsong of a man selling fruit on the street. "Cherries, cherries, señora, have a look at these red cherries, señora, good cherries, señora." Unexpectedly I hear a woman's voice that I recorded while waiting for the light to change on Velázquez Street. She was speaking calmly in a high, clear voice, just a few steps away from me. People talk loudly on the phone without realizing others could be listening in or spying on them. I have to play her monologue a few times to catch every word. It was a young woman, I remember. She was pushing a baby stroller with both hands and holding the phone to her ear by craning her neck against her shoulder, almost between her chin and clavicle. "Dinner was good, very good. It was with the American ambassador. And you'll never guess who came along with him. Harrison Ford. I swear. Oh, it was great, just so cool. Just great. So cool. Wonderful people. Harrison Ford was totally down-to-earth, with that beard of his. I mean, I don't think it suits him. And everyone was really pleased about the elections. It was great, really great."

YOUR TOP FITNESS MOMENTS. There are rare stretches where all you can hear is traffic and the sound of footsteps. Nobody's footsteps. My voice, which can usually be heard repeating a phrase I read on the street or re-counting what I see, has disappeared. There's a sound like the sound of wind blowing through the trees or of waves crashing on an empty shore. Someone listening to these fragments wouldn't be able to tell in what city they were recorded. A ceaseless sound without a name. Whenever I stop speaking into the phone I turn off the recorder, but sometimes I forget, or miss the button, and the seconds and tenths of a second keep ticking away in an accidental recording that sometimes lasts for several minutes. I walk in silence and the phone continues to record inside my pocket. Sometimes the noise grows faint and distant. I must have turned off an avenue and gone down a quiet street. My footsteps are heard more clearly, and bird-song, too, faint but perceptible, sparrows in the branches of an acacia tree on some side street in Madrid, or a magpie, the screeching of parrots. A specialized sound engineer could find this recording and begin to catalog each of its acoustic signals, lifting them apart like layers in an archeological site. The sound of shutters being abruptly lowered. An automatic garage door being raised. The birdlike clamor of children playing in a schoolyard. Sounds from a different era, a different century. A knife-grinder's whistle. The sea, which had been calm, is suddenly stirred, revealing a vast expanse of sound stretching in a series of receding planes to the horizon. The wail of a police siren in the far distance. An ambulance, faint at first, then drawing near, drowning out all other sounds, then gradually diminishing until it is finally lost in the great acoustic fog.

CELEBRATE EVERYTHING YOU HAVE. My voice is gone and so am I. There are just footsteps, which don't seem like mine, don't sound like footsteps at all but rather like a hollow pounding or the heartbeat of a very large creature, the uneven steps of a heavy man, limping, perhaps a man with a big shoe and a brace of metal rods and screws around his leg. It sounds like a piston or a pair of bellows, opening and closing, an ivory leg, a wooden leg striking rhythmically on a wooden floor. In the background there is a kind of clumsy, groaning accordion. For a moment, the sharp click of high heels sets off a counterpoint to the clomping of the orthopedic shoe, of Ahab's shoe, old Ahab wandering around Madrid. I go back to the start of the recording and it seems both stranger and more unquestionable that those steps belong to me. Then I listen more carefully to the faint metallic sound: keys, or coins, rattling with each step and striking against something. The reason the footsteps sound so deep and uneven is that they're recorded from the side pocket where I carry the phone. The metallic sound is the sound of keys and coins striking against the phone itself.

TRY ON A NEW IDENTITY. On a TV screen at the airport, a blond woman takes a cab in Copenhagen. She's wearing dark glasses, high heels, and a black suit. A moment later the city she glimpses through the window of the cab is London. She types something on her phone; when she looks up again the blue pillars and harp-like cables of the Manhattan Bridge are gliding past the window. This time yesterday I was walking through Madrid on a warm summer evening, now I watch a red sky turn purple from a sidewalk in Paris, breathing in the same balmy air. The sudden sense of distance alters and widens my spirit, heightening within me a feeling of anticipation or of trembling premonition, as if these were the last days before some great event, the last night of an era that only in retrospect will be seen clearly to have been drawing to a close. Days that feel like photographs, touched by the faint aura of what will come to be remembered, to be witnessed years later in a documentary: people walking down the street in period dress, or seated outside a café, unaware of the future archaism of their clothes or of the faint archeological air that clings to them, their hats, the way they wear their hair, the cars going by, which already look like museum pieces.

OFF TO THE CITY AT THE LOWEST POSSIBLE PRICE. To walk through Paris with nothing to do and no one to meet after a day's work is to be here on this precise evening in June and simultaneously to remember it years or decades later, when things that are hazy or even entirely invisible in the present will appear in the crisp, irrefutable outline of their historical becoming. Crowds of young people are drinking and chatting under the bridges along the Seine, their bare legs dangling from the stone embankment and their cheerful voices ringing out as on a square in Madrid. The river's current is swift, rough, powerful, with an oily sheen under the street-lights like the back of a huge aquatic creature. By the flowing Seine I remember the Hudson. I lose track of how long I have been walking. There are squares and avenues flooded with a stifling crowd of tourists, like Venice on a summer day, and then, a step away, smaller squares and narrow streets sunk in a kind of antique silence, the black-and-white Paris of Brassaï. All day the sun beat down on the limestone buildings. After months of gray skies and ceaseless rain, women are out again in skirts and blouses, baring their shoulders and their pale legs. Time and space seem to distend in the thick, warm air and in the lingering daylight, inviting people to drift lazily along. At ten in the evening there is still light. Young people wade into the fountain on the Place Saint-Michel, beneath the bronze archangel treading on a demon with his wings outspread, raising a sword.

WE HAVE EVERYTHING YOU NEED. At street corners, or in the hollow doorways of shuttered shops, large families or tribes of Romanian gypsies have set up camp, taking over the sidewalk with their mattresses and their old blankets and sheets. Men and women with children, or alone, or holding babies in their arms; small flocks of lively, ragged children with flashing eyes and dirty faces, the racket of a gypsy camp right next to the luxury shops and the lights of the cafés. At the outdoor tables there are open newspapers with alarming headlines, as in a documentary about the 1930s. And just as in those old pictures, there seems to be no connection between the ominous news and the placid normalcy of life. My verbal tenses slip into the past. The Brexit referendum just took place, but the results will not be known until dawn. Outside the brasseries there are piles of oysters and shellfish half-sunk in glaciers of chopped ice that are lit to heighten their freshness. Trays of beer mugs capped with foam seem to glide in the air, held aloft over the waiters' heads.

AN ANSWER TO EVERY QUESTION. It could all be a mirage. The dazed, fragile mirth of a vanished world. I was told that in the outer neighborhoods of Paris there are groups of Muslim watchmen patrolling the streets to impose Sharia and punish women who go out without covering their heads. The bookstores that stay open late into the night are as resplendent as the brasseries. L'Écume des Pages is as full of customers and as well stocked with all kinds of appealing books as always. In Paris you swim in the high spectacle of the city, giving in to an endless craving for bookstores and for the French language, for hearing, speaking, and reading it, a language as sumptuous as French food and producing in the returning enthusiast a mild inebriation like that of French wine. The Rue des Beaux-Arts is so quiet that I can hear my own footsteps as I look again for the facade of the hotel where Oscar Wilde once lived and died. I have walked for hours on an empty stomach and I'm starting to feel hungry. At an old bistro named Chez Fernand I dine on boeuf bourguignon and drink plenty of red wine served in a carafe. My feet are sore and I am sated and happy and keep walking until midnight. Almost every corner is haunted by some revered ghost. Brassaï went through that doorway on the Rue des Grands-Augustins many times to visit Picasso and photograph his sculptures. Balzac lived and wrote nearby as well. Oscar Wilde checked into the Hôtel d'Alsace under the name Sebastian Melmoth. In New York, in a glass case at the Morgan Library, I once saw a bill bearing that name. Wilde got very sick and was never forced to pay it.

YOUR ROAD THROUGH THE WORLD STARTS HERE. Insomnia breeds inside a hotel room like moss in a shady place. I go to bed dead-tired but I stay up, avidly reading and examining the books I just bought until my eyes close. Sleep, though not fatigue, dissipates as soon as I turn off the light. A captivating book is a kind of stimulant similar to caffeine. I find in what I read an intimation of a loose and scattered music that I would like to capture in my notebook, clipped and supple, the honed precision of Marguerite Duras or of Paul Valéry. I wake up suddenly from a deep and troubled sleep and am lost in darkness, unable to remember having turned off the light or even where I am. I dreamed of the facade of a hotel that looked like this one, whose name I could read on a bright sign: Hotel Cólera-Miró. My phone, which had been off, is casting its white glow on the nightstand. I see on the screen the latest numbers from the British referendum, the calamity that no one thought would happen.

YOU WILL MEET NEW CHALLENGES WITH RESOLVE. I lie awake, then fall into short stretches of restless sleep from which I wake once more to fall asleep again, so that the night in the hotel seems to go on forever. I wake up and think that I've slept for a long time, surely it will soon be morning; I even mistake the glow of the streetlamp coming in through the curtains for the first light of day. When its true character becomes apparent, it seems impossible to have mistaken it for the sun. And when I pick up my phone, fumbling in an unfamiliar darkness where habit has not yet laid its signposts, the screen lights up and I'm astonished to see that it is three in the morning. Many hours of darkness remain. I go from sleep to waking and back again as if moving through a series of identical communicating rooms. I can't tell if they're always different or if maybe there are just a few rooms through which I pass again and again.

CUSTOMIZE YOUR PROFILE. In the meantime, silence is a sedative against what seemed like a return of anxiety. The gift of insomnia is a deep, broad silence that can never be found during the day or in the evening hours when people are still out. Insomnia is a place of hidden crypts and sound-proof chambers, of subterranean lakes whose smooth, translucent waters are lit by glowing microscopic organisms. It's precisely in this silence that the task can come to life, become auspicious and appealing, a promise of effort-less absorption so enjoyable that it doesn't matter if it turns out to be useless or to dissolve into nothing, just one among the many projects that rise like splendid clouds in your imagination, taking the shape of continents, arctic cliffs and archipelagos, cities full of terraces and golden galleries and domes like the ones De Quincey saw in his opium dreams—until they waver and begin to lose their shape, and finally dissolve without a trace into the blue.

THE BEST THINGS CAN'T BE LABELED. I once met a scientist who had a passion for clouds. He always carried a camera, knowing how crucial it was to photograph them quickly. Sometimes if he saw an interesting cloud while driving he would stop the car on the side of the road, even on the highway, and hurry to take its picture. He was a specialist in fluid dynam-ics, and also, he said, a member of the International Cloud Appreciation So-ciety. Could this be what your writing and your projects are like? Currents of air and molecules of water vapor coming together in bizarre yet predict-able shapes, following a fixed repertoire that can be ordered and classified like plant or animal species. Writing takes shape and sculpts itself out of a material nearly as intangible as water molecules suspended in the air. And once it has a shape, acquiring a clear outline in the mind of the reader, it vanishes spontaneously after a few moments or a few minutes, dissolving like a cloud or like the geometric shapes carefully composed in multicol-ored sands by a Tibetan monk in a mandala, which, once finished, he will erase just as conscientiously with the palm of his hand.

OUR PASSION IS TO TURN YOUR DAILY ROUTINES INTO UN-FORGETTABLE MOMENTS. They arrived with merciless punctuality at eight in the morning, taking the house by storm like a methodical commando. After a few minutes they were moving through the rooms with strategic swiftness, as if they had studied in advance the plans of the fortress they were going to invade. Outside the house they parked a huge truck that took up half the street. They came equipped with tools, dark blankets, coils of rope and twine, unassembled cardboard boxes, retro-futuristic guns that will allow them to lay down and snip long strips of adhesive tape in one motion, a tape that will squeak throughout the day as they apply it and smooth it down and cut it with a quick, loud, repetitive tearing noise. Their blue shirts look vaguely like police uniforms, with sewn badges and epaulettes. The women are female commandos as tough as the men. They wear their hair up in a ponytail and issue curt commands. Some of the men are older but still quite sturdy, strengthened by a job that keeps them relentlessly in shape. The younger ones are foreign, Latin American, perhaps Romanian. They have tattoos and beards and their stiff pants are tucked into their hiking boots. As soon as they arrived, the house ceased to be what it had been for the past twelve years, up until the very instant we woke up this morning, which is our last. The house is an encampment now, a warehouse, its doors thrown open so that people can rush up and down the stairs while we grow smaller and more irrelevant with every passing moment, a pair of inept and puny individuals standing in the way and hesitating when decisions must be made, watching like the weak victims of an invasion as all of their possessions are taken down and packed away, dozens of books pulled off the shelves by the armful to be shoved carelessly into cardboard boxes that the workers carry off with gruff annoyance.

YOU CAN ACHIEVE YOUR DREAM AT ANY AGE. I walk around the house feeling daunted, standing always in the way of someone in a hurry to get through with a heavy load. I watch them empty my record shelves and can't bring myself to ask them to be careful. I start assembling a cardboard box and one of them walks over, puts it expertly together and sets it at my feet politely though with a hint of contempt. Some of the women look even more imposing because they carry walkie-talkies. The men only pause to give or to receive instructions on their phones. I start putting things away that, in the midst of the maelstrom, suddenly seem like the strange and elaborately ridiculous contents of a junk shop: paintings, souvenirs, photographs, documents that lay forgotten for years in the back of a drawer, things that accumulated over time from sheer inertia and that I did not remember keeping: drawings that my children made when they were little; telegrams from a not-so-distant time when one still sent such things; old batteries, keys to unknown doors, charging cables for lost and obsolete devices, for digital cameras we never used again, all of it in one big jumble and almost none of it of any use, relics, trash. And there I am, staring at a faded Polaroid or at a note I scribbled long ago on the back of some official invitation, while behind me a group of burly men is carrying a sofa as big as a rhino, sweating and cursing as they try, though it seems hopeless, to twist it through a door, onto a landing, and down a flight of stairs.

TECHNOLOGY APPLIED TO LIFE. And just when I think I've finished, when it seems there's nothing left to put away in this strange and empty room where until a few hours ago I used to do my work, and read, and listen to music, one of the movers carelessly picks up a drawer of my disassembled desk and a box falls to the floor. When I open it, I find things inside that I hadn't seen or even remembered in over a decade. Memory betrays us.

I recognize my father's wristwatch, his last ID card, his driver's license, a lottery ticket, things of his that I kept after he died, surfacing now as if by sheer chance from an archeological site, the watch especially with its big face, the glass a little cloudy and scratched, the steel strap that used to go around his wrist, which was always much stronger than mine. Looking at the watch hands, I suddenly find myself wondering if they could be pointing to the exact time of his death.

ENJOY IT AT YOUR NEAREST BURGER KING.

"Peaches, *niña*, look at these peaches from Aragón; good peaches, *niña*, for cheap. Look at these peaches from Aragón."

"If there's no government there's no order, which means there is disorder."

HELP US CUSTOMIZE YOUR MORTGAGE.

"When I was little you promised you would take me to the river and you never did. You promised you would take me on the cable car and you never did."

"*Niñas*, *guapas*, don't miss out, just look at all these apricots and peaches."

HI, I'M A TWENTY-NINE-YEAR-OLD BLIND GIRL AND I'M OUT OF WORK.

"He calls me up at ten at night and says, where are you, and I say, I'm at home, where else would I be?"

"Take some home with you, *niña*, good peaches, fresh peaches, cheap as they come."

CUSTOMIZE YOUR SHOPPING CART HERE.

"Have you ever been to the Ice Palace?"

NOW YOU CAN DRIVE THE CAR OF YOUR DREAMS.

"As soon as I open my eyes in the morning, I thank God because He gives me whatever I ask for."

"When I get out. After I see the oncologist, which is at five."

JESUS THIRSTS FOR YOU.

"Just go to the website. I'm telling you, by November you'll have a boyfriend."

A WIDE SELECTION OF KNIVES AND MEDIEVAL WEAPONS IN TOLEDO STEEL.

"*Guapas*, here's your chance, try what you like, look at these peaches and apricots, *nena*, the freshest, the best, just wait till you taste them."

DON'T SETTLE WHEN YOU FLY.

"The problem is, you've lost that person, and now you can't get them out of your head no matter how you try."

IT'S TIME TO EXPERIENCE SOMETHING DIFFERENT.

"These are the best peaches, *nena*, the best apricots, try them before you buy them."

BORN WILD, RAISED IN THE CITY.

"Okay, okay, you'll let me know. Or you can send me a WhatsApp. Okay."

"Sweet summer peaches *niña*, from Aragón, give them a try, don't buy them if you don't like them."

OUR OFFERS ARE AS AMAZING AS YOU.

"You're wondering why she went back to live with her parents? Because her husband used to beat her to a pulp, that's why."

MURDER VICTIM'S FINGERS PRINTED IN 3D. There was an underwater quality to the Café Comercial, a twilight brightness shot through with shadow. The morning light of Madrid poured in through faintly frosted windows and fused with the inner dusk as in the deep recess of an old warehouse. The gray-black marble-top tables and wood chairs absorbed the light and softened its sharpness. There were crisp echoes, like the clicking of dominos, even if no one was playing. A wisp of tobacco seemed to hang in the air from all the ghostly cigarettes once smoked by generations of vanished patrons. I usually took the Metro there. I would come out opposite the roundabout of the Glorieta de Bilbao, stop at the newsstand, buy a paper or two as well as some obscure and fortuitous DVD, then walk happily into the great inner space of the café as if entering a parallel Madrid or a different region of time; not a portion of the past, somehow pooled or preserved as in a sanctuary, but a present time whose ties to the past had not been severed. There was a particular atmosphere that is rare in Spain, as of a place where dignified and well-worn things endure and are cared for. It seemed more Portuguese than Spanish. This feeling was confirmed by the waiters' crisp white jackets, even if only to be instantly dispelled when those same waiters, in all their faded Portuguese elegance, opened their mouths to list the spartan offerings of the café in the harsh accent of Madrid. They were as gruff as old school proctors, seeming to take pleasure in informing customers that they were out of churros or of any of those fancy sodas with elaborate names like Nestea or Aquarius. They had Pepsi and Fanta and that was plenty, as one of them might have said.

ARE YOU SOMEONE LOOKING FOR NEW EXPERIENCES? Once, on a different day, when I went in and walked to the banquette by the window,

I thought I recognized the man with the satchel whom I had seen peering into the café. I realized that I had felt a sense of familiarity even on that first occasion. I must have recognized him by the satchel, which lay next to him on the banquette. He made a gesture inviting me to join him. It was clear that he was not very good at preambles or that he simply didn't care for them. He only knew how to get straight to the point. The voice was the same I'd heard a few days or a few weeks earlier: deep, a little raspy, with an accent that was impossible to place. Spanish seemed to be his native language, but it was a Spanish unlike any I had ever heard. It seemed to come from far away, either in space or in time.

NOW IS THE TIME TO RECOVER THOSE LOST MOMENTS. "You may not remember, but we met once, in Granada, more than thirty years ago. You came a few times to the house where I lived in the Albaicín. Or I should rather say the *carmen* where I lived, to use the local word. It is an Arabic word. You used to say that the house was so hidden away, the only way to find it was by getting lost. I am not surprised that you do not remember. It was a very small house, narrow and steep, like a spiral staircase. A cubist *carmen*, if you will allow the comparison, a kind of Moorish, three-dimensional Juan Gris. Not a Picasso or a Braque. You understand what I mean. Juan Gris is "the man," as those jazz musicians you like so much might have said. There was a garden with a well, and a small balcony. You still don't remember? From the balcony you could see the Alhambra, long and low, like a whale, on the other side of the Darro. The reason you do not remember is not that so much time has passed, but that you have lived several different lives since then."

ENTER A NEW DIMENSION. "What people refer to, though in my view with a regrettable lack of precision, as the 'transmigration of souls' is in fact a perfectly common occurrence. Reincarnation could be studied as easily as a change of address. It *is* a change of address, to some degree. I, too, have lived a few lives since, though perhaps not as many as you. Of course, if we go back farther, I may be ahead. The possibility of rebirth as an animal

83

or as another human being is a metaphor. Primarily a Tibetan or a Hindu metaphor. It would be as mistaken to take it literally as to think that you and I believe the Earth is at the center of the universe because we say the sun rises in the morning. We say the walls have ears, but as far as we know there are no actual ears embedded in them, though occasionally they happen to be bugged. You are in fact reincarnated into someone who turns out to be yourself, though substantially altered. Some of our past lives leave memories behind, while others, most, do not. In severe cases a complete loss of memory is advisable and of course welcome. A clean slate, one might say. Yet another metaphor. Memories remain but we do not realize they are memories. They appear most clearly in dreams that vanish without a trace as soon as you wake up. Like the tape in the old TV show that would self-destruct five seconds after relaying its secret message. You think you are inventing a story when you are in fact remembering. You think you are imagining something that takes place in the future when in fact what your mind is picturing is a lost memory."

NIGHT OF THE BEASTS.

Man bludgeons his elderly mother to death with a hammer in Madrid.

Dirty war returns to the skies over Colombia.

More than a hundred dead in Nigerian church collapse.

Police officers are poisoned by the body of a man who committed suicide with toxic agents.

Eighty dolphins die in the sun on a Florida beach.

Patrons flee as a large deer enters a restaurant.

Faceless assassins cornered in Mosul.

Woman is found chained like a dog.

At least twenty dead after a car-bomb attack in Mogadishu.

Two girls set off suicide vests in a Nigerian market.

Security guard punches a young woman outside a nightclub.

Teacher arrested after putting a student in a garbage can.

Hottest summer on record.

Twelve-year-old girl dies from alcohol overdose.

Plastic surgeon arrested for fraud as he was operating on his own penis.

Wave of terror in the Near East.

Girl slept with rags around her neck so as not to be eaten by rats.

Brightest supernova in History was actually a cosmic cataclysm.

Death of Japanese flamenco singer.

Terrorism strikes at the heart of the Christian Copt community in Cairo.

Twenty-three dead after a bomb explodes in a crowded church during Sunday mass.

Woman bites off the nose of her boyfriend's ex-girlfriend at a nightclub.

Kurdistan Freedom Hawks claim responsibility following suicide attack that killed thirty-nine people last Saturday outside an Istanbul soccer stadium.

Egypt begins to export crocodiles.

Temple to an Aztec wind-god found in Tlatelolco.

Largest organ-trafficking network in the world dismantled.

Forty-five whales die on Indian beaches.

Large cities are flooded in trash.

City of nine million evacuated by orders of the Chinese government.

Thousands of geese die, poisoned by toxic lake in Montana.

Norwegian scientists find sixty pounds of plastic bags in the stomach of a dead whale.

Days on Earth are growing longer.

Will the sexual future of mankind involve carnal relations with robots?

Why are there winged ants in the fall?

What would you do if you knew the love of your life was guilty of murder?

REDISCOVER SENSATIONS THAT EVERYDAY LIFE WON'T ALWAYS PROVIDE. For the past few days I have been living in a hotel room in my own city. It makes me feel like I'm doing something secretive or slightly questionable, leading a double life. This morning I gave the house keys to the new owners. Now I no longer carry in my pocket a set of keys that jingles as I walk but a magnetic card that weighs nothing. This adds to my sense of lightness. I walk through the city where I live as if I were just a visitor. I step out of the hotel and find myself in a neighborhood that I only ever knew in passing. I've moved out of the house where I used to live, and the house I will move into is not yet ready because of unforeseen delays with the renovation. All of my belongings except for a suitcase and a backpack have been put away in a storage unit. My possessions amount mostly to what I carry with me when I go out on the street: a phone, a computer, some notebooks, a pen, an inkwell, a few pencils, two or three books, and an e-reader. Moving all the things that had piled up at home over the years required a truck. Suddenly all of it seems superfluous, a lead weight that shackled my feet and prevented me from walking as lightly as I do now, on these late days of June when it starts getting hot and a lazy holiday mood begins to slowly spread over the city.

WE ARE WORKING TO MAKE YOUR DREAMS COME TRUE. I make my way across the hotel lobby and am greeted by the doorman. All around me there are voices speaking in English or in Latin American Spanish. I live among travelers now, and some of their foreignness rubs off on me. I push the revolving doors and step out from the air-conditioned coolness of the lobby into the June heat. I've walked down this street many times before, but today I am a guest at the hotel and thus a stranger, if not a suspicious impostor. Places I once reached by taxi or by subway, or after a long walk, are now conveniently around the corner. I go out at dusk, freshly showered and in a light clean shirt, my hands in my pockets, a false traveler in my own city yet filled with the real anticipation of someone who has just arrived, and feels, on leaving the hotel, the mysterious promise of night as the windows on the buildings and the shop signs are lit, beacons calling out to him with a siren song. The woman I am meeting for dinner is my own wife. Afterward, when we come back together to our hotel room, the way we move and touch will have the fervent stealth of adultery. Our love is a different love and Madrid turns into a foreign city. Once again, as long ago, your only joint possessions are the few things you bring to the hotel.

TWELVE PEOPLE ARRESTED FOR SPREADING FALSE REPORTS OF CREEPY CLOWNS. *Clowns in vans. Clowns in the woods. Clowns lurking in the shadows. Clowns chasing people or committing crimes. Twelve individuals face charges of harassment, spreading false reports, or making criminal threats. Other reports may have been caused by children with overactive imaginations, by mischievous teenagers, or by other individuals impelled by their own motives to stoke the general panic. The hoax of the killer clowns is responsible for at least one death. In Reading, Ohio, public schools were closed last Friday after a woman said she had been attacked by a man dressed as a clown. A teenager had been arrested a day earlier for being allegedly involved in threats that clowns would attack students at his school. The first clown sightings were reported last August in Greenville, South Carolina. Individuals dressed as clowns were luring children into the woods with offers of money, or prowling near people's homes to frighten them. Subsequent reports spread like an epidemic, with clown sightings taking place in at least six other states: Alabama, Georgia, Maryland, New Jersey, North Carolina, and Pennsylvania. In one incident, in LaGrange, Georgia, four people were detained and charged with making terrorist threats after police received reports that individuals dressed as clowns had threatened to commit violent acts at three different schools. The suspects said they would be dressed as "creepy clowns" and travel in a white van.*

SI L'AMOUR POUVAIT ÊTRE TOUJOURS COMME LE PREMIER JOUR.
They have all they need to be happy, and perhaps they are, but there is an incipient sense of weariness, an apathy that they perhaps can't quite perceive. There is affection and trust between them, a complicity that is perhaps a touch excessive, a danger in knowing each other so well, in how it all flows naturally, without a hitch. Nothing is out of place, the apartment is pleasant and of course refined, with its high ceilings and gilt moldings, but modern too, like them, the perfect couple, as their friends must have said when they first saw them together: her passion and sophistication, her big dark eyes and luscious hair, a high-end Carmen, so to speak, or a Penélope Cruz. She's Spanish and he's Anglo-Saxon. Yet another perfect combination. She is dark like Carmen, he is blond; her eyes are black and his are blue; she has soft and beautiful skin while his face is rough and masculine, with an attractive stubble that makes him seem adventurous while also delineating the contour of his jaw. But there is something in the air, a secret disquiet between them, or in each of them separately. We see, from the outside, the lights go out in the apartment. But she is changing into different clothes, swiftly, silently putting on a raincoat and slipping a set of car keys in her pocket. Her languor turns into haste, her calm into determination. The car is a Mercedes sports car. She drives through Paris very fast, down avenues and through a tunnel that must lie parallel to the Seine. Beyond the profile of her face we see a luminous red fog. When luxury cars drive through splendid cities or down the highway they always have the road entirely to themselves. Behind her, in the tunnel, a motorcycle suddenly appears. For an instant the memory of Princess Diana's tragic death in a similar chase gives us warning of the frightful closeness between a great passion and a catastrophe. The motorcycle catches up with her. Concealed by his helmet like a medieval knight

in armor, the rider turns to look at her as he speeds by, then disappears into the distance.

YOUR MOST SECRET FANTASIES. She parks the car by a high gate. It could be a mansion on the outskirts of Paris. It is a luxury hotel. She glides through the lobby in her cinched black raincoat, on edge, aware that the women at the reception desk are watching her. She is someone who doesn't need to say much to express her will. A key is placed on the marble counter and her fingers close over it. As she rises in a gleaming elevator, the pulsing reflection of the city lights below is like the pulsing of her heart. She leans against the side, holding in one hand a flask of perfume. Outside the elevator there is a very long hallway that is lit like a spaceship. She touches the walls with her fingers as she goes. She leans on the wall, fainting with anticipation and perhaps with desire. Before using the key to the room, she stands outside and presses her forehead to the door. Her lips are parted as if about to break into a smile tinged with expectation, with impatience, perhaps with disbelief at being finally there. Her trembling fingers turn the key in the lock and she opens the door. The man who was waiting for her is him. The room spins as they embrace. The windows and the lights of Paris spin with them and turn into a perfume flask, Trésor, the treasure of a love that stays forever like the first day.

ONLY A MASTER CAN TRANSFORM YOUR SKIN DURING THE NIGHT. He often has a dream in which a threatening figure is drawing near, a vague shape emerging from dark depths, drawing closer and closer while he remains paralyzed in the quicksand of dreams, incapable of acting. He can never tell if it's a human being or an animal, or both at once, or something in between, a hybrid creature from the island of Dr. Moreau. Perhaps it comes from the beginnings of time, rooted in ancestral memory, a cluster of tightly packed neurons deep within the brain, in the tiny, almond-shaped mass of the amygdala. Perhaps it was already there when hominids sought shelter in the trees from carnivorous beasts that hunted them for prey. Even in his sleep, instinct warns him that something is silently approaching. Fear acts like a biological radar. It could be an animal that is drawing near, so stealthy and well adapted to the dark that it can only be discerned by the gleam of its eyes. Or it could be a human predator, faceless, or wearing a mask; a primitive mask in the shape of an animal or perhaps a cheap modern mask made of plastic or cardboard, stamped with the frozen, happy smile of a cartoon character. He is filled with terror by its approach and is unable to move, paralyzed like an ape before the gaze of a feline predator, like a rabbit or a deer in a car's blinding headlights. He must move, but he can't, and when he tries to speak or scream for help he finds his mouth and tongue will not obey him.

WE FOUND YOU. This time, in the dream, the figure is wearing a robe like a mandarin or a high Chinese official. Like the robe that Mao wore in some of his portraits. The robe reaches down to its feet, and on its head there is a monstrous, swollen mask. Or perhaps there is no mask, just a monstrous face, like the Elephant Man. It steps out of the darkness and the robe is blue, a muted blue. He manages to raise one hand as it draws near, to close it into a fist, like a prisoner struggling to free himself from his bindings. Then, while the rest of his body remains paralyzed, he gathers all his strength into his arm and brings himself to punch the air, causing a loud noise that frees him from the nightmare. He has punched the lamp on the nightstand and knocked it to the ground. But even now, as he lies awake in the dark, his sense of helplessness remains. The masked or monstrously deformed creature in the blue robe refuses to vanish completely into the surrounding darkness. Where does it all come from. Who wove together the scene in just a few seconds, selecting the costume, the mask, the dark background, the texture and color of the robe. He keeps his eyes wide open, trying not to fall back asleep. It would be like going back into the tunnel where his gruesome visitor awaits, a visitor that he himself has shaped and brought to life.

STRANGE THIRTEEN-LEGGED CREATURE FOUND ON THE OCEAN FLOOR. Somewhat immodestly, though also accurately, he prides himself in having invented no less than three new disciplines in the already extensive field of the humanities. It's true that several lifetimes would be required to establish their theoretical and methodological bases, as well as to complete a few research projects that would put their principles into practice and demonstrate their rigor, their efficacy, the wealth of new discoveries they could bring to light. The primary obstacle is neither the subject matter nor a proper access to sources, but rather the fact, irreparable at present, that he is the sole inventor and practitioner of these fields of study. At a time when science and the academic world in general are dominated by working groups and by increasingly complex crowdsourcing and management techniques, the realm of action for an individual is almost pathetically circumscribed. Not to mention that the individual in question lacks all academic credentials or connections, thus any access to adequate facilities or to sources of public or private funding for his projects. Even so, did not Santiago Ramón y Cajal work alone? As did Edward Gibbon, Louis Pasteur, Dr. Jekyll, Dr. Frankenstein, Pierre and Marie Curie, and Albert Einstein, when he was a young patent clerk in Bern. All those large, well-financed teams, all those brainstorming sessions, the whole tremendous apparatus of the universities not just in Spain but all over the world: How many concrete, verifiable, beneficial results do they usually produce? Lacking any academic affiliation, he will have to be entirely self-reliant. He will have to come up with the titles, programs, and qualifications. He will even have to print the business cards and diplomas for these new disciplines, being as they are entirely of his own invention and currently in a stage that is not so much preliminary as utterly chimerical.

WE ARE THE SOLUTION TO YOUR NEEDS. But in the end, he thinks, except in the physical sciences and in those that help people heal or that hasten their death, what's the difference between an official university degree and one that is fictitious or apocryphal? Don't we often see, he thinks, getting a little worked up, eminent academics adding to their curriculum by what would politely be called "borrowing" from other people's efforts, their colleagues, their subordinates, sometimes with their acquiescence, whether remunerated or not, sometimes without their knowledge? Is there not in recent scandals, which nonetheless, to the relief of all but a few vindictive individuals, have not managed to permanently damage the good name or well-being of the alleged plagiarists; is there not an underlying notion of individual "authorship" that is antiquated, elitist, and obsolete? At a time when so many other innovative degrees are being promoted in the world of higher learning, from Event Management to Spiritual Coaching to Translation Science, it doesn't seem far-fetched to him to launch these disciplines or fields of knowledge that he believes himself to have invented, or rather founded, just as much as Auguste Comte is thought to have founded sociology, or his cherished Erwin Panofsky is called the father of iconology. If UFO studies, political science, educational psychology, plastic surgery, communications, or literary theory are now fully acceptable fields, the academic community will no doubt soon embrace these new disciplines that have been inspired, and one might say pioneered, by him. He is too modest to imagine a future where he will be called "The Father of Instantaneous Archeology," "A Pioneer in Topobiography" or in perambulation studies, or in the history of accidental art. Merely to arrive at a sketch of each of these disciplines (better not call them "sciences," the term is already quite discredited in these circles) would require a lifetime of research, theoretical reflection, and documentation, not to mention all the activities related to fieldwork that in the academic world are comfortably delegated to assistants, graduate students, and postdocs.

BE YOURSELF, UNLESS YOU CAN BE BATMAN. New geolocation devices and techniques will allow for a huge leap forward in Perambulation

Studies, similar perhaps to the one brought about in neuroscience by magnetic imaging, even if limited by the current inability to employ them retrospectively, that is, to the walks that people took in the past. As its name suggests, perambulation studies deals with the physical routes taken by writers, artists, scientists, lunatics, prophetic seers, and destitute madmen: whether it be the habitual paths they followed all their lives—Kant's daily walks would be a classic example—or those sudden, irregular trajectories that only happened once. It remains unclear whether perambulation studies is an independent field or rather a branch of topobiography, whose end, as can be easily guessed, is the study of the various locations where these same figures live or lived, in order to establish, with the aid of detailed maps, the likely psychospatial or sociovital patterns involved. (The wholesale creation of a specialized jargon is another challenge beyond the powers of a single person.) Borges once referred disdainfully to those literary biographers who are "so enthralled by a change of address" that they have no time to look at the works of the authors they study. But topobiography can shed light on fundamental aspects of scientific and aesthetic creation, or simply of mental rambling, that have been little understood until now. No branch of knowledge, even in the humanities, can function anymore without a solid quantitative basis. In how many Parisian hotels, for instance, did Charles Baudelaire and Walter Benjamin live? What is the ratio of changes of address per period of time? And the ratio of pages written per location? In how many places did Thomas De Quincey live in England and Scotland, or Edgar Allan Poe in the United States, if we take Boston and Richmond as the limits of his geographical displacement?

THE PLACE YOU WERE DREAMING OF IS HERE. *Madame Bovary* was written over the course of five years in the same room of the same house. This sedentary state must somehow be part of the novel's DNA, to employ a distinguished though perhaps entirely useless term, just as Baudelaire's unsettled life during the years when he wrote *The Flowers of Evil* must have had strong creative implications, heightened by the fact—we trespass here on the territory of perambulation studies, given there is no cadre of specialists yet to jealously guard it—that Baudelaire composed his poems mentally as he walked. In how many rooms, on how many kitchen tables, in how many cafés, houses, and cities did Joyce write his *Ulysses*? A traveler just arrived in Trieste is excited to find a little plaque marking a house where Joyce once lived. But nearly identical plaques can be seen on corners all over the city, since Joyce moved houses with the same disastrous frequency as any of his fellow literary wanderers. Needless to say, a great deal of research has already been done and a wealth of materials is available. But a theory is missing, a method, a set of quantifying tools and of conceptual or maybe even neurological principles to really shed light on the likely correspondence between, on the one hand, the tangle of routes and locations that one can draw on a map, and on the other, the blazing neuronal connections that gradually gave rise to those rambling works of the imagination.

ALL THE SPACE YOU NEED IN YOUR LIFE. Each morning I am astonished to be back. Every single morning. Whether I am calmly making breakfast or whether I go out and see the great puddle of light on the sidewalk and the swaying shade of the locust tree that scatters its small white blossoms everywhere, dry as confetti in the summer heat. There is a sacramental quality to making breakfast, to the propriety of each necessary step in a ritual involving all the gifts of nature and of human labor, of plants and animals, a ritual that is best carried out in silence and that seems imbued with a tacit sense of gratitude: the cow, the grass, the bee that pollinated the flower of the orange tree from which the juice was made, the grain of wheat, the cup of water, the burnt coffee bean. And then, too, the biochemical, pharmaceutical, eucharistic sacrament of our daily pills, taken with a glass of water. I step out on the street, freshly bathed, absolved, prepared, alert. I have my backpack on one shoulder, my phone in one pocket, a small notebook in another, and a spring in my step. I walk down the street like water flowing downhill. My own steps carry and guide me as they please, my dusty hiking boots, my seven-league boots whose thick soles are worn along the edges and with which I've taken who knows how many steps in the past few months, mile after mile through different cities. I could know the actual number if I had downloaded an app for counting steps or if I wore one of those smart watches that take your pulse and calculate your breathing rate. Perhaps I feel a special attachment to these boots because I was wearing them when I lost my way in the world, and also when I found my way back. They carried me through those months when I was just a shadow, when a sense of dread weighed down my head and lay on my shoulders like a heavy burden. They carried me when every street was a dark tunnel and every room a suffocating cell. Anxiety would force my eyes open at dawn like the prodding muzzle of a creature, a faithful vampire waiting at the foot of the bed to feed on my fear. A clot of darkness would adhere to my back as soon as I found the strength to get out of bed, gathering the small bit of courage required not even to face the world but simply not to stay hidden in my room all morning with the curtains drawn, or look through the peephole to make sure no one was in the hallway before stepping out, or go out on the street to be instantly dazed and cast down by the blinding light. The same dark shadow that forced me awake robbed me of the strength I needed to leave my bed.

YOU'LL WANT TO HOLD IT IN YOUR HANDS. I made it back, seemingly intact, and each morning I realize with gratitude and incredulity that the old terror is gone, that it vanished in the air without leaving any traces on all the things it used to pollute. It went away as suddenly as it first came, as it had come at other times before. Or even faster, from one day to the next, like someone who used to take up the whole world but now is gone. I came out of a citadel and the enemy that was laying siege to it turned out to have withdrawn silently during the night. I breathe again, like an asthmatic who can suddenly inhale, marveling each time at just how clean the air is, and plentiful, and at the strength and clarity he feels as the oxygen spreads through his brain. What used to be impossible is now entirely natural. In the bright air I can distinguish colors again. Sounds and smells are extraordinarily sharp, as when someone stops smoking and one day the scent of a tangerine being peeled across the room bursts into his brain. It is my own face in the mirror that reminds me of how long I spent in the dark. There is a trace of fear deep in my eyes, a faint dread of the visitation of darkness. When the subway comes into the station I no longer watch it approach with a kind of morbid magnetism. But I am not entirely at ease. I go out every morning just in case, to get away from a threatening presence to which my nervous system has become habituated, the small nucleus of the amygdala releasing deep within the brain the chemical signals of fear. Sometimes I'm able to forget it for days, even for weeks at a time. But I know it too well to be entirely unafraid. It has disappeared before only to come back gradually, like a faint sound of steps I can recognize from afar. I've felt it drawing near without being able to move or to defend myself in any way, yielding to it in advance.

YOU WILL GLOW WITH AN INNER LIGHT. Literary wanderers make a living as best they can by writing for the newspapers. They have no other job. They have no private means, or they lost them if they ever had them. No patron to protect and support them. They give up the rights to their work as soon as they accept whatever amount some editor is willing to pay. They earn so little that they must write as fast as possible. The medium in which their writing appears is as new as the world they describe or as the literary forms they must create to recount things that have only recently come into existence. The newspaper and the modern city explode in tandem. Both are part of a general conflagration unleashed by ceaseless growth. Growth in the population, the size of cities, the goods that are sold in their markets, the factories that rise around them, the number and the circulation of periodicals. Poe comes up with made-up news that drastically increases the sales of the papers he writes for, but receives no compensation for the benefits their owners accrue. One of his stories claims that a new and incredibly powerful telescope has revealed cities and fields on the moon, and even what look like inhabitants. Thomas De Quincey, who writes for magazines in London and Edinburgh, collects newspapers from all over the world. He stacks them in piles in his rented rooms and moves among them as through a swamp or a wasteland of printed matter. Poe discovers De Quincey in the pages of English periodicals that reach the United States, and begins to imitate his style.

WHEN ITS END APPROACHES. The tempo of the city and of the newspaper gives rise to a literature of frantic urgency. The urban wanderer writes for a pittance and as fast as possible. Their work does not appear on the refined pages of a book but on a sheet of newsprint, in tiny type, lost in a sea of advertisements and random stories. Its reading audience is composed of the same strangers who furnished the subject matter. De Quincey says that the street is a pageant where a writer procures his characters like a farmer looking for cattle at a county fair. De Quincey's readers cross paths with him on the street without knowing it and pay a few cents for the newspaper that prints his stories. Baudelaire tries desperately to get his pieces in the papers while at the same time despising their vulgarity, just as he despises photography, gas lights, advertising posters, and the long, straight boulevards that are changing the face of Paris. "I do not understand how an innocent hand can touch a newspaper without convulsing in disgust," he says. The urban literature of the newspaper spreads swiftly and contagiously, like the deadly epidemics brought about by poverty, overcrowding, and a lack of public sanitation.

EVERYTHING REVEALED. The paths of literary influence spread as quickly as the growing network of roads, railways, telegraph lines, and steamship routes that are gradually covering the globe: star-shaped patterns of frost spreading and converging on the surface of water when its temperature drops beneath a certain point. In his youth, De Quincey traveled by stagecoach or went on foot from one city to another. In his old age he took the train. In Baltimore and in New York, Poe reads De Quincey's writings and contracts the virus of his dark imaginings, his visions of nocturnal cities that are theaters of crime and delirium. In Paris, Baudelaire reads Poe and De Quincey in periodicals sent from England and the United States. He translates their work out of admiration and also to earn some money. He seems to recognize in Poe a fellow soul, as if his own life had been prefigured by another man. In De Quincey and in Poe he finds a fellowship of restless urban wandering, of doomed writers and opium addicts who must barter away and even degrade their talent in order to make a living. In Berlin, Walter Benjamin translates Baudelaire. Unable to find a teaching post, and having lost to the convulsions and the raging inflation of the early twenties the secure bourgeois existence into which he was born, he finds that he, too, must write for the papers. The future of the works these men compose is as erratic and uncertain as their lives: scattered essays in the most unlikely publications, in periodicals of such obscure or short existence that every single issue was lost; essays submitted by post or by hand that were never published because the newspaper in question had already gone bankrupt. Baudelaire died without seeing his prose poems gathered into the book he always dreamed of. Walter Benjamin conceived immense works for which he never had the time or the peace of mind. He had to write short pieces to pay the rent, to buy a little food. He kept changing address or moving to another city, another country, never able to gather all his notes and bring forth what already existed in all its dazzling completeness within his mind.

DYING IS A PART OF STREET ART. *Vhils, Portugal's most renowned graffiti artist as well as an artist of international repute, splits his time between the quiet neighborhoods of Lisbon and the hectic streets of Hong Kong. "Each city has its walls; each wall has its own layers, its own life. The process of renewal and decay is faster over there than here, but that's precisely what inspires me." We are in his studio, a huge abandoned warehouse that he refurbished in the town of Barreiro, on the banks of the Tagus overlooking Lisbon. Soon he will go to a different body of water, Kowloon Bay in Hong Kong. "There's more in common than one might expect," he asserts.*

TALENT DRAWS ITS INSPIRATION FROM THE STREETS. *Alexandre Farto, Vhils, age twenty-nine, continues to be dazzled by the streets where he became an artist: the chaos of the big city, with all its human depredation and its endless cycle of production and destruction. He is not a critic of consumerism or an apostle of recycling, but rather an observer of the ceaseless, hectic, fleeting life of cities. His huge portraits, pockmarked by the imperfections of the walls on which he paints them, express perplexity more than suffering or grief. They are calm faces. I am here to stay, they seem to say. You, most likely, are not.*

TELL ME IF IT WAS A DREAM. *"Public spaces make the work more human. It doesn't bother me that it's ephemeral. I live implicitly with that fact from the moment the work is born." This summer, in just a few days, the pickax destroyed two of his most emblematic works in Lisbon. One of the derelict walls on which they were painted was needed for a private hospital. A dock* *for cruise ships is being built where the other one stood. Vhils is unfazed. "I'm not worried about copyright or about the destruction of my work. Destruction is part of creation. People sometimes rip out pieces of the walls where I do my work. But it's just to take them home, no one has tried to sell one so far."*

WHERE IT ALL BEGAN. *Vhils grew up on the other side of the Tagus, in Lisbon's anarchic suburbs of Seixal, Barreiro, and Almada, where as a teenager he would make his graffiti paintings as quickly as possible before the cops arrived. A world that all big cities have in common, including Hong Kong. No matter how far apart or how ethnically different two cities may be, in the end there is always soul and cement. That is why he set up his second studio in a Chinese city that at times resembles London and at times Beijing. He spends about half the year there, and this past spring the HOCA Foundation hosted the largest ever retrospective of his work. It was shown not only on the walls of the museum but also on subway cars and streetcars, which were used as ephemeral moving platforms for his work.*

THEY GLOW IN THE DARK. *After experimenting with cement, acids, screen printing, and even polyethylene, Vhils came to embrace neon in Asia. "It came from a similar influence. The city, the big signs on the bay. It's an urban advertising technique at risk of extinction. And it doesn't mean I'm giving up on any other materials. My work is a bit anarchic; I choose as I go, I don't have to quit one material to take up another." In Hong Kong, the biggest show in town is the lighting of the neon signs at dusk over Kowloon Bay. It looks like Blade Runner, with Batman directing traffic down below, beneath those immense lights that shine as if only for themselves, conveying a sense of sheer mass. "In Hong Kong I felt compelled to use neon. It wasn't easy, since there are barely any craftsmen left to teach you how it's done."*

ALWAYS WITH YOU, WHEREVER YOU GO. *Vhils takes in everything he sees on the street but he is also influenced by the films of Wong Kar-wai, the* *paintings of Cabrita Reis, or the latest hip-hop. He always perceives analogies between the deconstruction of sound and image, and has even deconstructed a train car into slices. Nearly fifty people have worked on the large exhibit in Hong Kong, which will travel to Shanghai, Rome, Cincinnati, and Rio de Janeiro. Meanwhile, through art galleries in London, Berlin, and Beijing, his work is sold all over the world. Alexandre Farto, Vhils, has become, according to various international publications, one of the most influential artists alive today. But he has a skeptical view of it all. "I never wanted to be anyone," he says. "Just going across the Tagus was a big deal for me."*

THE PULSE OF THE FUTURE IS STRONGER THAN EVER. Every surface must be entirely covered. Every bit of open space, every inch, like the walls of the Alhambra covered in Arabic lettering and glazed tiles, or like a body covered in tattoos. Messages can be inscribed absolutely everywhere: on a milk carton, on the postman's sack, on the back of a seat in a taxi, an ATM screen, a streetlight, the back of a traffic sign, the side of a bridge across the highway that goes to the airport. At the arrivals terminal, people wait in front of large automatic doors that are entirely covered by an advertisement for a line of cruises. The whole side of the bus passing next to you is painted front-to-back in the bright green color of a Heineken bottle. Its windows swim in a frothy, golden sea of beer. The word *Heineken* is printed many times on both sides. Time is occupied as thoroughly as space. The voices on the radio ads are loud and very fast. The radio hosts speak hurriedly as well, as if they caught it from the advertisements and were now eager to rush to the next commercial break. The same announcer who a moment ago was informing listeners of something that actually happened proceeds without changing her tone of voice to what seems like a news item but is in fact an advertisement.

EVERY MINUTE COUNTS TO MAKE SURE YOU WIN. The same ads in the same voices that seem unnatural or dubbed are broadcast simultaneously on every station. The same voices of presenters, celebrities, politicians being ceaselessly interviewed. The same voices everywhere, in a kitchen, in the wireless earbuds of an elated and exhausted man at the gym, in a psychiatrist's waiting room, all through the day, in a taxi driving you from the airport into the city at dawn after a long night of travel, in the high cabin of a trailer truck, in a car with a nervous woman and her children in the middle of a traffic jam, in the nurses' room in a cancer ward, in the ears of a cleaning woman or of an employee pretending to work at a computer, in a sacristy, inside a convent, in each of the taxicabs that are driving at this very moment through Madrid, often blasting the radio so loudly that its passengers are unable to have a conversation. Enthusiastic voices, hysterical voices, tempting, familiar, urgent, complicit, confidential, impatient voices urging you to act as soon as possible, to come to a sale, just two more days, to take advantage of this offer now, become a millionaire, have it all, voices that become even more pressing when they relay their catchphrase in a bastardized English, "people in progress," "power to you," "gourmet your experience."

EXPERIENCE YOUR FAVORITE MOVIES FROM THE INSIDE. To occupy space. To flood it. To exhaust it. I, too, have an instinct to fill every page of every notebook. A blank sheet of paper is as tempting to me as a freshly painted wall to a teenager with a spray can or as a patch of open skin to a tattoo artist. Once I start a notebook it must be filled to the last page. To leave it halfway and start another is a failure, a weakness of will, or worse, a loss in the urge to create. In exile, in growing poverty, Walter Benjamin would write in a smaller and smaller hand to make the most of every piece of paper. He wrote on used envelopes, on the back of handbills or movie programs, on random scraps of paper that he kept in his pockets for the moment when he felt the urge to jot something down, even if he was increasingly bereft of everything, of time, of money, watching in Paris as the great catastrophe approached like a slow-moving tsunami until it suddenly sped up, slow motion giving way to the frantic sequence of a silent film while he kept writing at his desk in the Bibliothèque Nationale, on the back of a lending card with his beloved fountain pen, the one with the extra-fine nib.

YOUR ULTIMATE A350 EXPERIENCE. Baudelaire says that he suffers from "*l'horreur des affiches.*" Before 1860 most advertising bills were relatively small and consisted primarily of words. In 1861 the art of lithography is perfected, making it possible to print posters more than six feet tall and displaying images in several colors. Baudelaire watches in anger as posters and bills spread through the city covering every wall, from the chimney tops to the very ground, as one witness relates. An encroaching blight of slogans and gaudy pictures of figures in motion: women dancing with their legs in the air, acrobats, huge bottles of liquor, galloping horses, locomotives, steamships, the huge face of a laughing clown. Around 1880 the first ordinances are imposed to limit the surging flood. Entire buildings are made off-limits. Special columns are set up on the street where advertisements can be posted. As a child, Marcel Proust would stand in front of one of these columns gazing ecstatically at a playbill for a performance by Sarah Bernhardt.

JOIN THE NEW DIMENSION. The city is tattooed in words: its bridges, its highway embankments, every bit of space has been inscribed. The city is submerged in a flood of simultaneous words as in a vast cloud of pollution. All the words that people whisper, yell, say to each other, mutter to themselves, speak into their cell phones to be scattered through the air in ceaseless bursts of electromagnetic radiation. Over rooftops and terraces, a constantly expanding array of relay towers that no one can see will send its signals to orbiting satellites and then all over the Earth. The hive of human voices down below merges with a skein of voices wrapping itself around the planet. Radio stations send their advertisements and their prattling, swindling, phony voices into every taxi in the city, filling it with toxic words. Words and voices pop up frantically on cell phone screens. In bars and restaurants, inaudible words flow in streams of subtitles beneath a talking head on a giant TV. The city is a body tattooed even to its inmost folds, the root of each hair, the ear canal. The skull is shaved so the tattoo can spread further. Even the highest floors of a recently abandoned building are covered in graffiti. Screens are installed on every street so there can be more moving images and words, and not a single place be left where the eye can turn without finding an advertisement. One day, electronic panels will identify you on the street and instantly project an advertisement that is custom-made for you.

THE NIGHT OF THE LIVING DEAD IS BACK. Fat, destitute, ungainly, wearing rouge to conceal his eczema, Oscar Wilde shuffles down the boulevards of Paris and the narrow streets of Saint-Germain-des-Prés, home to the cheap hotels where he finds lodging. When he asks for a room he uses the same name that now appears on his visiting card, Sebastian Melmoth. When he removes a glove to shake someone's hand or to offer his card, his own hands are big and coarse, bright red, like those of a manual worker or a stevedore. He is the Shadow, the Invisible Man, an apocryphal descendant of John Melmoth, a character in a gothic novel who lives as a wandering outcast for centuries, turning up now and then in surprising and even impossible places, the mountains near Valencia on a stormy night, a dungeon of the Inquisition, the cell of a man condemned to death, the bedroom of an agonizing man. The huge, wavering shadow of Oscar Wilde is cast on a wall by gaslight as he goes back to his hotel, drunk on absinthe and muttering to himself. When he meets an old acquaintance, he is, like Melmoth, mistaken for an apparition or a revenant. Some cross to the opposite sidewalk when they spot him in the distance, or simply avert their eyes and pass by as if he were invisible. Melmoth-Wilde is a ruined Golem, bloated with alcohol, a mop of dirty hair above his loose and jowly face. His steps are crooked and he walks in an insalubrious fog, reeking of alcohol and perhaps of jail. He is back in Paris after an absence of a few years but he might as well have returned from the past century or from another world. When he was here last he was a celebrity. His plays were staged in the best theaters and he was flattered and praised wherever he went. Now he is an outcast, more dead than alive. He keeps the hours of a vampire, sleeping all day and going out as it grows dark. One night someone saw him sitting at a table in the rain when the waiters had already rolled up the awning and turned off the lights in the café. An old friend, a woman, turned a corner and ran into him, the slow bulk of his body filling up the narrow sidewalk. She greeted him with pity, with sadness. He reached out a hand and asked her for some change.

LEARN TO READ YOUR BODY. In space, though not in time, Walter Benjamin and Oscar Wilde cross paths. They walk down the same streets and frequent some of the same cafés. Wilde may have stayed at one of the same seedy hotels for dubious characters where Benjamin now lodges. Benjamin, too, is a foreigner, a survivor from a vanished world to which he can never return. He has no money and his nationality is uncertain. He goes from one government office to another, obtaining and presenting documents that Wilde would not have known, passports, visas, temporary residence permits, photographic identity cards, documents that are hard to obtain and that can be revoked at any moment. Documents he must carry on his person at all times, to produce immediately should a policeman ask—he, who loses everything, whose hands are clumsy, who walks a great deal but looks, when he is tired, like a plodding turtle, according to the description of a woman he was in love with. He always carries with him a black leather satchel filled with all sorts of things: books, papers, antique toys.

YOU ONLY HAVE TO CLOSE YOUR EYES. In time, but not in space, Walter Benjamin crosses paths with Fernando Pessoa, restless wanderer of a city that Benjamin hoped to reach but never did, Lisbon, his intended port of transit in the attempt to flee to the United States. Some of his friends and acquaintances had passed through Lisbon and may have sent him letters while there. The world was coming to an end but the post office continued to work just fine. Pessoa walks through his city at exactly the same time as Benjamin through Paris. Both are nearsighted, wear round glasses, dress with a meticulous if rather run-down formality, and have an interest in graphology. Both carry at all times a big black satchel. Wilde had tried to hide under a false name. Benjamin published articles under a pseudonym when his name was proscribed in the German press. Pessoa conceals or multiplies himself through his various fictional identities. His doubles or his shadows walk the streets of the Baixa, the banks of the Tagus, the hills of the Chiado and the Bairro Alto. In photographs, Pessoa and Benjamin greatly resemble each other, as if they were doubles or what Pessoa himself called heteronyms. Pessoa reads Melville and Walt Whitman and is carried away in drunken flights of poetic creation. As a teenager, he went on the only great trip of his life, from Cape Town to Lisbon. Baudelaire, too, had a single, great, defining trip that took him down the Atlantic and part of the Indian Ocean to the island of Mauritius. He always lied and said he had reached India, where he claimed to have hunted tigers from the back of an elephant.

RIGHT WHERE IT SEEMS THERE'S NOTHING TO BE FOUND. Forgotten and discredited after the failure of *Moby-Dick*, Herman Melville works in an obscure post at the New York Custom House, the kind of position Poe unsuccessfully tried to obtain to escape poverty. Each morning at exactly the same time, with disciplined sadness, Melville follows the same path through lower Manhattan and up along the Hudson to get to work. Fernando Pessoa and Bernardo Soares, his heteronym or double, also gaze at a river on their daily walks to work, the Tagus. Melville dreams up Bartleby the scrivener, Pessoa the accounting clerk Bernardo Soares. Both sit at their desks writing with meticulous devotion, leaning over thick ledgers and office manuals. Bartleby lights a candle when it grows dark, Bernardo Soares turns on a light bulb. Bartleby's office overlooks an inner courtyard while Soares's looks out on the attics and the upper stories of the buildings on the Rua dos Douradores.

CHANGE YOUR EYE COLOR. Slim, nearsighted, formal, and disheveled, James Joyce walks through the streets of Trieste and is forever late to his next English lesson. He walks as briskly through Trieste as Pessoa walks through Lisbon in those photographs where he is hurrying past the window of the Bertrand bookstore. Perhaps the reason for Pessoa's haste is not that he has to be somewhere, but simply that he'd prefer to elude the wandering photographer who earns a living by snapping portraits of people on the street and trying to sell them their picture. There is a kind of family resemblance between Joyce and Pessoa in their photographs: the glasses, the mustache, a dignified bowtie that is always askew, a satchel or briefcase crammed with papers and books. Engrossed, barely able to see where they're going, and sometimes quite drunk, they walk through seaside cities that are also mysteriously similar. Some of Lisbon's official buildings have a kind of crumbling Austro-Hungarian grandeur. What the Praça do Comércio most resembles is the Piazza Unità in Trieste; both are monumental spaces open to the sea. Joyce and Pessoa are both polyglots in love with a language that is not their own. Joyce and Benjamin cross paths in Paris as the German invasion and the great European collapse approach, stateless fugitives living precariously from day to day. Both are so nearsighted that they would probably fail to recognize each other if they ever met. Joyce, in Trieste and in Paris, is always really walking through Dublin in his mind, just as Benjamin perhaps is walking through Berlin. Neither one will ever return to his native city. At the very same time, Virginia Woolf is walking through London or down an English country path near her house, imagining as she wavers between reason and madness that the Germans are about to invade. She wears simple English shoes and her hair is dripping with rain. She pokes the tip of her cane into the muddy path before her. There is a river nearby. Its sound is like an invitation.

DINE IN THE DARK SERVED BY BLIND WAITERS. In Trieste, in Paris, James Joyce invents Dublin. In Lisbon, Fernando Pessoa invents Lisbon itself in minute detail. Walter Benjamin visits Baudelaire's grave in Montparnasse and Proust's and Oscar Wilde's in Père Lachaise. I, too, in a former life, went to Proust's grave, a dark, austere block of marble, and saw Jim Morrison's grave as well, covered in graffiti and strewn with plastic flowers. Leopold Bloom and Stephen Dedalus wander through Dublin like Bernardo Soares through Lisbon. In 1914, during the war, Proust walks through the streets of Paris by night after the curfew, when all the lights are out and the city glows beneath a full moon that is as slow and stately as a German zeppelin. Soldiers on leave are out on the streets and Proust sometimes follows after them, tempted by their youth. He is fifty but he looks much older, heavyset, feverish, dressed in a thick coat and wheezing on account of his asthma. Faint lights call out to him in the dark from the doorways of the male brothels that he visits with some regularity. Wilde may also have gone through those doors, mumbling his assumed name, Sebastian Melmoth, the perpetual wanderer, as if murmuring an incantation to conceal his true identity. Clarissa Dalloway steps out one morning into a fresh and sunny London street to purchase flowers. Doctor Yuri Zhivago searches Moscow for a blond woman he will never see again. Sometimes, for an instant, he experiences the false joy of thinking he has recognized her in some other woman who resembles her. In Paris, Walter Benjamin likes to go to the last showing at the movie theaters, usually to watch American films. He falls in love with Katharine Hepburn. He pays close attention to the actors' voices because he is determined to learn English, a step toward a planned immigration to the United States that he can never quite set in motion. Peter Lorre wanders by night through a dark, expressionist city, like a vampire or a Mr. Hyde, whistling *Peer Gynt*. On the other side of the world Juan Carlos Onetti walks down a brightly lit avenue in Buenos Aires with nothing to eat. In London, on successive nights during the early fall of 1821, Thomas De Quincey stays up for nights on end walking through the city in a kind of temporal hallucination, wandering through the same streets that he had roamed many years before when he was looking for a prostitute he never found again, a girl he knew only by her first name, Ann.

OUR DIGITAL EXPERTS WILL DESIGN YOUR SMILE. Summer dresses that give a supple outline to the body, to the legs, exactly like the skirts Egyptian dancers wear on bas-reliefs, on carvings of young women bearing gifts, or that wooden statue of a girl carrying on her head a platter with a goose: such ease and lightness, not just to the clothes but to the hair as well, falling loosely over their bare shoulders and backs or covering half the face down to the collarbone. The sandals too seem slightly Egyptian, supple on their shifting feet, and then the flowing motion of the hand as they sweep their hair from their faces or type a message on their phones: long, swift fingers tapping the screen with delicate precision, the merest brush, hovering in the air above the small, smooth screen with a sense of imminence or wonder, as if the paint on their fingernails were still fresh and they needed to be held up in the air to dry. Styled hair and polished, painted fingernails and pedicures, the exquisite ministrations of the beauty parlor and the salon. Pamper your feet. Put a little style in your step. Feline beauty. Slim legs. Sandals are in. Latin American or Asian immigrants, probably undocumented, bend over a pair of bare feet with a reverential care that could itself belong in an Egyptian bas-relief, their mouths and noses covered by masks that will not protect them from the toxic vapors of the products they employ, solvents and lacquers that poison their lungs just like the chemical waste of textile factories poisons the rivers of their native countries.

ONCE I GAZED AT YOU IN WONDER. Beauty flows in sandaled feet. In currents of air scented with fragrance and shampoo. Hair and skin as smooth as silk, glowing lips and nails, smooth legs made supple with moisturizing creams. There is a plenitude, a consummation, the beauty of the body and the artifice employed to heighten it in order to instill desire or contemplation, not a rancorous and perhaps at bottom hostile craving, but simple gratitude, a momentary joy in apparitions that meet us on the street and then are quickly gone. What Salinger said of joy can also be said of beauty, it is not a solid but a liquid; not a stable, predictable assemblage of perfections but a kind of visual tremor, neither fully tangible, nor purely momentary, nor merely an illusion. A figure seen in profile from afar or looking away in the distance. A pair of crossed legs on a nearby seat in the subway.

WIN AN EXCLUSIVE PACK. Sometimes, too, a gesture. A woman fixes her hair or stands a little straighter because she realizes she is being watched. Or a smile that could be a mere reflex, a crossing of glances in which nothing is requested and nothing is offered, just a flash of mutual recognition, discontinuous, without consequence, too brief to even leave behind a memory.

COLLECT THESE WONDERFUL GIFTS. I'm always watching, waiting for the sudden apparition of beauty, calmly, without masculine bitterness or craving, just heedful, passionate, observant, grateful, like the boy of eleven or twelve who knew nothing about sex but would look entranced at modern girls in miniskirts, falling hopelessly in love for a few minutes with certain bodies and faces but not with others, not because he chose to but only in response to a feeling that flared up in an instant, as irrevocably as when you heard certain songs.

FEAR THE WALKING DEAD.
    Southeast Florida overrun with putrid algae.
    Three suicide attacks sow fear in Saudi Arabia.
    Germany urges its citizens to stockpile food in case of an attack.
    Hate spreads through social networks.
    Biodiversity at risk everywhere on Earth.
    ISIS carries out deadliest massacre of the year in Turkey.
    Major cities are besieged by deserts.
    Starving vultures attack cattle.
    Terror strikes again in France.
    Millions of players all over the world take to the streets
    to hunt down monsters.
    Dozens dead after truck plows through a crowd
    in the Promenade des Anglais in Nice.
    Biodiversity at risk everywhere on Earth.
    Barbaric attack spurs outrage.
    Bodies were flying everywhere.
    "I saw shoes, glasses, bags strewn on the ground."
    People jumped into the sea to take cover.
    "Everyone turned around and we saw
    a thirty-ton truck plowing into people
    and driving onto the sidewalk to crush them."
    A huge white truck drove at full speed
    into the crowd swerving to hit
    as many people as possible.
    It passed just a few feet away from me
    and I didn't even notice it.

I saw bodies flying like bowling pins.
I heard noises and screams that I will never forget.
I saw horrible things that will haunt me for the rest of my life.
I saw two children crushed under the truck's tires
while their parents screamed in desperation.
I was paralyzed. I could not move.
All around me was sheer panic.
I saw the path of destruction.
People were running, screaming, crying.
Then I realized what was happening. And I ran with them
toward the Crocodile, a place where everyone
was taking shelter. Only a few seconds went by
and it seemed like an eternity.
"Take cover," "Don't stay here," "Where is my son?"
I heard these voices all around me.
Then I went out. I wanted to know what had happened.
The promenade was deserted.
Not a sound. No sirens. No cars.
I ran into Raymond, a man in his fifties.
He said to me, crying, "There are bodies everywhere."
It was true. Right behind him
there were corpses every ten or fifteen feet.
Lifeless. Some of them were missing limbs. They brought water
for the wounded and towels to cover
those who were beyond hope.
At that moment I lacked courage.
I would have liked to help, to do something, but I wasn't able.
I was still paralyzed.
A second wave of panic
made me go back to the Crocodile. The killer truck
came to a stop a little farther on,
riddled with gunshots. I didn't hear the shots.
Just screams, "Come back, come back," and crying.
"We were all like zombies, just running and screaming."
I kept walking. I got on my motorcycle

to get as far away as possible from this hell.
There were bodies and wounded people everywhere.
The first ambulances began to arrive.
Followers of the terrorist group rejoiced
on social media over the attack.
"If you do not have bombs, or bullets,
do all you can to find infidels
and break their heads open with a stone, slit their throats
with a knife, run them over with a car, throw them down a ravine,
strangle them, poison them."

THE PULSE OF THE FUTURE IS STRONGER THAN EVER. I like the look of painters, except when they dress up consciously to look like painters, or even worse, like artists. A great artist doesn't need a costume. I like their attitudes, the sturdy, healthy air they have about them, which often lasts until a ripe old age since many painters live long lives and stay active to the very end. There is a glowing vigor to their faces, to their gaze, the look of people who work hard at something they enjoy, thoroughly absorbed for hours and days in a fully imaginative yet also fully material task to the point of losing all sense of time, or rather of finding within themselves a different kind of time, a pure, inward present in which they live and work as much as within the four walls of the studio, among their tools, jars, brushes, palette knives, their own works lying carelessly about and then a thousand things they keep at hand in the hope of putting them to use some day, stained rags, pencils, cans of turpentine, large sheets of paper from a drawing pad as well as tiny notebooks where they make sketches or scribble notes. Useful things, and useless too; things that seem like junk but end up being revelations, and things that go the other way, the coins and cigarette butts that Jackson Pollock picked up off the floor or took out of his pockets to stick into a thick dab of paint on the canvas.

TECHNOLOGY MOVES YOU. I like the picture of Alex Katz that I am looking at now, a color picture that I cut out of a magazine and glued with admiration and a bit of envy to a blank sheet of paper, wanting to experience myself some of the glorious feeling of working with one's hands. Katz is leaning back in an old folding chair, a solid piece of 1930s office furniture that he may have found at a secondhand store or picked up off the street.

He's close to ninety but he seems much younger, in sneakers, a T-shirt and sweater, his arms crossed in an attitude that seems either pleasantly idle or slightly and calmly arrogant. His powerful shaved head resembles that of Paul Motian, who lived to be almost as old and who always stayed so active and free, unpretentiously original, perpetually inspired, faithful to himself yet never going back to what he did before, free of all nostalgia for his own past mastery, when he was young and played drums with Bill Evans in the early sixties. The last time I saw him play at the Village Vanguard was on a weeknight after a snowstorm and there were only a few people in the audience. He was a last-minute replacement for a then-famous singer who had been unable to get to New York because of the snow. He played with a small band, three or four musicians who were all young and deferential, perhaps a bit intimidated by his legendary status. He was generous with them, discreet to the point of furtiveness so as not to overwhelm them, trying rather to raise them into his own splendid mastery. They finished, thanked the small audience, and sat down at a side table to have a beer. I remember Paul Motian's shaved head, his broad back, a turtleneck of the kind an old-time boxer might have worn.

BOOST YOUR CREATIVITY. Alex Katz has the sober, solid presence of an American artist strengthened by work and by an active life, in the manner of Edward Hopper. David Hockney looks like a klutz who other than drawing, painting, and smoking would be incapable of doing much with his hands. A frail old smoker who stays up all night; with those pale, watery eyes that stare so pointedly in his late self-portraits, still so curious and so fiercely inquisitive, the eyes of an old man who will cast off his age and seem like a man of thirty as soon as he starts working. Thirty being the perennial time at which the consciousness of your own age seems to stop for someone who, like him, devotes himself to a task that never changes, whether in the studio or simply at a bar, looking at people and thinking what it would be like to draw them, or driving down a highway in California or a country road in the region of England where he was born, eyes eager and alert, fingers tinged yellow from smoking and perpetually busy with a pencil, a camera, a brush, an iPhone, an iPad, anything at all. Hockney can draw like

Ingres or Picasso; much better than Matisse. I like his vigor and vitality, the way he fled England to find a new life in Los Angeles, the sharpness of his interviews and writings, the nerve with which he sets upon new tasks despite the years, exploring innovations in technique, as rapt over a sheet of handmade paper as over a digital screen, with an air of stupefied amazement reminiscent of Peter Sellers and wearing all the stylish props of his public persona, the messy mop of yellow hair, the glasses and suspenders, the perennial cigarette. "When I paint, I am thirty years old," he says. I, too, am thirty when I begin to write and forget everything around me, or when I cut and paste newspaper headlines, or stop in front of a shop sign to write down what it says in pencil in a notebook that I take out of my pocket, holding it against the wall or on a trash can for support. But being an eternal thirty now is different from when I was really thirty. In the limpid temporal illusion of the moment, as I begin to work, as I take pleasure in my life, I am younger even than I was back then.

WHEN SILENCE SPEAKS, LISTEN. If astrophysicists can hear through their telescopes the cosmic background noise, that fossilized remnant of the big bang, it will surely one day be technologically possible to hear city noises from a hundred, a hundred and fifty, two hundred years ago. If scientists found a way to take a picture of the universe as it was being born, they will likewise be able to devise a telephoto lens that, just as current lenses can reach into the depths of space, will reach into the depths of time. Who could have imagined just twenty years ago that we would be able not just to walk down the street talking to someone on the other side of the Earth but even to see their faces, the room behind them, the light coming in through the windows. He finds it regrettable that having developed so many technological devices that are entirely useless, or worse, horribly destructive and even lethal, we have not been able to produce even a rudimentary version— say, the equivalent of Edison's first wax cylinders—of the parabolic chronoscopic antenna (to give it a name) or a temporal photobathyscaphe capable of diving to ever greater depths of time.

3D IS EVERYWHERE. He imagines himself inside the cockpit of the chronobathyscaphe, as cramped a space, due to the technological constraints involved, as the capsule of an old Apollo rocket. He is surrounded by lenses, cameras, electronic depth gauges, keeping an eye on the space-time coordinates and peering through the glass (perhaps a small round window, as in a bathyscaphe) into a pitch-black darkness where gradually a few uncertain shapes begin to be discernible: bits of light, figures that are not immediately resolved, in part because the instruments have a limited range and in part because what can be seen "out there," as they say in the movies, is a dark and murky medium like the bottom of the sea. "Oxford Street, London," says the future onboard equivalent of Google Maps. "August 19, 1821." A day on which De Quincey says in his diary that he's sat down to write after going for a walk: the fog rising from the river, the smoke of chimneys broken here and there by gaslight, and that figure, that silhouette of a man walking down a street that is nearly deserted now, close to midnight, when London lies wrapped in a glowing fog that Turner might have painted. Or the chronobathyscaphe could explore the streets of Baltimore between the nights of September 26 and October 3, 1849, piercing the gloom with the lamp on its prow, like the *Nautilus*, following each stumbling drunk that passes by and shining its light on their faces as they lean against a wall to see if one of them is Edgar Allan Poe.

SPECIALIZING IN ALL MANNER OF OCCULT WORK. In the end, he would settle for just putting on a pair of large headphones, like a sound engineer, and listening to the past, acoustically exploring it as he explores the present when he listens through white earbuds to the recordings on his iPhone. There would be a faraway sound, as when you put a seashell to your ear, in this case the faint rumor of time rather than the sea or the circulation of the blood. The neighing and clopping of horses, the bugle of a stagecoach, the cries of street vendors, the barrel organs that made De Quincey shiver with grief each time he went back to London. "The rolling clamor of the omnibus," as Baudelaire says, the footsteps of a lonely figure on an empty street, and then suddenly other sounds as well, as he slowly turns a knob on the control panel or touches an icon on the screen and the numbers begin to rise on the display: the ring of a streetcar, the horn of an early automobile, the growing roar of traffic drowning out sounds that used to be habitual not so long ago.

IT WILL TAKE YOU TO AMAZING PLACES. It would be a reductive view of perambulation studies to suppose it concerned only with tracing out physical paths, even if that in itself is already an inexhaustible field of inquiry. Something glimpsed at random during a walk can be the crucial stroke of inspiration for a poem or a novel. Max Planck, walking hand in hand with his son through the Grunewald in Berlin, suddenly intuits the principles of quantum mechanics. Darwin pieces together the theory of evolution as he walks each morning on the gravel path around his house, etc. Also within the purview of our discipline are issues such as the swiftness or slowness of a person's walk at different stages of life or of a creative process; types of footwear and their virtues and deficiencies; the posture and attitude of the body when it walks. None of these matters are superfluous, none are irrelevant when considering a particular set of stylistic or imaginative traits. "Style is the man," says Buffon, who as it happens used to walk with vigorous solemnity through the Jardin des Plantes in Paris. Style is the entire man, the person, not some nonexistent (if highly celebrated) disembodied quality of mind or "ghost in the machine." Style is the entire body: its height, the way it leans, its heaviness or lightness, the particular force of its steps, the way the heel strikes the ground.

NIGHT DOESN'T ALWAYS MEAN THE DAY IS OVER. Proust writes about the way that certain men, on leaving a place of ill repute, a brothel or a gambling house, walk in a rapid sideways motion to present the least visible surface to those who could be watching, like infantrymen trying to elude the enemy's sharpshooters. Science is distinguished exclusively by the capacity to make predictions. The ideal aim of perambulation studies is to analyze a literary text and be able to deduce, in a manner subject to verification, the height, age, health, and way of walking of the person who "produced" it, to employ a respectable academic term. By reading one of Frank O'Hara's rambling New York poems you will be able to develop a virtual model of O'Hara's walk, to be then confirmed by looking at films that actually show him walking. By watching a short film of Cartier-Bresson walking through Paris and by noticing how he holds his camera (discreetly, but not covertly) you will learn more about his style than from any number of lengthy monographs—at least those written prior to the rise of perambulation studies in colleges and universities, a rise which will perhaps be even more sweeping than that of structuralism or of semiotics once was.

YOU'LL GET SHARPER PICTURES. A great step forward will take place when different routes are juxtaposed. From 1846 to 1849, Poe, Whitman, and Melville are all living, working, and walking simultaneously through New York City, orbiting around a small number of magnetic poles: a particular bookstore, the offices of a handful of literary journals, the houses of a few cultured people that hold soirees. The study of the ways in which their paths meet, cross, or collide, all within the map of a city that barely rose above Twenty-Third Street, can be as rich as tracking a set of elementary particles in a linear accelerator. There is no evidence of any personal relation. But we know that Melville and Whitman read Poe. They must have known people in common, and they must at least have recognized one another when they crossed paths. Did Melville, Dickens, and De Quincey walk past each other or collide in London during the winter of 1849? Melville then traveled to Paris, leaving London after witnessing a public hanging. Did he ever walk past Baudelaire? What we need is facts, not hypotheses that cannot be verified experimentally.

OUR GREATEST GIFT IS KNOWING YOU. In Paris, among millions of footsteps and by using cutting-edge perambulation techniques, he will search for Walter Benjamin's clumsy tread. His geolocator shows the streets where Benjamin used to walk. His audio-chronoscope is set to June 1940. Suddenly every needle on every gauge drops to its lowest level. The city is silent. Measurements can be imprecise for periods of less than twenty-four hours. It could be daybreak, since a great concave clamor of birds is heard, a sudden irruption of eternity that seems to do away with history. Then his instruments begin to pick up a signal, a faint and nearly indistinct rumor beneath the frequencies perceptible to human hearing. Little by little it grows into a tremor that delicately shakes the needles of his most sensitive gauges, a vibration that travels deep beneath the ground and up the walls and window panes, to the jug of water on a nightstand by a sick man's bed, or a small spoon resting on a saucer. It's the armored cars, the trucks and motorcycles, the gun carriages, the rhythmic strike of German boots entering Paris, parading in front of no one in the glorious light of an early summer morning. In the apartment that Walter Benjamin hastily vacated a few days earlier, some of his belongings can still be seen. Papers and books; clothes in the drawers; a gas mask on a shelf like some kind of brutal idol, with its ribbed hose like a rubber trachea and the leather straps, the metal buckles, and the round pieces of glass to look through—a mask out of an old black-and-white horror film.

CITY OF NINE MILLION EVACUATED BY ORDER OF THE CHINESE GOVERNMENT. Empty streets, dark buildings, shuttered shops. What is happening in Hangzhou, one of the most flourishing and populous cities in eastern China? The Chinese government, wishing to prevent disturbances during the G20 summit it is hosting as rotating president of the group, has taken measures that would be unthinkable in a Western democracy. Picture a city as densely populated as New York emptied from one day to the next. No cars on its wide avenues except for armored vans carrying soldiers and police. The wail of their sirens is louder and seems to last longer and carry farther in the surrounding silence. Every traffic light blinks amber and red. In the city's newest neighborhoods, where identical buildings rise fifty stories high with empty plots of grass between them, every window is dark, though there are blinking red lights at the top, on lightning rods and helicopter landing pads lit by floodlights. Nine million people have abandoned the city in perfect order in just a few days.

WE LOOK AFTER EVERY DETAIL. In cars, buses, and trains. In slow, massive traffic jams that blocked every highway out of the city. The government wants to make sure there are no disturbances during the stay of the G20 dignitaries. Helicopters fly through the glass canyons of the business district and over peripheral neighborhoods and flat expanses of factories and shopping malls. Their floodlights sweep the darkest alleys, the entrance to a tunnel, the upper floors of a skyscraper. Army trucks are posted at large intersections or move slowly on patrol along the sidewalks, the barrel of an assault rifle jutting out the window or from the tarp in the back. In the nightlife district, glowing theater marquees and digital displays show advertisements for musicals, cell phones, luxury cars. *Beauty and the Beast*, *The Lion King*: images of pseudo-African masks and dances followed by Chinese characters. Men fly over an abyss in motorcycles. Languid teenage girls gaze vacantly with parted lips. Brand names glow in the dark like constellations. Huawei. Vuitton. Max Mara.

YOU ARE THE FOCUS OF OUR ATTENTION. Thirty stories up in the air, a young woman in a tight skirt and high heels walks down a red desert road carrying a Louis Vuitton bag. A caravan of limousines and of black armored SUVs drives down the highway from the airport into the city, very much like cars in an advertisement, racing toward the horizon or down an empty road between tall mountains. They are preceded and followed by military convoys and flashing police cruisers; by policemen in white helmets on enormous motorcycles, like high-tech Transformers in which all distinction disappears between the human body and the machine that carries and engulfs it. There is no one to watch this fearsome parade, this triumphal procession of the lords of the Earth and their praetorian guards. No one will be able to see the people riding in the back seat, behind dark bulletproof glass, sitting in leather interiors aglow with the light of cell phone screens and security cameras, surrounded by Herculean bodyguards with massive necks and military haircuts, dressed in dark suits and wearing dark glasses even in the gloom of the vehicle, a wireless receiver in one ear, a microphone on the lapel.

WE HAVE A PLAN FOR YOU. The convoy moves at full speed so as to reduce even further the risk of an attack. Police and army units in gas masks and combat gear patrol the great labyrinth of sewer pipes beneath the city, shining their headlights into every corner. Furtive animals venture out onto the asphalt near the shuttered parks. In a room as large as a space-flight control center, high-definition screens display simultaneous video feeds of streets, highways, empty parks, subway stations, parking lots, pedestrian underpasses. For a few seconds a lone figure traverses one of these images like a furtive shadow. A moment later it is gone. They search in vain for it on every screen, on every camera pointed at a street corner or a bank. They freeze the image, enlarge it, enhance it digitally as much as possible. All they can make out is the shadow of a human being. The more they expand the image the fuzzier it becomes, blending into the darkness of the empty city.

FIND THE PERFECT CONTENT FOR YOUR NEXT CREATIVE PROJECT.
". . . the great poem of our century can only be written with rubble and debris," he said to me on our second or third meeting, after setting down his heavy satchel by his side. We were at the Café Comercial. He kept his eyes on the marble tabletop and spoke quietly, in a measured tone that stood in contrast to the vehemence of his words. "With the waste products of language: the mistakes and mistranslations of a poorly dubbed American film or series; the cheap language of consumer advertising and of public relations and politics; the nonsense of technical jargon; the pseudopoetry of perfume ads and the language of self-help, of horoscopes, of flyers offering girls, massages, bank loans, mortgages; the grand compendium of food products in a supermarket flyer or of daily specials on a sign outside a restaurant at noon." Only garbage itself can give a proper account of such an overabundance of garbage. "I kneaded mud and turned it into clay," poor old Baudelaire used to say. With all due respect, that is not a great achievement. Mud is a noble material, or at least it used to be, before it was polluted by chemical and radioactive residues. Some of the greatest works of mankind were made out of mud. In one of your many former lives you were a child and played with fresh mud in the streets after the rain. People throughout history have done what needs to be done with the materials they have at hand, and what is presently most at hand is garbage, junk, detritus. So that is what will have to be used for the poem. It will perhaps be very long, an immense amount of material will be required, but there's no risk of it ever running out. On the contrary, the more time passes, the richer we become in that particular form of wealth. It piles up in mountains, Everests of trash reaching higher at every moment: a vast midden of words, a landfill as large as the ocean, which has itself become a dump, filled with tides and currents

of trash that will soon be visible from space like storms and cyclones. The poem will require long dedication, perhaps a lifetime. A lifetime to make and a lifetime to read. It will probably be anonymous and cumulative, like the Homeric poems. None of its verses, phrases, or words will be the creation or personal contribution of its author, or authors, if such a term really applies in this case."

THINK DIFFERENT, CHOOSE TACO BELL. "It will be like the first naves of the Great Mosque of Córdoba, built purely from pillaged materials, disparate columns, random capitals found here and there, taken from masonry dumps or salvaged from demolished buildings. The poem will doubtless consist of thousands of lines and every one of them will have been plundered and stolen. Not from other poems, or literature, or anything else that is respectable: only from the purest garbage. Great discipline will be required in this respect. No style at all, my friend. As for your 'personal sensibility,' ladies and gentlemen, stick it wherever it happens to fit (with all due respect). Your personal sensibility is fully known to data collectors, most of it from information freely furnished by yourself. Any computer program can decompose in a few minutes, one by one and with the utmost quantifiable precision, the celebrated traits of anyone's "personal style," and I apologize if my hands rise on either side to form a pair of air quotes. Any day now some start-up will offer to design your very own personalized literary style. So let's get off the high horse."

READERS ALL OVER THE WORLD WILL KNOW YOU. "As to the poem's length, I'm afraid there can be no middle ground. Enormities or miniatures. The *Aeneid* or a haiku. You will understand if I cite your respected pediatrician, Dr. Williams. It's either four verses about a red wheelbarrow and some plums in the fridge, or the three hundred crowded pages of *Paterson*. Dickinson or Whitman, a bacchanalia or a Buddhist fast. In times of upheaval one must make urgent and radical aesthetic decisions. The poem must be contemporaneous and extemporaneous; of this world and out of it; for a select minority and for the masses; yours and anybody else's. It will be explosively original and strictly impersonal without ever putting on stylistic airs. Just pillage, plunder, and hoarding. A giant sack where anything can fit, like those sacks of ultra-strong plastic fibers used to carry rubble, or those metal containers where for several weeks they dump anything that comes out of a demolished house, and which the neighbors use as well to discard whatever they please without a second thought: a door torn off its frame, with the hinges and peephole intact; a wheelchair-accessible toilet; a metal filing cabinet with folders stuffed with X-rays; a bag of rotting garbage. The poem will be like one of those landfills that after a few years are covered in plastic sheeting so they can be topped with fertile soil and turned into parks. Except this park will remain a landfill."

THERE'S NEVER BEEN A BETTER TIME TO TELL YOUR STORY. "What is the most outsize piece of contemporary art you know? What is our equivalent to the *Ring of the Nibelung*, the palace of Knossos, or the *St. Matthew Passion*? The most immense. The most colossal. I'll tell you what I think. It's *The Clock*, by Christian Marclay. An artist of debris. A Michelangelo of refuse and remnants. A Cologne cathedral, a Himalaya of recycled materials. *The Clock* is a movie that lasts twenty-four hours. Not a minute more, or less. It's made of very brief fragments taken from over three thousand films. Masterpieces, blockbusters, failed movies that no one saw, horrible pictures, forgotten TV shows, crime movies, disaster films, Westerns. Movies of all kinds and from all periods; the entire history of film, surveyed and plundered. None of the fragments lasts for more than a few seconds. There is just one organizing principle, which is quite simple and which generates the entire work in an immutable manner that, like a process of nature, can nevertheless be performed with great variation. Like bacterial reproduction or the development of a baroque fugue, or a piece by Steve Reich that never becomes monotonous. There are two conditions: the first is that a clock appear in every shot; the second, that the time on the clock coincide exactly with the time of day or night in the location where the film is being projected. You go into a dark room and find a screen as large as that of an old movie theater. You go in one morning at eleven o'clock. Four minutes past eleven, to be precise. On the screen, you see a movie fragment showing a clock that points to four minutes past eleven. A little later, when you take out your cell phone mechanically to look at a text message, the time on the small screen of the phone is the same as on an alarm clock on a nightstand next to a bed where a woman is being strangled. Now you're caught. You can't look away, and decide to miss whatever appointment you were heading to when you happened to walk by the art gallery. You fall asleep exhausted after looking at the screen for two or three hours. You wake up with a jolt, not knowing where you are, thinking you've woken up in a movie theater where your mother used to take you at four o'clock on Sundays all through the winter, a theater that was demolished and that's now a hole in the ground fenced in with large cement blocks. Out of sheer habit you tap the screen on your phone to check the time. But there's no need. The time is always the same in the room and in the film. Godzilla rears over buildings that are clearly miniature models, crushing them beneath its webbed feet. With one swipe of its hand it destroys a tower on which a clock marks the very same hour and minute of your present life."

MORE THAN ENOUGH SPACE FOR ALL YOUR MULTIMEDIA AR-CHIVES. ". . . The size and complexity of the poem carry their own risks. The word *carry* is quite fitting in this case. The foremost danger is that it remain unfinished. One could die, or simply give up after too many years of solitary devotion to the same task (even if literary solitude, though highly touted, is in fact neither indispensable nor even desirable: the impersonal nature of the process would allow a well-trained team to expedite it by being placed in charge of gathering and organizing all the materials). Nor can the risk be ruled out that the poem become unmanageable through sheer overabundance and complexity, making it impossible to establish the least amount of order, or better still, to foster the rise of an implicit and spontaneous order of the kind that occurs in nature. I believe *emergent order* is the proper term. A building of such mass and immense complexity can collapse and sink under its own weight. Not that this would be a problem either. It might even be preferable. Unfinished things are melancholy, but what is overly finished and complete can produce a sense of horror. The Escorial, for instance. A frightful building. St. Peter's Basilica in Rome; that gruesome baldachin, with its twisted columns of gilt bronze! Centuries of neglect would perhaps improve them, or perhaps a large earthquake or a fire. Nature rising from the rubble; fallen columns lying like colossal tree trunks in an American national park; cats in the Colosseum. Entire colonies of cats, a lineage going back for centuries like the patriarchs in the Book of Genesis. Splendid blades of grass between the paving stones and a wild fig tree growing out of a crack in the wall, life itself spilling out and burgeoning in the heavy rain and the fertile, humid heat of Rome. Imagine how horrible, how vulgar a building like the Colosseum must have been when it was just finished. Covered in marble and gold like a Vegas casino mimicking the Colosseum, with a big neon sign on top, or better yet, a name in solid gold letters: TRUMP."

WE WANT OUR EXPERIENCE TO IMPROVE YOUR FUTURE. ". . . It will be the poem of Trump's century, just as the *Aeneid* was the poem of Augustus. This is your catastrophe, I am only passing through. France under Louis XIV, China under Mao, Athens in the time of Pericles, the age of Trump. Each figure placing its name and its dreadful monuments on an entire age. The horror of Versailles, the merciless geometry of its terrifying gardens, the very trees and bushes ranged in regiments like a troop of Brown Shirts in Nuremberg. What Versailles needs is to be abandoned for a few centuries. Not even that, just fifty years. Nature acts quickly in wet climates. I'm not losing the thread of my argument. Or I lose it and I find it again. Theseus in the labyrinth, etc. What matters most about the labyrinth is that when Theseus arrived it was already in ruins. The best thing about the *Aeneid* is that it remained unfinished. Virgil had no time to spoil it by giving it a polish that is entirely alien to life: a shine, a finish. Look at the *Divine Comedy*, so horribly well-made, so complete and perfectly conjoined; one verse following another, eleven syllables, then a tercet, and another, and another, until you can't bear another set of three, and then another canto, thirty-three, and then three parts, always three, like the Holy Trinity. The Holy Trinity! How can such an abstract abomination have been tolerated for so many centuries? Paradise, the angels, the archangels. Can anyone stand it?"

WE SHARE ALL YOUR DREAMS. "An unfinished *Divine Comedy* would have been more human and much more interesting. A pile of drafts and loose sheets of paper in a trunk up in an attic in a house somewhere, perhaps the house where Dante died. The trunk that held Pessoa's manuscripts. The leather binders that Benjamin entrusted to that lunatic George Bataille when he was about to flee Paris. It was a great good fortune that Proust could not entirely revise the final volumes of his novel. Hundreds of nearly indecipherable handwritten pages fallen at the foot of his bed or mixed up in the sheets. Galley proofs with endless marginal additions, with pasted notes, and poor Céleste Albaret doing what she could so it wouldn't all fall into complete disorder. Pascal was just as lucky (which is our own good luck as well) in dying without ever writing the theological treatise for which he kept jotting down notes here and there. Picture that treatise, as solid as a tomb, instead of the squiggles and scrawls, the flashes of lightning of the *Pensées*. Can you stand Camus's novels? And those pompous philosophical essays? But just open any of his *Carnets* and you won't be able to put it down. Or read the unfinished novel he was carrying in a suitcase in his car when he was killed in a crash. Give me works that are unpublished, posthumous, unfinished, failed, half lost. Give me *Billy Budd*, written in longhand and put away in a drawer from which Melville never brought it out again. Give me the monstrous novels, never to be published, that Henry Roth wrote in an RV parked in the middle of the desert in Arizona. How *could* he have published them, when what he wrote in them was that he and his sister had been lovers. There he is, sweating, sitting at a camping table, typing in his underwear in the desert like a hermit with a picnic cooler, as if he had survived a nuclear apocalypse. Just him, the typewriter, the RV, his folding chair, and a rickety table that must have shook each time he struck a key. Writing and writing as if an abscess had burst; feeding a tumor that grew with every page he wrote. Inspiration like an open hemorrhage, the catastrophic flood after a dam collapses . . ."

CHOOSE THE WILDEST CONTENTS. "You are right in that respect," he said, as if he had only become aware of my presence at that moment, following a brief silence, his thoughtful eyes remaining perfectly still behind the lenses of his glasses as he took a sip of water and wiped his lips with a paper napkin, his pale hand over his face like a shifting mask. "It's true that some writers were able to finish their projects without falling into anything too heavy or monumental. Which no doubt was for the best. Cervantes finished *Don Quixote*, and Joyce finished *Ulysses*. Melville finished *Moby-Dick*. But don't all three of those books seem like they move almost at random? Remember, *Don Quixote* is not a novel. It is two different books, published a decade apart and written in the course of fifteen years with an improvised, cumulative structure full of sizeable oversights that became the bread and butter of generations of academics; made up, in fact, of quite diverse materials that seem taken from all over. Not to mention that the second volume was finished in great haste, in a burst of anger against the author of an apocryphal *Quixote*. We have that wonderful word in Spanish: *a vuelapluma*. Who wants to read, who has the patience for jewelers and goldsmiths? Perfection is just jewelry. Cervantes, Joyce, Melville, all three of them work with waste materials. They reach into the alluvial deposits of stories written by others before them. They steal. They cut and paste. They let themselves be carried away by reckless digressions, courting disaster, almost wanting the book in progress to collapse, to burst and spill until it becomes impossible or nearly impossible to control, as *Moby-Dick* exploded in Melville's hands after a few chapters to become a wild, chaotic mass of words, a flood, a pastiche, a thing of rags and tatters. *Moby-Dick* was a landslide that buried poor Melville's name and reputation for the rest of his life; an explosion that destroyed whatever it found in its path . . ."

GREAT BALL OF FIRE FLIES OVER SPAIN AT 60,000 MPH. *It can take a glass bottle up to four thousand years to decompose. There are nearly four thousand chemical substances in a cigarette, among them nicotine, tar, ammonia, and Polonium-210, all of them carcinogenic and capable of contributing to the death of over six million people per year. Given its composition, a cigarette filter can take one to ten years to decompose. Chewing gum is 80 percent plastic. It takes an average of five years to decompose and the process requires oxygen, which during the first stages causes the gum to petrify. Polyethylene terephthalate, used in the manufacture of most of the world's water bottles, is immune to nearly all naturally occurring decomposing microorganisms. It can take between a hundred and a thousand years for a plastic bottle to begin losing its toxicity and start dissipating in the air. By 2025, about 155 million pieces of plastic waste will have been dumped into the Earth's oceans. Two hundred years is how long it can take a sneaker to decompose. A household battery can pollute up to three thousand liters of water and take between five hundred and a thousand years to decompose. In addition to arsenic, zinc, lead, chrome, and cadmium, almost all batteries contain mercury, one of the most toxic metals known to humankind. In contact with water it produces methylmercury, a by-product that severely pollutes the ocean's biosphere. Glass bottles are made of calcium, sand, and sodium carbonate. It can take four thousand years for a single bottle to decompose.*

TRUE LUXURY SHOULD KNOW NO BOUNDS. *By 2025, the world will produce six million tons of waste a day, twice the current level. If you weigh around 150 pounds, you should know that each year you produce six times your own body weight in trash. Humans produce 3.5 million tons of waste* *each day. By some estimates, total waste production could rise to eleven million tons per day by 2100. The economic model of consumption is at its most extreme in the city. These frenzied nodes of manufacturing and consumption produce enough trash in one day to fill a convoy of trucks stretching for more than three thousand miles. After the 2015 Paris summit, it was concluded that if no measures are taken the entire planet could collapse by 2050.*

YOU'LL HAVE THE TIME OF YOUR LIFE. *El Salvador, currently the world's most violent country, was shocked by the death of a hippo after suffering a gruesome beating. Gustavito, as the hippo was christened by popular vote, was the only one of its kind at the National Zoo. Weighing more than three thousand pounds, it lived precariously in a pond that was far too small for its size. The government confirmed that the death of the animal was caused by severe blows inflicted by one or more unknown persons who illegally entered the zoo. Blunt and sharp instruments were employed. Gustavito, a sixteen-year-old hippo and the only one of its kind in the entire country, suffered "massive hematomas and lacerations on the head and trunk" that proved fatal. Judging from the type of injuries it received, the authorities believe it was attacked with rocks, ice picks, and sharp knives. Deep gashes on its snout and head have led experts to believe it tried to defend itself. Many public complaints have been made in recent years about living conditions at the zoo and the state of its facilities. A cobra and an African lion starved to death prior to this latest incident. Severe behavioral disturbances have been documented among the animals, including a tiger that tried to eat its own tail and birds that plucked off their feathers.*

OREGON MAN BEHEADS MOTHER AND WALKS INTO A SUPERMARKET WITH HER HEAD UNDER ONE ARM. *Three minors arrested in Seville for beating a man to death. Man dies after being attacked by a pack of dogs in a village in Alicante. Four dogs covered in tar and left out in the sun so they would stick to the ground. Film actress attacked by shark while shooting a commercial in the ocean. Dead wolf found strung up from a traffic light.*

This is the third instance of dead wolves strung up in Asturias in the past three days. All of the animals were killed by gunshot and displayed in public places. Intruders enter Paris zoo at night to kill a rhino and saw off its horn. Crocodile stoned to death by a group of visitors to the Tunis zoo. According to the mayor's office, the animal died "of severe internal bleeding" after being hit by a large stone. The crocodile was killed by two heavy stones that struck it near the eye. The same group of visitors threw stones at wolves and hippos. Man brutally kicked by ostrich in South Africa.

I CAN'T STOP LOOKING. It was the summer of Bosch at the Prado, Caravaggio at the Thyssen, Torres-García at the old Telefónica building and Fantin-Latour, Hergé, René Magritte, and Baudelaire in Paris. The photographs of Miroslav Tichý were on show in a small room at the Museum of Romanticism in Madrid, which was even emptier than usual in the general exodus of the summer holidays. *"Glorifier le culte des images,"* says Baudelaire. The cult of images had much to do with the constant, vibrant joy I experienced during the long and leisurely walks I took on those lazy days of summer. To set out toward the places where the images were waiting was to begin preparing my eyes in advance, my mind as well, which grew increasingly alert with physical exertion in the precious coolness of the early morning. My bicycle would glide in perfect silence down an empty tree-lined avenue. There was no traffic, the air was fresh, and by the time I went from one part of the city to another my mind felt sharply focused and my eyes wide open. In a dimly lit room inside the Thyssen there was a single painting, Caravaggio's *Saint Ursula*. The darkness of the room and in the painting fused together. It was like going from the blinding sun into the gloom of a chapel deep in an Italian church. Looking at that painting requires a special patience; what it depicts seems to be happening very slowly. Gradually my pupils began to discern the metallic gleam of sword and armor; the soldier's sunburned rustic faces; the paleness of the martyr pierced by the arrows of her torment and beginning to bleed out. Caravaggio put himself in the painting, craning his neck among the other witnesses like someone at the scene of an accident on a busy street. Saint Ursula spreads her wound open with her pale fingers as if she was spreading open her sex.

A NEW WAY TO LOOK AT LIFE. To get to the Prado and look at the paintings by Bosch I had to cross El Retiro. Walking through the park was in fact a good preamble to Bosch. It looked very different on the way back from the museum than on the way there. The ordered rows of trees stretching away over tidy lawns to an umber horizon was like the modest, practical view of *The Garden of Earthly Delights* in Bosch's painting. Groups of young girls—foreign tourists—leaned their heads together to take pictures, holding out their cell phones and laughing joyfully as in an advertisement. Caravaggio's Abraham, about to slit Isaac's throat, pressed his son's face against the sacrificial stone with the same fierce determination with which a jihadist had beheaded an octogenarian priest in Paris in front of the altar where he celebrated mass. There was an advertisement on every bus stop with a joyful group of fearless young people jumping off a cliff, throwing their arms up and flexing their knees as if taking flight. On every corner store there was a cardboard panel with an advertisement for Magnum chocolate ice cream bars. The same pair of catlike eyes stared at you all through Madrid, the same face split vertically in two: a young, dark-skinned girl on one side, a leopard on the other. On one half a human nose and lips; on the other a muzzle. A leopard-woman, a panther, daring you and holding out to you the thrill of an urge as powerful as the one that turned Henry Jekyll into Mr. Hyde or an ordinary man into a werewolf. Dare to go double. RELEASE THE BEAST.

TERRIFYING INCIDENTS. It was the summer of Bosch. There were as many bodies crowding around and in front of the triptych as there were bodies painted on its panels. Flushed, well-fed bodies with cameras and iPhones gazing at emaciated medieval bodies. Packed into the room where *The Garden of Earthly Delights* is displayed, visitors pace slowly around it in a circular motion, a motion that is very similar to that of the mounted figures riding around a small pool in the central panel. The bodies in the painting are all the same: tiny copies of the same man and woman, seen from a distance that grows even greater given how difficult it is to approach the painting in that crowded room. People get as close as they can, eager to look, to make out little figures and small details, hideous creatures, symbols that in most cases remain entirely unintelligible. People glutted with pictures of overabundance and with televised visions of paradise gaze in a slow stupor at barbaric and infernal scenes where every torment lasts forever. Tourists flock like anxious pilgrims desperate to touch a sacred relic. Those who get too close receive a warning from a guard. Unlike the figures they are looking at, they are as varied as a crowd of people strolling through an airport or as the multitude that will be summoned—as many of them doubtlessly believe—to the Final Judgment. Some of them, listening to the audio guide, nod as if receiving a secret message. The figures in *The Garden of Earthly Delights*, by contrast, are all alike. There are no children or old men. No one is fat, or skinny, or ugly, or handsome, or aged, or in their prime, and there is barely any difference between the sexes. The crowd in the museum moves around the room in all its chaos and variety. Fat, exhausted tourists sweating in the summer heat and shuffling their feet, red-faced, fanning themselves with the visitor guides they were given at the ticket counter. In *The Garden of Earthly Delights* it is never hot or cold. Bodies do not sweat, or weigh anything, or cast shadows.

DON'T MISS YOUR CHANCE. If you look closely, no one seems to be enjoying themselves very much in this Earthly Paradise or whatever it happens to be. Men and women surrender themselves to pleasure with a neutral and conscientious expression, as if taking part in an orgy that was also an assembly line. The catalog of their sexual postures and acrobatic maneuvers displays all the exhaustive and rigidly regimented variety of pornography. Instead of being aroused by watching or embracing others they seem lost in thought. Each of them, with the right software, could be given a little cell phone. They could hold it up to their ear or look at the screen, or type a message with those little hands that look like the tiny paws of lab rats. They walk through Paradise and are as lost in what they alone can see as people tracking Pokémon in the park outside the museum.

TURN YOUR ASPIRATIONS INTO REALITY. Eventually I had a realization. I would meet him at a certain place, but I never saw him arrive or leave. He would be sitting at a table in the Café Comercial and the next moment he was gone. If he wasn't there already, he never turned up, and if he was, he had gotten there before me. It seems odd that it took me so long to notice, but going back in my mind to each of our meetings I couldn't find a single memory of him arriving at the café when I was already there, or leaving before me, let alone together. Once or twice, when we made plans to meet, I got there early just to make sure I was on time. Ten or fifteen minutes early. But he was already there, sitting at a table halfway between the front windows and the back wall, where light began to give way to shadow. One morning I looked in and didn't see him. I had in fact arrived twenty minutes early. Pleased with myself and with my punctuality, I went to the newsstand to buy some papers and maybe a cheap DVD. I kept an eye on the subway exit. I looked down Fuencarral and Sagasta, saying to myself I would surely see him come, since it was almost time for our appointment and he was never late. I remember the film I bought that morning, a rare find I couldn't have come across anywhere else in Madrid: *The Hands of Orlac*, a movie that Buñuel was quite fond of. A pianist who has lost both hands in an accident receives as a transplant the hands of a murderer, and then, possessed by them, becomes a strangler. I stood on the sidewalk holding a couple of newspapers under one arm and a silent movie in my hand (which seemed to emphasize even more my perennial anachronism) and looking at the crowd that periodically came out of the Metro even though it didn't seem like a means of transportation he would use. At one point, since I was standing outside the café, I looked in through the window. And there he was, perfectly settled at his usual spot, with his satchel or briefcase to one side of the marble-top table. Had he been in the bathroom when I went in? Was that why I had missed him? But I had no memory of him ever getting up to go to the bathroom or walking back to our table.

SITTING DOWN CAN BE A GREAT ADVENTURE. There was always a moment of strangeness right before I recognized him. He had a quality, or suffered from a condition, that I have noticed in just a few people over the course of my life: his physical features were forgotten as soon as he was gone. As if he were impermeable to recollection, covered in an insulating film that prevented the mind of anyone who knew him from clinging to his image. I must add that, in his case, this peculiar quality was strengthened by a kind of talent he possessed never to be seen head-on. I can picture him clearly with his back to me or in profile, or if I do have an image of him sitting directly across the table at the café, what I remember are his hands or the gleam of his glasses, the tilt of his head, never his face looking me directly in the eye; never his features in the pale light that came in from the street, the gray light coming through dusty glass into the Café Comercial.

YOU'LL WISH THE ROAD NEVER ENDED. In Edinburgh, in a museum as small and intimate as a private home, I saw a pair of boots that belonged to Robert Louis Stevenson. They were high boots, strong and supple, with thick soles and many laces, the kind of boots an explorer or a horseman in the Far West might have worn, or perhaps a hero in an adventure novel or travel book of the sort he used to write. Not, however, the kind of boots in which you would explore a city. It made me wonder what kind of boots Baudelaire wore when he roamed Paris (stylish, perhaps, though battered by his long walks down dusty, muddy, unpaved boulevards) and what kind of boots or shoes Dickens wore in London when he spent entire days walking and avidly watching people and places, fleeing as well the black spectral shadow of depression. I picture Dickens's boots as larger than Baudelaire's, the shoes of a strong, active man without the least trace of foppishness, someone who never fell prey to the languid fumes of opium or the toxic luxury of any other artificial paradise—a literary workhorse, a family man with many obligations rather than an idler like Baudelaire. As for Poe, he must have worn the kind of boots that you would find on a drunk or a dead man; on one of the living dead, a man embalmed in alcohol and opium. Probably a pair of narrow, pointy boots that a young rake from old Virginia could have worn. The boots as well of a wretched man crushed by addiction, heartbreak, and financial ruin; soiled by the muddy clay of graveyards and the urine and sawdust of tavern floors. Apparently they were literally falling to pieces: one of Poe's friends saw his boots come apart and fall into the mud as he jumped over a puddle.

THE PERFECT WAY TO START A TRIP. There is a picture of Fernando Pessoa in a pair of laced-up, thin-soled shoes that would be rather useless for a long walk, let alone the steep hikes required by the streets of Lisbon. Coming down the Chiado and hurriedly turning the corner of the Bernard bookstore, Pessoa looks a bit like Tintin: a man in round glasses, a thin mustache, a trench coat, and a pair of tapered pants that expose his ankles, carrying a satchel under one arm like a valiant comic-book character flitting here and there through Lisbon without in fact ever straying very far: the Baixa, the arcades of the Praça do Comércio, the banks of the Tagus, the Chiado, and little else. Bernardo Soares, his shadow or literary counterpart, never seems to wander very far from the Rua dos Douradores, where he lives in a rented room that is just a stone's throw away from his office. Just once he mentions taking a streetcar. The longest journey he recounts is a short train ride to the neighboring town of Cascais and back, a trip from which he returns as exhausted as if he'd taken the Trans-Siberian Railway to Vladivostok. Despite their thin, partly patched soles, Pessoa's shoes probably never became too worn or soiled with dust and mud. He must have carefully cleaned them every night in his lonely bachelor's quarters, with that widowed air that always seems to haunt him in photographs.

THE TOUGHEST CHALLENGE FOR AN AVID RUNNER. Lester Young only wore loafers made of the lightest and softest leather. He must have walked in them as stealthily as he played the saxophone, like a Zen master, shifting weightlessly from place to place, much like his melodies gradually trace the contours of a song without the least effort. Lester Young's loafers must have gotten soaked in the snow and in the sharp, freezing rain of a New York winter, even though he rarely went out on the street, just to get from his hotel to the club where he was playing and back: wet socks, frozen feet, a chill that lingered under the thin blankets in one of those seedy hotel rooms near Times Square with a tall vertical sign glowing with spurious poetry in the dark of an alley.

THIS SUMMER, TRAVEL BACK IN TIME. I picture a museum for the shoes of literary wanderers. A somewhat funereal place, given the stark, posthumous air that always clings to shoes even when you simply leave them at the foot of the bed, those twin, sepulchral witnesses to the journeys and travails of life. A museum filled with all their boots and shoes, from generation to generation. Poe, De Quincey, Baudelaire, Charlotte Brönte, Charles Dickens. Emily Dickinson's tiny boots and house slippers; Charles Dickens's shoes; the shoes of Benito Pérez Galdós, who did his share of walking in London and Madrid. Virginia Woolf's austerely proper English shoes and Vivian Maier's big, ugly, flat-soled shoes. Diane Arbus's shoes, whose heels must have been bent out of shape from so many hours of wandering through New York City among the freaks and the insane. Frank O'Hara's elegant (I imagine) shoes when he went out to lunch in Midtown, in the fifties, walking in a kind of quick and volatile tap dance. Truman Capote's little black shoes. The sober though unkempt shoes that must have carried John Cheever like a helpless sleepwalker to the nearest liquor store.

GET READY FOR THE COLD. When people are shot, or when they die in aerial bombings, they are often missing a shoe. The bare yellow feet of the dead poke out of their pants as if they were already lying on a marble slab at the morgue. One foot is bare, the other is wearing a sock, pulled down to the ankle, a toenail sticking out through a hole. One wonders what shoes Federico García Lorca was wearing when they beat him with the butts of their rifles and loaded him onto a truck to drive him to the place where he was going to be shot. Whether it is true that he was in pajamas. Whether he put on his shoes in a hurry and didn't have the time to put on socks, and couldn't quite manage to tie his laces. Sometimes when a man was shot in a decent pair of shoes one of his executioners would steal them, or someone else would take them, coming by early on the following morning to look at the corpses.

TRAVEL TO ANOTHER WORLD WITHOUT LEAVING YOUR COUCH. I often think about the shoes or boots that Walter Benjamin must have worn. According to some of his acquaintances, he had a strange way of walking, abrupt, then slow, like someone in a great hurry who a moment later is idling in front of a toy-store window. We know as well how Lorca used to walk: clumsily, on account of his flat feet, which also pointed out, and of his build, which was short and thick, like a peasant's; a big head, dark hair, a wide and weather-beaten face. Was he taller or shorter than the men who shot him, or than the other men facing the firing squad beside him, in the glare of the headlights? How strange never to have thought of this, the shape of his figure next to the others, the school teacher Dióscoro Galindo and the two bullfighters. Galindo, who was missing a leg, must have hobbled on crutches over the dark earth and the dry brambles on that summer night. The final, adventitious camaraderie of death, the bond between four men who only met a few minutes before they died.

AT A HOTEL BY THE SEA. Although the beach is nearby, you have to make an effort to hear the sound of the sea from the balcony outside the room. There are dim, discontinuous strokes, some faster than others, the faint slap of little waves against the shore, the echoing sound of those that are farther out. Trees sway in the breeze like ocean fronds, pulsing creatures that are neither plant nor animal in this liquid night where no distinction holds between air and water. Voices ring as clear as echoing sounds in a vaulted room: a burst of laughter, a couple speaking quietly as they come down the promenade between the sea and the hotel, and then a pop song, far away, and the voices of children who have been allowed to stay awake until almost midnight on this summer night, tired and elated, farther out beneath the lampposts where the darkness begins. If you listen more closely you can hear the chirping of crickets. As Borges famously said of the rain in one of his sonnets, the chirping of crickets always takes place in the past. This night turns into a different, distant night that happened many years ago. The breeze picks up, stirring the pages of the notebook and shaking the crowns of the trees with a rustle of branches and leaves.

PERHAPS ON AN ISLAND. Beneath the various sounds, so clear and distinct, there is a silence as deep as the bay. Drifting voices reach your ears much like the glimmer of lights reaches your eyes across dark water from the opposite shore. The crash of a larger wave lingers on the curving shore. Each branch, each leaf and pine needle quivers with its own particular motion. Palm trees sway more readily than pines. I could stay all night here, on the balcony, never going back to the warm, thick air inside the room. I could stay until they close the bar and the last few children have gone to bed and no more voices are heard; until, if someone passes by, you can hear the sound of their footsteps distinctly against the backdrop of the sea, whose brief, transparent waves keep vanishing into the sand. Life always begins in a salty fluid, whether inside a cell or in the mild, calm waters of this bay. When I go down to the beach the water is lit by the lights of the bar, which is empty now except for the waiters clearing the tables. In the water, floating over the sand and pebbles among the ragged seaweed, there is a school of little fish, each as transparent as the water itself, darting and flickering as swiftly as sperm cells in the salty medium of semen.

DRAW A PICTURE OF WHERE YOU WANT TO LIVE. Draw her outline on the surface of her body with the tip of your finger. Draw with three trailing fingers the loose strands of her hair. Draw the curve of her forehead and the shape of her eyebrows. Draw her lashes as carefully as possible and the shape of her eyelids, feeling the faint throb of her eyes just under the skin. Do not forget to draw her ears, the inner groove of cartilage, the softer outer part, which is a little like a cup handle, and then the earlobe, softer still, hanging like the dot beneath a question mark. Do not forget the contour of her cheekbones, perceiving, beneath the smoothness of her skin, the solid bone, its pure and formal beauty. Draw her thin lips, too, and then the smile that starts to form the more you draw, two tiny creases of delight appearing at the corners of her mouth. Touch her tongue and let it wet your fingers with saliva as you draw, so that, moistened like a brush or like the thick tip of a pencil, they can go back over her lips to darken them. Go down to the chin, conclude the drawing of her face in profile, which began with her forehead, her hair, and went down to her nose, and now continues sliding from the chin down to her neck. Draw her clavicles, spread like wings in flight, and draw the frontal volume of her naked shoulders, each one rounded like a fruit, an apple or a peach, one that you should graze lightly with your lips or gently bite.

LEARN TO READ YOUR BODY. Draw this body, so familiar and beloved, lying on the bed like a model for a painting who will also be the canvas and the drawing itself. Graze the areola as if to shade it with a bit of charcoal, draw the nipple, which seems to rise just as your circling finger begins to faintly trace it. Spell the letters of her name softly on her stomach as if drawing them on sand, the sand where even now, through the curtains, you can hear the ocean breaking feebly. Draw the belly button with a slight, twisting motion, then downward, a simple stroke to show the body's symmetry. Give the utmost care to the place where her naked skin, a little sticky now with sweat, shades into the faint beginnings of her pubic hair, a darker area that, to draw it, would require neither the tip of your finger nor even the edge of your fingernail but a brush as fine as a single hair. The warm gloom is always the same, the lazy air of midafternoon, but the faint light coming into the room will do so now through drawn curtains in a hotel by the sea. Trace the twin line of her thighs, and as you reach their meeting point let your fingers delve a little deeper. Do not stop drawing, do not stop looking until the very moment when you close your eyes, like a thirsty man who, bending down to drink, undoes with his mouth the perfect image of his face on the still surface of the water.

SILKY FEET IN JUST A FEW MINUTES. One night you can't hear the sound of the sea no matter how hard you try. The air is so calm that even the tips of the leaves are perfectly still on the palm tree facing the balcony. The bay is as smooth as a pool of India ink. The near presence of a silent sea turns the acoustics of the balcony into those of an old town square closed off to traffic on a summer night. High up in the sky a full moon casts a dusty glow. Voices ring clear in the warm, motionless air and over the still surface of the water. A tinkle of glasses, cups and coffee spoons, of ice cubes in a glass or in a metal bucket. They have turned off the noisy, manufactured music, and only a few voices remain. I can't quite tell what they are saying from this far, I can only recognize the sounds and the cadence of British English. The only branches beginning to stir again are those of the palm trees, the most sensitive to the breeze. Every night I like to stay on the balcony and notice how the voices gradually disappear: a last few peals of laughter, then silence, deeper than ever, now that even the soft ripples on the shore become too faint to hear. A jug, a glass, when struck, will make a sound as pure as that of a Japanese gong or one of those Tibetan bronze bowls that are struck or rubbed along the rim with a wooden handle. Voices seem both very near and very far against the clear backdrop of the sea. I can faintly hear conversations, the soothing sound of people talking calmly. Voices that are speaking here and now yet also seemingly on some distant night, past or future, any of the identical nights they've spent in this hotel over the course of many years while we were somewhere else. Men and women who are now grown were still teenagers or children when we were last here. Suddenly a sound I was not aware of ceases. The silence grows even wider, spreading in the hollow of the bay, and I can hear the voices of the last few customers finishing a drink or having a conversation long after the bar has closed. I become aware as well of a stereo effect: there are voices coming from the beach and voices coming from the balconies of nearby apartment buildings.

BECAUSE YOUR FUTURE BEGINS NOW. An illusory sense of timelessness arises in this calm. To have arrived a few days earlier, to remain a few days more seem like superfluous circumstances. Nothing exists right now except this night, there's no before or after. Nothing but this moment and this bay, ink-black, with tiered dots of light far in the distance. I can see the mute, gliding headlights of cars along a curving road that must follow the opposite side of the bay. When people speak or laugh, the sound echoes like a clap. The trees are as still as the artificial vegetation in a diorama. The sharpened tip of the pencil makes a steady grazing sound as it moves across the page. Once I place the final period, only the white silence of the blank portion of the page will remain. I will take care this time not to give in to the vice of filling every bit of space with writing.

AS IN THE WORLD'S BEST AIRPORTS. Recent memories are blotted out: lives in transit, caught in a dead time. Airports are impervious to memory or presence. All time becomes a dead time. The memory of something seen or done at an airport dissolves a few hours later without a trace. By the following morning nothing is left. Fear, too, is more abstract in airports. Two ordinary-looking men can be seen pushing luggage carts in a grainy clip from a security camera. They slip away in the crowd and afterward no one can serve as a reliable witness. The more a space is regulated and closed off, the more complete our loss of memory. If we do remember something that happened in an airport it is only by a sudden chance association, like a dream that we forget on waking and that unexpectedly returns while we're having lunch or in the afternoon, slipping its strangeness into our lives when we are most awake.

THESE CREATURES COULD BE ANYWHERE IN REAL LIFE. Two or three nights later, the memory comes back to me on the balcony of our hotel room. It comes back because I see a man go by in a wheelchair. It can't be the same man. This one is older and very thin, elderly. The other, the one I saw among a group of people waiting for passengers to emerge at the arrivals lounge, was fat. Tall, fat, and muscular. He was wearing a pair of wristbands and he kept his hands on the wheels of his chair. He had long hair that fell down his back, and he was wearing a baseball hat and a tight black T-shirt with gothic lettering and heavy-metal skulls over his disproportionately muscular chest. Strapped to the back of the chair was a plastic bag filled with ice cubes from which the neck of a champagne bottle was poking out. Someone was supposed to pick us up and take us to the hotel, but they were nowhere to be seen. After hours of travel and waiting in two different airports crammed with holiday crowds, this new delay had deepened our dazed feeling of fatigue nearly to the point of collapse.

PURE ADRENALINE. I felt dizzy staring at the luggage belt as we waited for our huge suitcase to appear. Up on a screen, Penélope Cruz drove a Mercedes sports car through the Paris night. The Eiffel Tower or the Arc de Triomphe glowed in the distance. When the automatic doors slid open we saw people waiting behind the barrier. We were so tired that we seemed blurry to each other in the general turmoil. None of the signs held up by drivers had our names on it. Life was suddenly an endless wait that began as soon as you felt relieved to be finally done with some prior delay. Standing near the man in the wheelchair there was a woman whose eyes were also fixed on the automatic doors that periodically opened and closed. Sometimes they opened and no one came out, or just one person, lost, belittled by the collective indifference of those who waited. Then a horde of people would come through. The reason I noticed the woman was that, along with the man in the wheelchair, she was the only person to be waiting alone, surrounded by a large group of noisy kids on a school trip and by families with signs, balloons, even costumes. The woman was pressed against the barrier, directly facing the doors. Because she was alone, and silent, the urgency of her waiting became more evident. She held a large handwritten sign that had no name on it, just a heart that she had drawn in red: THE LOVE OF MY LIFE.

THIS SUMMER, PLUNGE INTO A NEW REALITY. While I was looking at her face and at the sign, the man in the wheelchair had met the woman he was waiting for. She was a brunette, the kind of woman who would've once been called a bombshell. She had sat down on his lap, straddling him, and they were kissing and pressing up against each other, a pair of fleshy bodies stuffed into pants and shirts that could not really contain them, her thick thighs clad in tight, torn jeans. There was a tattoo of the Egyptian symbol for life on the nape of her neck. The crowd of arriving passengers flowed around the wheelchair on both sides while the two of them continued kissing and embracing, murmuring to each other without minding anyone else. Now she was holding a plastic champagne flute in each hand. He opened the bottle, struggling a bit to get it done since she was pressed so closely against him. The cork came off with a dry pop, eliciting some alarmed reactions that quickly subsided in the general hubbub. A jet of foam spurted from the bottle as from a fountain and got them both wet. She was laughing loudly now, shaking her head vigorously as if she was dancing or coming out of the water.

JUST LIKE YOU ALWAYS DREAMED. Passengers kept arriving and being met by people who clapped and shouted with joy, calling out their names, taking pictures with their phones, surrounding them with balloons. Small flags held aloft by tour guides fluttered over people's heads. Whoever was coming to pick us up was now apparently on the way. So many people came to the island during the holidays that the roads were backed up, especially entering the airport. A hundred eyes would not have been enough for me to take it all in. The constant visual and aural stimulation turned fatigue into a kind of giddiness while at the same time sharpening my attention. I looked back, fearing I'd missed the moment when the woman who was standing alone had met the person she was waiting for. I wanted to know what he or she was like, this person whom she openly called the love of her life, even going so far as to draw a heart and color it red. She was blond, and she seemed German, perhaps Scandinavian, attractive though a little wan, with a beauty that was perhaps a bit austere. I couldn't see her anymore. I thought she must have left, hurrying to meet her lover. Then a group of Chinese tourists followed its guide away from the barrier and I saw her standing where she'd been before. She was still holding the sign in her hands, though a little lower now because her arms were getting tired.

THE POWER OF DREAMS. The doors remained closed now, opening infrequently. They were entirely covered by a large photograph of a family at Disneyland Paris. A young couple with their children, a boy and a girl, all four in harnesses and helmets, shooting down a water slide fearlessly, with ecstatic joy, in a kind of rocket piloted by Mickey and Minnie Mouse. Win a once-in-a-lifetime experience for the whole family. The woman must have gotten to know those faces in every intimate detail, the big smiles, the water spewing all around. The doors open and their whole span is suddenly filled by a new throng of travelers. The lovers on the wheelchair drink from one another's glasses, in a tight knot of tangled arms and tattoos. Seeing more people emerge, the blond woman lifts her sign again. Did she just smile? I turn to look, but no one comes her way. She must think at every moment that she sees the face of the person she loves. *The love of my life.* The other woman kisses her man voluptuously on the mouth, leaving marks of lipstick on his face. Her mouth gleams with lipstick and champagne. He holds the empty bottle by the neck, letting it dangle alongside the chair.

SATE YOUR DESIRE. Our driver calls to say that he is at the arrivals lounge but cannot find us. Now I want to stay and see how it all turns out. The man in the wheelchair rolls himself vigorously with his big hands. His knuckles are tattooed and he wears black leather wristbands. His lover walks by his side, pulling a pink suitcase and caressing the back of his neck with her long fingernails. Our driver is here, flushed, embarrassed, dressed in a formal shirt and tie though his face is glistening and there are big sweat stains under his arms. He is one of those people who sweat profusely and smell strongly, and have a kind of soft, overripe skin. The lounge is nearly empty now and the doors remain closed. The happiness of the family in Disneyland Paris is as invulnerable as the perfect blue sky over Sleeping Beauty's castle. The woman takes a few steps, holding her sign in one hand like a discredited banner. She looks at the doors, which no longer open, and then at the other set of doors leading outside. Our eyes meet for a moment, though I am sure she does not see me.

SPEND AN EXTREME SUMMER WITH US. *A prank played by five German teachers was mistaken for a terrorist attack and caused a man to go into cardiac arrest. The offending tourists had pretended to spot a celebrity on the promenade, yelling and waving selfie sticks and toy guns, which caused a stampede. The incident produced "horrible panic" among visitors spending their holidays at this Catalan seaside town. Eleven people had to receive medical attention for minor contusions and anxiety attacks. Emergency services received 178 calls reporting the alleged attack. Many claimed that guns were being fired. In seconds, panic seized hundreds of visitors walking on the promenade of Platja d'Aro.*

SINISTER PRANKS SOW PANIC. *Townspeople mistook the flash-mob performance for an attack involving firearms. Chairs and tables outside local bars were overturned during the panic. Some people were injured after falling to the ground as the crowd fled in all directions. People ran carrying children. Bags, cell phones, and all kinds of personal belongings were left behind in bars and restaurants. Police officers armed with assault rifles assumed strategic positions along the streets. It was shortly before ten o'clock and the streets were filled, as they usually are throughout August, with tourists looking to enjoy themselves in one of the Costa Brava's foremost tourist destinations.*

ACCORDING TO WITNESSES, EVERYTHING CHANGED IN A FEW SECONDS. *Laura and Manolo, waiters at the Llevant restaurant, saw hundreds of people fleeing the promenade toward the main street of the town. Four hundred customers were dining at the restaurant, some inside and some* at outdoor tables. In just a few seconds, they say, noises that sounded like gunshots and subsequent cries of "bomb, bomb" and "terrorist attack" unleashed a state of collective psychosis. Tables were overturned, dishes and drinking glasses shattered on the floor. Some customers fled down various streets, but most ran inside for cover. Some locked themselves in the bathroom, others went to the kitchen or to an inner courtyard. A young woman fainted and collapsed at the entrance of the Dino ice cream parlor. Large numbers of people came up from the beach yelling and crying. Women and children wept in a state of great anxiety. Similar scenes took place at the Sant Lluís pizza parlor. Its customers rushed out in a panic through doors and windows. The inside was littered with bags, phones, and other objects left behind by those who fled when they heard hundreds of people yelling, crying, and running through the streets. Ramón, a security guard, described the scene as follows: "I saw a frenzied father run out carrying three children in his arms; a woman in a wheelchair going so fast you wouldn't believe it; a woman who snatched her child from the baby carriage and sprinted off." Ramón adds: "Another woman fell down. She cut herself and started bleeding, but she kept running." One of the waiters who lived through this bizarre incident says, "The best thing was how it ended, given how it might have turned out."

WHERE THE DAYS ARE NEVER THE SAME. I always bring with me my traveling office. My office of lost moments. Clippings, headlines, notebooks filled in pencil from the first page to the last, interleaved with old newspaper articles or brochures and glossy ads from fashion magazines: slogans, silhouettes, single words that I glue into the notebook like the illustrations in a book, sometimes on the cover, or wherever I can find a little space. Terrorist attack leaves eighty dead in Kabul. Scientists say humans and robots will one day fuse and become indistinguishable. I've set up my office in so many places that I can hardly keep track anymore, especially now, during this summer of borrowed rooms, hotels, keycards in my pocket. Child suicide bomber kills fifty at a Kurdish wedding in Turkey. Perhaps the act of wandering spurs the imagination. Without a home you live inside your notebook, attached only to the few objects you carry on your person. For a while my office was in an apartment in the neighborhood of Moratalaz, near El Retiro, where I could see from a window the tall buildings of the city center rising deceptively behind a thick expanse of trees, looking even more distant in the summer haze. Then for ten days the office moved without a hitch to a balcony in a hotel on a secluded bay in Mallorca. Everywhere it was the same office, succinctly deployed before me in the small space around my hands, enclosed in a circle of lamplight late into the night.

IF YOUR DREAMS HAVE NO LIMITS. Only the background changed, the view out the window, like a flickering movie still. An overcast sea with a string of lights tracing the contour of a bay in the distance. A view of locust trees seen from above, and of the cool canopy of shade they cast over a sidewalk in Madrid. An inner courtyard in Paris that was sunk all day in the same static gray light. At times the office has been quite minimal: a pencil, a notebook on my lap, the voice recorder on my cell phone as the number 20 bus climbed up and down on its way to the center of Madrid, toward a red evening sky that spread beyond the tall buildings on the Gran Vía and the Calle de Alcalá, with the terrace of the Círculo de Bellas Artes rising over the rooftops. Whenever the bus stopped I hurried to write down whatever words I overheard or could see through the window on an advertisement, knowing it would be impossible to write once we began to move again, to pick up speed and tumble up and down a hill. *Are You a Nower?* We Always Knew They'd Come Back. Collision Course, Now in 3D. Another time, I set up the office on a dining-room table facing a pair of sliding glass doors and an austere garden in Lisbon. The lamp stayed on till very late, through long, sleepless nights of silent work. Often it was lit at the very moment I reopened my eyes, still caught in an amphibious state between sleep and waking.

BREATHE NEW LIFE INTO YOUR SYSTEMS. What a relief it's been to be unexpectedly without a home this summer. What a blessing in disguise. Not to have to sit each morning at the same old desk like a bureaucrat or a clerk, tired of my own work, of a vocation dangerously transformed into a lethargic routine. Not to be tied down to the ergonomic chair and the laptop screen, hemmed in by memories and books and photographs, everything I've collected, everything that simply gathered over the years out of sheer inertia, the thick sediments of a long employment. Now my office is just a notebook and a pencil, a pen, an inkstand, a sharpener, a pair of scissors and a glue stick, a folder with some clippings in it, a couple of pocketbooks. *O livro do desassossego* is bulkier than the rest, though the writing is so light, so clean in its precision and its fogginess that it seems devoid of weight. Now when I work I am no longer sitting motionless before a screen, dazed by its glare, the tips of my fingers gone numb from pressing on the keyboard. I work without working, moving from one place to the next. I work by dictating notes into my phone. I see a headline in a free newspaper that someone left behind on the counter of a bar and I tear out the page and put it in my pocket. The killer walked through the scene of the crime shooting people as in a violent video game. New sensors developed by scientists will one day allow humans to expand their senses. Goebbels's secretary claims she was entirely ignorant of the Holocaust. Outside the door to the bar, a woman who stepped outside to smoke and to finish her beer begins to cough as she speaks into her phone in a cracked voice. "I asked you a question, and the fact you didn't answer is an answer in itself."

MY OFFICE IS ALWAYS WITH ME. This is not work, but a task. A task that I carry out wherever I go and whatever I do: sitting at a bar listening to other people's conversations; hearing the rustle of palm trees from a hotel balcony in Mallorca; riding the Metro; carefully picking withered flowers off a thick jasmine bush in a garden in Lisbon. Late in the afternoon the stretch between Moratalaz and Cibeles on the number 20 bus feels like a grand journey. Work has a purpose, a direction, a beginning and an end. A task is fulfilled at every instant. It suffices unto itself and it seems to lack any particular direction, which is why it benefits from any chance accident that would have interfered with work. There is no setback that the task cannot turn into a fortuitous advantage. When you're not there to perform it, the task continues on its own.

WE HAVE EVERYTHING YOU NEED. For the last few days the office has been a table facing a garden. It might seem that I will be here forever, given how well suited the place is to my routines, but in fact I will probably never see it again after next Saturday. The house belongs to a stranger. I am an intruder or a guest in a place that has been shaped by someone else's tastes for a life of which I am entirely ignorant. This doesn't bother me at all. I feel fully at home and in a few days I'll leave and there will be no trace that I was ever here. A dog, when it enters a room, examines various places, corners, cushions, before selecting with mysterious certainty the exact point where it will settle down and curl into itself. After a few different tries I finally decided to set up the office on this breakfast table facing the garden rather than in a more sheltered corner of the house where I found a desk with a lamp. It's a big table, with a dark marble top as smooth and aseptic as a Mies van der Rohe. I can spread my notebooks, newspapers, clippings, and scissors on the surface and there is always room to spare. Each day it becomes less of a desk and more of a workbench. It stays pleasantly cool in the summer heat. The garden is small and can be seen in its entirety from where I sit. It's graveled, with a few steps of dark wood that are as thick as roof beams. A heather screen divides it from the garden next door and there is fresh soil along the perimeter as well as in the center, where a jasmine bush grows as thick as the crown of a tree. Stalks of bamboo rise higher than the walls. All you can see is the sky, as in a Japanese garden or in a walled courtyard in Granada's Albaicín, places that are entirely closed off to the outside world, invisible, unknown to those who pass by on the street. The breeze makes a different sound in the jasmine bush than in the thicket of bamboo. Now and then the silence is broken by an airplane making its descent along the mouth of the Tagus. Other tiny planes glide in silence up above, at cruising altitude, leaving Europe to begin their journey over the Atlantic.

NOW IS THE MOMENT TO SEIZE THE MOMENT. The house is a recess of shade between two forms of brightness: the blinding glare of the windows facing the street—the Rua Nova de São Mamede, in Lisbon—and the soft inner light of the garden. Even the bedroom, which faces the street, is quiet and cool. Soundproof windows keep out all external noise when they're closed and white shutters block the light of the sun except for a thin vertical stripe in the middle where the two panels meet; a bright, thin crack in the shade of the bedroom like a shaft of light coming into a chapel. In the morning the air in the darkened room is heavy with the warmth of sleeping bodies. In the quiet of the afternoon the eye gradually adjusts to a dim light that spreads through the room, casting its soft gleam on two embracing figures, shiny with sweat, intertwined simultaneously on the bed and deep inside the mirror that stands at its foot.

I'M ONLY AN APP AWAY. A faint slapping sound, a quick wet snap, a warm parting of flesh like a flower whose thick leaves have not yet come unstuck, damp with fluid and saliva, the spit of mingled mouths. A shared and secret thing, the face you love, the face you truly see only at this very moment, so close to you that touch and sight become one thing, the seeing hand, the eye that feels, astonished, rapt in observation of this moment that is always the first time, eternally the same in endless variation, each small thing so familiar yet unlike it ever was before, a smile that suddenly contracts with pleasure, gone as soon as it begins to form around the corners of the mouth, a sharp, exquisite throbbing that never quite turns into pain, a readjustment, the unfamiliar features of a horizontal face rising or emerging, the stubborn, childlike chin, the cherished hardness of her cheekbones rising from her tousled hair, the way her forehead now seems broader, higher, curving where the hair begins, the hard and beautiful and clear curve. There is a joint rhythm, quickening or slowing like the rhythm of a hammock swaying on its own. Like palm leaves or a thicket of bamboo on a windless night, ceasing, slowing to a moment of ecstatic stillness, of pure and mutual imminence.

FEELS LIKE THE FIRST TIME. Pay attention then. Slow down your breathing. Listen to the sound, the way it starts and stops, the way it seems to waver without haste, a secret innocence, the purity of sacred things that would be spoiled if they were shown. The sound of water slapping gently on the shore at midnight, in a cove, and something warm, wet, sticky, quickly growing cold outside, preserving for an instant the temperature of bodies, the sweet and harmless fever inside them and between them, "secrets which do not permit themselves to be told," as Edgar Allan Poe said in the opening lines of "The Man of the Crowd." All that is demurely sacred, incorruptible. All that happens privately behind closed doors, for no one else's sake.

GRAND OPENING OF THE CONSUMER ELECTRONICS SHOW. One morning like any other, I arrived at the Café Comercial and found it closed. When I came out of the Metro the windows were boarded up and there was a chain with a big padlock securing the doors. They had closed it without notice, from one day to the next, without explanation or even a sign saying thank you or goodbye to their longtime customers, people of all ages who suddenly found themselves in a kind of exile, rudely banished from that gloomy and austere place that, though never too inviting in its decor or in its service, had nevertheless grown so indispensable that we now found ourselves condemned to wander aimlessly during that early time of day when a lazy, retired, or superfluous person, or one devoted to essentially concocted occupations, has nothing better to do in life than sit in a café. We were banished to bleak diners, fake artisanal bakeries, the poor imitations of a real café; or to the local branch of an international chain, the corporate regularity and rapaciousness of a Starbucks or of something even worse, absurdly named, Pans & Company, things of that sort. Places that force their employees to wear caps and uniforms with their first names written on a label over their chests; where you have to stand in line to order breakfast and then carry it on a plastic tray while looking for a table in a space as inhospitable as an industrial warehouse—even if decked in artsy, pseudo-artisanal, or downright poetical decor, with color photographs of adorable old bakers or of tiny villages that look like a Christmas ad for Nescafé. On top of which you had to drink your coffee in a paper or a plastic cup, leaving behind when you were finished a trail of unsalvageable waste: straws, forks, spoons, disposable plates.

BE THE STAR OF YOUR OWN MOVIE. Standing outside the Comercial, on that street corner that was suddenly shuttered and cold, I thought dejectedly that from that morning on I'd have nowhere to rest when I walked through that part of Madrid. I realized as well that I had no idea where to find my friend—or acquaintance, or accomplice in extravagant and rambling conversation—since I had only ever met him at the café. I didn't have a phone number or an email address. I could no longer ask the waiters of the shuttered café. Instead, without any real hope of receiving an answer, I went over to the newsstand and asked the man that sold discounted DVDs. The closing of the café would surely be a catastrophe for him as well. But he didn't know what I was talking about. It's true that I did not provide him with a description that could have helped identify the man. How could I, when it was so hard to remember him, to recall even his most concrete and recognizable features? Which in turn led me, on that morning of crushing discoveries, to another realization: I didn't even know his name, or if I did I had forgotten it, just as I always forgot between one meeting and the next whether he wore glasses, or if his hair was gray or white, or whether in fact he was bald. "A middle-aged man," I told the owner of the newsstand, "maybe a few years older than me." "Middle-aged, or old?" He spoke with the characteristic bluntness of Madrid. I felt a little hurt. "Hombre, I wouldn't really say old." I found it hard to retrieve any accurate visual details. "He usually wore a coat, and he carried a satchel. A black satchel, I think." "Did he wear glasses?" he asked in his harsh voice. "Well, I can't quite remember. He used to put them on and take them off. He would clean them with a wipe. But I'm not sure if he was taking them off to clean them or if he only had to put them on to look at things up close."

MAKE AN ADVANCE APPOINTMENT ANYTIME. The owner of the newsstand looked at me from up on his perch, behind the counter and among his magazines, reigning over an expanse of merchandise that had been prosperous until quite recently but was now threatened with decline by the closing of the café. Cardboard boxes filled with movies cataloged by genre: silent films, monster movies, Spanish soft porn, Westerns, horror movies, each set of DVDs in perfect order in a shoebox with a hand-made label. I selected two or three movies, feigning—in a servile attempt to befriend him or at least to invite some concern no matter how conde-scending on his part—an interest in film that was not especially strong at the moment. I went on, handing him the movies, while he quickly tallied up some number in his head that was no doubt completely arbitrary. "I'm sure about the satchel. He always carries it." But he demolished my sense of certainty as swiftly as he calculated an inflated price for my secondhand movies. "Does it look like a briefcase or more like a backpack?" I wasn't sure about that either. Perhaps both. Sometimes he carried it by the handle and sometimes under one arm, depending on how full it was. Sometimes it seemed empty and sometimes to weigh a lot, as if there were bulky things inside, books or packages.

THERE ARE 1,440 MINUTES IN A DAY. Late on a summer day the poet Catulle Mendès arrives at the Gare du Nord station in Paris. In the crowd of people filling the platform he sees a familiar face. It is Charles Baudelaire, carrying a suitcase in one hand and looking a little lost. For Mendès, Baudelaire is a master, a sacred and heroic figure. It was when he read his poems as a teenager in the countryside that his own vocation was awakened. He used to scour the newspapers for his articles and his short essays on art. Now, seeing Baudelaire alone in a crowd of strangers, he gathers up the nerve to approach him. He notices that his clothes are elegant but also old and frayed: the jacket and trousers, the boots, the limp knot of his cravat. Unlike most of his contemporaries, Baudelaire is cleanly shaved. His skin is smooth but he is very pale, probably sick. His hair is combed back and thin and gray, almost white, even though he only just turned forty-five. Mendès notices how people's faces change when they are alone in a crowd, unaware they're being watched. He sees Baudelaire stripped of the arrogance that he puts on when he enters a café or poses for a photograph. When Mendès addresses him, Baudelaire reacts with the bewildered and alarmed gesture of someone lost in his own thoughts. He says that he just missed the night train to Brussels and must now look for a hotel to spend the night. There's no other train until the morning. Mendès tells him that he has rented a room not far from the station and that it has two beds. If he does not mind sharing the room, it would be a great honor to have him stay the night with him. Then, in the morning, he will be conveniently near the station.

WE DEVISE A WINNING STRATEGY JUST FOR YOU. Mendès puts out the light and notices that Baudelaire is restless, tossing and turning in the other bed, unable to fall asleep. He came from Brussels to Paris for a few days to see if he could find an acceptable offer for some of his work, but had no luck. The contracts he was offered and that he had no choice but to accept deprive him of his rights to the work in exchange for very little compensation. His creditors are after him wherever he goes, in Brussels or in Paris. He doesn't want to stay in Paris but he doesn't want to be in Brussels either. He hates Brussels, Belgium, the king of the Belgians, all Belgians, all of humanity. No one has written more offensively about a country than Baudelaire in his rantings against Belgium. Three years ago he went to Brussels in the hope of finding good publishing contracts and making a little money by giving conferences. It all turned out a failure. So few people came to the conferences that the organizers canceled them outright. In Brussels he lives in extreme poverty, no friends, no newspapers willing to publish his essays. He fears he will be forgotten if he stays away from Paris for too long, in a city he finds dreadful, with its terrible weather and its muddy streets that won't allow him even the brief solace of a pleasant walk; with its coarse men and its fat, rumpled women. The lady who owns the hotel where he lives is constantly torturing him with demands for payments that are long overdue. The only respectable thing about the hotel is its name, the Hôtel du Grand Miroir. Ever since he squandered his father's fortune in his youth, Baudelaire has been without the least financial security. He has always depended on his mother's scant and humiliating generosity; staying in filthy hotels and rented rooms, always on the move, besieged by creditors, chasing editors to see if a newspaper will publish his articles or to demand whatever pay is owed to him. Increasingly the tragic wandering life of Edgar Allan Poe seems like a prefigured version of his own. He doubts he will live much longer than Poe, dead at forty in complete ruin; a heroic failure, a martyr of literature in a crass society where money is the only thing that matters. He is ill. He has fevers and spells of dizziness and nausea. He is forty-five and wrecked by syphilis. Years later Mendès will recall how Baudelaire spoke all through the night, muttering in the dark. Out of curiosity, out of respect, Mendès did his best not to fall asleep.

TURN YOUR ILLUSIONS INTO A REALITY. Baudelaire's rambling soliloquy gradually acquires the strange, arithmetical character of a delirious act of bookkeeping. Bemoaning his poverty, he goes back over every payment he ever received for the essays, poems, and translations he published in the course of more than twenty years. He seems to hold it all in his head like a deranged accountant, incapable of sleep, caught in the delirium of an endless sum. Perhaps he has taken laudanum. Mendès hears his voice close by in the dark and it all feels like a dream, though Baudelaire is actually there, whispering almost directly in his ear, obsessively rehearsing sums and dates of publication, adding, multiplying, while the young man, whose own health fosters and requires sleep, dozes off and wakes up to the endless singsong tally and the bitter complaint, to work so hard and for so long and to receive so little, to reach his age and to have nothing, not even one of those bureaucratic sinecures that clever men of letters know how to procure, or some official recognition, a decent editor, a paper that would pay him well and treat him with a measure of respect. Calling back to memory the ancient journals and the measly payments, Baudelaire begins to realize how many pages he has written, all those pieces that his young disciple has been reading and rereading ever since he was an adolescent, all the things he gradually discovered, the objects of his passion, the things he wanted to disseminate during his life, contemporary painting, music, the masters of caricature, his defense of Poe and Wagner when no one cared for them, his permanent rebellion against public indifference and the stupidity of critics, and that long poem in prose, *The Painter of Modern Life*, where he defined before anyone else a liberating and exacting notion of modernity, a word that he himself invented.

THE VOICE OF EXPERIENCE. Baudelaire runs through it all in his mind on that sweltering night in July when the heat may have made it even harder to sleep, placing next to each title the sum, the paltry amount that is now added to the rest. Being very tired, and confused, he frequently loses the thread and is forced to go back, to begin again, wrought up by his own mental turmoil. At last he reaches a satisfactory sum, it seems that he is soothed and that he will finally allow Catulle Mendès to fall asleep. But then he wonders out loud how much he earned on average during each of the twenty years of his publishing life. He carries out the calculation in his mind. Assuming he earned some fifteen thousand francs in twenty years of steady work, how much is it per day? What have been his wages as a writer and translator? He falls silent, but Mendès can hear him whispering, speaking in a faint murmur under his breath, as if he were falling asleep but the numbers kept seething in his fevered brain. "One franc and nine centimes," he finally says. "That is all I was able to earn. Less than a factory worker or a tradesman." Catulle Mendès thinks with melancholy outrage of the paltry wages given to the most acute mind and the greatest poetic talent the French language has seen in a century. Finally he falls asleep, unable to tell if he is dreaming of Baudelaire's voice or if he truly hears it by his side. When he wakes up in the morning Baudelaire's bed is empty, and he never sees him again.

CALCULATE THE PRICE OF YOUR ALARM SYSTEM. Twenty years earlier, the photographer Nadar frequently catches glimpses of Baudelaire walking down the street. Both of them live on the Île Saint-Louis. Baudelaire's clothes are elegant and eccentric: a blue working smock, an unstarched white shirt, leather gloves that have been dyed pink. He is a young man of twenty-four, with a faint goatee. Nadar remarks on an additional extravagance: he doesn't wear a hat. He says that Baudelaire walks through the neighborhood with uneven steps that seem at once languid and anxious, like a cat, choosing carefully where to step, as if the streets were covered in eggshells he was afraid to crush.

MULTIPLY YOUR HAPPINESS. Once or twice I thought I saw him walking down what always struck me as an implausible street, either because it was far from the neighborhood of the Café Comercial or because in some instinctive way I couldn't connect it with his reclusive manners. In fact, I had no reason to be surprised, since I had never managed to discover where he lived. Once, riding a subway that was just leaving the Cruz del Rayo station, and looking distractedly out the window as the platform vanished into the tunnel, I saw him or I thought I saw him sitting on a bench, his satchel on his knees, poring over what looked like a travel agency brochure. And I saw him, on a cold and clear morning in winter, looking into a crate of old books at a stand along the Cuesta de Moyano.

TO LOOK INTO THE EYES OF CATS. The only time I felt truly certain, the only time I saw him from up close was in a room at the Museum of Romanticism that had at first seemed empty. There was an exhibit of the work of Czech photographer Miroslav Tichý that must not have been attracting many visitors. I had gone early, right as the museum opened, to avoid as much as possible the terrible summer heat. The sky was a dirty white, presaging a stifling afternoon. It was in the emptiest days of August, after the fifteenth, when everyone who planned to leave the city has already left and no one has come back yet. We had finally settled into the new house after a long series of delays that forced us to travel or to stay in borrowed homes and hotels. The house was half furnished and seemed as barren as a warehouse or a sound stage, too much space all around, a sense of vacancy, of encampment, rooms without furniture, bare bookshelves, stacks of boxes filled with books in the middle of a room, paintings leaning against the wall, a sound system in pieces on the floor and its tall speakers still in their boxes. In the kitchen, which we were already using, the cabinets and drawers were mostly empty and the dishes and cutlery were not entirely sorted and put away, so in order to find anything we had to open each cabinet, each supposedly helpful drawer where you always found things you weren't looking for. A bed lay on the floor with its legs off in a room that wasn't quite a bedroom yet. The nightstand was a cardboard box with a desk lamp on top.

MY JOURNEY THROUGH THE WORLD STARTS HERE. It was a warehouse and a campground. A campground inside a warehouse, in a hangar where the house we already lived in was still being built. The two of us stood out even more conspicuously against that nearly blank background, as empty and bare as the windows in the walls. The view through their frames was the only thing in the house that seemed finished. At the foot of the bed, the large suitcase we had dragged behind us for months was still open, at hand, like an affirmation of a perpetually nomadic life. I still kept my notebooks and pencils in the backpack to make sure they wouldn't get lost. Our voices seemed different in those empty spaces where nothing absorbed sound. They seemed like new and younger voices, imbued with the sense of newness that reigned through the house, a blank slate, the smell of plaster and of paint and varnished wood, of all that has been freshly finished and unveiled. The TV set and DVD player were in place on the low table where they belonged, but the colored cables hanging down in bundles seemed to us beyond all possibility of ever being reconnected. Going out and walking down the street still felt like exploring a new city. Everything was so new that we were a little abashed to see each other naked, and the first night was even more of a first night because we had never been in the house after dark. It was when we first had sex that it became our house, even if the walls were bare of photographs and paintings and our books were not yet on the shelves. As I drifted off to sleep, eased by love, I resolved to remember every bedroom, every room where we had sex for the first or the only time; to mark on a map each and every city where we ever made love.

LIFE BEFORE YOUR EYES. Since I still had a backpack, a pair of sandals, a good pair of hiking boots for days when I walked far; since I still had a notebook, a credit card, a pencil, a sharpener, an eraser, I kept up my active and irresponsible summer life. I had to plan new routes, calculate new walking distances from our new address. A serious wanderer will not rely entirely on Google Maps, but rather carefully keep track of time, distance, useful shortcuts, and auspicious detours. One morning I set out at nine-thirty and by ten-fifteen I was already walking down the Travesía de San Mateo to the Museum of Romanticism. The uniformed guard looked up from her cell phone, a little surprised to see a visitor. Then she became absorbed again in what seemed from the sounds that came out of the phone like an engrossing shoot-'em-up game. I had discovered Tichý's photographs a few years back in New York. I was glad they had come to Madrid, and that a persecuted and derided body of work that was seemingly doomed to oblivion had nevertheless become known and attained a certain posterity. Life can play out in strange ways. I saw one of Tichý's cameras displayed in a glass dome, with its lens that looked like a castaway's spyglass and its bits of rope, rusted gears, discarded odds and ends precariously held together with electrical tape. Unexpectedly, I saw as well another visitor, a man sitting with his back to me on a narrow plastic chair that was barely wide enough for his buttocks, looking at a monitor as it silently played a documentary about Tichý. He was wearing headphones, so he hadn't heard me come in.

THEY WILL STAY WITH YOU FOR THE REST OF YOUR LIFE. As always, I failed at first to recognize him. As always, I was surprised a moment later not to have known immediately who he was. This time my confusion was dispelled more quickly because he was easier to recognize from the back than from the front, and also because the setting—an antiquated and rather ill-fated place—seemed already to anticipate or to favor his appearance. Something in him was contrary to the sensuousness of sweltering heat, light clothes, bright colors, the turmoil of a summer crowd. So there he was, large and furtive, heavier now than I remembered, not because he'd put on weight but due to the peculiarly erratic traces he left in one's memory, which had led me in the past to be surprised at how much taller, shorter, thinner, balder, or less formal he seemed. Perhaps it was the fact that he was wearing glasses, or that he wasn't wearing them. But there he was, on that chair that would have needed to be wider or sturdier to preserve his dignity. His satchel or briefcase was beside him on the floor, and when I looked at it I noticed too that his trousers rose a little high above the ankles, revealing a pair of dark socks that didn't quite manage to cover his pale, fleshy calves, which were hairless where they rubbed against the edge of the sock and which had rarely been exposed to the air, the sun, or the healthy shock of the sea. You could tell his shoes had never trod on sand.

TELL ME WHAT YOU SEE. I saw him, not without a pang of joy, sitting perfectly still, his broad, upright back like that of a Buddha made of bronze or terracotta, and on his head a pair of large and ancient headphones befitting an obscure cultural institution of scant means, a pair of clunky headphones that made him look like an engineer or a Soviet spy. Over time, laziness and misanthropy—though mostly laziness—have left me without friends. So I was even happier to suddenly run into him, even if I wasn't exactly expecting a hug or a slap on the back, or even a handshake. He was someone I knew, after all, someone with whom I had a relationship, even if I couldn't remember that earlier life anymore, that pristine time, never to return, of a nascent vocation, the joy and the uncertainty of all beginnings. I felt that I could not approach him without giving him some kind of notice; first, so as not to startle him, and then because a rigid, almost mummified or sepulchral formality had gradually established itself between us, partly from reserve and partly out of masculine ineptitude. I was wondering how to approach him when my cell phone rang. The phone was new, because I'd managed to lose the old one, with all the recordings of voices and city sounds I had made in the past few months. I was not familiar yet with the jingle that rang by default when a call came in, nor had I taken the time to replace it with something less irritating. I patted my pockets frantically while the merciless tune kept ringing at full blast, aware that I had jolted the guard out of her pleasant absorption in the video game and feeling the brunt of her censuring glance, the way she rose up in her seat to direct at me the full weight of her uniformed authority. Who could be calling me at ten-thirty in the morning on a Saturday in August. With an anxious sense of guilt and a pathetic clumsiness that will accompany me forever, I finally found the phone, its much-touted slickness rendered even more slippery by my sweat, and I walked hurriedly out of the room, tapping the screen repeatedly to pick up the call or at least to put an end to the vile tune, pursued by a forbidding glare from the guard that was reinforced by the penal sternness of her uniform. A girl with a gentle Venezuelan accent addressed me warmly by my first name, said her name was Maika, and joyfully, urgently announced that I still had time to take advantage of the Love Is All You Need Family Plan by Orange. I pictured her sitting in a white plastic cubicle in front of a computer, in a building without natural light or air conditioning in an industrial park (for instance) on the outskirts of Ciudad Juárez. The way Maika said my name as if she knew me made it hard to hang up on her without a word. But that is what I did, cravenly taking advantage of the distance between us and the lack of any foreseeable consequences. I put away the phone. My fingers were a little clammy from agitation and a sense of my own baseness. The guard, appeased, had now sunk back into her game, her belly strapped and harnessed in a military-looking contraption that held a gun, a baton, and a pair of handcuffs that would surely never be needed. The chair facing the monitor, however, was empty. The headphones had been carefully placed on the seat.

MEXICO SHOCKED BY MYSTERIOUS BUS VIGILANTE.

Mexico is searching for an Exterminating Angel.
He has no name, age, or face.
But everyone knows what he did. Last Monday
at six in the morning
he spread the wings of vengeance
on an intercity bus
and killed four robbers without hesitation.
It was a chilling, merciless,
abysmal execution. He waited
in the shadows
of the back seats
for the robbers to ransack the passengers,
and when the robbery was nearly complete
he stood up and killed them one by one.
Then he returned the passenger's belongings
and was lost in the lawless Mexican night.
None of the witnesses would give a statement, not even
the bus driver. All of them claimed it was too dark
so as not to have to describe him.
There are some who openly approve of the killings.
The incident took place between five and six in the morning.
It was still dark and the bus was heading
from San Mateo to Mexico City.
Forty miles of good road.
Fifty-three passengers were dozing in their seats.
The robbers got on the bus when it stopped in San Pedro Tultepec.

A few miles later the robbery began.
Their leader held the driver at gunpoint.
The others began to take money, jewels, credit cards,
and cell phones from the passengers.
There were insults and blows. One man put up a fight
and was subdued by force. Knives in hand,
the robbers stuffed their loot in a pair of backpacks.
After driving another twenty miles
the bus began to slow. The leader of the band
had been on the phone the whole time.
They had almost reached the appointed place
and the robbers began to move toward the door.
That was the moment when the man
sitting in the back chose to get up.
He took out a gun. He took aim silently
and squeezed the trigger four times in a row.
Each bullet struck one of the robbers.
The bus kept moving.
The first to fall was the leader. The bullet
went through his left shoulder blade and pierced
his carotid artery. He bled to death on the floor.
His three companions, wounded and terrified,
huddled by the door. From the back of the aisle
the Exterminating Angel came for them.
The bus screeched to a halt.
Its doors opened. The body of the leader
tumbled out. Then the three other robbers jumped.
They tried to flee, but vengeance
would not let them get very far. One after another
dropped by the side of the bus
as they tried to flee.
With death in his eyes, the Exterminating Angel
took the blood-soaked backpacks
and after returning what had been stolen
he asked the passengers not to give him away.

He stepped off the bus
in the middle of La Marquesa National Park
and walked into the woods.
The mystery of his identity fuels speculation
and there are almost no clues. The hope of finding him
has waned. No one knows
where the Exterminating Angel might be.
His tracks are lost in the night.

FIND THE PERFECT CONTENT FOR YOUR NEXT CREATIVE PROJECT.
Miroslav Tichý was a Robinson Crusoe in castaway rags, walking through
his native town as if it were a desert island or one of those large cities where
any eccentricity is accepted as a regular part of the landscape. He carried
with him a strange camera made of discarded materials. A reversed bottle
cap pierced by a thumbtack served to advance the film, while the lens was
like a section of a spyglass salvaged from the sea and held together with bits
of rope and tape. Tichý lived in a kind of shed or hut, surrounded by all
kinds of junk that he found here and there, like flotsam that is cast ashore
or like the contents of a dumpster next to a construction site. Out of it all
Tichý gradually built himself a shelter, chaotic but inhabitable, like a castaway on a desert island who has no access to the benefits of civilization
and must make use of whatever is at hand. He lacked all human company,
but he made up for it in his desert island with a few animals that became
his only interlocutors—an audience for his soliloquies, as well as the sole
witnesses to his feats of domestic ingenuity. Rats, mice, cockroaches, birds
that came in through a cracked and dirty windowpane, ants that marched
in line across the floor to harvest bread crumbs or to plunder the grand
organic feast of a dead cockroach. An empty space would form around him
as he walked down the street, like a leper or an untouchable, protected from
intruders or any excessive closeness by his stench and his misanthropy.

BECAUSE OUR DREAMS ARE NOT CHEAP. Some of the artistic sensibility that he stopped exercising when he gave up painting was surely
channeled into perfecting his image as an anchorite, which made him look
exactly like a nineteenth-century illustration for a castaway novel. Only by

renouncing everything could he make himself invulnerable to coercion, to the threat of having things taken away. Instead of meekly or cynically submitting, instead as well of an active resistance that would have meant immediate self-immolation, Tichý chose or found a radical form of disobedience by becoming marginal, by giving up all needs and so never having to ask for anything, shipwrecked in the desert island of his own provincial and terror-stricken town, lonely as a hermit in the hovel of his own house, the desert of his own land, tyrannized by the Communist bureaucracy and the secret police. Since he had nothing, nothing could be taken away from him. By giving up painting he spared himself the need to purchase materials, plan exhibits, or look for galleries. No one could deny him things he hadn't asked for, or take away a job he didn't have, or purge him from organizations to which he didn't belong. No one could ruin his artistic career, because from a young age he had decided not to pursue one. It was useless for them to try to silence him, since he had long ago decided not to speak; nor could they forbid him to do anything, since all he ever did was walk around, or sit in a park scratching himself in the sun when the weather was nice. They couldn't make him an outcast, since he had embraced being one from the start. He was not afraid of being forcibly marginalized since for a long time he had been perfecting his own marginal existence. He might have said something similar to what Borges once said to a student activist who was threatening to turn off the lights if class was not suspended to join a strike: "Go ahead, turn them off. I have taken the precaution of being blind."

CHOOSE THE KIND OF PARTY THAT SUITS YOU, AND MAKE IT A REALITY. But total renunciation can devolve into sterility, turn in the end into a barren gesture unless it arises from some kind of passionate affirmation. By giving up on being someone, on having anything, Tichý achieved a disinterested celebration of the variety and abundance of life. The asceticism of his indigent existence was made up of irony and guile. His laughter remained just as splendid for all his missing teeth. Poverty sharpened his wit and his ability to make the most of anything that came his way or lay at hand; to always manage on his own, a castaway who must invent and improvise at every step because he is bereft of all, except perhaps for the providentially selected wrack that the sea always casts ashore in novels. His princely patrimony was the vast endowment of all that people threw away. His darkroom supplies cost nothing and there was no danger that a manufacturing or distribution mishap would prevent him from procuring them. Living nearly on nothing, he had all the time in the world to enjoy his free occupations and to practice his art. Even amid the shortages and rationing of a communist economy, the air and the light of day remained not only free but inexhaustible. When they threw him in jail or put him in a psychiatric institution, he enjoyed the comfort of an assured and decent meal, a relatively clean cell, a comfortable bunk, veritable luxuries in comparison with his own disastrous domestic arrangements. In jail and at the mental hospital he passed the time chatting with the other inmates and the staff, even earning a bit of money by painting portraits of some of the higher-ups.

CHANGE YOUR EYE COLOR TODAY. He lived for his art as completely as Picasso for his paintings or as Flaubert for the precision of his prose. But he was spared the torment of vanity, since there were no critics to judge his photographs or collectors eager to buy them; no praise to be received or denied; no peers with which to draw comparisons. Tichý didn't have to measure up to anyone because no one else did anything remotely resembling his work, if it could even be called work. He would go out in the morning and spend the day walking around looking at people and things, especially women, young women, bathers in swimsuits at the local pool, girls sitting on a park bench after school in pleated skirts and socks. Desire for him was equivalent to the contemplation of beauty; always spied from a certain distance, often from behind a fence or some other kind of barrier that is never breached even though it wouldn't be hard to do so. The destitute photographer's desire does not expect, request, or even imagine any reciprocity. Things are as they are. Even when he photographs them from up close, the women seem enveloped in the haze of a conclusive distance, a distance assumed and accepted by a hand that doesn't want or is unable to reach out. A deep remoteness is established over a very short physical distance, like glass made cloudy by breath. The distance of one who looks but is not seen, devoting to others an attention they do not perceive; or one who, being very close, remains invisible because his presence causes physical revulsion, discomfort, disdain, or apprehension. Beggars share in this invisibility, as do people standing on street corners trying to hand out flyers while everyone eludes them without a glance. Making eye contact even for an instant would mean acknowledging their existence, establishing a bond.

WHAT GOES INTO A CUP OF COFFEE. But in his town, everybody knew Tichý. He was like an assiduous but harmless stalker, an impassioned ogler, considerate, respectful, not just out of shyness but out of gratitude as well for the beauty he was being allowed to witness—a momentary beauty that was quickly gone but that he captured with his makeshift camera and then developed in the darkroom as if drawing with shadows—a Zen-like artist without brush or pencil, molding light and shade into the figure of a woman who remains unknown and radiant, a bit ethereal always on account of the precarious methods he employed to develop and print his pictures, and also, above all, because her beauty is seen through a barrier, the metal mesh of a fence, some trees, a window frame, the muggy summer haze in a park or in a swimming pool that he himself will not enter. Tichý turns the crudeness of his methods into a stylistic trait. Some of the women who later recalled having seen him or exchanged a few friendly words with him did not remember that he had a camera. It was such a bizarre object that they would have maybe failed to recognize it even if they saw it. The strap, the cardboard box, the lens tube held together by masking tape, the bits of rope, etc., it could all have been part of his extravagantly elaborate outfit, a king of trash, a dandy in rags. Sometimes he concealed the camera in those rags and took the picture by pulling on a string or a piece of wire, a quick dry yank like a fisherman's when he feels the bite; a painless kind of fishing, that harmed no one and took place unnoticed.

FIND OUT RIGHT NOW IF YOU'RE A WINNER. The process didn't end when the picture was developed. His prints varied according to whatever random tray or support was available, and this impoverished delight in his materials affected the outcome of the work, as did the equally impromptu backboard on which he stuck the picture or the unavoidable accidents resulting from his precarious process: spots, blemishes, areas that were out of focus, defects in the paper or the piece of cardboard or the chemicals. No accident could spoil the outcome: each, as it took place, became a necessary part of his creative work. There was no need for proper storage, since damage and decay were like additional touches: a rim of moisture; the nibbling of a moth or mouse; the layer of dust that in such a dirty house began to cover the print even while it was still wet. Disorder, carelessness, forgetfulness, and neglect carried out a selection that he would never have bothered to make. The anonymity of his subjects and the passage of time gradually gave his pictures the very mystery of temporality, a sense of the frailness of the past. There is a tremulous freedom to the women in bikinis whose pictures he took in the sixties and seventies, a half-fearful yet assertive sensuality that would not be as alluring or as intriguing to us if it did not shine against the backdrop of time. Those public swimming pools and lazy summer days are tinged with the uncertain quality of weather that will soon turn gray and cold. That barely tasted freedom, like water in a pool that is a bit too cold, is the freedom of the Prague Spring, even if Prague was far away and Tichý had no TV or radio, and never read the papers or spoke with nearly anyone, or would have shown much interest in whatever happened to be taking place. Tichý's lens, which he used as an improvised spyglass to look at what was right before him, is now a telescope through which we glimpse a distant world—more distant still on account of its apparent nearness, of how his pictures show us the beginnings of a modern way of life that is, for some of us, our own.

FEEL THE CONNECTION. We, too, were shy and secretly fervent witnesses to the opening of the first swimming pools, the girls in bikinis or miniskirts. Tichý comes from that same past, a castaway outside of time, a Robinson Crusoe wandering down our century, quite old, unkempt, and toothless in those color pictures of his final years, burned by the sun, coarse fingernails edged in black, like a pauper's, and yet as well a kind of king, sarcastic, skeptical of his own abrupt celebrity, a more or less unscathed survivor of the communist regime that tried to crush him with its power only to sink into oblivion as he strolled along, a kind of Buster Keaton, dazed, unharmed, while all around him the house collapses. Scratching with gnarled fingers at his filthy hair and beard, Tichý laughed a toothless laugh at his success just as he had laughed before at anonymity, at tyranny and destitution. And now he turns up like a ragged, glorious ghost one August morning in Madrid, in a museum, on a monitor that shows a documentary about his life to an empty chair. He turns up here just as he turned up at the great communist parades and patriotic celebrations on the main square of his city, among the flags, the crowds of docile citizens in traditional dress that looked away and wouldn't even stand beside him, waiting for a police van or a psychiatric ambulance to come and take him out of circulation until further notice. Tichý would amiably climb into the van and take a seat, politely greeting the policemen or the orderlies, some of them by name.

WHEN YOU'RE ON YOUR CELL PHONE YOU LEAVE THE WORLD BEHIND. The painter tells me that he wakes up every day around four in the morning, rested, alert, clearheaded, and begins to think immediately about the painting he is working on or a new idea that came to him suddenly in the dark. Not a complete image, just a glimpse, an intimation that is nonetheless enough, a kind of little crack or signal, perhaps a figure or a silhouette in a corner of an empty canvas, one of those dark spots that were formed by damp patches on his bedroom ceiling when he was a child, which quickly and without the slightest effort on his part turned into clouds, ships, horses at a gallop, elephants, or lion heads. It's the urge to work that gets him out of bed, so briskly that he forgets he is quite old, soon to be eighty-one. He washes his face with cold water. He puts on an old pair of pants, slippers, a smock, and goes downstairs to his studio. Through a big glass door he sees the garden still in darkness. If the weather is nice, he goes outside and stays there for a while, doing nothing, lifting his face in one direction or another—like a dog, he says, lifting its muzzle, recognizing smells and sounds, so fresh and clear at this time of day.

FIND A NEW REASON TO KEEP ON SMILING. He drinks a glass of water from the tap and he begins to paint without having had anything to eat. "It's only now," he says, with an accepting, retrospective smile for all the oddity and weakness of human beings, that he truly enjoys his work. I ask him why and he takes a moment to consider it. "I'm not afraid now," he says. "I'm not afraid of anything. I find it hard to believe it took so many years. But I find it even harder to believe that I am not afraid. I'm not afraid that the gallery will not like the painting, or the critics, or that no one will want to buy it, given the current state of the art world. I'm not afraid that it will turn out worse than other paintings I have done, or worse than other people's paintings. I don't compare myself to anyone. That is the greatest relief. It has taken me my whole life," he says, "my whole life. But I could have died without ever getting well. Not to look askance, not to feel stung when someone else gets a fancy retrospective at the Reina Sofía and I don't, when a price is announced for someone else's work that I'll never even approach. Nor am I afraid that the painting will fail, that it won't work, that it will start off well and be spoiled as I go, or that it won't match what I imagined. If it doesn't work, I put it aside and start a new one, or I just paint over it."

YOU WILL HAVE A NEW LIFE. His studio is tidy and clean. He says he doesn't like to get things—or himself—dirty. "Strange, for a painter, right?" In a kind of cupboard he keeps rows of jars, tubes of paint, pigments, brushes, palette knives, and pencils. There are pencils of various thicknesses, and cases of cheap school pencils with which he also enjoys working. In school, he says, as a child, they were a luxury. He didn't have colored pencils then, or anything else. The room was cold, he says, and he was hungry, and the teachers used to hit the kids. During the war the teachers kept disappearing and classes were canceled half the time. They couldn't find replacements quickly enough for the ones who were put in jail, or murdered, or purged. The war was not a bad time for children in Madrid, at least until food began to run short, and especially until "those people" arrived. "Those people," he always says, without further clarification. There are areas of time that never came to an end for him. "In school we had no pencils or notebooks," he says. "Just a piece of slate, a rag, some bits of chalk that you had to care for as if they were made of gold—or bread, rather." He remembers how much he enjoyed writing on the smooth black surface of the slate with a piece of chalk. "Have you seen the paintings on slate by that Russian or Lithuanian painter—what's her name—Vija Celmins? Try remembering a name like that when you get older," he says. "That woman knows. Artists can only work with what they truly know."

THE YOUNGER I FEEL. He gets excited when he talks about chalk or charcoal, about the stains they leave on your fingers. He looks at his own thin fingers, the fingers of an old man, tinged yellow even now from when he used to smoke, so many years ago. He used to take a sharp piece of charcoal and draw comic-book characters on the walls of his father's little coal shop, or characters from the cartoons they played at the neighborhood cinema. "Like a child painter in Altamira or Lascaux," he says. "Did you know they found out that some of the cave painters were children? They can tell from the size of the hands." He drew pictures of Diego Valor, Donald Duck, Mickey Mouse. "I was doing pop art before its time and never knew it. I was a prehistoric pop-art child painter." He says it took him his whole life to be able to draw again with that careless joy. The wonder of tracing an outline that is recognizable, a silhouette, a shadow, the shape of a hand on a wall.

THE BEST OR NOTHING. He paints before sunrise, by electric light, in a silence as deep as the silence of a well, a cave in Altamira. "Why did they go so far inside, what did they see when their shadows were projected on the walls?" Time passes so quickly as he paints that it takes him a while to realize there is daylight in the studio, that many birds can be heard, not just blackbirds anymore, and there's the noise of traffic on the expressway, people driving anxiously to get to Madrid. He doesn't have the radio on when he paints, or play any music. He used to listen to the classical music station, Radio Clásica. Now he listens to his own breathing and to the sound of his feet coming and going on the linoleum floor, approaching the painting, stepping back, facing it, viewing it from a certain angle, from another, in silence. I picture him in his black slippers, his smock and his black pants, moving through the studio as slowly as if he were practicing Tai Chi. He says that silence sharpens his ability to see. It works like an extremely clean and polished magnifying glass. He never stays still for very long. He learns what he needs to do a few tenths of a second before he does it. Not being as physically strong as he once was, he no longer makes those big gestures that pivoted from the shoulder and left behind a streak of color or black ink across the canvas. "It was a little theatrical," he says with a laugh. "We wanted to be abstract American painters." These days he gets closer to the canvas, painting, as he says, not with his whole body but with the wrist, and lower still, with his fingers, as if he were writing in pencil. Sometimes the difference between a good painting and a failed one is a tiny mark, a small spot that creates or fails to create a sense of balance across the whole composition. "Look at those drops, those tiny spots of paint in Bosch," he tells me. "Look at them closely. The merest dab of white and you have the medieval headdress of a woman seen from the back, far away, in a forest, on a field where a horrible army approaches."

NO MATTER WHAT YOUR STYLE MAY BE. By nine in the morning he is tired and hungry. He makes breakfast, and now he does turn on the radio. He eats facing the garden. A good breakfast, but not too abundant. "A piece of toast with oil and tomato," he says, "toasted just right, not so lightly that it stays white and porous, but making sure it doesn't burn." He talks about the toast as he would about an artistic question. He loads the dishes in the dishwasher, wipes the table, sweeps any crumbs that may have fallen to the floor, and turns off the radio. He brushes his teeth and gets in bed and sleeps until noon. "Like a child. As I have never slept before." For the rest of the day he doesn't feel the slightest need to go into the studio. He doesn't really remember what he did, he says. Some days he sleeps so soundly that when he wakes up and takes a shower it seems to him that he only dreamed he was painting. "But one *should* paint while dreaming," he says. "It's the only decent way to paint. Much of what they call primitive painting, the art of the Aboriginal Australians or the Native Americans, is made of dream visions."

REASONS TO STAY HOME. There is a deliberate aesthetic quality to everything she does, a thoughtful yet fluid and natural ease, like a musician improvising, simultaneously aware of the general shape of the music and of the next step to be taken, though not perhaps of the one after that. She is attentive to every detail of her presence and to every little thing around her. She looks at herself carefully, though out of the corner of her eye, in every mirror and shop window. And she wanders, curiously attentive though lost in her own thoughts, through the city where she has lived all her life, a space as familiar and well-known to her as her own house. Her aesthetic sense turns into spiritual alertness when she watches other people. She's as sensitive to the ways in which others see her as she is to the outward signs of their character or the inner life that is sometimes revealed in their gestures, their attitudes and words, more often still in the particular way they say them or in the expression on their faces as they speak. She's endowed with extremely delicate sensors that pick up the most subtle variations in other human beings, her loved ones, her acquaintances, even total strangers whom she encounters only once, in passing. She can readily imitate voices and facial expressions, how people walk, how they sit at the table, gestures that are visible to others, too, but which she alone seems to notice. When she imitates a voice, she imagines that she is inside the person, looking through their eyes, moving their mouths and their facial muscles, which at that moment seem connected to her own, like a mask.

THE SLEEPLESS EYE. She is keenly aware of herself from the inside and the outside. She carefully observes and studies her own reactions and moods, and tries as well to see herself as others do, whether it be a casual observer or someone as close and as attentive as she is. She walks down the street absentmindedly, as when she was a young girl crossing El Retiro to get to high school, but noticing everything that takes place around her: the people walking by, the shops, the architecture, the light, the first signs of a change in fashion, of a new expression, or a turn of speech. She looks affectionately at the older women, the waiters, the children, the grandmothers, the store clerks, the animals—cats, birds, dogs, a caged parakeet inside a store in Cádiz, a noble, tired horse yoked to a tourist carriage in Central Park, a raccoon, its snout and bandit eyes peeking out behind some bushes. She dresses and she puts on makeup very slowly yet with careless grace, as if she were writing something destined for others and in equal measure for herself, for the cultivation and delight of her own senses. The knowing wisdom of her eyes as she looks in the mirror, the feel of her clothes and hair, the pleasure of breathing in the scent of soap, of shampoo, a bit of perfume redolent of flowers and of talcum powder.

WHAT THEY NEVER TOLD YOU. She watches those who are dearest to her with great attention. Solicitous, a little anxious, intuiting their burdens or their sufferings, their sadness. Anticipating, too, their needs, thinking of possible work connections for them, a friendship, a relationship, practical advantages that would improve their lives. She takes nothing for granted and she accepts nothing as set in stone. She lives in hope and fear, in joy at being alive and in troubled awareness of the fragility and the shortness of life. Her amiability softens her critical sense of others. Her judgment of herself is usually less lenient, and can at times be punitive. But it doesn't weaken her sense of fairness or her anger at being treated unjustly, the old wound of failing to be recognized when she knows she deserves it. She is sensitive to affronts, which makes her more vulnerable but also sharpens her love of justice.

NOW IT'S EASIER TO FIND WHAT YOU NEED. I am all ears. Her steps, soft as silk on the wood floor; then the bathroom faucet, the bidet, the stream of urine behind the closed door; and then, earlier, her shyness, which is as arousing as her wantonness, the way she breathes through parted lips, the signs, contained yet undeniable, that she is coming. To see, to hear and touch. To touch her face, pressing her bones, her cheekbones beneath the skin, the throbbing pulse of her eyelids, which my fingertips touch, caressing her as avidly as if my hands were the hands of a blind man. *Au bout des doigts. No limits. Everything you desire. The moment is now. Come and let me show you what you will never see without me.* "Let me see your beauty when the witnesses are gone," says Leonard Cohen in one of his songs.

WE GO WITH YOU WHERE OTHERS CAN'T. An immediate and pragmatic sense of beauty is at play in everything she says and does, the clothes she wears, the way she sometimes tosses her hair to give it volume, the objects she finds to outfit and to decorate the house. Nothing is left to chance, yet the general effect you feel, consciously or not, in every space she has arranged is of a natural and balanced spontaneity, as uniquely hers as the pure simplicity of everything she says or writes or of the conversations she so quickly enters into with a stranger—a waiter, someone working at a store or at the bakery where she selects a piece of bread and some croissants for breakfast as attentively as she once chose the cups, the tablecloth, or a particular butter dish. She has, instinctively, a Japanese sense for the beauty of ordinary things and places: fluid yet formal, ruled by an inner restraint even at its most free. She has an utmost gift for what is near and concrete. Neither abstractions nor generalities entice her. She is puzzled by people who display a great sensibility toward the artistry of art or the poetry of poems but are unable to perceive the beauty or the ugliness of the prose of life, or take pleasure in the poetry of reality. Even more puzzling to her are those great benefactors of humanity who champion grand causes but in their private lives are miserly or inconsiderate; apostles of the people who can nevertheless be disrespectful to the waiter serving them, or speak sarcastically to those they scorn so as to wound them. Just as some people are allergic to the smallest dose of certain substances, she is allergic to sarcasm, and rebels against the thought of mocking those unable to defend themselves. She chooses her words in speaking as in writing with scrupulous precision and care. She wants to say what matters to her with the greatest possible clarity, but she does not believe that clarity has anything to do with crudeness, or truthfulness with aggression. She is never insensitive to pain, no matter who it is that suffers, a human being or an animal. She has gained her strength of mind and the freedom of her soul at a very high cost. It has taken her all her life to become who she is, all her life and a substantial part of mine as well. But you can tell, looking at an old photograph or at a family movie in the strident and now fading colors of the seventies, that as a child she was already the person she is now.

FIND OUT THE HIDDEN SECRET. The more that coarseness, negligence, and ignorance are touted as signs of spontaneity, the more she cares about preserving forms and manners. She takes pleasure in them in the company of others, when she goes out in public, but also when no one is around to see or to pass judgment. More so, perhaps, in those cases, since no one can watch her as closely as herself. She feels that forms and manners, in shaping our acts and organizing time, serve to order as well our moods and minds. She puts on makeup and tries on different pairs of earrings with the kind of deliberation and self-critique that a painter might put into a work in progress. She does not impose particular forms on herself or on the things around her: it all emerges from within, expressing her best possibilities, grounded in an acceptance of herself and of her limits. Limits are precisely what allow us to draw the contour of a shape: what's given, what you accept and take into your work, the materials and experiences that constitute a life, the time in which you happened to be born, and what the passing years have bestowed on you and what they took away, everything you didn't choose but must learn nevertheless to use, faithfully, cautiously, with civility and without waste. Putting together what she bought yesterday and what she happened to find in the pantry or the fridge she gives shape to a meal as she will then arrange and give shape to the table, sometimes also to the group of people she invited. A spray of flowers and the particular vase she selects for them are as important as the main dish or as the way the plates and the basket of sliced bread are set on the table. The potter's hands and wheel give shape to a lump of clay just as words give shape to a story, or as food, kindness, the glowing lights of a house, the darkness of wine in a glass give shape to a gathering of friends that transpires gracefully and leaves behind some memories. To preserve the proper forms, to tend to them, seems to her a noble exercise of our aesthetic conscience, action, and contemplation, a pageant where the actors and the audience are one, and there is no pretending. Forms are orderly and conscientious but neither solemn nor rigid. A truly expert musician seems to play without effort. Rigid strictness is merely protocol. Form lives in the simplicity of our daily rituals.

WHEN SILENCE SPEAKS, LISTEN. This may be why making breakfast is her favorite task of the day. A form is all the purer when free of any social obligations. Each properly repeated step is a minor consummation, an exacting pleasure. As she opens the coffee tin, the trapped scent spreads in the air, awakening her sense of smell and starting to rouse her. Scented air goes deeper into the lungs. She must place the paper filter in the coffee maker. She must fill the jug with water. After so much travel and change, so many temporary stays, she's starting to learn the layout of the house. Gradually her gestures fall into a fluid sequence as she grows accustomed to the kitchen, the smell of its fresh finish, its crisp echoing sound, and she no longer hesitates or makes mistakes, as she did before, when she looks for something in particular. After much training, each finger goes naturally to the right key. With every day that passes, each drawer and cabinet will offer more exactly what she needs. Where are the knives. Where are the glasses. How many doors will we have to open and close to find out which drawer is hiding the pot of honey or the vanished orange juicer. Bread can once again be sliced on the cutting board reserved specifically for bread; with the long, serrated knife that has just turned up compliantly where one expected. Each implement and tool has a single purpose, one that belongs to it alone on account of its shape, like the tools in a workshop. Milk and coffee come together in a kind of eucharistic mystery. So do bread and butter, quince and cheese, bread and olive oil.

ALL YOU LOVE. Once everything is finally in place, its proper form achieved, as simple and harmonious as a still life by Juan Gris, one should, before taking the first sip of coffee or juice, remain for a few seconds in a religious or simply astonished silence, and give thanks. What matters is the form, the ceremony. Juan Ramón Jiménez said that, in poetry, form is on the inside. Forms have their own intrinsic meaning, at once objective and symbolic. No need for doctrinal addenda, just as a work of art has no need for a label or a wordy explanation. The work, the form, explains itself, radiating silent meaning. She wants to give thanks for all that is obvious and ordinary: the fresh clean water coming out of the tap, the electric light in the kitchen at dawn, the stillness of the house, where she feels safe, the bees that pollinated the orange trees and made the honey that sweetens her coffee, the milk that ran in white rills from the udders of a cow, the elaborate chemical processes that pasteurized it, the skilled hands that picked the coffee beans in a farm that according to the label is in Guatemala. She wants to give thanks, with some remorse, for being safe, in a house, in a country that is not at war, for not hearing above her the engines of planes dropping bombs on a city from where even at this very moment a foreign radio correspondent is transmitting live. What seemed firm and indisputable just a moment ago becomes uncertain. She hears the cries of people mobbing a truck that is delivering food to a refugee camp. She hears the voice of hatred, making threats, basking in the triumph of its terrifying crassness. There are urgent slogans now, prodding her to buy, to try, not to miss this special chance. Call now. Live a unique experience. Take advantage of this offer. Don't miss out. Last few days. The car of your dreams. Unlimited calling. They speak so quickly and so loudly that each moment brings a new and crushing flood of words. Click now. People in progress. Experience the Champions League live. Power to you. She turns off the radio and is grateful for the fresh morning silence. It seems even purer, wider, unaccustomed as she is to hearing it in this house.

YOU CHOOSE WHAT YOU WANT AND WHEN YOU WANT IT. I want to live like this, unencumbered, taking walks, reading books, carrying a backpack with notebooks and pencils, wearing a pair of sturdy hiking boots that give a slight elastic impulse to my heels and to the muscles in my legs, the head of the femur sliding in the hip socket, the strength of the hip, an ancient bone, the base on which the spinal column rests. I want to live on foot, by hand, by pencil, at ease, responsive to whatever I meet, loose like the air that moves around my body as I walk or like a graceful swimming stroke. I want to remain astonished. To set aside or put on hold what I am and what I carry, and give myself instead to what I find or to the things that come my way, like a character in an old tale, without a past, with no biography aside from his fortuitous encounters, the travelers he meets and talks to or that he overhears when he stops to rest, when from a table nearby or from a different room the voices of a conversation drift his way. I want to wear light, practical clothes. To walk with my hands in my pockets. To get lost by stretches in the two-step rhythm of the walk. I want good pockets that can hold the things I find, a slightly larger one to hold a book—a pocketbook, of course, quite light, that I can read however I please, from beginning to end or by skips and jumps, at random. I want to settle into time as into a broad landscape that I am in no hurry to traverse, even if I enjoy the briskness of the walk.

LIVE ON THE ISLAND OF INVISIBLE THINGS. I remember in Holland the country paths outside Amsterdam, the flat fields and the wide Atlantic sky, which seemed to broaden space without making it alien or oppressive. I want to have a room, my room, with my papers and notebooks, my music, my pictures, my pencil cups and cases, the wide window that all through the day lets in a pale and clear light, the armchair with a footstool where I sit and read with a view of the sky over the rooftops of Madrid. But I also want to carry my room with me wherever I go, like an itinerant scrivener, able to set up at any moment wherever I may be. I want to spend hours in a café, reading the newspaper, looking out the window, or simply noticing the people walking by and overhearing conversations. I want to bring out my notebook and pencil at a reading table in a public library or in the restaurant where I eat alone, and take advantage of the wait to jot things down that I might otherwise forget, a quick verbal sketch of an interesting face at a nearby table. I remember Chez Fernand, in Paris, and the Café Guaraní in Oporto. I remember a table by the window at the corner of 113th and Broadway, on the second floor of the public library, where the homeless and the mentally ill seek shelter in winter. There is a café at the corner of Fernán González and O'Donnell with a wooden counter all along the plate-glass window and a framed poster of a drawing by Giacometti that I like to look at, the mere suggestion of a human figure, a smudge of charcoal that seems to vanish as if traced in smoke or dust. I like the silence of my room and I like the noise of people all around me in libraries and cafés.

TAKE ME WHEREVER YOU LIKE. When the Café Comercial in Madrid was closed for two or three years, I yearned for it with hopeless nostalgia. When I go back to The Hungarian Pastry Shop in New York, it feels like I was there the day before even if many months have passed. I want to live unhurriedly, without anxiety or haste, without remorse or artifice. I want to know that those I love are in good health and in good spirits; and not too far away, if possible, though I don't need to be with them constantly or to always know what they are doing. I want to read poems and to say each word softly to myself, to learn a few by heart so I can recite them as I walk or as I wait in line at the supermarket, at night as well when I can't fall asleep. I want to glimpse the sparks of poetry that suddenly shine forth in advertisements, or in the newspaper, or in a conversation that I overhear on the street. I want to make love with the woman I love, sweetly, without haste, and fall asleep beside her for a while, and then when I wake up remember having sex as if it were a dream, with all the poetry of dreams and all the visual, tactile, carnal poetry of real life.

WE ALWAYS KNEW THEY'D COME BACK. What I don't want is for that shadow to come back, that voice that I alone could hear even when it spoke softly in a crowded, noisy place; a creature with a dark muzzle that came to prod and wake me in the dark, urging me to open my eyes so I could hear the voice even before the sun was up, and all through the day, and then at night, from the moment I woke up to the moment I fell asleep, when as my eyes began to close I told myself, as if the voice itself were saying it but also to escape from it, as if it were whispering in my ear a command or a suggestion of the only way to finally escape from it forever, a thought that was my own, of which I felt ashamed: "I hope I never wake up." But it would seep into my dreams as well, arranging every detail like an exacting film director who takes care of everything himself, the plot, the dialogue, the music and lighting, planning each of the scenes of his horror movie. It weakened my legs to make it harder to go out, since in the open air and in the light of day its power would sometimes wane. It held fast to my knees to make it difficult to walk. It attached lead soles to my shoes while I slept. It climbed on my shoulders and pushed me down, forcing me to tumble forward. It squeezed my throat so I could barely speak. When I listen now to some recording of myself back then, I can't understand how I failed to realize how strange I had become, how weak my voice was and how shrunk with fear.

DARE TO LIVE THE NEOLOVE EXPERIENCE. "Who can stand it now, the artsiness of art," he said to me the last time we spoke, or rather that I heard him speak, in the Café Comercial, never raising his voice despite his distaste, never lifting his eyes from the marble tabletop, behind the lenses of his glasses which, by the way, were not very clean, a pair of round glasses that gave his gaze the startled fixity of an owl—a myopic owl, of all things, or some slightly deranged and erudite émigré in a Parisian café circa 1938. "Who can tolerate anymore the theatricality of theater, the filminess of films, the bookishness of novelistic novels, the wittiness of wit, the comedy of comedy, the Photoshopped beauty of beauty, so perfectly perfect, and the gimmicks that everyone can see coming a mile away, so when they finally arrive they fail to produce even a yawn or a slight stir of indignation; and the sentimentality of all those sentimental effusions, of put-on candor, offered to the public as shamelessly, though more hypocritically, as the stumps and medieval deformities displayed by a Romanian beggar on any corner of Madrid. The only beauty I find boring is the official beauty of all the famous actresses and models. On any given street I can find more beauty and feminine grace in ten minutes than in all the pages making up those massive blocks of glossy paper they call magazines, or in one of those red-carpet galas with photocalls (as you can see, I am familiar with all the latest terminology)."

MERCURY WILL BRING SUCCESS TO YOUR LIFE. "And tell me, is it possible not to be sickened by the poetical poetry of poems, or the artistry of artists who call themselves simply 'artists,' without qualification, artists of Art, even when they haven't actually made anything. Can they really say calmly of themselves, 'I am an artist,' as who should say, I am an accountant, I am a lion tamer? Even worse, how is it possible to call oneself a 'poet'? How would you know that you're a poet? Because you write verses that sound poetic? Art just happens, my friend. Poetry flashes forth. It comes of its own accord, a sudden, dazzling apparition that somehow remains, sending forth a kind of radiation, like uranium dust, for centuries or even for millennia. '*Une étincelle qui dure,*' says poor Apollinaire, his head all wrapped in bandages on account of a war that was brought about by the patriotism of patriots. He knew what he was talking about. He could find beauty in the flash of a mortar in the night. A spark that endures: the sudden glow of a firefly; images and words that have a kind of bioluminescence, like microscopic algae or crustaceans lighting up the sea at night or glowworms deep inside a cave; diamonds, gold pips in the ore and slag of a ceaseless logorrhea that can never be turned off. You have to dig up mountains to get a single gram, though sometimes an entire lode is found at once. Each fragment of poetry is one of those millions of oysters at the bottom of the Hudson Bay, cleaning and filtering the toxic waste out of the water. Doesn't a single battery pollute three thousand liters of fresh water? A poem does the opposite with three thousand polluted words. Like blades of grass or the leaves on a tree, taking atmospheric CO_2 and turning it into fresh sap while clearing it from the air."

BITE INTO OUR FLAVORS. "And when I speak of art and poetry, I include what is disdainfully referred to as 'craft.' The craftsman does not impose a personal will on his materials. That's what artists do. His work depends on having as thorough a knowledge as possible of his materials and the rules of his craft, which are as impersonal as those of meter or of tonal harmony. The rules have been so thoroughly assimilated and have been practiced for so long that they seem to become unconscious habits. Which is not to say they are mechanical. It only means they're not applied or governed by an act of will, a whim, a random preference. Technique only becomes fertile once you're able not to think of it. You don't think about the letters in a word before you write it. You don't even think about the word, or choose it. The word appears in your mind or on the tip of the pencil and you decide to write it down, or not, but you were not the one who summoned it, detaching it from a warehouse of available words, as in a dictionary. You only get to decide if you leave the word on the page or you replace it by another. André Breton and his fellow bureaucrats in the department of surrealism were quite skilled at claiming authorship of what is already obvious to everyone. There is no writing that is not to a large degree automatic."

CREATE YOUR OWN CUSTOMIZED PACK. ". . . There is no orchestral effect anymore that I don't see coming, no false note that I miss. It can be irritating, but it is also freeing, and a relief. I no longer have to like anything other than what I truly enjoy. Every trick seems an affront to me, a kind of personal betrayal, unless it be the shameless trickery of melodrama, of a bolero, or the cynical impudence of advertising. I don't mind reckless imperfection, or what is done with daring inspiration even if without technique or expertise. What I can't stand, what strikes me as debasing and even as a kind of crime, is shoddy work covered up in grave solemnities. I love the literature of newspaper headlines, the way they compress a wild story into a single phrase. Man dressed up as Hitler arrested in Hitler's native town. That is true concision, my friend. Kinky girls are here to take you for a ride. Scarlett Johansson opens gourmet popcorn store in Paris. I love the stories in the back pages, the news wires that read like fiction. I love the mercenary poetry of an ad for makeup or perfume, or for a trip or a luxury car. The graphic power of a photograph cut out of a magazine. The visual plot of an ad that pops open when you read the paper online, or one of those videos playing simultaneously on many screens at airport terminals or subway stops. I have developed particular food allergies, so serious and acute that the smallest dose of certain harmful things will make me quite ill. The sports pages, the editorials, the opinion pieces, the political stories, the arts and culture section, my God, that is by far the worst, the culturedness of culture."

FEEL LIFE THROUGH YOUR EARS. The voice, the spoken word, exists for a few seconds, a few minutes at most, and is lost. So many billions of human voices, each one completely distinct from the rest ever since hominids began to produce articulate sounds with precise meanings—so many voices, and almost all of them are lost. What was the voice of Socrates like. Of Buddha, Sappho, Sor Juana Inés de la Cruz, Emily Dickinson, Herman Melville. What was the voice of Walt Whitman like. How strange to think that Cervantes had a voice as distinctive as yours or mine, and as familiar to those who knew him. I find it hard to recall my own father's voice, and he only died twelve years ago. And the voice of my grandfather Manuel, and my grandmother Leonor, and my grandfather Antonio, who spoke so softly and so little, a bashful man who didn't feel at ease with words, and who, for many years of his life, had no need of them as he worked silently on his small farm. Two decades ago it was reported that a radio recording of Federico García Lorca might have surfaced in Buenos Aires. I asked his sister, Isabel, a strong, lucid woman in her eighties, and she said to me, "I wouldn't be able to tell. My brother was killed more than sixty years ago. I don't remember his voice." There is a temporal boundary for voices as there is for faces: before and after the invention of recorded sound; before and after photography. That is why the voices that are just on this side of the line, the first ever to be recorded, are so moving. The first photographs, the first daguerreotypes: Emily Dickinson at seventeen, or that devastating picture of De Quincey taken in his old age, which makes him seem even more distant. What was it like, the voice that issued from that fallen, shrunken mouth, De Quincey's toothless mouth, as full of malice as his eyes. For years, in Berlin, Benjamin took part frequently in radio programs, reading short essays that he composed expressly for an ephemeral and instantaneous medium that he found very inspiring. None of those recordings have survived. How strange, to suddenly think that we have no access to the voice of someone as near to us in time as Benjamin.

ONCE NIGHT FALLS YOU'RE NO LONGER SAFE. You think you remember a voice clearly, but it's not true. You realize this when you actually hear it, or when you unexpectedly hear another voice that resembles it. Once, I called my uncle Juan on the phone and suddenly heard the exact voice of my father, his older brother. I wonder if in my children's voices there is something of my own that I don't recognize, just as their faces have some of my features, which others see but I cannot, since closeness blots out a likeness that is visible from afar. I remember well the fresh, deep voice of the man who was my second father, Manuel Lindo. After his death, we found it unexpectedly on messages he'd left on our answering machine. Only now do I realize that in moving to a new house and changing our telephone number, those messages that seemed to come from the other world were lost. I can't remember the voices of my children when they were little, though surely they exist in some recording, some family video that has gradually been tinted with strange hues, the chemical reactions of what moves into the past. They used to record our greeting on the answering machine, back when that kind of thing was done. Time passed and their real voices changed, but their old ones remained, squeaky and shrill, almost unrecognizable, leaping out at us each time we called that number and no one answered. What is it about a voice that makes it more distinctive than a face? I call my mother on the phone and the voice I hear is the same she had when she was young. The telephone preserves our voices from the effects of time. When I was a child the world was richer, acoustically, because we lived among the faceless, disembodied voices on the radio: presenters, actors, actresses in radio plays, people we never saw but with whom we felt a deeper closeness because it came only from their voices. On Sunday evenings my father would listen to a show about the bullfights. You could hear the music of the band, the *pasodobles*, the roar of the crowd. When the bugle calls rang out, my father would explain what each one meant. On New Year's Eve you heard the frail, high, singsong voice of General Franco. Falling in love meant the feeling you had when you heard the sound of a voice that was unlike any other.

YOU CAN'T IMAGINE WHAT AWAITS YOU. I like to listen to recordings of her voice from the time before we met. I like it and I experience as well a retrospective envy, a desire to amend that portion of the past. I get to hear her voice because back then, in her twenties, she hosted a radio show. It was in the 1980s, those years of manic freedom. Everything was yet to be done, to be invented, nothing of any value or luster could bear the slightest trace of the past. The young were bursting into the world and taking the place of the old, who were stunned, bewildered, hopelessly discredited by their complicity with the dictatorship or simply by the fact that their lives had coincided with it. Suddenly youth was an advantage, a natural condition of the times. The new socialist president was forty years old and some of his ministers were just over thirty. Today, this precociousness is inconceivable. The old, the very people who were young back then, have ensconced themselves more thoroughly in their entitlements and their positions than the heirs of the dictatorship ever did. She was twenty-three or twenty-four and she had a radio show where she did interviews. Pictures show a girl in short hair that is dyed red. Her lips are bright red as well and she's smoking a cigarette in front of the microphone, holding it at the very tips of her fingers. There was a time when those recordings would have been lost, or would have been inaccessible. Now I can listen to them quite easily on the internet. It's still her voice, but a bit different, more youthful, of course, but not higher; actually the opposite, a deeper voice, youthful and assertive, with that conscious and almost boastful confidence one heard in Madrid back then, when the young jumped as brazenly into their newfound political autonomy as into the maelstrom of their personal freedom. A confidence that had rushed into the radio stations, those heavy, somber buildings that might as well have stood somewhere in Ceaușescu's Bucharest, filling them unrepentantly with pop music and racy shows about everyday life, the frivolous wonder of nightlife and popular fashion. She was very young and she was a woman, so she had to stand her ground in a world of older men who spoke commandingly and categorically, having inherited, whether they were politically on the left or on the right, a congenital sense of masculine self-assurance.

MAGIC IS A GIFT. I listen to that voice again, to its cadence, and I feel like I am doing something slightly illicit, listening in on something private. Back then I used to fall in love with voices on the radio even more than I do now. So I am certain that I would have fallen in love with her voice, with her, as soon as I heard her speak. Now I play a recording of her old show and in the few seconds it takes me to recognize her voice I have already fallen in love. I am annoyed at myself for not having listened to her show back then. What was I doing. Sunk in what thoughts, what fears and distractions. I am flooded with a retrospective love for that woman and that youthful voice, a stranger I might have never met, whose face I might have never seen. And through that voice, as through a veil, I fall in love again with the woman she is now.

WOMAN BURNED ALIVE IN NICARAGUA. *Her name was Vilma Tru-jillo and she died after being burned in a bonfire. Aged twenty-five, the mother of two fought to stay alive in agony for over a day after sustaining second- and third-degree burns that scorched 80 percent of her body: her breasts, her thighs, part of her face, and all of her back were charred. This was the punishment she was forced to undergo after members of her church determined that she was possessed by the devil and must be burned in a bonfire to cast him out. She agonized, gruesomely burned, in the remote hamlet of El Cortezal in an eastern province of Nicaragua.*

THE NEFARIOUS BELIEF IN THE DEVIL. *El Cortezal is a no-man's-land. There is no municipal building, no hospital, and no police station. Religion is the only law. The local priest is the highest authority. El Cortezal is not even a village, just a dot on the map. It is located in the high mountains of Nicaragua's central region, surrounded by bean fields and by wide pastures stripped from the tropical jungle. Getting there from the nearest village requires a four-hour drive down a terrible road with large potholes filled with mud. The car tumbles along until it reaches the end of the road. Then one must walk for three hours through the jungle, crossing rivers, climbing steep, rugged mountains and ravines where a single false step could mean falling to one's death. Frequent rests are necessary so as not to collapse in the high heat and the stifling humidity.*

IMMERSE YOURSELF IN NATURE. *The earth in El Cortezal is black and stony, under a bright blue sky that can change to a stormy dark gray in an* instant. The evangelical church stands on a hill, a crude wooden building where the congregation meets every Saturday under its pastor, Juan Rocha, who is twenty-three, and who gave the order to burn Vilma Trujillo. Facing the church is the pastor's house, also made of wood, with a dirt floor, a door, and a single window for light. The dark, stifling room where the pastor lives is also where Vilma Trujillo was confined after her sentence was passed. In one corner the floor is charred. The congregation made a small fire to burn Vilma's feces since she was forced to stay inside at all times. A few feet away, at the foot of a hill, some blackened stumps and branches remain from the bonfire where she was burned.

STRENGTH AND POWER TO THOSE WHO ARE BRAVE. *The population of El Cortezal is made up of poor farmers who grow beans and raise pigs. They live in flimsy wooden huts that always seem about to collapse under the strong winds that batter the region. They are reclusive people, unaccustomed to strangers. There is no electricity or running water. Their only connection to the outside world is through a few battery-operated radios that are always tuned to religious stations. Children run around, dirty, some of them with bloated bellies or ridden with sores, poorly fed on beans, corn, and green plantains cooked over an open fire. Their lives are entirely subjected to religious belief. Faith rules everything they do. Days begin at three in the morning and end at eight in the evening. Everyone attends mass. Adultery is a crime punished by banishment. And every single person believes in the devil.*

HER FLESH SHOWED THROUGH AND HER SKIN WAS COVERED IN CRUSTS. *On the afternoon of February 15, Juan Gregorio Rocha, pastor of the Church of the Celestial Vision of the Assemblies of God, visited Vilma Trujillo. He said that she was sick, that she suffered from hallucinations and did not answer when addressed. Her family, which is deeply religious, allowed the pastor to take her away and to declare that healing prayers be said for her. Vilma remained in the pastor's house, bound hand and foot, until February 21. The pastor decreed a period of fasting and long communal prayers. He* was aided by two members of the congregation, Franklin Hernández and Esneyda del Socorro. They concluded that Vilma was possessed by the devil. After six days of fasting and prayer, Esneyda said she had received a divine revelation. God told her they must light a bonfire and cast Vilma into the flames to release her from the devil's grip. The ceremony was carried out at five-thirty. The men lit a bonfire and Vilma was thrown in, bound at the wrists and ankles. The young woman frantically resisted. The fire burned through the ropes and allowed her to jump out of the flames when her body was already charred. "When I saw her, it was night already," says a witness whose initials are M. T. G. "She was all burned. She was writhing and saying, 'Ay, ay, I'm going to die.' The pastor was happy. He kept shouting, 'She's going to die, and then she'll be reborn! As soon as she dies we'll take her into the church and deliver her to God, then she'll be healed and she won't have these burns anymore.'"

TIME IS THE ESSENCE WE ARE MADE OF. The novelty of being back is a blessed shock. I am back from absence, darkness, the depth of something like a coma, a long trance, or a seizure. I am as weak, grateful, and fearful as a convalescent. I am back from something that has no name, though one might give it one, or several, the old literary names or the modern names of psychiatry and neuroscience, clinical labels, diagnostic words of suspect accuracy. I am back from waiting rooms that usually have no windows and are stocked with stale, wrinkled magazines. In one of them, New Age was playing in the background. In another, Kiss FM, rather loudly. Those who wait, alone or in someone else's company, hold an open magazine on their lap but look down at the floor or at the opposite wall, never saying anything when someone walks in, or else just muttering a vague greeting without lifting their eyes. I am back from rooms where the curtains are drawn during the day, as if they were meant for vampires. A coma or a seizure would have been better, then at least I would have been unconscious. I would have felt no fear, that sharp, clear stab of fright when I woke up, the hypnotic menace of the subway entering the station at a propitious speed. I am back from evenings like long tunnels, nights without sleep, a morbid sense of clarity that furnished me exclusively with reasons to sink more deeply into darkness. I am back from pills, from nausea, from despondent monologues given to strangers who looked at me from across a desk, the bookshelves behind them filled with psychiatric volumes, pretending to take notes on a sheet of paper while they looked sideways at their watch. Their secretaries charged for the visit in cash, with a polite, discouraging smile that foreclosed in advance the possibility of a receipt.

ENJOY THE IMMERSIVE ENTERTAINMENT EXPERIENCE YOU WERE WAITING FOR. I could be coming back from farther away. From twenty years ago, to a present time that was once the future; from a dream or a coma that lasted twenty years. No one then would be more of a stranger. So little time would have passed, yet I would no longer recognize the world. I go looking for a telephone booth, to call people, to tell them I am back, walking down one street after another without finding one. When I finally do, there is no phone inside. In the next one there is a phone dangling from a cable but it has no dial tone. I grow more and more anxious, the way one does in dreams. When I finally reach a cabin that seems undamaged I realize that I don't know how it works. None of the coins in my pocket will fit into the slit. As if Clark Kent got back to New York and started looking desperately for a booth where he could turn into Superman, but lost his powers and the chance to display his heroism because none could be found. Searching for some kind of refuge, I wander toward my old neighborhood. I get to the square where my house used to stand and recognize it with immense relief and with bewildered gratitude. The fruit shop next door is still open and still called Casa Aragón. The newsstand still stands at the corner by the church railings. I realize that, until then, I hadn't seen a place to buy the paper. Buñuel once said he would like to come back from the grave every few years, buy a newspaper and find out how the world was doing before happily going back to his eternal sleep. But the newsstand, which used to spread onto the sidewalk with its large offerings of magazines and papers, is now shuttered and abandoned, tagged with graffiti, the words and cryptic scribbles of the strange language of the future. The awning hangs in faded tatters. Beneath its frame there is a pile of bags, suitcases, old clothes. An African woman in exotic rags has set up camp next to a mangled beach umbrella that remains half open.

ALL THE MYSTERIES OF THE UNIVERSE WITHIN YOUR REACH. There is a café down the block with a framed poster of a drawing by Giacometti. I look at it every day when I go in to have a bite to eat, or to buy bread or a couple of croissants for breakfast. It's a narrow place without any tables, just some barstools and a counter that runs along the length of the plate-glass window. It's run by a couple of Venezuelan émigrés who are turning more and more into exiles with each day that passes. Jazz is always playing discreetly in the background, so those who care for it can hear it and others can ignore it. The day's papers are on the counter along with some new and some old magazines. Sometimes in the morning I like to take my time over a cup of green tea, facing the window, looking out into the street at the passersby or waiting to cross at the light. I flip through the papers, and since I always have my notebook and pencil handy, I sometimes jot down a headline or a phrase in an ad. Israel launches cyber campaign to conquer the desert. Dare to feel it. Climate change exposes buried Cold War secret. Lady Gaga unveils in LA the outfits for her upcoming tour. I listen to someone talking on the phone by my side. "You're wearing it right now? Really? You put it on to talk to me?"

YOU DON'T ALWAYS WANT EVERYTHING. My eyes always wander to the Giacometti drawing. It's a human figure sketched in pencil with a few thick strokes, a man in a hat who seems to be turning around as if someone had called out his name. He seems about to vanish, to dissolve into the white surface of the paper as if the pencil marks were drawn in smoke. A passing shadow made of smoke and graphite, as faint and fading as a handful of dust that's blown or scattered into the air. He is transient, both in the sense that he is passing by and in the sense that he is on the verge of disappearing. He is visible and invisible. A silhouette cast through a window into a basement as someone passes by outside. A figure dimly seen through frosted glass or on the other side of a lit cinema screen: the Visible Invisible Man, a comic-book hero from the forties or fifties, Shadowman, or from a low-budget science-fiction film in black and white: vaporized, perhaps turned into a shadow by exposure to a radioactive flash, like the Incredible Shrinking Man. His misfortune gave him powers that set him apart from other humans, a curse that's also an extraordinary gift. As a shadow he is capable perhaps of going through walls and closed doors; or he can follow people to spy on them, perfectly concealed as their own shadow. He walks down the street like a busy ghost, a little like the green man in the crossing signal or like those white figures in New York that mark the paths belonging to pedestrians from those reserved for bicycles and joggers.

SO IMMERSIVE YOU'LL FORGET YOU'RE LOOKING AT A SMARTPHONE. As I look at the Giacometti drawing, something makes me realize that I wasn't paying attention to the music. I like listening to it like this, through the voices of the customers at the café, the gentle Venezuelan accent of the waiters, the noise of traffic that periodically grows louder when the automatic doors slide open and shut. Following the music as one would follow a person in the crowd, someone we know and want to be with. Now I pay more attention because Thelonius Monk is playing "Crepuscule with Nellie," a ballad of enduring conjugal love that is suddenly threatened by the fear of loss, written when his wife was sick and in the hospital. The melodies are as simple, as free, as intertwined as the lines in the drawing, a wisp of smoke, Thelonius Monk's bejeweled hand tracing figures in the air like a sleepwalker, up on a small stage at some club. Thelonius Monk. Thelonius Sphere Monk, one of the most magnificent names in all of music, as worthy of his supreme extravagance as his hats, those fedoras, trilbies, and caps that could have been the headdress in a Rembrandt painting. Among the musicians who played with him there was one whose name was nearly as powerful: Rossiere Wilson, otherwise known as Shadow Wilson. While others played, he seemed to gently move around them, appearing, disappearing, like a shadow. He got his nickname from "his beautiful light touch with brushes," the way he grazed the cymbals and the snare. He, too, seemed to be drawing in sand, in dust and smoke, each bristle leaving behind its delicate trace like Giacometti's pencil, which must have made a similar sound, rich and secret, as it slid across the sheet of paper leaving a trail of graphite particles behind. Shadow Giacometti, rapt in the unique absorption of working with one's hands, of drawing or playing the drums, when you allow yourself to be carried by the act instead of trying to direct it, an expert mastery that has no need of an intention or a will.

YOU CAN GO TO PLACES BEYOND WORDS. The less he feels like traveling, the more he likes a travel agency, an advertisement for a Caribbean cruise, or a tour of the Greek islands, a full-spread advertorial about some luxury resort in Cuba or Santa Domingo. Gorgeous color brochures on glossy paper, free, sometimes with a picture of a woman gazing at the sunset from the deck of a luxury liner with a smile of inner joy on her face, the wind playing with her hair and sculpting a light white dress against her body or spreading it behind her like a nuptial train. He copies down the slogans or he cuts them out with scissors and glues them carefully. Choose the right experience. Choose your destination and be free. Find your private paradise. A journey you'll never forget. He stands outside, looking through the window at posters with pictures of tropical paradises that he never plans to visit. Names that seem taken out of a novel, golden temples in the jungle, Balinese dancers with heavy makeup on their eyes, joining and lifting their hands, or an arctic landscape lit by an aurora or the midnight sun, the natives smiling in their furry sealskin jackets and their bright wool caps. The flukes of a whale rise like a glorious, instant monument out of an explosion of foam off the coast of Patagonia.

DARE TO GO FURTHER. He looks at the pictures and reads the names, saying them out loud to savor their geographic poetry, extracting from each one the pulp or juice of its promise of adventure. Experience South Africa. Cuba, the Genuine Island. Exciting El Salvador. What he likes best, however, is to peer inside the agencies themselves, through those plate-glass windows that keep them isolated from the noise and light, sequestered in a green and pleasant shade, calm and air-conditioned. Travel agents sit in front of computers whose large screens can better display the exact colors of those dreamed-of places, the clear blue waters, the dress of tribal dancers, while all around them are posters with amazing views of man-made or natural wonders: the snowy summit of Mount Fuji or Kilimanjaro against a deep blue sky; the Taj Mahal; a Mayan pyramid rising from a Guatemalan jungle that is probably (he thinks maliciously, though reproving of his own sarcasm) infested with mosquitos that transmit malaria and with squads of drug dealers and *sicarios*. From the street you can see a long line of desks, all in a row so as to greet in unison whatever would-be traveler comes through the door. Each agent sits by a computer and is provisioned with an endless supply of free brochures printed on fancy paper that imbues the pictures and the place names with an added glow. They are pleasant to hold in your hands and even more pleasant to cut with a pair of sharp scissors, slicing melodiously through the kind of glossy paper that is used in fashion magazines or catalogs for watches, sports cars, cruises, a heavy paper that makes them thick and dense like metal ingots, with a foldout to encompass the whole spread of a long beach with palm trees and thatched huts equipped with all the amenities, or to suggest the span of the horizon from the deck of a yacht in the South Pacific, the emerald glow of the big ball of the world itself.

IT'S TIME FOR YOU TO KNOW WHAT IT FEELS LIKE. On the wall, above each head bent studiously over a monitor, different clocks tell the time in cities around the world. The name of the city and the face of the clock combine to show the vastness of the Earth, all the different time zones, climates, distant lands one must traverse to reach those places. New York, Hong Kong, Tokyo, Sydney, Istanbul, Bangkok, just reading all those names and seeing all those time zones makes him feel a little drained, a little dizzy, and it gets worse if he looks at the map of the world hanging like a backdrop behind the silhouettes of all the travel agents, a map of such colossal size it might contain the actual oceans and the continents.

THE PERFECT PICTURE AWAITS. He has noticed, with a little dismay, that travel agencies are becoming harder to find, like newsstands, stationers, hardware stores, grocery stores, birds, gorillas. For some reason he can't understand, almost everything he is fond of is going extinct. Recently, however, he was pleased to find a travel agency that looks auspiciously prosperous, even affluent. The premises are large, well situated, as spacious as the inside of a bank, with a big window where he always stops to look at posters for tourist destinations he will never travel to, safaris, desert crossings in all-terrain vehicles that leave you heroically covered in dust. A world of unique experiences. On the photographs of tropical islands and coral reefs there is no sign of the mountains of plastic waste that are carried there every day by the currents of the Pacific. El Salvador is a lush hillside where an endearing peasant in a straw hat offers a handful of coffee beans to a tourist couple. On a dirt road in Africa, tourists aboard a Land Rover smile joyfully at the sight of a dusty rhino that is at no risk of being killed by poachers who will leave its huge carcass to rot in the sun because they only care about the horn, which they will sell to a Chinese billionaire eager to regain his sexual powers by drinking it as an infusion once it has been ground into a powder. Being a loner, he stares a little enviously or with a faint sense of spite at the posters for honeymoon destinations. The bride and groom appear happy and relaxed in a pair of white bathrobes, gazing dreamily into the distance from the end of a long pier that juts out into the sea. Have your honeymoon anywhere in the world. Guatemala, land of the Mayas. Experience the magic of Cuba.

SUNNY DAYS ARE BACK. One day he will pluck up his nerve and go in. Confidently, with a slightly formal air, inquisitive, polite, carrying his satchel under one arm. He would prefer it if the agents (are they called agents, since they work in an agency?) were busy when he came in, first because it would be a good sign that business is going well, and then because he'd have more time to look around and enjoy the silence, so well preserved by the double-paned window, and to enjoy as well the temperature, so pleasant in the midst of a merciless summer on account of the soft, cold breeze blowing from the AC, which is turned up a bit high, even if he has wisely taken the precaution of wearing a light jacket. An agent who is taking care of another customer will greet him from behind her desk and ask him to take a seat. He thinks approvingly of a phrase you hear frequently when placed on hold during a call: "All our representatives are busy at this time." The best travel agencies have a waiting area with comfortable chairs and glass tables stocked with a pleasant abundance of catalogs and brochures. Paris for lovers. All the allure of the Far East. Discover the Amalfi coast. Unforgettable Vietnam. Mythical Cambodia. He has to make an effort not to open the satchel right away and stuff it with flyers. The noise of traffic in the background is as delicate as the sound of palm trees in the breeze or as ocean waves breaking on a reef. The air conditioner makes everything as cool and fresh as when he walks down El Retiro in the early morning, when the fragrant lawns have just been watered. He can't imagine a better destination than this travel agency.

DISCOVER AS MUCH OF THE WORLD AS YOU CAN. A map of the world as wide and as blue as the sky; a row of identical clocks, each telling a different time; beautiful city names that are always more beautiful than the cities themselves; lavish photographs that promise paradise, and couples more joyful than Adam and Eve in the Garden of Eden, and families, too, happily gathered around Mickey Mouse in Disneyland Paris or sliding fearlessly in a welter of laughter and water down a chute in a theme park in Florida. Not only are these lavish documents—produced and printed regardless of cost, with the largesse that only the old international photo magazines could once afford—not only are they given as freely as the fruits of paradise to our first parents, but the employees (the agents) want to make sure that you take as many brochures as you like, even looking through their drawers for other, more sumptuous brochures. Then they swivel their screens to show you pictures of the seaside bungalow where you can stay once you've completed a twenty-hour trip filled with the serial humiliation of clearing multiple security checkpoints. Going one by one through every pamphlet and brochure within his reach, in no kind of hurry to see an agent, he enjoys a breeze that seems to come not from an air-conditioning duct but from the very beaches in those photographs.

THIS IDYLLIC RETREAT WILL PUT YOUR SENSES TO THE TEST. Comfortably seated in an ergonomic chair he looks at the customers, who are treated with the exceptional solicitude shown by the staff at a grand hotel or a luxury cruise. Most of them are young couples, soon to be married, looking at honeymoon options that seem as varied as their own prospects in life. They share complicit looks, happy to agree on a particular option, worried about prices, packages, discounts, payment plans, the best date and time to fly. When they are not seeing a customer, the travel agents type on their keyboards with a look of busy concentration, as if they were not just making travel arrangements but also coordinating weather patterns, temperatures, sunsets, the right phase of the moon, a herd of gazelles crossing a plain at the perfect moment.

SOMETIMES A LIE CAN HELP PEOPLE LIVE. He puts the brochures in his satchel a little stealthily, admiring the quality of the paper, which is as pleasant to hold and touch as it will later be to cut through with a pair of scissors. All those magnificent monuments lit up by night, the Colosseum, the Great Sphynx, the Taj Mahal; all those rich fonts and poetic phrases; all those pictures of white, sandy beaches that are never touched by an oil spill, never reached by dying birds whose stomachs are filled with disposable lighters or by whales that die stranded, crazed, disoriented by the engines of oil tankers, cruise ships, or cargo ships carrying mountains of metal containers. No hurricane will raze those thatched bungalows offering complimentary Wi-Fi. No logging companies will profane with controlled burns, bulldozers, and massive tree-cutting machines these forests that are home to gorillas, wild orchids, luxury resorts with tiki bars where exotic, dark-skinned girls discreetly serve you specialty drinks with Polynesian names.

DISCOVER THE LAND OF THE RISING SUN. He watches and waits, affably, at ease, appreciative, making small involuntary gestures of approval and holding the satchel on his knees, a satchel that is in itself a kind of credential, the sort of thing a serious if slightly antiquated man might carry, made of supple materials that age well, "bonded" leather, as they say. He stands up perhaps a bit too quickly when the same woman who greeted him as he came in—perhaps a manager, her hair is dyed and she wears eyeglasses with a little chain around her neck—comes over and asks him to follow her, to take a seat on the chair (still warm) where the future bride was sitting a moment ago. One forgets that the human body has a constant temperature of around 98.5 degrees. It's precisely as he notices the warmth of the seat, which, unlike the synthetic texture of its lining, is not unpleasant, and as he looks at the smiling woman, who folds her hands over a mouse pad with a picture of the Iguazú Falls, that he realizes he has forgotten to think of an excuse, a travel plan that would justify his visit. His mind goes blank for a few seconds, during which he has the impression that the woman's smile begins to fade and that the knuckles of her clasped hands (she is wearing several rings and some bracelets that look vaguely tribal or ethnic) begin to whiten. Her question hangs in the air, among the various objects floating around him at different heights, the clocks, the city names, the domes of the Taj Mahal and of Hagia Sophia. "Well then, what destination do we have in mind?" Her use of the first-person plural gives him a little comfort. He looks stealthily around, somewhat overwhelmed by the weight of that word, "destination," so many destinations, so many destinies before us at every moment. He catches sight of a poster with a picture of some towers rising from a jungle canopy and looking like a nightmarish cross between a skyscraper, a temple, and one of Jean Nouvel's obscene cylindrical buildings. He reads the name and says, too quietly at first for the woman to understand him, "Kuala Lumpur."

DO SOMETHING INCREDIBLE NOW. A camera mounted on a tall crane moves down the nave of a church filled with people. A bride and groom are kneeling before a priest dressed in lavish vestments who is about to give his blessing. But the woman shakes her head. The priest, the groom, and the groomsmen exchange stunned glances. The woman turns around and breaks into a run, the train of her dress spreading on the crimson carpet and her veil flung back in the rush of her flight. Running is difficult because she's wearing high heels. The camera frames her in a new aerial shot as she runs down the church steps. The landscape seems Italian: hills, olive trees, pine groves, blue mountains in the distance. The church could be a village church or a private chapel in a princely estate. The bride runs down the steps, stumbling but keeping her balance, and then continues to run down a gravel path leading her through gardens and trees. The camera stays with her as she runs, as if it too was taking part in her escape. Suddenly it rises higher, as if lifted not just by a crane but by a helicopter, showing the white figure below, the trailing dress, the veil, the fields and crops. Now the camera swoops down like a hawk, straight, swift. Now it shows a close-up of the bride from below, the heaving of her chest, her tousled hair against the bright blue of the sky and the dark green of a double row of cypresses. Her face is shining with sweat. She smiles, joyfully, a little recklessly. She takes off one shoe and then another, even as she continues to run, flinging them furiously away. She can run faster now, even if she's barefoot. She casts away the bouquet of flowers, which lands on the path at a little distance from the white shoes. Still running, she tears off the veil with the same anger and joy.

LET YOURSELF BE TEMPTED. The veil floats down in slow motion while she runs away. There must be music, to accompany her flight and to exalt it, but it can't be heard on the plasma screen at the duty-free fragrance section in the airport. The daring bride leaves the path and begins to run through fields and orchards up into the hills. She doesn't feel the cuts on the soles of her feet. Then, instead of just holding up the skirt of her dress as she runs, she tears it off in a single motion, emerging, sweaty and fit, in a rather improbable skintight suit that a swimmer might wear. The camera rises to show a helicopter flying low to the ground and reaching the crest of the hill she is climbing, which suddenly turns into a mountain. The helicopter comes closer. The meadow ripples like water in the wind of the rotors, which tosses her shining hair in the sun, a whirling halo of gold around her face. She's soaked in sweat, but she's not tired. Without ever stopping, she leaps and grabs one of the skids on the helicopter, swaying and giving herself momentum like an acrobat to come to a kneeling posture. The helicopter rises and the former bride lets her legs dangle in the air. An arm, strong and tanned, a powerful hand reaches down to her, wearing a multifunction steel watch that flashes in the sun.

FIND OUT JUST HOW FAR YOU CAN GO. Now we see the pilot's face for the first time. He's in his thirties, his bronze skin has been hardened by expeditions and adventures, his hair is a dark blond or chestnut brown. He may be David Beckham or someone who looks a lot like him. He wears sunglasses, and a dark stubble covers his jaws and his strong chin. She sits next to him in the helicopter and caresses his face, the muscles and the bulging veins of his neck. Her pupils dilate with desire, her nostrils flare at the scent of Dior Homme Cologne. Suddenly she is back in the church, as if it had all been a dream, and the priest, with all the temporal incoherence of dreams, is about to resume the blessing motion of his hand. But she shakes her head, jostling the bridal veil, and she turns around and runs toward the door, followed by the stunned faces of the wedding guests as she rushes down the steps.

NOW YOU'LL KNOW WHAT YOU WERE MISSING. Ten screens in ten different places of the same concourse show ten different but equally frantic stories to people hurrying to their boarding gate. You will end up watching some of them, no matter where you're standing. Unless you are already watching them, or something like them, on your phone or on the computer you hold open on your lap to pass the time a little faster, like a smoker taking a few quick drags from a cigarette. People fly and float with ease. Gravity is optional. People jump from a seaside cliff or from the edge of a glass building and stay afloat. They laugh wildly and their hair blows in the wind. They fly like swimmers in a dream over the rooftops and the streets. They jump from a tall building into the void, and their calm, elastic leap transports them to some other building nearby. You can have, if you so desire, the flying and the acrobatic powers of a superhero. You can drive luxury cars down highways that are always empty, on winding seaside cliffs, at sunset. "The North and the South are mine. The East and the West are mine. All seems beautiful to me." The voice falls silent, the car speeds away on a desert road, the word VOLVO rises from the earth like the red ball of the sun at daybreak.

OVER THIRTY-FIVE THOUSAND PROFESSIONALS TO LOOK AFTER YOUR ORAL HEALTH. Every few seconds the shot changes as the camera veers in its fluid motion. You and a group of your friends are in a Jeep Renegade, laughing excitedly, probably on a Friday night. Your hair blows in the wind as you speed along. Everyone is young. Men, women, mostly white, a Black man too, perhaps, or at the very least dark-skinned, with dreadlocks, and all the men wear scruffy beards, headbands, T-shirts or unbuttoned shirts, and all are muscular and have tattoos. You raise your arms up high in celebration, like people on a rollercoaster do. Then you're dancing wildly to the pulse of electronic music, each of you lost in the huge crowd, joining in the general rapture, but always in the end together, complicit, waiting to get back in the Jeep. Time is compressed into a series of strobe-like flashes. You're outside the night club, wolfing down some hot dogs at a street stand to regain your strength, lit by its neon sign and by the light of early dawn. All of it happens silently across a series of screens mounted high up in the airport's shopping area. Now the Jeep is no longer driving through city streets, but down a muddy road with lush vegetation. Mud and water spray under the car's powerful wheels, which easily gain traction in this wild terrain. The car bounces and you laugh and fall over each other. You laugh so hard now that your mouths no longer close and you can see your tongues, your gums, the almost frightening teeth of a cannibalistic joy. You experience everything at full intensity, top speed, without fatigue. The tempo never wanes and there is never a dull passage in your life.

I'M SEARCHING FOR A NEW SKIN. The entire story of that endless night cannot be more than sixty seconds long. Now the Jeep is parked in the sand, at the end of the trail that its own wheels have left on the beach. You've lit a bonfire without much trouble and you're dancing around it, silhouetted against the flames, which cast a red glow on your glistening faces and on your legs and your bare shoulders. It's a cross between a tribal dance and a cool party that is also countercultural. Then, instantly, as soon as the word JEEP and the evocative name of the model—Renegade, with its alluring sense of rebellion—have risen over the beach, the story starts again, looping back with the same exact euphoria, a superhuman joy that suddenly seems ghastly in its eternal return: the same highway, the same town, the same club, the hot dog stand, the fire, the beach, never giving way to rest or sleep, but only going back to the beginning, again, forever, on each of the many screens that are playing the ad throughout the airport.

THANK YOU FOR GIVING US LIFE. You have to be young, but not too young, perhaps thirty, thirty-five, no more than that. You can be in your twenties if you're enrolling in the study abroad or the master's program of your dreams, or if you're requesting or deserve one of the tuition scholarships offered by a bank. In that case you'll be a girl with long, straight hair and glasses, pensive and hopeful, smiling as you ride a bicycle through the cobblestoned streets of a peaceful university town somewhere in Europe, carrying a bag on your shoulder that is made not out of plastic but from recycled materials, with maybe a long celery stick poking out one side and your books and notebooks in the bicycle basket. You'll be talking on the phone or looking up your route on Google Maps, so people can tell that as a native of the digital age you're comfortable with the newest technology. It's acceptable to be older and to have gray hair if you're going to drive luxury sedans through cities with skyscrapers and empty streets, or through the mountains or a desert, or a cliff overlooking the sea. You can also be over forty, even past forty-five, if you're tanned, in perfect shape, and wearing a very expensive watch. Beyond that age, the possibilities narrow: you can be sixty, just a little over sixty, and have white hair, and be a couple, so you can take a winter cruise or walk barefoot on the beach at sunset with your pants rolled up, enjoying the peace of mind provided by a solid pension plan.

YOU FEEL YOURSELF CONNECTING. After that, all that's left is to be an endearing grandfather or grandmother, probably the former, with a good set of teeth that can glisten a bit excessively when you walk hand in hand with your grandson enjoying the things that really matter in life or laughing together as you sit on a couch sharing an iPad. A good head of white hair also goes well with hearing aids. Hear your life again. Shrunken old people who lead an active lifestyle can wear Apple earbuds, since age is not at odds with technology or with physical exercise. I am growing young, says, or thinks, a slim, attractive, and supple woman with short gray hair, standing on the beach wearing a T-shirt in an ad for a pension fund. Whenever white-haired people stand on a beach there's always a beautiful sunset, to suggest tactfully, discreetly, that their lives are setting too. Whether they are at the beach, leaning on the white railing of a cruise ship, playing with a grandchild in the dining room, or in an office in a bank where they've just signed some papers related to their pension plan, white-haired people smile as if lit by an inner joy that often leads them to gaze dreamily into the distance, filled with all the experience of a long, rich life and all the hope for what is yet to come. Do you know when *you* will be able to retire?

RAISE YOUR ADRENALINE TO THE MAX. In order to observe the smallest details, and to better carry out his task, he sometimes uses a magnifying glass that he keeps in the satchel or in one of his pockets. Inspecting an ad on the window of a bank, he's like an expert standing very close to an old master painting with a powerful loupe in his eye or lifting his glasses to study a particular stroke, a stylistic trait that can establish its authorship almost as indubitably as a fingerprint might. This is how Sir Anthony Blunt must have inspected a Poussin in the collection of the Queen of England, to study a mythological reference and to ascertain from the nature of the brushstroke that it was authentic. Poor Anthony Blunt, concealing his homosexuality as well as the fact that he was a Soviet spy. In fact, he thinks, being a spy and studying the form and the hidden or overt meaning of paintings are professions that complement each other well. An advertisement in the window of a bank; a video that pops open as he reads the paper online; a TV ad; a glossy magazine generously given away at a travel agency or a cell phone store; these are his Hermitage, his Tate, his Frick, and his Wallace Collection. A private and highly distinguished museum—never mobbed by crowds of tourists wielding selfie sticks—of which he is the sole curator, a kind of disciple of Aby Warburg or Erwin Panofsky in a tweed jacket with elbow patches, pale from staying up all night looking at old drawings under a powerful lamp, masterpieces of doubtful authorship whose analysis requires an even greater effort if one is to trace their origins, their story, the meaning they once held for their contemporaries, which once was obvious but is now entirely lost or very hard to decipher.

RECAPTURE THE FEELING OF DISCOVERING SOMETHING NEW. You might call this field "high-precision iconology." If a man and a woman, young, maybe in their thirties, are smiling, together or separately, they must have found the perfect loan to grow their business or to renovate their house; that or a mortgage specifically tailored to their needs. Let your project take shape. If you're a couple in that age group you must live in very spacious rooms, sunny, with light-colored furniture; and you must sit side by side on the couch as you look together at something really fascinating on a cell phone, or better still a tablet or a laptop resting on your knees. Whatever you're looking at is making you smile what could be called a complicit smile. Perhaps a picture of the new house you can finally afford, or of the beach where you will spend a well-deserved vacation; or why not, the table with the payment periods and the highly advantageous mortgage rates offered by your bank. Get the most for your money quickly and easily. Or you could be a youthful entrepreneur meeting other entrepreneurs around a big glass table, holding cell phones and tablets, casually dressed, perhaps jeans and a wool sweater that looks vaguely Scandinavian, sometimes a knit cap on your head at a jaunty angle, or a three-day beard, or alternatively a long and carefully groomed beard like the ones you might see in an Assyrian bas-relief. Best of all would be a flannel shirt over a T-shirt. We believe in your dreams, and we can help finance them.

ALL I DO NOW IS SMILE. It's permitted to have children, who can be of various ages, though never sullen teenagers. You will play with them on a rumpled bed, mom and dad together, confident that their future is secure thanks to the bank's warm generosity, or enjoying all the fun and connectivity offered by the latest cell phone models and an all-inclusive family plan. Discover a new dimension of games and entertainment. There will be joy and camaraderie, as if you were friends or colleagues, really, instead of parents and children, and you'll sit on a couch gathered around a screen or several screens, each member of the youthful family enjoying their own device, though all together in convivial warmth. I can share my gigabytes with anyone I choose. Get a second 3G phone line free. A father who is perhaps divorced will make breakfast for his two children, six and eight, on a splendid kitchen island. A call will have come in on the father's phone, and in answering it he will have caused a minor but very amusing mishap, perhaps involving the scrambled eggs or the orange juice. The son will laugh at his father's endearing clumsiness. The girl, by his side, will hold a banana up to her ear as if it were a telephone. Sometimes a couple, lying very close together in bed, will be thinking confidently about the child that is visibly about to arrive, and this will lead him to rest his hand on her round belly with an intimate closeness that is not without a slight air of mischief. If a pregnant woman is alone, she'll stand and gaze firmly into the distance, sometimes shading her eyes with one hand as if to discern the future. We have the right plan for you. With a deeply humane and touching sense of sympathy.

WE UNDERSTAND WHAT YOUR MOST IMPORTANT PROJECT IS.
Couples will tumble festively onto a comfortable couch or a wide Scandinavian bed with their small children. So I can think more about my life, and less about my mortgage. A bright, cheerful, Sunday morning light will filter through the curtains. We want your dreams to become a reality. Generally, books are not allowed. There can be at most a few art books on a low designer table. The couple will be lying in bed, smiling, heads touching, with a child between them. It's not mandatory, but the child will probably be a boy, with blond hair. Sometimes it will be a girl with very curly hair, dark-skinned, or Black, pleasantly exotic and commendably adopted. Her curls, or her braids, or maybe the colorful bands in her hair, will provide a welcome multicultural air. We bring you closer to what really matters.

IN THE SHADOW OF YOUR EYELASHES. He wakes up in darkness and silence, in the pure abstraction of time. He floats in black space, a time without shape or outline since he doesn't know how late it is. He only knows it is Sunday. Last night, when they went to bed, she closed the shutters completely, an old pair of large, heavy shutters with wooden slats that block out all the light. Nor do any sounds come in from the outside, since all the windows are double-paned. He feels entirely clearheaded, without a trace of fatigue. It could be three in the morning or ten in the morning. If he reached for his phone on the nightstand he would know, but he decides not to. He is ensconced in bed like a silkworm in its cocoon or a fetus floating in amniotic fluid; enveloped in successive layers of comfort: the sheet, the light blanket, so pleasant after months of stifling heat, the warmth of her embrace and of her body as she sleeps in her underwear beside him, a human warmth that in the course of the night has been gradually communicated to the air in the room. He is sheltered and at the same time suspended, enveloped in a sense of weightless freedom as if floating in water. Waking up without anxiety is still a source of wonder, of astonished gratitude. In the darkened room, as in a camera obscura, parts of his dream persist and are projected in bright colors and rich detail, a strange blockbuster movie that is screened exclusively for him. He dreamed he stood on the shore of a lagoon from which large, widemouthed fish began to emerge. They crawled to the shore and then kept crawling swiftly on the ground. Pebbles and aquatic fronds glimmered in the green and clear water of the lagoon, which seemed a memory of the glassy waters of the bay in Mallorca. When the first fish came out of the water and crawled toward him he felt afraid. Now he gazes at the fish with curiosity and wonder, as if watching a scene from *The Origin of Species* or Genesis, the moment when aquatic creatures began to colonize the earth. They are also the fish in the creation panel of *The Garden of Earthly Delights*. Except the fish in the painting, after crawling like tiny seals around the grassy shore and in the shade of the trees, plunge back and disappear into the pool.

FORGET WHAT YOU KNOW. Then he is standing in a square in Granada, at dusk, in early summer. The trees are the same that stood at the edge of what was perhaps the Earthly Paradise: trees that you might see in a painting by Bosch or in a well-tended garden or a park. The space around him is so broad and open that it can only be the Plaza Nueva. He sees a young woman coming his way in a light summer dress, with a pair of sunglasses on her head. Although he thinks they've never met, he says to her, "You got a haircut." She looks at him, pleased. "You noticed." He can't see her face clearly in the dream, or at least he's not able to remember it now. The facade of the Real Audiencia rises like a stage set behind them. He says to her, "I will be in love with you my whole life." He doesn't want the images to fade; he doesn't want to forget them. The fish coming out of the water, the pebbles and the fronds near the shore, the trees—privets, perhaps, or orange trees—the silhouette of her light dress. He thinks about the possibility of inventing a camera that would take pictures of dreams, instant pictures with the processed, slightly faded tones of an old polaroid. He realizes that the mesmerizing beauty of a polaroid came from the fact that it portrayed the present moment as its own preemptive memory, tinged already with a sense of distance and of disappearance.

THE FUTURE BEATS STRONGER THAN EVER. He reaches for his phone; the screen lights up and casts a glow over the nightstand. Somehow its effulgence seems part of the strange light of the dream. It's eight-thirty in the morning. No need to rush. He gets up, pleased with the thought of going for a walk. A shirt, light trousers, espadrilles, a sense of ease, so many hours still ahead of him and nothing in particular to do. His neighborhood is as empty on this Sunday morning in September as if it were still August and everyone had left Madrid. As if it were all a stage, still free of memories and habits, arranged as for an apparition or a viable dream.

DISCOVER YOUR DS3 PERFORMANCE LINE. They jump up in the air, separately or in groups, squinting their eyes in a big happy smile or laughing outright with glee; all of their desires coming true without the slightest effort as their youthful bodies rise into the air and float suspended, like seagulls swaying motionless in the breeze. Express yourself in every dimension. They rise like pole-vaulters who never had to strain their muscles in any way, or, needless to say, subject themselves to the tedium and discipline of training; like members of a modern dance troupe, impossibly suspended in midair. Thirteen cyclists defy gravity in China. Performance in your hands. A unique flight experience where every detail counts. Express yourself in motion. Boost your senses. They launch themselves fearlessly on hang gliders from a cliff, floating over landscapes of green hills or over deserts stretching all the way to the horizon. Virtual landing takes place in Pluto. Fly at the best price. Find a new dimension. They fly whenever they want. Don't settle for a lesser flight experience. They fly without even realizing it, transported by their own joy, looking at an iPhone, maybe listening to music, closing their eyes and tossing their hair, caught in a dance that's the more enjoyable because it's solitary, the white cord of the earbuds tangled in their hair. Once I learn to fly, I'll never come down. We'll give you all the hits of summer, and add another thirty million songs. Picture a world without gravity. They rise in the air holding a frosted beer bottle, a bottle of Coca-Cola, a lottery ticket that will no doubt win the prize. Enjoy the moment. Fly over land and water. Three young models, as severe as vestal virgins, walk in single file in the desert wearing boots and long black dresses. They leap and rise in slow motion as if they were dancing and their stage were the blue sky and the desert sand. Are you afraid of flying? Join our Fearless Flying workshops. Take a chance. On the fly. Be the first.

TECHNOLOGY THAT'S CHANGING THE WORLD. They glide horizontally over rooftops, parks, and busy streets as lightly as in a dream, without any effort or any sense of vertigo. A long-haired girl in a summer dress flies barefoot over a spring meadow, picking a flower and smelling it as she goes. Dive into the now. Lightness you can feel. The power of dreams. They jump like superheroes from the edge of one glass building to another. Show us your most fun and adventurous side. Fly Vueling. They fly from the sheer joy of starting a master's program at the business school of their dreams: a backpack on their shoulders, their arms wide open, hovering a dozen feet above a campus that is even more ideal because the sun is setting and a golden glow spreads over the redbrick buildings and the grassy lawns. They float and move as slowly as astronauts in a space station. Are you the kind of person that looks for new experiences? Feel the call. Start your adventure. Fly through the air. Abuse your imagination. Celebrate everything you have. Free unlimited. Hurry up and live. *Cammina nel blu.* You won't know if you're on the ground or in the sky. Defy gravity with the newest breakthrough from Shiseido. A young couple flies hand in hand over a city on a bright day, against a blue sky, freed by ING from the dead weight of banking fees. Do you know how to fly?

OPEN YOUR LIFE TO THE CELEBRATION OF NEVER MISSING OUT. Their laughing mouths are stretched painfully wide by a terrifying joy, a fanatical, collective, unanimous euphoria. They are the suicide squads of happiness, its fundamentalists, caught in a gruesome glee that forces them to jump from cliffs and trampolines. Any day can be a party when you have everything you need. They laugh in a circle, looking separately at their phones and at the same time joined by the excitement radiating from each glowing screen. They all laugh: couples, families, friends, mobs of people. They also laugh alone, as if they were insane, taking a selfie, listening to something on their headphones, looking at their phone or at an iPad. They laugh, they roar and bellow, contracting the muscles of their jaws so that their teeth and gums and tongues show even more. They clench their fists, puff out their chests, the veins and tendons in their necks become so taut that their faces turn crimson. Enjoy the wildest content. Watching commercials on YouTube, or peering through his magnifying glass at the pages of the magazines he gathers everywhere, he studies those big happy smiles and feels a kind of admiration that may be slightly tinged with resentment. He does not remember ever having known such joy or having burst into that kind of laughter, strong enough to shake the needle of a seismograph.

LEARN THE MAGIC OF REMARKETING. Perhaps he secretly envies their youth, their gleaming teeth, the flagrant promiscuity between men and women. Perhaps he envies their nocturnal lives, the sandy beaches where they take selfies, laughing wildly, raising bulbous glasses with tropical drinks; or the collective trance of soccer games and concerts, the swarming, bouncing crowd inside a disco, if such a name is still used. They wear sunglasses, swimsuits, colorful bands in their hair, and they get covered in sand and are always laughing. The reason they laugh is that they're enjoying a cold beer or a certain brand of gin or just a soda, which seems to turn as soon as it touches their lips into a powerful laugh serum. They laugh joyfully as they hold an iPhone 6 or a Huawei 9 up in the air like a trophy; they laugh when they discover the huge variety of sports and movie channels, the many series they'll enjoy on a 4G network. So you can talk as much as you like. So you can always stay connected to the ones you love, no matter where you go.

YOU'LL HAVE THE WHOLE BEACH TO YOURSELF. When the analog or digital needle reaches its highest levels, a warning signal will begin to flash. A light comes on and the needle quivers as if confused. It detects a dangerous point where laughter could turn convulsive, the jaws become unhinged, the lungs begin to fail, their breathing turning to a dry and spastic heaving, and the eyes, growing wider and wider with joy, come out of their sockets like the eyes of zombies in a film, and the veins of the neck begin to swell until they burst, bleeding out internally, and the face turns blue from lack of oxygen. At the very end, a moment will come when laughter will give way to barking and then to a pure and frantic chattering of white teeth, like a windup toy or a sewing machine, quite capable of severing their tongues. You'll split your sides. You'll die laughing. You'll have the time of your life. Enjoy without limits. Never stop.

SIDEWALK NARRATIVES. A woman in a red business suit and red heels walks magically through a city as if she were floating, impelled by a breeze that quickens her step without ever lifting her entirely off the ground. She steps off the sidewalk and the white stripes of a crosswalk turn red beneath her feet, a glowing, Estée Lauder red, the same red as her shoes, blazer, handbag, and lips. She walks under a tree and one by one its leaves turn red as well, as does its spreading shade on the pavement.

I CAN'T STOP LOOKING. There is only one face that you will fall in love with. One alone among all other faces, the hundreds of faces you meet and notice on the street every day. Proust says that beauty is "*le charme indivi-duel,*" a face whose utter individuality takes you by surprise and at the same time fills you with a sense of instant recognition. You see it for the first time and it feels like you are seeing it after a long and distant separation. You find it so beautiful that you begin to fall in love with it, weak with desire and at the same time filled with a heartbreaking tenderness. It only happens a few times in life. Perhaps at each of those decisive ages, those various lives into which we are reincarnated with no memory of who we were before. It doesn't guarantee you will be happy, much less that it will be reciprocal. It is a game of chance where you stake your life or at least one of them. Nothing is possible, after all, without a sense of beauty, which in the end has little to do with objective criteria. It's all or nothing. "All or Nothing at All," as in the old song that Billie Holiday sang best. Like Baudelaire crossing paths in Paris with a mysterious woman in mourning, or James Joyce finding Norah on a Dublin street, or Pierre Bonnard getting off the tram to follow the young, short-haired woman that he will spend the rest of his life painting. Like Wal-ter Benjamin seeing Asja Lācis walking the streets of Capri. All of the discov-eries that follow, the tracing out of mutual sympathies, affinities, may deepen your initial fascination or belie it, but they will not replace it. You either fall in love or you don't. And once you have fallen in love, you either fall in love even more deeply or it all comes apart like an illusion. Time will either strengthen love or make it dissipate. With every step that draws you closer there's a risk that the spell might be broken. The fleeting nature of a mirage does not de-grade its beauty. But the most precious spell is one that grows and is sustained by both physical attraction and impassioned talk, weaving together instinct and reason. The moment when you fall in love shines with complete clarity, as does the mystery of a lasting desire. When you saw her for the first time, you instantly felt you had known her forever. From this moment on, through the years, if you meet her unexpectedly at a restaurant or a hotel that you came to separately, you will feel again that you are seeing her for the very first time.

ALL OUR ATTENTION IS CENTERED ON YOU. Asja Lācis recounts the first time she met Walter Benjamin, in Capri, in 1925. Two people from cold northern countries who found themselves in the summer light of the Mediterranean. She and her daughter had gone into a shop to buy almonds but she did not know the Italian word. A man standing next to her at the counter translated her request and offered to help her. "Would you allow me to walk with you and help you carry the bag?" She was a modern, independent woman, involved in theater and the avant-garde, as well as a militant Bolshevik. She must have been surprised by this old-fashioned and ceremonious man. She said he walked like a turtle. "Glasses that sparkled in the light; thick dark hair; a thin nose; clumsy hands. He kept dropping the bag." Lācis wrote these words years later, when Benjamin had been dead for a long time and she had survived the Gulag. He told her that he had been watching her in the square for days. "I have been watching you for two weeks. In your white suit, with your long legs, you seem not to walk but to float across the square." He would watch her go by with her daughter. Perhaps the visible resemblance between them made him fall in love even more.

EVERYWHERE YOU LOOK. In September the city seems about to overflow. Too much traffic on the streets, too many people on the sidewalks, a sign outside every bar and restaurant with a long list of daily specials; and then the cluttered corner stores, one after another, and the bakeries with light wooden counters and young, polite attendants in aprons made to look handcrafted or from an earlier era. Too much of everything, a flood, a dizzying profusion—especially of trash, which pours out everywhere like water from the drains after a storm. The garbage cans are brimming with paper waste and plastic containers, and the ashtrays on top are stuffed with cigarette butts. The metal dumpsters on the sidewalk outside building sites are spilling over too, not just with debris, which they are meant for, but with all the things that people discard as they go by: doors, toilets, bidets, broken furniture, pipes and faucets, tangled skeins of insulating material, smashed dresser drawers, piles of binders stuffed with bills and papers, bursting garbage bags. Every tree grate becomes an ashtray crammed with cigarettes that spill onto the sidewalk too, trampled by people's feet just like the crumpled packs that are thrown on the ground, each with its gruesome color picture of a dying person or of some internal organ eaten away by cancer or embalmed in tar. Shuttered shop windows are covered in a thick layer of posters and signs, freshly glued or old and tattered, like ivy taking over an abandoned house. Covered in graffiti, the old signs continue to repeat their dire warnings, LAST CHANCE, EVERYTHING MUST GO, FINAL DAYS, in big red letters on a white ground.

WHEN THIRST CALLS. Lampposts and streetlights are covered in signs that have been glued or attached with masking tape, even surgical tape. Sell your car. Bolivian girl available for eldercare and housework. Freight and moving services. We buy gold. We buy silver. A locksmith you can trust. Window repair. Spanish house painter. Cars that stay parked in the same spot for a few days begin to bristle with flyers stuck under the wipers or in the windows. Massage, Asian Girls, Latin Bombshell, A Volcano in Bed, Master Doma Grand African Seer. Since it hasn't rained for many days, and since the street sweepers have not been out, the edge of the sidewalk is covered in a thick compost made of many different kinds of garbage mixed with dry leaves. Master Suleh Seer Medium Medicine Man, Professor Dide Famous African Seer. There are piles of dog shit on the ground like little stinking monuments. Master Bamba Seer Fortune-Teller Medicine Man. A sidewalk bench is littered with empty beer cans, squeezed ketchup packets, plastic containers for prepared foods. Master Ma Djeneba the Greatest African Shaman. If it's Saturday there is a smell of uric acid and fresh vomit everywhere from last night's revelers. Beautiful feminine feet, pedicured and sandaled, step swiftly around the bits of trash on the sidewalk. The shuttered entrance to a travel agency is littered with pieces of cardboard and old clothes strewn on the ground, the remains of a now abandoned shelter put up overnight by a beggar who must have woken up early.

FOUR SECONDS ARE ENOUGH TO CONTROL YOUR IMPULSES. Urgent, barking, prodding voices tell, implore, command, or warn you that time is running out, the offer will expire. Pulsing in a corner of the screen, entreating or demanding, or, if necessary, making you feel anxious, they give out curt instructions, pushing, pointing, barking like a drill sergeant, elbowing and urging you to find out more, search now, ask for more, explore. It's now or never. Buy it now. You drag the little icon of the open hand and click on the word *now*, or the word *more*, and every possible desire is revealed and instantly fulfilled. Learn more. Visit now. Start here. Click here. Sign up. Click to buy. Search now. Find a doctor. Shop here. Find your sign. + Info. Book this minute. Experience it now. Book now. One-syllable English words quicken the pace and urgency of their demands. Shop now. Skip ad. The simplest rhythm, the most effective, the most primitive, one that is not consciously felt by areas of the brain related to higher thinking but by the cerebellum, which governs the most basic bodily motions. Get more. Shop here. Your heart quickens, just as when you hear the beat of electronic music on the street or the thumping bass of a passing car. Buy it now. The rhythm of your steps and of the beating of your heart, one-two, expanding and contracting, the breathing of your lungs, the pulsing of your blood. Click here to learn more. Buy now. Everything in the curt robotic syntax of the imperative. See more. Ask now. Skip ad. A voice accosts you on the street or lies in wait for you inside your phone, which buzzes frantically each time you click on a website to follow the news. Read more. Click here. Try it now. Find out what you like. Find out more. Just for you. It knows exactly what temptation it should place before you.

IT WILL TAKE YOU TO AMAZING PLACES. Walter Benjamin was carrying a kind of black leather briefcase when he tried to flee to Spain across the Pyrenees. He was never without it. That briefcase, or satchel, made him seem all the more bizarre as he walked down some wild country path in his glasses and tie among smugglers and sheep herders, dressed in his incongruous city clothes in a sweltering heat that was unusual for late September. He suffered from heart disease and had the weak lungs of a smoker. He pressed the briefcase to his side and said its contents mattered more to him than his own life. It must have held the documents that he thought would save him: an entry visa to the United States, a permit to cross into Spain and Portugal. He would stop to catch his breath, to wipe the sweat off his face with a handkerchief, and the other fugitives in the group would gradually leave him behind and have to stop and wait for him, always fearful that the French guards would find them. That briefcase, or satchel, or travel bag, seems to have still been in his possession when he checked into a room at the Hotel de Francia in Portbou. It appears in the final list of his belongings, yet it was never found. The gas mask he carried with him when he fled Paris, on the eve of the German entry into the city, must have been left behind somewhere else. Nor did anyone ever find his pocket watch, inherited from his grandfather, which used to dangle from an old-fashioned chain attached to his lapel—the sole surviving relic of the bourgeois existence he once led in Berlin.

EVERY PIECE COMES WITH A STORY. Whenever you move houses, certain things disappear and others turn up again. I was in the study in the new house and she brought me the lighter she gave me when we first became lovers, the one I used when we were first together in New York. It must be twenty-five years since I last saw or thought of it, ever since I gave up smoking. It is made of steel, with a curved surface that makes it pleasant to hold. It retains a certain glow but is scratched and dented along the edges, worn smooth like any small everyday object that is used frequently and kept in a pocket. You had to flip it open in order to light it. There is a kind of Art Deco sensuousness to its shape, its curved metallic surfaces, pleasing to look at and to hold. My hands were much younger when she gave it to me, and the skin around the nails of my index and middle fingers was tinged the faint yellow ochre of nicotine.

YOUR FINGERS DESERVE A BETTER FATE. She gave it to me one morning when I went to see her in Madrid, a visit that was going to be even shorter than usual. In a few hours I would take another plane that would carry me much farther away. We fell into each other's arms with the ardor of arrival and of separation, and of the promise of a new encounter in a city she had never seen before and I had been to only once. The lighter was a kind of keepsake for my trip. It lay on the nightstand with the ashtray and the cigarettes, next to the bed where we were already embracing a few minutes after I arrived. Our breathless kissing in the taxi, at the entrance to the building, in the elevator and the hallway was all the more arousing from the scent of nicotine, the way it seemed to faintly veil her lips. The gift of the lighter stood for other gifts: her bright and sudden nakedness;

the reckless way she gave herself to me completely, without conditions. Taking it with me would be like having her by my side. Whoever noticed that peculiar lighter would inadvertently perceive as well her presence in my life; the mark of her aesthetic sense, quietly at work in everything she wore, her things, the places where she lived, the space I entered into when I was with her. To carry the lighter, to light a cigarette with it, to bring it out when someone asked me for a light was to profess to a secret flame that would burn inside me all through the trip, fed by memory and expectation. Whenever I set it down on a table or as soon as I took it out of my pocket people would notice it. She conferred on me a touch of distinction even when she was far away. All through the nights I spent across the ocean, in some huge hotel room in the Midwest, her gift on the nightstand or between my fingers was a light to outlive distance.

THIS IS YOUR CHANCE TO TAKE OFF. We used to listen to boleros back then. I would lie on a huge hotel bed thinking about her, looking out the window at one more endless parking lot or at a wheat field stretching into the distance. Lighting a cigarette meant repeating the gesture of her hands when she would do it for me after we made love. Her body would have been even more slender and youthful on that immense bed. An enormous room in Columbus, Ohio, became the small bedroom in Madrid where we spent entire mornings with the shades drawn. The afternoons would darken into evening long before we turned on any lights, and waking up in the middle of the night was as sweet a pleasure as falling asleep exhausted. In one of our favorite boleros Moncho used to sing, *Darling, don't smoke in bed, no fumes en la cama.* Now I place the lighter on my desk, moving aside some papers and notebooks to make room for it next to a photograph I took of her on a bench in Central Park, not long after she gave it to me. It's not so much that memory can bring back the past faithfully (it almost never does) as that every now and then, time just ceases to be. Those days are as tangible as the lighter I hold in my hands today, twenty-five years after I last touched a cigarette.

WELCOME TO A NEW ERA. He notices so many things now that he never did before, he explains—before the project, when it all became an obsession and he couldn't help it anymore, especially after finding the whale. "You wouldn't believe it," he says, stopping on the sidewalk to emphasize his words, stretching out his arms as if to encompass something impossibly large. "Ten thousand pounds. Broader than the sidewalk and longer than a city block." He stands there like a man from an earlier era, a time when people went on walks to have a conversation, and as he speaks about the whale I begin to notice more closely the heft of his body, the complexion of his face, his beard and his tousled hair, which are both white despite the fact that he is still quite young. His evocation of the whale seems even more powerful on account of his strong hands and a jacket that is like the coat of a sailor or a mountain man. The same species, by the way—he adds—as Moby-Dick: a sperm whale. One day it turned up on the beach like a giant heap near the marine station where he and his colleagues had been working on the project for several months, and it was like a flood, a ravaging tsunami that alters everything; even though his obsession had been with him for months already, a constant presence that never seemed to fade, even at the end of the year when they were done compiling their tables and counting and classifying all the objects they had found.

LOOK AT LIFE WITH DIFFERENT EYES. "And it's still there," he says of the obsession, "right now, even as we speak, as we walk down the street, and earlier, while we were having coffee. I'll be thinking of something else, or talking to someone, and suddenly I realize that I'm no longer paying attention or that I lose the thread of my thoughts because I'm looking at someone flicking away a cigarette without a thought or walking out of a drugstore with a plastic bag in one hand that holds maybe a single bottle of pills. Things like that. Do you know how many cigarettes are smoked in the world in a year? Over five trillion. And one way or another, all those cigarette butts and the thousands of toxic substances they contain will end up in the sea."

TECHNOLOGY MOVES YOU. "Look at that, for instance," he says, pointing to a soda bottle and a takeout container that someone left behind on a bench along with a torn, empty bag of potato chips lying on the ground. "You'd have to follow one of these people," he often thinks, "and keep a record of the trail of plastic trash they leave behind in a single day, or a year, or in the course of their lives. Imagine the kind of biography that would make: what we all leave behind us without even remembering we did, or being able to help it. Even me, despite my obsession. I'll buy a pair of scissors or a toothbrush and injure my hand trying to open the stiff plastic cover. Then I think that those sharp edges will tear like a knife at a sea turtle's throat, for instance, when it tries to swallow it mistaking it for a squid, and I remember the burst stomach inside the whale when we cut it open, all the plastic waste and debris that spilled out. There was no food at all," he says. "Its intestines were empty. It died from a gastric rupture, but it was already very weak because no food could reach its stomach. And I can't stop noticing, looking," he says, "no matter what I do. Sometimes I can't help it and I tell someone to pick up the plastic bottle or bag they just threw on the ground. I mentally classify each thing I see into the list of categories we created for the project. Bottle, food container, beverage can, hygiene product, fishing net, farming equipment . . ."

MAKE THE MOST OF IT. He stops again, this time at the busy corner of Goya and Alcalá, among the profusion of people and things, a big Corte Inglés department store with a boatload of merchandise in each of its floors and basement levels. "When I go by this store, for instance, I remember all of the Corte Inglés shopping bags we collected in the course of the year, or rather the bags the fishermen collected for us, just on that small section near the coast." He looks at the people going by with their shopping bags and thinks of the big warehouse where the objects they collected gradually piled up during the year when his incurable obsession began. "It was a reverse Corte Inglés," he says, "a great department store of garbage." And, since his imagination is prone to quantifying and classifying, he provides figures to illustrate. "Forty-seven thousand items in a year. Forty-seven thousand and one, to be precise. For a whole year the fishermen along the coast near the research center brought in whatever garbage they picked up in their trawling nets. We were especially interested in trawling boats because their nets sweep the ocean floor," he says. "Seventy percent of all plastic in the sea lies at the bottom. Each day we got a new load." At first they used a system of waste classification developed in Norway. But they soon realized it was not what they needed, because the Norwegians did not pick up waste from agriculture. "Whereas here," he says, "we're right next to all the greenhouses in Almería, and all the ones being built each day in Granada and Murcia. There were thousands of pounds of the clear plastic sheeting they use for roofing material, square miles of it, and of the stiffer sheets of black plastic they lay on the ground to preserve heat and moisture. For years they've thrown into the sea the plastic sheets that are too worn out to be used anymore. Or if they're not thrown in, they're snatched by the wind and carried into the sea. Plastic crates, rope, netting, plastic pots. We found two plastic pots and twenty pounds of plastic sheeting inside the whale's stomach."

ALWAYS A STEP BEYOND. With each passing day, as the truck came and dumped its muddy, jumbled load, a kind of taxonomical delirium took hold of him, an urge to classify every single bit of waste and garbage. Objects larger than two inches had to be washed, dried, labeled, weighed, and measured. Snarled-up nets and skeins of shredded plastic had to be untangled. Once, they found a huge ball made up of eighty-nine different kinds of netting. When they were finally able to untangle it, they found that it had formed around a teddy bear with a conical wizard's hat. Entire shelves were devoted to toys that were then classified into smaller subdivisions: plastic superheroes; articulated dolls; drowned Barbies with big eyes and drenched hair; teddy bears of all sizes; plush penguins; a strange zoology of hippos and giraffes and tragic babies with finely rendered human faces, of Disney princesses whose hair was tangled up in mud and algae.

I MAKE A PAYMENT AND I HAVE IT ALL. "And TV sets," he says, "old ones as well as newer plasma screens, and whole refrigerators, dishwashers, portable fans, toy cars and trains and fighter jets and spaceships, and wool or rubber gloves like hands coming out of the water begging for help, and plastic swimming pools and floaties, sneakers, plastic sandals, condoms, swimming goggles, birdcages, traveling crates for pets, buckets, engines, bicycle tires, whole bicycles, synthetic sponges, car tires, huge trailer-truck tires."

WHEREVER AND WHENEVER I WANT. "And the plastic bags," he says, "the plastic bags and bottles and food containers, which are the three most frequent items. Such a huge quantity of plastic bottles," he recalls, "carefully arranged, like an army or like the pieces in a deranged game of chess. Soda bottles, laundry bottles, cleaning products; bags and plastic cups and plates; plastic knives and forks for some huge feast, and rows of toothpaste tubes, toothbrushes, plastic straws, baby diapers, plastic kitchen sets, candy wrappers, bags that used to hold potato chips or cheese puffs: bright, intact, still shiny once you washed them."

EXPERIENCE INCREDIBLE SENSATIONS YOU'LL NEVER FORGET. One day someone came and told them about the whale. It seemed even more immense on that sheltered cove. To get on top they had to climb its slippery mass, moving around it in their orange body suits and safety goggles like deep-sea divers or astronauts as they cut it open with chainsaws. In the black rampart of its head there was an open eye that was already swarming with flies. Working very quickly so the growing stench would not spread over the beach, they arranged on the sand the various objects that would later be taken to the warehouse to be permanently classified. "It was like being on a different planet," he says. His eyes no longer dart sideways as he speaks. They are fixed on that memory. The whale, cut open like a trench filled with innards and organic matter; the burst sack of its enormous stomach, from which they kept removing things; and all the human figures walking on top of the dead animal in rubber boots and masks to cut it into pieces. A crane and a bulldozer waited to one side. "You may not be able to actually imagine it," he says. "It weighed nearly five tons. There were forty pounds of plastic in its stomach. The record for that species currently belongs to a whale that was stranded on a beach in California with 161 pounds of plastic in its gut. Most of the plastic inside our whale was greenhouse sheeting. But there were also nets, plastic nursery pots, a spray can, plastic bags, cigarette lighters, food containers."

CALL US, WE CAN HELP. But he is not a gloomy or a bitter man. His voice is as calm as his face, which seems youthful by contrast with his white hair and beard. He counteracts the dizzying welter of apocalyptic figures by an inclination to think concretely, attending to what is feasible and near at hand: the well-defined parameters of an experiment; the time span of a project; things that can be measured, counted, and reliably assessed. Sometimes, when work was done for the day, he would stay behind in the warehouse, alone, surrounded by the forty-seven thousand items they gathered and classified that year, wandering among his collections with a certain sense of pleasure that belonged not so much to a proprietor as to a kind of museum director. Some small corner of reality had been organized and measured. I tell him that perhaps at those moments his satisfaction was more aesthetic than scientific, and it makes him smile. But then he looks serious. "Why should there be any difference," he says.

BE THE FIRST ONE TO OWN IT. It's a little before noon and we're having a beer and some tapas at a bar on Menéndez Pelayo. October in Madrid. All around us people are talking and drinking, sharing plates of tapas at the bar. Some rest their elbows on the counter with an unconscious air of easy wisdom. The broad sidewalks and its closeness to El Retiro give this part of Madrid a sense of openness, like that of a city by the shore. Along with our beers they brought us a few slices of bread and a tin of mussels in oil and vinegar. There is a kind of perfection to each small thing, a consummate coming together of pleasure and common sense. The walk, the conversation, and the glass of beer give a glow to his face. He speaks in a soft Andalusian accent, calmly, without emphasis, his words trailing off into their aspirated endings. "The worst part is not what we saw," he says, "but what we never found. All the plastic that is swept to unknown depths by marine currents stronger than large rivers; all the plastic that gets broken up into microfibers measuring five millimeters or less. Plastic never goes away. A water bottle or a silly shopping bag may disappear after a thousand years, but that's irrelevant: the microfibers remain and are absorbed by living organisms, causing unknown reactions at the cellular and molecular level." He points his fork at the mussel he is about to eat: it surely contains traces of plastic, pesticides, antibiotics, antidepressants. "A smoker even inhales rat poison," he says, "and pesticides, and heavy metals that will pollute the bit of ground next to that tree where people throw their cigarette butts when they're done smoking them by the raised tables that the owners of the café have installed on the sidewalk."

WOULD YOU LIKE TO BE HERE TOMORROW? He is ever watchful. Nothing escapes him. A waiter just threw away a small plastic basket with several untouched slices of bread; the attractive woman who stepped out with her glass of beer to smoke on the sidewalk crushed an empty cigarette pack and threw it on the ground. He watches with amazement but without misanthropy the irrational or simply catastrophically careless actions of human beings. His erudition ranges in peculiar directions, and he turns out to know a lot about Proudhon and other utopian French socialists. He shares one of Proudhon's sayings (he may be the first person to mention Proudhon to me in more than forty years): "Well-being without education turns people into brutes and makes them insolent." He has begun another project related to the problem of Chinese tires. On a virgin and nearly inaccessible cove he found a tire dump. People buy Chinese tires because they're much cheaper, but since they are illegal in the European Union, they can't take them to official recycling centers when they wear out. Instead, they dump them wherever they can, including that exceptional beach. Since it lies far down at the foot of a nearly vertical cliff, all they have to do is tip the dump truck from a bend in the road. So he started a project. He got some funding. Someone said they had a crane he could borrow. Members of a mountaineering club will rappel down the cliff. He thinks there are two to three hundred tires on the beach, all in a black heap like the stranded whale at the edge of the sea—a deep blue sea whose waters no longer contain the least speck of plankton, and are thus empty as well of all the fish that once came to the cove seeking food and a shelter from predators.

I AM FULL WITH A THOUSAND SOULS. There is a kind of invisibility to Herman Melville, as if lost or perpetually estranged among the people walking down the street with him, or in the smaller sphere of his literary circles, the bookstores and cafés. Walt Whitman, who was his exact contemporary, must have crossed paths with him. When Melville's first book was published Whitman wrote a favorable review in a Brooklyn paper. Melville was a reader of Poe, and both frequented the same bookstore in New York, whose owner they knew well. But they never met, or if they ran into each other now and then, to the point of becoming familiar strangers, we will never know it. Melville walked quickly, in long strides. He said Broadway was a Mississippi flowing through Manhattan. During a trip to London in 1850 he spent his days exploring alleyways and courtyards, bookstores, theaters, cafés, dubious streets he would have avoided in other people's company, where women stood at the corners offering themselves under the gaslight. De Quincey was still alive and it is very likely that Melville had read his *Confessions*, as well as Poe's "The Man of the Crowd." Melville took quick notes in his journal as he traveled. *Moby-Dick* must have been taking shape in his imagination, its first episodes, Ishmael's first night in New Bedford rising dimly in his mind like a dream or like a memory. One day, in London, he lets himself drift in a festive crowd that fills the streets. At some point, when it is too late to step aside or to try to turn back, he finds out that all those people are going to a public hanging. "The brutal multitude," he writes with disgust in his journal. There was another witness elsewhere in the crowd that day, one who was just as repelled: Charles Dickens. Dickens and Melville, standing separately in that moving mass of people thirsting for cruelty, so unknowingly close to each other.

WE SEE REMARKABLE THINGS IN YOUR FUTURE. Starting in December 1866, and for the next twenty years, Herman Melville takes the same walk through the streets of New York City six days a week. Leaving his house at 103 East Twenty-Sixth Street, he takes the tram, which is still horse-drawn but already on rails, and heads south. He gets off and walks west, toward the piers along the Hudson, the scenery of his youth. His father used to take him for walks along the piers when he was still a well-to-do businessman, before he became ill and went bankrupt. They would walk hand in hand. Now Melville wears a blue cap and a dark-blue uniform with gold buttons. His official title is Assistant Inspector of Customs. Poe had sought a similar position a few years earlier to no avail. A friend arranged for an appointment with the president at the White House so Poe could offer his services and explain his precarious situation. He got so drunk the night before that he never turned up. Melville's task is to ensure that proper dues are paid on the merchandise coming to New York on ships from all over the world. He works in a kind of large wooden shed. The job is especially unpleasant to him because everyone around him is corrupt. Fifteen or sixteen years later he will change his route, though not his job. He is transferred to a dock on the East River, far north, near Seventy-Ninth Street. The city is undergoing rapid change. Now Melville goes to work on the elevated train that runs along Third Avenue. There are no tall buildings yet to block the view. From the window of the train, the seated traveler can see the broad span of the city: the two rivers girding it on either side, and the docks bristling with masts and as the years go by, with the tall stacks of steamships belching out black clouds of smoke and sounding their deep horns.

JUST WHEN YOU NEEDED IT MOST. No one knows or remembers who Herman Melville is anymore. Tall, serious, sitting on the train with the same fixed, distant gaze he has in every photograph, with that grand old-fashioned beard that has now turned gray, he is as imposing and as anachronistic a figure as the rare sail ship that now and then still docks at the piers. The same man who sailed so widely in the first part of his life would never go to sea again. No one remembers any of his books, not even the first ones, which had turned him into a somewhat scandalous literary celebrity because they told tales of cannibals and of the sensual natives of the Southern seas. Henry James, who knows everyone in the literary circles of New York, never mentions his name. Of the 3,000 copies of *Moby-Dick* printed for its first (and only) edition, 2,400 remained for years in the printer's warehouse, entirely forgotten. Then they were burned in a fire that destroyed the building. The flames must have spread quickly through that mass of paper, that purgatory of unwanted books, the same words and the same pages identically repeated over and over again. Gross sales of *Moby-Dick* in the United States amounted to $556.37. There is a rather ghostly photograph from around 1890 showing the esplanade of the Battery at the tip of the island, with a railing over the Hudson and the bay. Several male figures appear at a certain distance, each standing alone, men out in the sun in dark formal dress and top hats on what seems like a winter morning. One of them could be Herman Melville. In the 1920s, when *Moby-Dick* was printed again and *Billy Budd* was first published, an old man who had worked in his youth as a clerk in a New York City bookstore said that he remembered having seen Melville many times. He said he was a private man, always kind and generous to the employees who worked in the shop.

THE WHOLE BEACH, ALL TO YOURSELF. For the first time in months there is rain and a wet wind. For the first time I see the new house in the gray light of an overcast day. It feels like truly moving in, as if we were already living in the winter days that are to come. The future, dimly discerned, reverberates in memory more than the nonexistent past. To go outside and feel the fresh, wet breeze and smell the rain and hear the trees tossing in the wind is like arriving in a different city, farther north and closer to the sea. The sidewalks are full of swirling fallen leaves that seem to have come out of nowhere, since the trees are still green. They are not autumn leaves but rather leaves that were scorched by the summer heat. To hear again the sound of the trees in Madrid is like hearing the ocean. When there is no wind in the city the trees are silent. Now the yellow awnings and the flags high up on the buildings are flapping and bits of trash get caught in short-lived whirlwinds and are swept along with paper flyers, cigarette butts, plastic cups, ads for massage parlors, gold buyers, and car lots, tossed together with the shriveled leaves and with the quick, sputtering drops of an invisible rain that feels like pinpricks on your face; a rain that pierces your light summer shirt and trickles down the windshields of cars that have been parked on the same spot for a long time, turning to pulp the flyers trapped for many days under the wipers.

EXCLUSIVE PRIVILEGES JUST FOR YOU. Since it's chilly and overcast, people walk a bit faster in the morning. Many women are still wearing sandals but they also wear jackets and shawls. There are groups of children on their way to school, mothers holding slow, sleepy kids by the hand, urging them to walk faster. One woman is pushing a double stroller carrying a pair of identical babies, guiding it with one hand while she arranges her hair and lights a cigarette with the other. She is talking on the phone, which she holds awkwardly between her cheek and shoulder. Awkwardly too she takes a cigarette out of the pack and lights it with one hand, her neck all twisted. Each of the babies is gazing at an iPhone. There are many private schools in the neighborhood and the children wear uniforms. There is a powerful sense of newness, of beginnings, a September sense of promise, the smell of fresh notebooks and pencils in one of those stationery stores that will perhaps soon cease to exist, as every useful, lasting thing seems fated to die off when it is suddenly declared—who knows by whom—as belonging to the past. Just as the radio was going to vanish once television arrived, and theaters were going to be shuttered. Just as all those experts on urban planning and architecture decided that sidewalks, streetcars, bicycles, and corner stores had to go, since walking itself was a thing of the past.

BEFORE IT RUNS OUT. I used to feel a little embarrassed by my allegiance to the things I had always enjoyed: notebooks, pens and pencils, printed books that you buy in a bookstore. Now I couldn't care less. Not because I've come to terms with being almost an old man living in the past, or because I am resigned to the loss of the things I love, but rather because that loss, that long chain of gleefully anticipated extinctions that until just recently seemed such a certainty, is no longer so clearly going to happen. The people I know who are most passionate about printed books and good typography are thirty years younger than me. Almost none of the practical, valuable things that experts said were outdated have actually disappeared. The more pervasive and ghostly the digital world becomes, the more we care for what is truly and uniquely there, between our hands. Timeless things seem obsolete only to those who don't realize they belong to the future as much as the past. What is outdated suddenly becomes futuristic: bicycles, streetcars, farmers' markets, crowded streets, public squares with trees, the fertile mingling of commerce, work, and life.

WE HAVE AN AMAZING OFFER JUST FOR YOU. Today I leave the house early, skipping breakfast since I need to have some blood work done.

At this early hour I find the city in a morning bustle that I enjoy all the more because I rarely get to see it. Walking down the street on an empty stomach, in crisp weather, wearing a jacket for the first time in several months, heightens the sense of lightness and novelty, as of a promise that need not be voiced to be fulfilled. I move down the sidewalk through flurries of conversation, the smells and the soft din of breakfast being served at the cafés, the fragrant scent of soap and shampoo from people who just showered. Here and there on street corners I see smokers who seem to have gotten up early for the sole purpose of poisoning themselves as quickly as they can, replacing as soon as possible the fresh morning air with hot, toxic smoke. Outside the hospital there is a cloud of smoke and a carpet of cigarette butts. Some of the patients are out smoking in their slippers, in big overcoats and a hospital robe over their pale blue pajamas. A kind, careful nurse sticks the needle in my arm without any pain and switches the plastic vials as they gradually fill up with suctioned blood.

FIND THE EXPERIENCE YOU ARE LOOKING FOR. The color of blood is always surprising. When she was finished she placed a bit of cotton on the puncture and wrapped it with a bandage. Instead of feeling weaker from the loss of blood, I feel lighter. I walk down familiar corridors and waiting rooms, the human bustle of a public hospital, as crowded and busy as a marketplace. The sun has not yet warmed the narrow tree-lined streets that lead to El Retiro. Doormen are out hosing down the sidewalk and it looks and smells like morning rain. At the local café, sitting by the Giacometti drawing, I have a larger breakfast than usual to recover my strength after the loss of blood. Coffee, orange juice, toast with olive oil and tomato. The taste of coffee and of dense, nourishing milk are strong and distinct to my grateful palate. Smells linger in the warm air inside the café, sounds blend in the background: people on the phone, the Venezuelan accent of the waiters, the noise of the espresso machine, Bill Evans playing "My Favorite Things." On the front page of the paper there's a big picture of Donald Trump standing in front of a slew of American flags. It is nine o' clock in the morning and the whole day is ahead of me, and my whole life. Inside the light sleeve of my jacket I can feel the tightness of the bandage covering the tiny prick of the needle. A woman next to me is talking on the phone. "I mean, I'm pretty stubborn too, I know I can be a lot to take." She falls silent as she listens impatiently to the other person, who speaks so loudly that I can hear the voice coming through the phone. She has long, red fingernails and her knuckles are white from pressing the phone against her ear. "All of you can just leave me alone. Just let me be, I can't take it anymore. Just let me be."

YOU'RE MISSING OUT. All the voices turn out to be just one voice. The names of songs seem to change, like the tunes and the lyrics, but it is more or less the same song repeating itself endlessly. All those ads, songs, and political slogans in the second person are referring to you, just you. Every song is about you. Our best player is you. You are the star. You are the journey. We have a Volvo just for you. Every voice is urging you to find out, to go on, to try it, to dare, to push open a door, to enjoy an experience, to click on a banner pulsing on your laptop screen. The best Mediterranean beaches just for you. Visit now. Learn more. Find out more. Click now. Click here. It's the voice of desire, speaking in suggestive and inviting tones. The voice of someone who knows what you want, what you think and what you fear, long before you ever say it. It knows you so well that it can anticipate your desires before you become aware of them, even things you wouldn't admit to others or to yourself. It knows your needs and places itself at your service without having to be asked. The ancient, sacred magic of augury and divination is now deployed through unfailing automated algorithms. Someone loves you. We know where you are right now. I know at what time you wake up each morning as if I were sleeping by your side. I know the precise moment you look at the cell phone on your nightstand, and where you go each day, and what the likelihood is that you will do a certain thing or take a certain route. You are our only concern. You, yes, you. The expression on your face—a little tired after a sleepless night, a little dazed and impatient—has been recorded by a camera in the ATM. Show us what makes you special. Hello, I am your new bank teller. We've improved our navigation so you can enjoy a better experience. We know the clothes, the flowers, and the brand of condoms you purchased today, and whether you changed your clothes since yesterday, and if you showered, and if you went to the hair salon and left a trace by making a call or checking your mail or paying with a credit card.

WE MOVE HEAVEN AND EARTH TO GIVE YOU THE BEST. You will never get lost again, because we know at every moment exactly where you are on Earth, what city, which block. We know more about you than anyone else, more than all the people who think they are close to you, more than your priest or your analyst. Even when you pay in cash, so your analyst does not have to declare it, we know who it is, how frequently you go, and where. We can predict with almost complete certainty which of the carelessly strewn magazines in the waiting room you will casually flip through. You open the website where you get your news exactly when we knew you would, to find on the front page a list of breaking stories that we have chosen, selected, tailored just for you. Since we know what book you briefly did a search for yesterday, we can offer it to you today on sale, flashing on the front page of a newspaper that we designed exclusively for you. We work for you. Let us drive for you. The old traffic safety ads used to say, "We cannot drive for you." That's no longer true. We can. Let us drive for you. We are always with you now, as faithful as your shadow, not just following your steps but predicting and directing them. Before long, there will be advertising screens on the street that will know when you go by and quickly offer you products suited just for you, temptations that exactly match your secret desires. Go where you didn't know you wanted to go.

WELCOME TO THE YOUNIVERSE. It's time to live a unique experience. Your time is now. The person of the year is you. You are on the cover of *Time* magazine. The cover is a mirror, a flexible mirror of reflective paper where you see a blurred image of your face. It looks good to be you. Now you'll see what you were missing. The world will be seduced by you. You will unleash uncontrollable passions. You choose how you live. A new world of sensations awaits you. You can make it come true from your cell phone. Manufactured just for you. Everyone's eyes will be on you. You will be a millionaire. Readers all over the world will know you. You're more than just another person. Every great story starts with you. You, yes, you. Nonstop you. Christmas is you. Your story awaits. You are the solution. You can drive the car of your dreams. Equipped with everything you need. Your style is always a step ahead. You can attain your dreams at any age. The smile you always wanted. All you need this summer. Performance in your hands. You are about to live the best moments of your life. You can start your journey today. You can go to places beyond words. The power is yours. You'll wish the road would never end. Life is smiling on you. What you need, when you need it. Seduction unleashed. Anytime you want it.

THE IRRESISTIBLE PULL OF FORBIDDEN DESIRE. Hot girls. A volcano in bed. Come see me. Unforgettable pleasure for body and soul. You walk through the city and the siren voices call. Young girls in flower sing just for you, tender girls in lovely harmonies that circle all around you, come be with us, or just one voice, melodiously calling. Drop your routine and come see me. I am real. I am waiting for you naked. An endless hum beneath the city noise, the flood of all the other voices, emitted at a frequency that is undetectable to the ear but not to the eye. You walk through the city and seem not to hear, not to notice, but a secret part of you answers to the ringing of that chord, that message that someone left under your windshield wiper and is waiting for you in the morning when you walk to your car, or in the door, or even on the sidewalk, left as if by chance or accident among the bits of trash, the cigarette butts, a bright piece of paper not much larger than a business card, whispering, confiding, six girls, new to the neighborhood, call us, free drink, total privacy. Five little friends are waiting for you.

WE'LL TAKE YOU TO THE LAST GREAT PARTY OF SUMMER. There's a telephone number, never an address. A code you can scan with your cell phone. They are always waiting for you. They go wherever you ask. House or hotel. Taxi fare not included. They sweetly specify how many minutes you can spend with them and what each minute costs. Sometimes there's a tempting parity: fifteen minutes, fifteen euros; each caress is timed, each soft rhythmic slap or thrust, each promise. Asian massage. Enjoy a little extra. The link between "Asian" and "massage" belongs primarily to the imagination. Body rubs. Happy ending. In this polyphonic siren song, ethnic and national variations are as rich and promising as the sound of a voice or an allusion to a special skill. Jenni from the Canaries. New in town. Elena from Paraguay. Dana from Poland. Crisna Supergreek Blonde. The language can suddenly turn corporate, its eroticism made even kinkier by its resemblance to motivational speaking. Specializing in all kinds of service. Maximum involvement. *Premium Massage.* Stunning Deborah. All in. Busty. Tight little ass. Each statement is a luring prophecy. My hands will soothe you. My mouth and body will give you pleasure. The city is a secret garden of fulfilled desires, a harem you can hire by the minute, a cloistered paradise that will open its doors to you when you show a little card somewhere or other, private apartment, total privacy, secluded house, having dialed a certain telephone number and followed a series of steps as in an old initiation ritual where you have to wear a blindfold. It's essential that there be a mystery to be gradually unveiled. Women display their breasts or lift their haunches up in the air, but their faces are concealed behind long, flowing hair, or blurred and pixelated, a little clouded oval that is all the more tempting by contrast to their brazen bodies and the exotic beauty of their mercenary names. Marilyn, Nikol, Karina, Karla, Martha, Anita, Dianita, Alicia, Lorena, busty, come and see, Latin, native French, I'm so lonely, all in, barely legal, thirty euros, real picture.

DOGS CAN SPORT THE NEWEST FASHIONS TOO. The end of summer in Madrid brings to a close as well a life of Edenic leisure. It was a summer of espadrilles, light shorts, a backpack, lazy weekends that seemed to stretch forever. Madrid in August is a rustic idyll that remains entirely unknown to those who leave and never see it. All that is bleak about Mondays is then gathered into the first working day of September. You go back to the office mournfully, back to your obligations and your pressing deadlines. You put on a kind of outward persona, like a formal suit that you kept in the closet for the past few months. You stick your hands in your pockets and find forgotten things. A ticket to a movie you cannot recall, despite the information tidily printed on the piece of paper, the time and day, the theater number, and the name of the movie itself, which draws a complete blank. A supermarket receipt. A restaurant bill. A flyer that you folded several times. A credit card receipt for a purchase at a bookstore. If you were in fact the person who bought those books, you never saw them again. You put on a jacket and feel as if you were usurping someone else's identity. The task must be deferred so you can make a living. You must go back to things that have an immediate practical purpose. You must submit to scrutiny and judgment.

THE NEW ICON OF MASCULINITY. But as I put on less casual clothes and leave grudgingly on a trip, a kind of traveling salesman for my own work, I realize that this will not in fact break off the task but rather blend with it, expanding it. The trip turns into the task without effort or forethought. The task was to wander through Madrid like a pilgrim or a traveler, recording conversations and picking things up off the ground. Now the task is to go to the airport and travel to France. Precisely that. And to listen to the radio in the taxi, and to look at every screen and every sign in Terminal 2, graciously receiving every flyer for a credit card or for an electronics store that is thrust in my path. There is a photograph of a Black woman with slightly parted lips that are painted a reddish gold. Unexpected. Unboring. Unlimited. Sitting at the gate, I record a conversation between two women behind me whom I cannot see. They talk enthusiastically about medical congresses and Caribbean resorts. "The international thyroid congress was in Orlando. Everything was fake. The lakes, the rivers, everything. We were taken to our sessions in canoes." "The next neurology congress will be in Alicante. They'll have real heads, you know, from cadavers." Across from me, a fat man with a mustache that is surely dyed is eating slices of salami, grabbing them from a plastic container that he ripped open in his eagerness and hunger.

BRING BACK CAPTIVATING FRAGRANCES FROM YOUR TRAVELS.
I carry with me everything I need: a pencil, a notebook, an eraser, a small
pair of plastic scissors so they won't be confiscated when I go through security, my cell phone with its camera and voice recorder. The pencil, which I
bought on my last trip, is already shorter than my thumb and hard to hold
between my fingers. I have a new one but I'm not ready to throw this one
away. It is immoral to throw anything away, anything that is worthy of respect and can be used again. Devout Jews did not throw out their copies of
the sacred scriptures when they began to come undone. They buried them
in special cemeteries, piously, with a ceremony. Throwing out written words
would be as inexcusable as throwing out bread when I was a boy. I keep my
used pencil in a cardboard box that once held a tin toy. I will put away my
pencils there when they can no longer be used. Suddenly I remember how
my grandfather, my mother's father, used to stick his cigarette butts with a
bit of saliva on a whitewashed wall in the garden, so he could smoke them
later if any tobacco was left.

**CHAQUE ACHAT DESSINE UN PEU PLUS VOTRE PROCHAIN VOY-
AGE.** Now I go to Paris and return to the same hotel where I stayed at the
start of summer, when the task was just beginning and I did not know exactly where it would lead. Not that I do now. There is no need for a project
when what I simply do by habit can give me such complete and childlike
fulfillment. When I first came to this hotel, I was about to move out of my
house and I had no idea how long it would be before I found a new one:
how many hotels, and trips, and stays in rented or in borrowed rooms.

While several hours each day will have to be devoted to work, I will also have long stretches of idle time. The receptionist at the Hôtel de l'Abbaye remembers me. I switch languages just as I switched out of my summer clothes to come here. The brain has strange unconscious mechanisms. I change coloring like a squid diving into a language I enjoy so much. The trip awakens a mimetic disposition that grows stronger with age. I would like to be able to change as easily as Thelonius Monk changed hats, with that mix of humor and calm earnestness. "A man of many hats," as they say. I'm always intrigued by the ability some people have to be eternally themselves no matter where they are or where they go, impervious to the surrounding atmosphere, never giving in to its flux, possessed of a cease-less constancy that is seemingly without effort. What I enjoy most about wandering on my own or speaking a different language is the partial in-terruption of identity. A brief holiday from yourself. Like the shopkeeper who hangs a sign on the door that says he will be out for a short while. He hasn't gone far, he will be back soon, but he will nevertheless have disap-peared, going off on his own or with someone else, in private, secretly, I wonder who. One of Eric Dolphy's greatest albums is titled *Out to Lunch!* I will have to try in the next few days to find these absent intervals among my obligations. You come back more clearheaded after a quick meal, a cup of coffee, a walk around the neighborhood, ready to be moored again in normalcy, to be with others. I need these intervals and I enjoy them. They have something in common with a hurried encounter between lovers or with the warmth of friendship.

THE PERFECT WAY TO START YOUR JOURNEY. There is no ambient music in the hotel lobby, just the sound of quiet conversations among guests. French hotels are free of that panicked aversion to anything old-fashioned that makes the common areas of Spanish hotels so unpleasant. Someone is coming soon to pick me up. I go into the courtyard to have a cup of coffee and I look around in the hope of seeing Isabelle Huppert again, as on that afternoon in June, the glow of her fair skin and the reddish gold of her hair. I could fall in love with Isabelle Huppert's face. I wonder if in the thirties this hotel might have been the kind of slightly sordid place where Walter Benjamin found lodging. There are iron chairs and tables in the garden and a large fountain in the shape of a tortoise. It was at the Hôtel de l'Abbaye that I woke up remembering a red sign for a hotel called the Cólera-Miró. Before leaving my room to come down to the lobby, I made sure to carefully arrange on the table the various implements that make up my office.

MALGRÉ LE TEMPS QUI PASSE. Looking at Fantin-Latour paintings in the Musée du Luxembourg I am seized by a powerful feeling that is shot through with grief, a kind of overwhelming joy imbued with gratitude and melancholy. The beauty of pure contemplation in his portraits and his vases of flowers holds me in its mesmerizing spell. Fantin-Latour depicts the very act of contemplation and so induces it as well in the viewer. He captures like no one else the spirit of pure absorption in a task that fills our inner life, stopping time or reaching beyond it: a woman reading; a man writing; a woman starting to draw and then pausing, standing still by a blank canvas facing a vase of flowers that contains at that moment all the mystery of reality and painting, the presence of motionless things. I try to imagine Emily Dickinson painted by Fantin-Latour. His vases of flowers radiate a sense of calm and spiritual contemplation as powerful as the statue of a meditating Buddha. Looking at his family portraits, and learning to recognize the faces that recur in them, I have the impression that he may have been in love with his sister-in-law, Charlotte, a haughty redhead that looks straight at the viewer, unlike her sister, Fantin's wife, who always avoids our gaze by taking refuge in a book or in a reverie. I too would have fallen in love with his sister-in-law. I even like her name. There is a sensuousness in names. One of the early signs that we are in love is a predilection for a certain name, a name that suddenly becomes mysterious, that we think about or whisper as if it were a secret, or say aloud and shiver.

A 3D JAW CAN GIVE YOU BACK YOUR SMILE. Charlotte's profile is that of a beautiful and assertive woman, her attitude suggesting imminent motion. In a family portrait where her parents and sister stay seated, statically ensconced in a rather bloated bourgeois domesticity, Charlotte is on her feet, dressed to go out (one glove is already on, she holds the other in her hand), eager to look out into the world, to go give German or English lessons to some pupil who must be secretly enthralled by her. Unless the private lessons are a lie, and Charlotte is on her way to meet her lover. It suddenly seems like a great pity that her brother-in-law never painted a nude portrait of her. Charlotte painted in the nude by Fantin-Latour would be more brazen and perturbing than Manet's Olympia. It is like imagining Caravaggio painting a nude portrait of his venal muse and model, Fillide Melandroni, with her mane of red hair. In each portrait he paints of Charlotte, Fantin-Latour watches her more intensely, discovering a new angle, a different aspect to her beauty. Love is a gaze that never rests and is never satisfied. His portraits are filled with a lover's joyful rapture at all the variations of the face he loves, like the changing beauty of the phases of the moon. In profile; foreshortened; facing him directly; smiling furtively to convey some secret that exists between them; or serious and composed; or restless. Perhaps I am just making up what I want to believe. But I feel as if I have been in those rooms, breathed their atmosphere, faintly veiled, the way the texture of the canvas shows through a most delicate layer of paint. Fantin-Latour is married to one sister but in love with the other, and what the three of them know but can never say is disclosed with cautious impudence in his painting. It is disclosed even now, right now, in the present, on this afternoon in late September 2016, in a room in the Musée du Luxembourg that is almost entirely empty.

YOU WILL TAKE INVISIBLE PICTURES. There is a chilling portrait of Baudelaire by Fantin-Latour: he is seated in a group, but completely alone. His face is pale, thin, smooth, clean-shaven. His long hair, combed back, is of a dark gray that seems at odds with the ravaged youthfulness of the face, the high forehead and the fixed, commanding eyes that seem to look at you from a height and also from deep within. In the empty room of the museum, Baudelaire's eyes seem to notice me and to exchange a glance.

AS UNIQUE AS YOU. Courbet, who painted a portrait of Baudelaire as a young man, complained of how difficult it was to achieve his likeness. The look on his face was too shifting, too fleeting to be captured by a pencil or a brush, a moving target that made it impossible to take aim. At a time when most men wore big beards and great mops of hair, his shaved face and lank hair, which was always combed back to reveal his forehead, gave him the striking aspect of a slightly sinister priest or (as an acquaintance once said) of a bishop in traveling clothes. Only priests used to shave back then. In Brussels it was rumored that he was an agent of the French secret police. In a self-portrait in pen and wash he appears as a dark, muffled figure; the lapels of his coat are turned up and the brim of his top hat almost covers his eyes. He looks sideways, as if plotting or keeping watch, a lit pipe in his mouth and the gaslights of a dark city behind him. He could be Dr. Henry Jekyll or Mr. Hyde. He could be Detective C. Auguste Dupin wandering through Paris at night, or Sherlock Holmes paying a visit to an opium den in the sordid alleys of the London docks.

HOW FAR WILL YOUR STYLE TAKE YOU. Baudelaire is that impassive, distant face that a young Catulle Mendès recognized in a crowd of strangers at a train station in Paris. He is an inquisitive figure strolling among the people and the trees on a sunny Sunday afternoon in the Tuileries, while a band plays in the distance. His friend, or rather his disciple, Manet, who knew him so well and was so fond of him, chose to draw his portrait as a stranger in the city crowd, one more among the bourgeois gentlemen dressed in a black coat and top hat. But it takes some effort to recognize Baudelaire among so many people, a crowd that seems festive at first but gradually becomes more and more stifling. He is off to one side, in profile, in the back, seemingly talking to others, recognizable by his mane of gray hair and his neatly shaven face. Then, as you look more closely at the painting, clicking and expanding that small area of the screen, his face turns out to be without features, just a dab of paint, barely outlined. The futility, which so alarmed Courbet, of trying to depict what is in constant motion. In a picture that Nadar took of him in 1855 his features are once more a little blurred and hazy. Sitting for a photograph back then meant keeping perfectly still for several minutes. Quick motions were invisible to photography. Of all surviving portraits of Baudelaire, the most mysterious was found just a few years ago. We cannot be certain it is really him, just as we do not know if Herman Melville is one of those bearded figures in top hats in an old photograph of the South Ferry, or Emily Dickinson one of two slightly aged women standing very close together in dark dresses and forbidding hairdos in a photograph I saw this winter at the Morgan Library in New York. Uncertainty heightens our desire to know. In the foreground of the photograph in question there is a man with big whiskers and pale eyes sitting in front of a studio curtain with a top hat on his lap. In the back, standing behind the curtain, barely pulling it aside with one hand like a person peering cautiously into a room, there is a figure with a blurry face that would appear to be, or one might say is almost surely, that of Baudelaire: straight hair, high forehead, shaved chin. And if it *is* him, one wonders what he was doing in that studio, what connection he had to the man sitting for his picture, whose identity has not been ascertained. It's like looking into a precise moment of the past through a time machine or bathyscaphe that is equipped with, among other instruments, a photographic camera.

DISCOVER THE SECRET OF YOUTH IN A PILL. Nadar lived until 1910. He survived his friend by forty-three years. During the first decade of the twentieth century, in those years before World War I that saw the rise of cinema, the automobile, the airplane, and the electric light bulb, there were a few people at least who would have remembered seeing Baudelaire fifty years earlier, in a long-lost Paris. Oscar Wilde, in his Parisian exile, could have met Nadar, and chatted with old people who would have told him what it was like to catch a glimpse of Baudelaire on the street; to recognize his face, his silhouette, to see him staring into space through the window of a café. Toulouse-Lautrec drew Oscar Wilde exactly as Manet had painted Baudelaire: as a stranger.

THERE COMES A DAY. At a certain point, the last thread of living memory snaps. When Walter Benjamin arrived as an émigré in Paris in 1933, no one who ever knew Baudelaire remained alive, though there were still people who had known Wilde, and Proust, and Degas. I once had dinner in New York with the poet Paul Pines, who in his youth had been a pupil of Heinrich Blücher, Hannah Arendt's husband. Suddenly, as in a blinding sequence of neural connections, an evening in March 2017 became linked by a string of memories to a past that had always been, for me, purely imaginary. Pines, a working-class Jew from Queens who had been in Vietnam during the war and later in the jungles of Guatemala, and who now lived in a house in the woods near the Canadian border, told me in that noisy restaurant that in the sixties he had been to Arendt and Blücher's house on Riverside Drive and 109th. Years later, in hindsight, Pines told me how grateful he was to have been a disciple of those German exiles, the last beacons, he said, and bearers of the great humanist culture of Europe. In Blücher's classes, and from their conversations in an apartment that was filled with books and whose big windows faced the Hudson, Pines said he had learned things that were vital to his intellect, his life, his rebellious sense of civic duty, and his calling as a writer. Had Benjamin lived, Paul Pines would have met him in Arendt and Blücher's apartment. James Joyce says that future events cast a shadow on the present. A past that might have happened throws a similar shadow on what came after. That is where the ghosts live, in that bit of conjectural space-time, their blurred faces peering from behind a curtain, moving incognito through the places where they might have lived.

DON'T MISS THIS ONCE-IN-A-LIFETIME OPPORTUNITY. "Too Much Happiness." That is the title of an Alice Munro story about a Russian mathematician, Sophia Kovalevsky, who was Fantin-Latour's contemporary. It is like a great Russian novel with all its scope and all its twists and turns compressed into thirty pages. Who knows how many times I have read it. The main character experiences a secret, inner sense of fulfillment during the same trip back from Paris to Stockholm where she contracts the illness that will kill her, on one of those trains that tunnel through the darkness of a European night in Russian novels. Often, during these past few days in Paris, or in other French cities to which I travel by train, I experience feelings that are too intense, as if I had been granted a secret explosion of momentary joy that cannot last, cannot exist without some kind of retribution or reversal. I gather precious mental images that are connected only by the motion of the train. Fantin-Latour's redheaded sister-in-law. Isabelle Huppert smiling as she talks with friends over a cup of tea in the courtyard of the Hôtel de l'Abbaye. The portraits and manuscripts of Baudelaire in the Musée de la Vie Romantique, which is housed in a small villa with a garden that could be in the middle of the countryside but actually stands at the end of a narrow, tunnel-like alleyway in Paris. The paintings and drawings he loved; the fierce handwriting of his letters and his dedications; the delirious, hypnotic quality of his eyes in those photographs by Nadar. Also the walk I took in Nantes this morning, the garden I found behind a church, with a fragrant fig tree, an inexplicable palm tree, a fountain that was level with the ground, from which fresh water gurgled. I had an hour on my own between two engagements and sat on a bench to hear the sound of the fountain and breathe in the scent of the fig tree, sheltered beneath its autumn splendor. Too much happiness. The silence and the sound of human voices in a garden tucked away behind a Gothic apse.

THE BEST MOMENTS ARE UNPLANNED. I recorded on my phone the silence and the sound of water that I heard in Nantes this morning, and then, this afternoon, I recorded the murmur of human voices in the squares of Toulouse, near the center of town, no cars, no horns, the brick facades were lit by the setting sun, the shops were closing, and all you heard were footsteps, voices, bicycles, the faint tinkle of their bells, people talking in the cafés. The sounds of the town and of people's lives could once again be heard. The sun was setting and a bit of soft, golden light remained on the upper stories of the buildings, all of them made of that red brick that seems devised expressly to reflect and to attenuate the sun. I went here and there, my hands in my pockets, tired and happy after several days of work, of meeting people, weighed down by the fatigue of travel and engagements but without any sadness, at peace with life in a town that seems expressly built to shelter and protect it.

ATTACKS ARE LAUNCHED ON CIVILIAN POPULATION TO FORCE REBELS TO A TRUCE. While I stroll through the main square of Toulouse, while I have breakfast at the café La Cigale in Nantes, beneath ceilings decorated with nymphs and diaphanous nineteenth-century ladies, in a room covered in green and yellow Art Nouveau tiles; while I walk along the banks of the Seine in Paris looking for traces of Baudelaire, Wilde, and Benjamin, or sit for a while by the great circular pool of the Luxembourg, looking at the toy ships, thinking about Temple Drake, Faulkner's beautiful redhead; while I fervently read Paul Valéry's writings on Degas, sitting by a window on a high-speed train that whisks me across the fertile fields and the ancient glow of Provence; all this time, as I do these things, bombs are raining down on Aleppo, destroying buildings that were already in ruins, finding their way to schools and hospitals, shaking the walls of basements filled with helpless people who will suffer and die, as in all wars, even though they had nothing to do with bringing them about, and have no interest in them. Along the Hungarian border, police are chasing people who fled Syria as they try to jump over coils of barbed wire. In the window display of an electronics store in Lyon an identical image of Donald Trump appears on a battery of curved-screen TVs, gesturing and moving his mouth as he stands before a sea of American flags. In the desert, on the outskirts of Amman, huge crowds of refugees gather among mountains of plastic trash, still terrified by the thundering noise of war. Right now, as I fly back from Lyon to Madrid over the flat and prosperous fields of France, the engines of military planes roar above Aleppo's battered streets, and bombs shake buildings and basements, blowing up windows, tossing up huge columns of debris into the air while people run blindly in a cloud of smoke and dust that blots out the light of day.

WE TAKE YOU WHEREVER YOU WANT. Insidiously, without warning, darkness returns like a familiar voice perceived from afar, among other voices in a train station. It may not be true darkness yet but rather the fear of darkness, an advance warning from a highly sensitive surveillance system. That sense of strangeness which suddenly comes upon you in a busy public place, perhaps a supermarket just before Christmas, or a train station, as you glide on a moving ramp down to the platforms and the waiting cars. It is not a localized pain but a vague discomfort that cannot be clearly defined, a grief that is all the more noticeable because it arrives suddenly and for no reason. You walk across the concourse and look up at the screens to find the platform number for your train. Suddenly you feel detached from everything around you, a sense of disconnection, a letting go, as if the ground had given way beneath you in a dream or gravity could no longer anchor your steps. You are now a stranger among your fellow human beings. Not on account of a subjective mood, or something in your character, but of a final separation, a fundamental difference that is hard to perceive from the outside; like a secret agent in a conquered country whose borders have been closed or like a traveler from the past—not the fixed and certain past of a history book but a recent past, just ten or twenty years back. It makes no difference that many of his old contemporaries are still alive and may preserve some memory of him. Even if they saw him, they wouldn't know what to say. There would be something monstrous in his strangeness.

AN UNMATCHED EXPERIENCE AT AN UNMATCHED PRICE. Ignorant of what everybody else knows. Dying without ever knowing that the Twin Towers would be attacked. Assuming there would always be telephone booths, video rental stores, well-stocked newsstands. Not realizing that those smooth black prisms everyone holds in one hand and mysteriously attends to are phones. Searching with anxious perplexity for buttons to press. Not knowing, when he is given by the receptionist what looks like a credit card, that it's the key to his room. Unable to recognize the faces in the paper, to understand most of the words it endlessly repeats, allusions that everyone else takes for granted, turns of phrase that became common during the years of his absence.

AS YOU MOVE YOU WRITE YOUR STORY ON THE EARTH. That is what you are when the darkness returns, the pain, the fear of fear, and of the poisonous voice that in fact disappeared not so long ago, just a few months back, not even a year. Then you see, far off in the crowd of travelers at the station, the figure you hadn't seen for several months, thinking it had vanished when perhaps it had only become invisible. You see it and you feel an urge to walk faster so as not to be found. You want to go down to the tracks as soon as possible and you also want to abandon your trip, fearing that you will see it in the train, in the next car over or the seat behind you, if not the one right next to you. It would be best to leave the station while you still have time, like a secret agent in a hostile country, giving those who follow him the slip at the last possible moment. Assuming you are still in time. Assuming there is not already someone following behind, unnoticed, watching your every step.

EXTRAORDINARY THINGS HAPPEN EVERY DAY. Officials have also expressed concern that returning residents could be attacked by the boars, which have settled comfortably into houses and farms in the years since the explosion, and lost their fear of humans. Photographs and video footage from the affected cities are reminiscent of Chernobyl, where wild fauna has continued to flourish despite high levels of radioactivity. Due to the absence of human beings, the region around the Ukrainian city of Chernobyl has become a sanctuary for all kinds of animals, including deer, brown bears, wolves, and lynx. Videos taken by journalists in Fukushima after the 2011 nuclear disaster show large packs of dogs roaming the roads. Colonies of rats have taken over the supermarkets. Agricultural lands have quickly reverted to wild prairies that provide a perfect habitat for foxes and boars.

BEYOND THE LIMITS. Damage by wild boars to farms near the reactor already amounts to $845,000. Local authorities are recruiting hunting parties in an attempt to reduce the wild boar population. But the species' reproductive capacity seems to exceed by far the number of animals killed. Authorities in the town of Tomioka say they have hunted and killed eight hundred, a number that does not seem significant. While the total number of boars hunted in a year was three thousand in 2014, it had risen to thirteen thousand by the end of last year. Aside from hunting, emergency measures being evaluated include installing special traps and using drones to frighten off the animals from inhabited areas. The neighboring city of Nihonmatsu dug up three pits to bury the remains of 1,800 boars, but local authorities say there is no more room for further burials, especially taking into account the risk of radioactive contamination entailed by such a large number of buried creatures. Last year the city of Soma installed specially designed incinerators to burn the remains and filter out cesium so it would not be released into the atmosphere. The project was suspended due to a lack of personnel to carry the carcasses and throw them in the incinerator.

3D IS EVERYWHERE. Walter Benjamin fled Berlin in March 1933 leaving everything in his apartment exactly as it was, his furniture, his library, his collection of children's toys and books. For the next five years he was without a fixed address, a home, a place to leave in the morning and lock the door and later go back to. An entire congress of Perambulation, a mountain of documents and research papers will be devoted to his comings and goings between the spring of 1933 and January 1938, when he finally moved into a small furnished apartment in Paris, tiny but with a balcony that looked out over the city, up on a seventh floor but a little noisy since it was right next to the big piece of machinery that hoisted the elevator. It was only for that reason, and because it was a very old apartment, that Benjamin was able to afford it. Tracing his movements during those five years requires a map of Europe and other maps as well: one of Ibiza, for instance, and one of Paris. In March 1933 Benjamin arrived in Ibiza after spending two weeks in the Hotel Istria in Paris. He had sold his collection of ancient coins. In Ibiza, where he had spent his holidays just a year earlier, in 1932, before he became an exile, he now found that life had become more expensive and noisier. From a plurisensory as well as a multidisciplinary perspective, one could speculate that Benjamin's movements were due in part to a permanent and hopeless attempt to find quiet. On the island, he tries to escape from the noise of the wind, the noise of the guests coming through the thin walls of the hotel, the noise of drunks at night, the noise of workers opening ditches and raising new buildings. In order to write in peace, he grabs a folding chair and table, as well as the satchel with his pen, his papers and books, and hides away in a pine grove. The wind blows his writing off the table. The prospect of making a living is highly uncertain. Jewish authors are not allowed to publish in Germany. The émigré newspapers pay almost nothing, or have no readers, or both. Benjamin rents a room in a boarding-house for one peseta a day. Soon after, he can no longer afford it. An acquaintance lets him have a room in a house that is under construction. The room has walls and a ceiling, but the rest of the house is a building site. In Ibiza he smokes opium with a German friend. There is a window in the room with a curtain that sways in the wind. Benjamin invents the word *curtainology*. He says, entranced, that curtains are interpreters of the language of the wind.

GET READY FOR THE COLD. His only steady income is the rent he receives for his Berlin apartment. "I have nothing and I am attached to nothing," he says in one of his letters. He suffers the additional calamity of losing his fountain pen. Without his pen and a good notebook, he is unable to write. His inspiration depends on his writing materials. An academic traveled to Ibiza in the nineties and interviewed some old people who still remembered Benjamin: his clothes, formal though quite tattered, and his plodding walk.

EXPERIENCE IT AGAIN LIKE THE FIRST TIME. He goes back to Paris in the fall, or the beginning of winter. He is horrified by the grayness of the city, the lowering sky and rain, the xenophobia of the French. At the post office he hears someone say, "The émigrés are worse than the krauts." Each day he eats at a cheaper restaurant. Every few weeks he changes hotels. With the aid of a map of Paris and some old telephone books it is possible to reconstruct his movements. His tangled path crisscrosses the city grid: Hôtel Régina, Hôtel Le Palace, Hôtel Floridol, Hôtel Panthéon, Hôtel Littré. He says he lives in the perpetual murmur and fog of depression. He knows he is entirely outside the world. His life takes place among strangers, surrounded by indifference and hostility. The people he cares for are far away and he can only communicate with them by mail. He avoids the cafés where the German émigrés come together only to embroil themselves in the same useless, passionate disputes as when they lived in Germany, nursing a hope of return that seems childish to him. He must have run into Joseph Roth without knowing it. He crosses paths with French writers whom he knows well and for whom he is invisible. He is forty-one, he has spent his whole life studying and writing and he has nothing, and he is no one. "The present intellectual industry finds it impossible to make room for my thinking, just as the present economic order finds it impossible to accommodate my life."

YOU THINK YOU HAVE DISCOVERED EVERYTHING. For a few months someone lends him a tiny room with a shared bathroom in an apartment with other tenants. Then he moves into a maid's room in the house of a family that is away on vacation. It is in a busy part of town, and the noise of traffic barely allows him to sleep or to do any work. During the summers he is invited by Bertolt Brecht to join him and his family at a country house they rent in Denmark. Brecht is a German exile, but a famous one, well known as a fugitive from the Nazis wherever he goes; someone, too, who will make it out in time and reach California, where he will join Thomas Mann, Arnold Schönberg, the upper echelon of the émigrés. Everyone seems better than Benjamin at making a go of it, at finding a position in life. Adorno travels to the United States in the company of his beautiful wife, Gretel Karplus, having secured an academic position at Princeton. There are always those who make it and those who drown; those who see it coming before others and take measures in advance; those who get there early and those who stay at the back of the line; those who outrun the rest and those who are clumsy and slow and let the devil take the hindmost. While others find a way out, Benjamin remains trapped in Europe, watching them leave, just as Miguel Hernández, at the end of the Spanish Civil War, saw his companions get on a plane but stayed behind because no one had saved him a seat.

DISCOVERING NEW THINGS IS WHAT KEEPS YOU ALIVE. To have a little distance from the racket of Brecht's family life—his children, his wife, his lover, his sycophants, his parasites—Benjamin rents a room in a nearby farmhouse. He finally has a large table to do his work. His friend Gretel Karplus has sent part of his Berlin library to Brecht's holiday house.

But the children are so noisy that Benjamin considers renting a room in a separate house, a place no one goes near because the owner is mentally deranged. There are no newspapers, or they arrive several days late, but every night the radio delivers its dark news. Hitler's barking in Berlin is heard through the airwaves in the Danish countryside. Benjamin plays chess with Brecht. They discuss the plot of a detective novel that they plan to write together.

ANYTHING YOU WANT, AT A PRICE YOU'LL APPRECIATE. He returns to Paris at the end of summer feeling increasingly trapped. He spends his days writing letters or waiting for them, filled with dread when they fail to arrive, sometimes having to gather his courage before opening an envelope. Letters fly from one European city to another, or they bear exotic postage stamps from New York, Shanghai, Jerusalem. His brother has been taken, tortured by the gestapo, and sent to a concentration camp. All traces of Asja Lācis have vanished in the great totalitarian silence that envelops Moscow. At least his ex-wife and son are safe in England. The names of New York City streets seem even more poetic to him because they appear on envelopes bearing letters from Gretel Karplus, now Gretel Adorno. The GPS of the past will show that Benjamin moves in an ever-narrower circle. The ground sways beneath his feet when he steps out each morning to walk to the Bibliothèque Nationale, in his dignified and ruined suit, his inadequate glasses, and his old satchel under one arm, like the professor he has not managed and will never manage to become. The world is crumbling around him, but slowly, silently, so no one seems to notice. People sit at the cafés, out on the sidewalk, smoking, sipping cognac, and calmly opening the newspaper, which is filled with terrifying headlines. Benjamin himself is crumbling inward beneath the weight of a relentless depression, a silent darkness that began to stalk him when he was quite young and that has now returned, strengthened and made more virulent by a real and external terror. He thinks he will be relatively safe if he can become a French citizen. To file his petition, he needs official documents that are supposed to arrive from distant offices in Germany. Everything takes a long time. Everything takes a long time and everything is urgent. Though it all seems fine on the surface, he knows, he feels that something awful is already taking place, that something beyond repair is happening to him. He is unable to separate fear from remorse. He is helpless and he is also guilty. If only he had moved when there was still time, if only he had gotten his papers together, made a real effort to emigrate anywhere at all, to Palestine or the United States. He thought as well of emigrating to the Soviet Union, but what he read in the newspapers and Asja Lācis's unaccountable silence made him abandon that thought.

SOMETHING EXTRAORDINARY EVERY DAY. He can't see well. He needed a new pair of glasses long ago, but he has no money to go to the eye doctor or to pay for them. What is most startling is not how desperately poor he has become, but that, having so few and such basic needs, he is unable to meet them. The more his expectations diminish, the more unattainable they seem to become. Soon he will no longer be able to afford even a humble destitution. Others indulge in political delusions, or get drunk, or dream of going back home. They try in one way or another to build themselves an artificial paradise. German, and now Austrian exiles too, argue heatedly in the cafés and claim that Hitler's days are numbered. Joseph Roth and Walter Benjamin cross paths on a narrow sidewalk but neither one recognizes the other: one of them can barely see, the other is drunk.

EXPERIENCE ALL THE EMOTION. But who is he to question other people's artificial paradises. He himself says in a letter that he must write a book in which he can take shelter. Even as the world crumbles around him in slow motion he never stops writing. During his years of exile, poverty, depression, loneliness, and panic, he writes better and more perceptively than ever. He would write even better if he didn't feel obligated to share in the fashionably obscure philosophical abstractions that are so dear to his friends. Several generations of college professors and questionable experts will live comfortably and parasitically on what he wrote during those years of anguish. Each morning, as punctual as an office worker, Walter Benjamin combs his dark hair in front of a cloudy mirror; puts on his jacket and tie; places his books, his notebooks, and his pen in the satchel; and walks to the Bibliothèque Nationale, trying unsuccessfully to ignore the day's newspapers that are already on display at the corner kiosks. At the entrance, he allows himself the humble satisfaction of showing the clerk his library card: name, address, photograph, some kind of credential or certificate; an official document allowing him, at least for now, free access to those warm, quiet reading rooms where he will spend the whole day and hardly notice it.

ALL YOU NEED AND MORE. His friend Gisèle Freund took several pictures of him at work in the library, surrounded by books and by pieces of paper and stacks of index cards. You don't realize—as you think absentmindedly about an idea, then jot something down, then set it aside to attend to something else—that you have begun a task that will last the rest of your life, that will in fact remain unfinished when that life is over. In one of his former lives, when he still had a country and his future seemed certain, he thought of writing an article about the commercial arcades of Paris. Nothing too long, something he could finish in a day or two. It was a random thought, an idea that came to him as he read somewhat distractedly a book by Louis Aragon, *Le paysan de Paris*. It was an appealing project but nothing too elaborate, one of those pieces that he enjoyed writing so much, a shining fragment, to be read in a café in the crowded pages of a newspaper. He only thought of it again a few years later, in 1934, when he was once again in Paris, though now in exile. What five years earlier had been an idea for a short article seemed to be turning now into an essay, maybe ten or fifteen pages long. The main obstacle was not a lack of inspiration or of sources but a lack of paper, or rather of the exact kind of notebook on which he had written the first few drafts, and which was unavailable in Paris. A book does not exist in a writer's imagination but in the blank pages of the notebook where it is yet to be written. He sent a letter to Gretel Karplus in Berlin asking that she go to a certain stationer's, buy the kind of notebook he required, and send it to him in Paris as soon as possible.

I WILL ALWAYS REMEMBER. What had lain compressed in a first image, a simple seed that might have yielded its fruit in two or three pages, burst suddenly in his mind and his imagination like a chain reaction, a blaze of connections and possibilities that seemed to encompass the entire city where he lived in exile as well as the century of its growth, spreading before him as stunningly in time as it rose all around him in space. He had started by wanting to write about a certain commercial arcade in Paris and had found instead a treasure map, the map of the city itself, and of all the successive strata of time that lay in jumbled sediments within it. It was Paris and it was Berlin, which he would never see again. It was him, in the present, reading, writing, taking notes in the Bibliothèque Nationale, and it was the man he had been in his youth, when he first found Baudelaire and began to translate his poems, and then, through Baudelaire, found other explorers who had roamed the cities of Europe and the United States before him: De Quincey, Poe, Melville, Stevenson, their horror stories, their detective stories, the seedy world of crime in the yellow press. He walked down the same streets where Baudelaire had lived. Just like him, Benjamin had to change his address repeatedly and to accept the humiliation of working himself to the bone without ever being free of the most destitute need. Baudelaire had depicted the simultaneous rapture and horror of Paris as an ever-changing modern city: the gaslights, the omnibus, the risk of crossing an avenue on foot while dodging carriages and horses, the dull, relentless flood of advertising bills and posters everywhere. Benjamin studied the city just as carefully, his senses sharpened by his foreignness. Paris was an endless roar of automobiles, a dazzling glare, now that the gaslights were gone, with galaxies of electric lights spreading across the facades of the movie theaters. Like Baudelaire, Benjamin saw everything through a fog of illness, knowing himself to be as alone and destitute in Paris as on a desert island, scavenging for scraps and waste and cheap attractions like those drunken ragmen that Baudelaire had elevated to prophetic greatness.

IT TAKES YOU TO AMAZING PLACES. He wrote hurriedly, with a fountain pen, on the sheets of paper that Gretel Karplus sent him or on anything else he could find. An uncertain and fugitive existence had taught him to write anywhere, in a crowded café, a subway car, the movies, using the armrest as a support before the lights went out. "Do not allow a single thought to escape you unawares, and keep your notes as strictly as the authorities keep their registry of foreigners." The more progress he made, the farther he was from an ending, since each new step unveiled uncharted possibilities that had to be pursued. If a particular book added to his knowledge and strengthened what he had already said, it forced him at the same time to revise passages that he thought were settled, and pointed to yet other books that he should find. As he wrote and read, he saw the richness of the work that opened gradually before him, but he became aware as well of the magnitude of the task he had begun, and of the time, the energy, the peace and quiet he would require to see it through. He was hobbled by ceaseless distractions, an article he had to write to earn a little money, filing forms to renew his refugee card or apply for nationality, the frequent need to change his address. He was disheartened as much as he was inspired by the profusion of materials involved, a maelstrom of names, ideas, and arguments that the work itself stirred up inside him and that never grew still. He could leave behind the dusty smell of the Bibliothèque Nationale, the tightly printed volumes from which he gathered facts about the nineteenth century, but once he set foot on the street there was no rest and no respite, since then it was the modern city that demanded his attention, surrounding him in even richer layers of materials to consider. He would go through bound sets of old magazines, gazing at lithographic illustrations and at advertisements for long-forgotten products, then go out and look intently at the signs over the shops and the cafés or at a color poster glued to the side of a streetcar.

THE IMPORTANCE OF LIGHT. He realized that, more than writing a book, he was assembling a collage made up of hundreds of pages of citations, fragments, sketches, drafts he had no time to develop. The further he went, the harder it became to order the materials he had gathered into an intelligible shape. Using a series of colored pencils, he devised an alphabetical system to classify his various subjects, which he then copied in his diminutive, meticulous handwriting, perhaps unaware that this attempt at clerical tidiness would nourish chaos instead of bringing it under control. Fashion, the catacombs of Paris, boredom, eternal return, cast-iron buildings, advertisements, the practice of collecting, architectural interiors, exhibitions, Baudelaire, imaginary cities, imaginary houses, dreams of the future, Jung, the theory of emotions, the theory of progress, prostitution, games of chance, mirrors, trains, conspiracies, painting, lighting technology, photography, dolls, auto-mata. Then, bleary eyed, pushing his glasses up to his forehead, he goes over the column he just wrote, the thin vertical thread of capital letters, sliding his pen down the page like a clerk going over a sum. As time goes on and disaster approaches, as it grows harder to keep up his spirits and even to main-tain his personal dignity, the project becomes more and more a matter of survival. "In this work I see the main if not the only reason not to lose cour-age in the struggle for existence." Quite near the end he begins to lose hope: "Whether the book will ever be written is more doubtful than ever before."

II.

MR. NOBODY

I'm Nobody! Who are you?
Are you—Nobody—too?

—EMILY DICKINSON

I, WHO HAVE BEEN SO MANY MEN. Opening his eyes in the dark, and hearing nothing but silence, he has no way of telling what city he is in or of guessing the time of day, the day of the week, the year, the period of his life. He has no name, at present, no face, and no biography. There is no clear boundary in his mind between sleep and waking, just as there is none between his shadowy limbs and the dark shapes of objects in the room or the very darkness of the air. He could be in Madrid, London, Paris, Lisbon. He could be waking up from a drunken stupor or an opium dream in a hovel crammed with manuscripts, books, and old newspapers, somewhere in Edinburgh; or on a tavern floor in Baltimore, his mouth pressed against the filthy boards, a thread of blood or spittle at the corner of his lips. He could be opening his eyes in a room with whitewashed walls inside a boarding-house in Ibiza or in Portbou. As it grows brighter, it will be possible to tell if the sky in the window is a flat gray, which could mean Paris in winter or perhaps Berlin. When the first morning sounds become audible they will provide him with further clues. The scrape of a shovel on the sidewalk will reveal that he is in New York, where it snowed all night and the doormen are busy opening paths outside their buildings. Or he may hear the bell on the watchtower, and then the one that rings the hours in the cathedral, and almost simultaneously the low tones of the Chancery clock. Then he would be in Granada, in an old house somewhere in the Albaicín.

THE WAY YOU MOVE CAN SAY A LOT ABOUT YOU. Today he woke up before dawn because it is the day of the journey. He had set an alarm to be safe, but there was no need. Occasionally during the night he surfaced from sleep and glanced at the red numbers on the clock. Then he plunged back, never quite awake, sometimes picking up the thread of a dream that he will probably fail to remember later. He opened his eyes feeling very alert and saw gray strips of light between the shutters. Out on the street the day is breaking, but in the bedroom it is still night. He can tell how early it is primarily because of the silence: the same silence that lay all around him when he fell asleep, the same in which he now spends so much of his time. He lives surrounded by a portable booth of silence. He is enclosed in it when he goes out and he reenters it when he comes back to the apartment and draws the safety latch on the door. All the voices are left behind. The written voices, the ones he overhears in passing, even the ones that speak to him in dreams. The insidious voice that used to perch in his ear whispering a black virulence seems to have lost his scent, along with the circling shadow that was beginning to lurk around him again. Now he does know where he is, as well as the time and day, though he may only have the merest inkling yet of who he is. I, who have been so many men.

TRAVEL LIGHTER, GO FARTHER. He has fled into silence. He has taken refuge in silence and distance as in a monastery. He starts making breakfast, but he only turns on the radio when everything is on the table. The inner courtyard is still dark outside the kitchen window. On the building opposite, just two or three windows are lit on different floors. They have an intimate glow suggesting sheltered spaces, bedrooms tucked away in the back of apartments. One of them must be the one that casts the reddish glow he sees at night. He arranges everything as carefully as if he were sharing it with someone else. People who are alone but wish to preserve a certain decorum treat themselves with a kind of sleepwalking politeness. Before sitting down he tunes the radio to a local station and the hosts with their familiar voices seem to join him at the table like guests or companions. Their voices reach him with greater clarity because his mind is as quiet as the apartment itself: a clapping of hands in an empty room. He hears the British voices of the BBC presenters. He hears the voices of people speaking in English with various accents and varying degrees of difficulty as they give witness to disaster, telling in their native languages (while simultaneously translating) the torture or abuse or persecution they endured. In the early morning silence you can hear helicopter blades, the clamor of starving refugees in makeshift camps, the toxic slogans of the demagogues, and the drone of charlatans. The roar of a tempest, the cry of birds in a tropical swamp are broadcast on the BBC. When you're alone you gain a strange intimacy with the voices on the radio, which are always the same, at the same time of day. It is as one-sided as an unrequited love, yet it is never painful, only melancholy.

ENJOY YOUR TRAVEL TIME. Today, aside from scrubbing and putting everything away after breakfast, he must make his preparations for the journey. Over the past few days he has traced the route with great care. He has made sure as far ahead as possible that the weather will be favorable, or at least not adverse. This will be a genuine expedition, but there will be no taxicabs, no rush, no traffic jams, no documents to verify, no security lines, no bewilderment or distress. It will be a real, substantial journey, a voyage of discovery, but it will take place in the course of a few hours. De Quincey says that under the influence of opium he sometimes lived a thousand years in a single night. More modestly, and in complete sobriety, he hopes to traverse a handful of worlds. He knows that in the absence of artificial stimulants he can experience the lucid inebriation brought about by solitude and exercise.

EXPERIENCE THE SPELL. The weather forecast on the radio belies the glow of sunlight that begins to spread over the window. It will be colder than this sweet, deceitful light would promise, but there will be no wind, or at least not much. You have to look at the people down on the sidewalk, see how bundled up they are, the early risers taking a dog to the park or hurrying the other way toward the taxis and the subway stop. Provisions are just as important. According to the radio, the temperature at midday will allow him to sit outdoors on a bench somewhere and have a bite to eat. There are several rules to the trip, one of which is that he stop to rest only once, and neither at a restaurant nor a café, given that another rule forbids any purchase except in an emergency or on a sudden whim, abiding always by a principle of frugality. You are only allowed to eat what you bring, and if you procure anything it must be as a gift, in barter, or at most in passing, from a street stand, since all stops must be kept to a minimum. The food must be nourishing but easy to digest and carry. There can be frugality without meagerness, a delight in what is flavorful, nutritious, simple.

CONNECT WITH WHAT YOU REALLY LIKE. He prepares, for instance, two slices of rye toast with olive oil, tomatoes, a few slices of prosciutto from the deli, and a couple of scrambled eggs. Each egg, as he cracks the shell, reveals a yolk as yellow as a sun, the bright color of autumn pumpkins and of taxicabs. The smallest detail is deserving of the right attention. He is the traveler risen at dawn to get underway, turning on one of the first lights in a building that is otherwise in nearly complete darkness. A Zen master is asked, What is satori, the state of enlightenment?: "Chopping wood," he says, "carrying water." Pressing down on the sandwich, he wraps it in foil and places it inside his worn, supple satchel of dark leather, the one with all the buckles, along with a canteen, a bag of dried fruit, and a small bottle of wine. He wipes the table and the kitchen counter and he scrubs the dishes, putting everything back in its right place. Disorder will enter an empty house if it is given the merest crack of neglect. Setting out on the journey without first making the bed would be like carrying a dishonorable secret inside. He checks to make sure the laces of his boots are tight and that his feet are snug and comfortable. His phone is fully charged. He has his keys. In the right pocket of his coat there is a small spiral notebook and a pencil. He is wearing his round glasses and his bewildered face, and he has his satchel, with a pair of added shoulder straps to make it easier to carry on such a long journey.

FIND EVERYTHING YOU NEED. He must bring a book as well, since part of the trip will be on the subway. Choosing it will take a little time. It must be thin, not too large, and weighing almost nothing, pleasant to hold and to feel inside his coat pocket; a book that opens and closes like a fan, somewhat confidential or perhaps elusive, flowing like a piece of music or a long walk or resembling an object floating in midair; a book combining the factual nature of a guide or manual with the impudent secrecy of an intimate diary; full of blank spaces, some visible and some invisible; a book that seems posthumous even though its author is still alive, and whose voice is anonymous and at the same time unique, seeming as if freshly written although it was published a century or two ago; a book with a beginning and an end that nevertheless seems unfinished, resembling at the same time a hastily improvised draft and a concise inscription.

WIN AN ONLY-YOU EXPERIENCE. Before leaving the apartment he takes a last look around. He feels there should be a kind of consummate perfection or civility to one's absence. A cautiousness as well: to leave, in a world of ceaseless, ubiquitous, invisible surveillance, as small a trace as possible. "He enters the woods without stirring a single leaf; he enters the water without causing the slightest ripple." Perhaps at some point in the past he studied Taoism in some depth. He will aspire, perhaps simply out of indolence, to the exacting wisdom of doing-by-not-doing. The less of a mess you make, the less you or someone else will have to clean up. He will have taken care when showering to use the least possible amount of gel, shampoo, and water. He has swept the crumbs off the table. He has opened the window, which is quite bright already, to let the cold and slightly humid air of late winter into the room. Whenever he prepares to go out, he tries to see everything as others would if they came in during his absence; what they would see or find if he never returned. Whoever comes will find a few small signs and traces, but no trash. They will be able to settle in as nicely as those travelers in fairy tales who come to a house in the woods that's perfectly arranged to receive them although no one is there. He wants to be conspicuous only in his absence.

UNEXPECTED DREAMS. This morning you have to bundle up to be outside. A hooded coat, a wool cap with earflaps, a scarf, some gloves, a thick sweater, a good undershirt. Keeping the cold at bay when you plan to be outdoors for many hours requires a certain expertise, the taking of particular precautions. From the window, the new day glows with a treacherous light, a glare of early spring belied by people's coats and hats, by their gestures as they walk down the street. He has wrapped in foil his hearty, juicy sandwich of olive oil, tomatoes, prosciutto, and freshly made scrambled eggs that give the bread a pleasant warmth. He has filled the canteen with water and a small plastic bottle halfway with red wine. He is also bringing some pistachios. Pistachios are an excellent way to replenish your strength as the hours pass and you start feeling weak. There is a sense of adventure to it all, a wealth of preparations, as at the start of an expedition.

SQUEEZE THE MOST OUT OF THE CITY. He believes that, whenever possible, it is better to go on foot to places that hold something precious that we wish to discover, something that cannot be found anywhere else and that is worthy of being honored by the effort of a walk. One need not go to extremes, like Catholic pilgrims crawling on their knees through stone and bramble to a miraculous shrine, or Buddhists lying prone, and getting up, and lying prone again for the entire length of their journey. Walking tones the body, oxygenates the brain, and predisposes the mind to a proper contemplation of the object one goes in search of. Thought and feeling are brought to order with every step. The body's external motion propels as well the flow of words and of ideas. A friend of Baudelaire's once said that he never saw him write a poem sitting down. He composed them as he walked, speaking quietly to himself. The rhythm of his verses was the rhythm of his steps. Montaigne paced back and forth in his round study, dictating to his secretary whatever came to mind, sometimes prompted by the spine of a random book on the shelves or by something he saw down in the courtyard or in a nearby field from the high casement of his tower.

VENTURE INTO THE WORLD. It's about eleven o'clock and he is walking up Broadway. Several hours remain to his journey. He wants to cover on foot the entire distance between the southern tip of the island and the house where Edgar Allan Poe once lived in the Bronx. He set off from South Ferry more than two hours ago, from the esplanade facing the mouth of the river at the southern end of the island. He pictured, as if it were an actual memory, Herman Melville as a boy, walking hand in hand with his father back when a forest of masts and rigging would have spread across the horizon. He saw the ocean crashing against poles where sailing ships once moored. He heard the horns of ferries coming over from Staten Island and of leisure boats packed with tourists heading out to the Statue of Liberty. Unnerving seagulls wailed and swung in the air above his head. Once, from this railing, he threw into the sea the core of an apple he had just eaten, and a seagull nearly grazed his head as it swept and plunged into the water to retrieve it, flapping and letting out shrill cries to ward off the other seagulls that wanted it too. He walked past the steps of the old Custom House that is now the National Museum of the American Indian. Herman Melville never knew this big, emphatic building with its marble and its statuary. He worked in a precarious shed-like structure by the river's edge. He was taller and more serious than the other men around him, a kind of Boris Karloff with the beard of an Assyrian potentate.

CONNECTED TO EVERYTHING. He came up the dark canyon of lower Broadway through the financial district, running into flocks of tourists and bank clerks and executives. The waves of tourists are as tightly packed as on the Rialto in Venice. From the loading dock for the Statue of Liberty to the bronze bull that symbolizes either finance or the stock exchange there is an overwhelming flood of tourists. They come from the far corners of the Earth to take selfies, raising extendable sticks high above the heads of all the other tourists. They crowd around a terrified squirrel to take its picture. They press against the bronze bull as if taking part in an atavistic ritual, circling, lifting the selfie stick as if it were a candle or a liturgical object. A very fat woman in a wheelchair is stuck in the middle of a crowded group of Chinese tourists. Garbage overflows from metal cans on every corner. Homeless people rummage inside to find slices of pizza, a half-finished bottle of Coke, a hot dog with the ends chewed off.

EMBARK ON A ONE-OF-A-KIND EXPERIENCE. He has seen the homeless stationed along Broadway at a certain distance from one another: the silent ones, who stay still, wrapped in blankets and sleeping bags, and the ones who pace the sidewalk, accosting people and shaking plastic cups with a rhythmic jingle of coins. The ones who sit on the ground are white and do not say anything. The ones who pace the sidewalk or prop themselves against a building or a piece of scaffolding are usually Black. He looks as he goes by at the signs written on pieces of cardboard. There are army veterans, HIV patients, blond kids, pale and staring into space or reading and writing, never asking aloud. A woman in her forties with disheveled hair is sitting on an upturned plastic bucket, smoking and holding on her knees the cardboard sign that tells of her misfortunes. Sometimes there are two of them, a boy and a girl, always blond, blue-eyed, with dirty faces. They huddle together or against a big dog dozing at their side. Today their faces and their hands are red on account of the cold, red and slightly blue. A young man sits alone by a cardboard sign that says he killed his father to stop him from abusing his mother and sister, and was then put in a psychiatric ward. Melville walked these streets and so did Bartleby, his imaginary clerk. A city of low houses, of docks and sailing ships, of churches, graveyards, darkness lit by whale oil. Only the churches and the graveyards with their worn headstones remain. Large open spaces used to spread to the north where the narrow streets gave way: Broadway ended and the old winding footpath of the Lenape began. It was an island of forests, hills, low swamps and marshes, streams and lakes. Trappers had killed off all the beaver for their fur. Of the Lenape, all that remained was a small population living on a patch of virgin forest at the island's northern end. Herman Melville witnessed all of this. Poe did as well, or some of it at least, during those last years of heartbreak and misfortune in the city, or rather in what used to be a rural area of Dutch-style farms and peasant houses lying well outside the town. Poe and Melville know each other. They cross paths on their walks through the troublesome city, a muddy waste of horse manure and filthy snow during the winter months, or they find themselves at the same book-shop or as guests at functions given by wealthy women with literary tastes. Melville has read Poe's tales of terrors at sea: the one about the shipwrecked sailors caught in the maelstrom; the one about the traveler who reaches the ice fields of the South Pole.

BEYOND ALL LIMITS. The Mississippi of Broadway, Melville says; the Amazon, the Nile. At Fifth Avenue and Forty-Second Street stood the city's water reservoir, which resembled an Egyptian citadel or temple. There was a prison known as The Tombs that had an Egyptian portico with tall, thick columns crowned by capitals in the shape of lotus flowers. The city grad-ually altered over time much as Broadway alters in the course of the walk. Avidly he traverses its many worlds, its times and places. To walk is to do something and to do nothing. It means wandering aimlessly along but also in a particular direction traced by the course of a street that he has fol-lowed from its very beginning. He stays always on Broadway and always on the west side of the street, the one in the sun. He has gone through noisy, crowded stretches and through places of sudden silence: the violent beating of a hammer on the metal plates with which they cover potholes; bulldozers digging into the asphalt and cracking it open to lift up piles of debris; pneu-matic drills that make the earth shake and the windows rattle; giant trucks from Canada or the Pacific coast. A ripped-apart, eviscerated city, a city under construction and under destruction. He has walked past trenches as deep as craters that take up entire city blocks where colossal buildings were still standing just yesterday. He has seen latticed metal structures rise and grow and turn from one day to the next into glass towers. This is the clat-tering work and the machinery of the world, the seismic and volcanic force of money shaking the island to its innards of hard schist.

COME EXPERIENCE SOMETHING DIFFERENT. There is a heartbeat, an ebb and flow to the slow and ceaseless shaking of the Earth. The noise attains a maximum and then subsides as you cross a street that acts as a border. North of Canal Street there are wide zones of silence. Also past the riot of construction and the crowds that spill a little beyond Times Square. Near Columbus Circle the road and the sidewalk grow wider. You can see far into the distance. Suddenly it seems impossible to have endured such a density of human beings; of noise, traffic, things, digital displays as large as the screens in old movie theaters; of beggars and of people in a rush, bumping and shoving each other, women striking the ground in high heels; colossal shops; cheap restaurants and fast-food places. Walking north, he felt a growing sense of suffocation. The endless repetition of bank branches, Starbucks, Duane Reades gives rise in him to a dull sense of timelessness and overwhelming corporate omnipotence. He walks and walks, and every corner is the same corner. The forward energy of the straight line crumbles into a circling vertigo.

THAT LONG CREVASSE OF SHADOW. He saw a massive, shirtless man coming down the street with a shaved head and a snake coiled around his neck like a scarf. He saw an emaciated woman holding in her hands what seemed like a basket or a tangle of wires or wickerwork, but turned out to be her fingernails. They were so long that they twisted and grew entangled like the nails of a strange predatory bird, a flying dinosaur, on a body and a face that were themselves a kind of corneous growth, skin as dry as parchment draped over bones and stretched over her jaws and clavicles. He sensed in the man with the snake and the woman with the long fingernails an intimation of terror, something like the start of a monstrous metamorphosis: Snake Man, the Clawed Woman, creatures out of a cheap horror film, sideshow freaks crudely advertised in garish colors.

THE RUMBLE OF THAT FEARSOME CROWD. He is no one. He feels devoid of weight. But the feeling now is one of fear rather than freedom. An inkling of how easy it would be to disappear, leaving no other trace than a black-and-white silhouette recorded in a flood of people as it streams past a security camera. Nobody knows him. He is one more among the city's invisible denizens. Not as invisible nevertheless as that undocumented Mexican tightening the bolts on a piece of scaffolding, or as the beggar dragging his loose pants along the ground as people pass him by without looking, a skill that is one of the city's distinctive traits. To see and simultaneously not to see. To determine within a fraction of a second who is visible and who is not; or who will become visible for only a few minutes and then be erased in the blink of an eye or the wave of a hand. No need to avert your eyes, since you made sure beforehand not to turn them in that direction. Put your guard up from a distance without seeming to notice the very thing you want to avoid. This is a city of zombies glued to cell phone screens, of invisible men and invisible women. Those who contract invisibility are changed by it over time. They turn into ghosts or into shipwrecked castaways gradually regressing to a savage state in the absence of human company. Again and again this morning he encounters people who look like they have survived for twenty years on a desert island and lost their minds. They walk down the street as through a forest or a heath where no one else is present. No one else is present because no one looks at them. As with all survivors on desert islands, they haven't had a haircut in years and they're still dressed in the rags and tatters of the clothes they wore when they were shipwrecked. Although they are surrounded by people, they eat in the middle of the street, or alone at a McDonald's or a Subway, in the savage solitude of hungry animals. They piss or shit wherever the need finds them. No one ever comes near, so they have gradually forgotten the habit of reserve. They scratch in the sun like sleepy beasts or they speak or yell at no one in particular. Silence, as much as the monotony of always hearing only their own voice, has driven them insane. On the island they've grown hairy and their clothes have spoiled. Their skin is hard and coppery from always being outside. Their nails are dirty and thick; it's been years since they cut them properly, given how unlikely it was that they'd find a nail clipper in the wreckage of the ship. Some carry on their backs the burrow, the hovel, or the cave where they go hiding. The hood over their faces is the entrance to the cave, so deep that no face can actually be seen; their rags are like a hut made of skins and furs on a winter steppe; the stench that envelops them marks the borders of their territory, driving away even more effectively anyone who comes near. They sleep in a corner of a subway car from which the rest of the passengers move away, anchorites in a desert that is also a garbage dump, cowled like misanthropic monks.

THE BEASTS ARE AMONG US. He realizes that he tends to keep his head down as he walks, looking at the ground. His eyes travel in a sweeping arc, from the sidewalk in front of his feet, to the faces of the people coming his way, to the heads and shoulders of those who walk ahead of him in the same direction. He has walked for so long through so many cities and never found sidewalks so agreeable to walking and looking as these. They are made of square or rectangular slabs of cement. The lines that divide them form a grid that helps measure the length of your steps. The cracks that spread over their surface trace winding patterns that often resemble branches, drawings of trees, rivers flowing into deltas, the outline of a mountain range. Arshile Gorky said the cracks on a sidewalk are always captivating. After they repair a sidewalk, when the cement is still fresh, shapes are impressed on it that last forever, hard and clear like fossil prints. Splayed hands, names, scribbled words and drawings, tracks of dogs and birds, human footprints. But especially hands. People walk by a slab of wet and freshly smoothed cement and they cannot resist the urge to press their open hands on it, just like twenty thousand years ago on the clay walls of a cave. On the city's sidewalks you find the palms of open hands and also little claw prints left behind by birds: pigeons, sparrows, starlings, species able to adapt and survive in an environment so hostile to almost any kind of life. Their tracks can form delicate, meandering lines across the width of a slab, like strings of leaflike hieroglyphs, schematic dinosaur prints, the scattered marks left by seagulls and plovers on a stretch of sand that has been smoothed by the receding tide. When a slab of fresh cement is poured in autumn, the shapes of fallen leaves are impressed upon it as precisely as on Egyptian bas-reliefs or as the leaves of fossil plants: a long wreath of tiny acacia leaves; the wavy fan of a gingko leaf with the small, clean stroke of its curving stem.

LIVE IT IN SUPER SLOW MOTION. Other leaves are imprinted like shadows or like old photographic plates. Wetted by the rain or trampled underfoot, they adhere to the porous surface of the slab and then, as they are carried away by the wind, or swept, or simply as they decay, their shadows remain on the great, gray sheet of the sidewalk as if drawn in charcoal, fading gradually through the winter months as they are altered by rain, snow, and changing weather. Sometimes an entire slab bears the imprint of a single leaf; sometimes, near the railings of a park, entire constellations can be found, pages of an herbal culled from various trees, arranged entirely by chance as if with a conscious sense of spacing. In the Great Encyclopedia of Accidental Art that he would like to oversee, he would reserve for himself the volume devoted to the sidewalks of New York, spread at people's feet like a canvas, like Jackson Pollock's canvas, which he lay on the studio floor so he could step on it and press into its surface whatever he could find, pennies, cigarette butts, the kinds of things that people toss on the sidewalk. That volume will include a full-page color illustration of a hand he saw one early April morning printed on the sidewalk. The sun was shining after several hours of that bleak, demoralizing rain of early spring that soaks your shoes and the bottom of your pants, and seems to punish people with its unacceptable lengthening of winter. It was a big hand, deeply printed, belonging to someone who had pressed quite hard on the cement. The gray sky had turned a clear blue, and in the hollow of the hand, where rainwater had collected to the brim, that very blue was shining even more serenely.

ENJOY THE BEST URBAN PICNIC. Out of prudence and even out of politeness he knows that he must curb the habit of looking into people's eyes. He knows it can be disconcerting and taken the wrong way. People here are not used to meeting a stranger's eyes. If someone tries to make eye contact with you, it must be for some unwelcome or at least suspicious or annoying reason: a panhandler, a crazy person, someone trying to sell you something, giving out flyers, hunting for signatures with a binder and an aggressively friendly manner, selling tickets for a tourist bus or for bicycle rentals. The thicket of glances that grows as Broadway nears Times Square must be traversed without encountering a single one, making eye contact at most for a few tenths of a second, never longer, so it won't be mistaken for an intention. Pupils dilate with a sense of threat. A glance that lasts a second too long gives rise to puzzled, mechanical smiles that turn a moment later into hostile gestures, a brusque turn of the chin. Some glances can elicit danger if they're taken to be defiant. Some dart from the shadow of a hood as from the depth of a basement or a den. Some glow with delirium. Children never look at you, unless they are foreign or very young, a year old or two at most. Children are trained never to make eye contact with strangers. Nor is one permitted to look at them, for that is as dangerous as touching them, even by chance, even simply by patting their heads or putting a hand on their shoulder for an instant. Children move in a visual vacuum from which even their parents' eyes are often absent.

GEOMETRY AND ANGST. Don't look people in the eye. Look ahead, or stare into your cell phone screen or into space. If you look, they will trap you, they will ask for something, give you something, steal a few minutes of your time, alter the straight course of your path. You must be like someone hovering around an object without ever brushing up against it. Notice every relevant detail as strangers come your way or you approach them, but do it surreptitiously. Or simply stare into your phone, giving the outside world only as much schematic attention as you need to go from one point to the next, like a blind man who can find his bearings with just a few scattered taps of the cane. Learn to look out of the corner of your eye. Instead of looking people in the eye, frisk and feel around their silhouettes, their figures, acquiring all relevant information without seeming to do so. Use a kind of radar, picking up irregularities in any movements taking place ahead of you. If a figure stands motionless in the middle of the sidewalk, it's already a sign to be on guard. Also if it walks from side to side instead of moving in a straight line. Even before you see the plastic cup or hear the jingle of coins you will detect him. Sometimes, without having to look, your sense of smell will warn you of a hideous stench. If the beggar is sitting on the ground or leaning against the wall, you only need to walk a little faster, staring straight ahead, and seeming not to hear anything at all, the endless litany, "spare change, spare change." The best way not to hear is to wear a pair of headphones, ideally the bulky ones that fit over your ears, allowing you to live in a closed acoustic atmosphere as sheltered as the inside of a car. If up ahead a human figure blocks the way, you must begin to veer slightly to one side before you draw near.

CATCH THE BEST FARE AND FLY. He crosses the island diagonally on the same path that was gradually traced over centuries by the footsteps of the Lenape. H. G. Wells's time machine resembled a bizarre bicycle. More than traveling, he is walking through time. Times Square was a lake surrounded by woods until the eighteenth century, and on its shores and in the streams that fed it, beavers built their dikes and lodges. For centuries the Lenape had hunted beaver to turn the pelts into winter clothing. The Dutch and then the English came to the southern tip of the island and began a trade in furs. They bought from the Lenape as many as they could supply, often in exchange for firearms that made it all the easier to hunt beavers. In less than a century there were no more beavers on the island. Soon after, the Lenape were gone as well without a trace.

RIVERS OF GOLD FLOW IN FROM ALL ENDS OF THE EARTH. Times Square is an aquarium and a lake hundreds of feet deep, an underwater park, a theme park sunk beneath the waves, like an exact replica of the city above. Rooftops and spires poke out of the water like the outcrops of a coral reef. Clouds and plumes of vapor drift across facades of blue or tinted glass. Large screens attached to buildings produce a swaying sense of moving currents or immense aquarium tanks, a silent flood where radiant creatures of the deep are seen to drift and glide sedately. Now you are forced to look up, raising your head, craning your neck. Different kinds of creatures teem on the ocean floor, in the muddy silt and detritus of the sidewalks and pedestrian zones. Tight groups of tourists move like shoals of identical fish, wide-eyed, open-mouthed, with fluttering gills, enveloped in the bioluminescent glow of their cell phone screens. Masked and helmeted like deep-sea divers, shod in heavy shoes, the superheroes, the Disney figures, and the Statues of Liberty wave their arms in big aquatic gestures as they try to call attention to themselves. At these depths there is a swampy thickness to the air. The superhero suits and capes are made of cheap, outworn materials, flimsy plastic breastplates, giant heads of greasy plush, tights that are patched and threadbare and full of holes, crudely stitched synthetic fabrics that make those who wear them sweat profusely. Abandoning their strictly separate realms, the mascots and the superheroes mingle like species native to distant oceans gathered in the same aquarium tank. Batman and Superman were already coeval, but they are joined by Spider-Man, Darth Vader, Wonder Woman, Captain America, the Teenage Mutant Ninja Turtles, and the Power Rangers, lumped together in the venal multicultural fraternity of degraded super-heroism, reduced to a spectacle for an idiotic tourist photograph, like Indian chiefs taking part in Buffalo Bill's circus with painted faces, decked in warrior headdress. Peering out of Mickey Mouse's gaping smile is the dark-skinned, frightened face of an undocumented Central American immigrant. The superhero costumes of Times Square are made in hidden sewing shops, in basements and industrial sheds in Queens and in the Bronx. The Statues of Liberty wear sunglasses and foam crowns, their faces are covered in glitter and the hems of their robes are soiled from being dragged over muddy patches of unmelted snow. On every corner, garbage spills and overflows from metal cans. The ground is a dunghill as thickly carpeted in plastic trash as the bottom of the sea.

THE BEAUTY THAT DWELLS IN THE CITY. Near the surface, in a brighter area, high above the tourists with their selfie sticks and the puppet-headed superheroes, higher even than the signs over the restaurants and souvenir shops and the theater marquees, flow the powerful currents of the advertising screens, swaying with a slow and silent motion. Moving cameras follow from above as cars race at strangely tranquil speeds through desert landscapes, on winding lakeside roads, along a cliff with breaking ocean waves or down the long, straight avenues of cities without any cars, pedestrians, or even sidewalks. People jump and stay afloat as if submerged, as if jumping in a space station or on the moon. Hair floats around women's faces like that of diving mermaids. Three girls, golden-haired, with glowing faces, run in light H&M dresses through prairies of high grass that wave and buckle in the wind. They run to the top of a hill with such ease that their feet don't seem to touch the ground, then they jump and glide through the boundless space that opens up on the other side. A man wearing a helmet and a pilot suit that make him look almost like an astronaut jumps in a parachute, swaying in a pristine sky that turns pink on the horizon where the sun begins to set. He loses altitude harmoniously, like a seagull soaring on still wings or like a hang glider. He lands on his feet on a paved road, a highway stretching away in a perfect line toward a mountain range. By the side of the road there is a Hyundai. The pilot packs his parachute with ease and stores it in the trunk. He takes off his helmet. He is a man with tousled brown hair, an explorer's sunburned face and a scruffy three-day beard. He gets in the car, turns on the engine, and drives away, disappearing into a horizon that is still aglow with a luxurious sunset. A moment later he is back in the parachute, descending just as slowly as before toward the same red car.

ENTERTAINMENT WITHOUT LIMITS. People rise and fall on digital displays at various depths with the same light grace. Rhinemaidens sway in submarine choreographies. A single ripple spreads across the screens, lifting all the floating people. Every thirty seconds it all repeats exactly as before. A lipstick tube is falling through the void, through a glistening darkness of silk or velour. Suddenly it shatters. A thousand particles of glass, metal, and red matter spread in all directions, blooming rapidly, expanding like a sea anemone. But just as quickly as they burst they fly back together and transform into a woman's red lips, then a hand with bright red fingernails pulls a zipper to reveal a nascent cleavage. The zipper's downward motion turns once more into the falling tube of lipstick which explodes again within its brief parenthesis of darkness, a lavish catastrophe, a burst of fireworks in the summer night.

ONLY THE BEST CAN REACH THESE HEIGHTS. Words, too, flow in streams along ribbon displays that curve around the Morgan Stanley building or the Fox News building nearby: a river and a sea snake of words curving like a whip around their facades, relaying share prices, financial news, warnings: St. Petersburg subway hit by suicide blast, rivers in flood leave hundreds dead in Colombia. The letters and symbols of a brand come together on a screen. The title of a Broadway musical, a car model, the latest Netflix series, the silhouette of a helicopter on a yellow background in an ad for *Miss Saigon*. A Norwegian Airlines Boeing 787 lifts off powerfully and flies in a straight line through a Himalaya of clouds. With dizzying swiftness, a cell phone screen transforms into a high-tech business park that opens its gates invitingly in Beijing: treelined avenues, glass buildings under clear skies, huge doors that open to let in a heavenly light. A muscular Black man leaps from a diving board toward a swimming pool of gleaming blue, his arms spread wide, a little like the Boeing 787 in the next screen over. In this oceanic trench, this theme park, reality has been abolished so completely as to unleash in everyone, including himself, this furtive traveler, a dizzying euphoria. The artificial paradises of the old city wanderers have finally become superfluous: De Quincey's laudanum, Poe's laudanum and cognac, Baudelaire's hashish, Walter Benjamin's opium and peyote. Urban hallucinations no longer need to arise from the mind, since they are made objectively available across a thousand simultaneous screens. The cars, the women, the tubes of lipstick that appear on them are as large as creatures of the deep, as whales and giant squids. Store signs attain the pitch of apocalyptic prophecies: LAST DAYS, FINAL LIQUIDATION, *everything must go*. Signs for clearance sales, worn as sandwich boards by men with drunk and ravaged faces, cannot be told apart from signs raised with vengeful zeal by preachers of the end of days. "You shopaholics," one of them yells, waving his arms among the tourists, "you better kneel down and pray for the mercy of the Lord."

THERE IS HORROR, AND PIERCING JOY, AND SOMETIMES CRUELTY. He feels that he will never leave Times Square behind. His steps seem weightless and anesthetized. He must reach a shore of reason and reality as soon as possible. He must leave Broadway's underwater canyon, emerge as quickly as he can from the liquid realm of screens. In broad daylight, its digitized glow prevails over the antiquated light of the sun. The world seems entirely submerged beneath the perfect unreality of advertisement. Families as softly obese as sea lions guzzle down manufactured foods in the corporate decor of a McDonald's, a Wendy's, a Popeyes, a Subway, a TGI Fridays. They eat meat drenched in hormones and antibiotics, French fries doused with saturated fat, drinks sweetened with genetically modified corn syrup. Each person leaves behind a trail of bags and plastic straws and food containers. Homeless people rummage in the garbage cans and find half-eaten burgers, nibbled bits of fried chicken smeared with ketchup, aluminum cans with dregs of hot soda inside. Pigeons as dirty and gray as the trampled snow peck at a slice of pizza. Now and then, seagulls come down from the cliffs of Times Square, drawn by the irresistible smell of melted cheese, burned fat, the cornucopia spilling out of every garbage can at the end of the day.

WILD CREATURES OF THE ASPHALT JUNGLE. He walks and walks. It's been three hours and it seems like days, or lifetimes. His walks form a thread that runs through many times and places. One of his rules is to stop only once, and only long enough to eat. If there's no wind he can sit on a park bench. Other than that, he only comes to a stop at red lights. There's no need to rest. He is the tireless little man in the traffic signal, the white silhouette marking the paths reserved for pedestrians in a park. The exertion of the walk generates the very energy that sustains it. He steps lithely on the firm rubber soles of shoes made specially for walking. The body's weight and balance are centered at the base of the spine. The head of the femur slides in its hip socket like a well-oiled piston. There is a sense of physical exaltation that is sharpened by the morning cold. The clarity of the air seems to transfer directly to the eye and mind. Walking is now a permanent condition, an organic rhythm as efficient and well-timed as the beating of the heart or the periodic intake of air into the lungs. There's a kind of folly in walking for so many hours; a stubbornness; a sense of incipient delirium, like drinking and drinking and wanting to drink even more. Walking is a gradual drunkenness without heaviness or hangover, a psychedelic trip fueled by oxygen and serotonin. The senses sharpen instead of growing dull, the will is perfectly at rest and simultaneously exerts itself along a constant path. The rule requires that he only stop for lunch and that he only make use of what he carries; he must not take anything that is not a gift. A newspaper is fine if it's free. Outside a tea shop, up in the seventies, a girl in a black apron is offering samples of hot tea. He takes a tiny cup and thanks her and drinks it as he goes. It warms his fingers, rouses his spirits and adds percussive force to his heels. The broad expanse of the river is now visible on side streets leading west. He is not allowed to browse through secondhand books at a street stand or to stop at the strange sidewalk bazaars set up on pieces of plywood laid across a pair of supports.

RELAX YOUR SENSES. He has reached one of the small triangular parks formed by Broadway as it cuts diagonally through the city grid. There are benches in the scant and deceptive February sun. There's a garden, a statue, a kind of recumbent nymph in Greek sandals with an ancient tunic draped over opulent curves and a hairstyle circa 1914. He has an old weakness for irregular city squares with gardens and statues. After three and a half hours of walking he is suddenly beset by great hunger, by soreness on the soles of his feet and weakness in the knees. There are lost souls and castaways sunning themselves on the benches. He chooses a sunny spot that is a little sheltered from the traffic. He takes the satchel off his back and takes out the sandwich wrapped in foil, the paper napkin, the canteen, the small bottle with its measure of red wine. Being a meek and fearful person, anxious to obey whatever rules are placed upon him and to read all prohibitive signs and regulations, he knows that consuming alcohol in public spaces is forbidden by the city, especially in parks, where one is not allowed to smoke either. But what could be a greater pleasure than a bite of rye bread, olive oil, fresh tomatoes, Spanish ham, and the drippings of a scrambled egg, followed by a drink of wine the more enjoyable for being surreptitious, while on a different bench someone sucks on a straw from a tub of soda overflowing with malignant sweeteners, stamped with the seal of Kentucky Fried Chicken and made of materials that, after being used just once, will take a thousand years to degrade into a cloud of toxic microfibers that will go on poisoning the water and our lives.

VOTRE VOYAGE COMMENCE ICI. I saw him in Straus Park, sitting on one of the benches facing the midday sun and the receding view of West End Avenue, which is rather stark and severe in the foreground but then turns blue and gold in the distance at that hour on a clear day. I thought I'd seen him the prior Sunday at the farmers' market, on that terrible stretch of sidewalk in the freezing morning shade up by Columbia University. What made him hard to recognize was that I'd never seen him so bundled-up before, dressed in a winter coat and wearing a fur-lined cap with earflaps. There was an incongruity between the elaborate hat he wore that Sunday—no doubt effective against the cold, but somehow archaic, like some piece of equipment for a zeppelin expedition to the North Pole— and the rather flimsy coat, which suggested a person lacking harsh experience with intense cold. He had been attentively examining the offerings at a mushroom stand. While the vendor, standing in front of his simple stall, stomped his feet and tried to huddle into his coat, he went on looking at the various types of mushroom with the calm attention of a naturalist, unaffected by the cold as the minutes passed. His mild and natural composure softened my surprise at seeing him, though just a moment later he was gone. A blast of freezing wind had shaken the frail arrangement of poles and the plastic sheeting protecting the stalls. One of them collapsed, dismasted by the wind, toppling a pile of crates that sent a bunch of apples rolling unevenly down the sidewalk at people's feet.

AN ÉMINENCE GRISE. The second sighting, to use a UFO term that he would surely have enjoyed, took place at The Hungarian Pastry Shop. Just as in Madrid, his movements, or apparitions, were circumscribed to a few particular areas and neighborhoods: Straus Park, the farmers' market up by Columbia, The Hungarian Pastry Shop, delimiting together a small area of ten blocks between two avenues, since the pastry shop, a less portentous place than its name might suggest, stands at the corner of Amsterdam Avenue facing St. John the Divine.

THE MOMENT HAS COME. One morning I was having coffee at the pastry shop and for a moment I felt sure I'd seen him walk past the door and turn to look inside, where he would not have been able to see much, given the contrast between the bright sun on the sidewalk and the relative darkness within; a darkness as pleasing as the murmur of conversation, the soft lamplight, the waitresses' voices calling out in thick accents the names of customers who had ordered something before sitting down at a table. Sometimes I would work there in the mornings, reading or jotting things down over a cappuccino. If I had to meet someone, I did so at the pastry shop. I liked that it was a real café, a well-stocked patisserie, with a certain Austro-Hungarian expertise when it came to pastries, yet with all the precariousness of a small American shop. I liked the coffee and the croissants, but I especially liked that it was not a Starbucks; that its tables were not taken up by zombies plugged into white earbuds and staring into screens; that real conversations between people could be heard and sometimes even laughter, and no music governed by a corporate algorithm, in fact no music at all. I liked that there were waitresses behind the counter or serving people at their tables, often politely, often even smiling, attractive waitresses who always seemed a touch exotic, perhaps Eastern European, moving among the tables and holding up a tray. Always, or almost always, there was a woman sitting alone with a book. I liked the absence of any design, corporate, hipster, bohemian, eco, ethnic, pseudovintage, pseudo-French, or any other kind. The walls had a yellow tint, as if they dated back to a time when people were allowed to smoke and had never been repainted. I liked to get there early so I could sit in a corner in the back, by the faint glow of a lampshade and with a good view of the narrow, cavernous length of the café, the to-and-fro of the waitresses, the air that grew thick in winter with the breath of people coming in from the street and with the damp steam of their coats and hats in the heated room.

THE WORLD AT YOUR FINGERTIPS. The day I saw him go by I was sitting closer to the door, facing it. On a different day, hurrying to get somewhere, I turned the corner and glanced inside. It was one of those cold mornings when the café would fill up right away and seem even fuller because everyone was bundled up. That time I recognized him by the Arctic hat. He was holding a fountain pen and looking over some sheets of paper on the table. He seemed so absorbed that I felt I couldn't interrupt him, couldn't draw him from that private rapture that enclosed him in a perfect isolation that was not, however, unsociable, partaking as it did in the sounds, the warmth of bodies, the smell of coffee and of pastries that filled the shop.

EVERYTHING OLD IS NEW AGAIN. Back then I had come to accept that my only meaningful connections in the city were with the dead, with absent or imaginary people, and only very rarely with the living, those who moved about me or who lived down the hallway or next door, even on the other side of the wall. I knew more about dead people I had never met and about ghosts of the past and figments of the imagination than about most of the living. The real ghosts were my closest neighbors. I knew of their existence only indirectly. A funereal cough would begin in the middle of the afternoon or in the middle of the night, somewhere in the building above my head, and it would last for hours. It was a man's cough, deep, rich, sometimes gravelly, as if stirring up thick matter, other times as dry as a slow bark. Sometimes I woke up at three or four in the morning and the sleepless cough was ringing, maybe it was even the reason I was up. In the lobby or in the elevator I never ran into anyone who coughed that way. It came in the dark, like the crazed sound of hammers or crunching gears when the heat came on and scalding water caused the old iron pipes and radiators to expand. Heavy blows like the fist of a revenant at the door, like the knocking that the dead apparently employ to send a message to the living at a spiritual séance.

A WORLD OF POSSIBILITIES WITHIN YOUR REACH. In the apartment next door, or perhaps in the one above, a woman would sneeze repeatedly and someone, before or after, began to play the piano. It was always the same sections of the same works: Bach, Schubert, Beethoven. Whoever was playing did so with ease, though not very fluently, getting stuck or stopping always at the same difficult part of a piece. I became as familiar with the repertoire as with the places where the music broke off. I knew Bill Evans had once lived in the building, around 1960, with his partner Ellaine and a cat. It allowed me to think of the possibility that Evans had lived in what was now my apartment. It was when he was recording his live albums at the Village Vanguard with Scott LaFaro and Paul Motian in June 1961. The muffled sound of his music as he practiced or composed would have reached me through these very walls. I would play one of his records and the music filtered through the walls and into the lobby as if it were 1961 and he were still alive. Bill Evans was much more real to me than the woman next door, who was perhaps the one who sneezed and played Schubert and Beethoven. Over the years I had run into her three or four times, and we never spoke for more than a few minutes. All I knew about her was what I could infer from the things that turned up at her door. *The New York Times*, *The Nation*, packages from Amazon, junk mail, letters soliciting donations.

DON'T WAIT ANY LONGER TO OWN IT. I never saw the people who delivered these things, either, just as I rarely saw those who left a different set of things at my own doorstep, adjacent to hers. On winter days there was sometimes a pair of muddy boots by her door, an open umbrella. Signs like these proved the existence of people I rarely ever saw. A Hillary Clinton or Bernie Sanders campaign sticker under a peephole. A pink umbrella, a pair of women's shoes, and a pair of girls' shoes at the foot of a different door. At first I thought my deep estrangement came from being a new arrival. Then I gradually came to realize that it would not be alleviated by the passage of time, but rather grow more consummate. The longer I lived in the building, the more invisible I became. Sometimes I would hear people laughing in the hallway outside my door, greeting each other with great American cheer. I would look through the peephole curiously, a little enviously, and the laughter was gone, the people had just vanished through doors that once again remained hermetically sealed, the door to the apartment opposite or the door to the elevator. I would come in from the street and greet someone leaving the building and it was as if he had neither seen nor heard me. I would go over to the elevator where somebody else was waiting and say hello again, and they would stand there, just a step away, without even performing the reflex action of turning to face the approach of a fellow creature. I began to think there was a border somewhere between invisibility and nonexistence.

WHAT YOUR IMAGE SAYS ABOUT YOU. Walter Benjamin says that to live is to leave traces. He knew what he was talking about. But if I thought about the traces I would leave behind me once I left, I might as well have never lived here. The only person who never failed to recognize me from a distance and to approach me with signs of joy was a Black homeless woman named Janis. She always wandered around the same part of the neighborhood, between 106th and 107th, near Straus Park. I would sometimes take Riverside Drive so as not to run into her. If I gave her a dollar she made a sad, disappointed face. If I gave her five she asked for ten. She was always decently dressed. She had a wide, pleasant face, with eyes that went in an instant from meek to sarcastic. The day I asked her what her name was she also asked me mine, and where I came from. When I said I was from Spain, she asked if it was true that in my country wild bulls were allowed to roam the streets.

THERE'S A NAME FOR WHAT YOU NEED. After so many years in the city I felt more and more like a ghost. As the time approached to leave for good—for it was clear now that I had come back only to say goodbye, to be there fully one last time—I noticed the same bewilderment as on the distant days of my arrival. Back then I thought the sense of foreignness would fade over time. Now I knew it to be an incurable condition. You think you've finally settled in, and it turns out what you have settled into is the small enclave of your foreignness. Half the people here—they themselves, not their parents or their forebears—have come from other countries around the world. My sense of foreignness was the same as that of many others around me, but that was not enough to form a fellowship. Not even a fellowship of strangers. Each foreignness is different from the next, and all remain mutually indissoluble. Religious or patriotic ties can sometimes remedy or soften it; not because they make it easier for people to adapt to this new world, but because they spare them the need to do it. They are here physically, but really they continue to live in the world they left behind, a world they are able to replicate to some degree with the help of their countrymen or those who follow the same religion. Neither option was available to me. Even language failed to establish a meaningful bond, not because it is spoken with different accents but because Spanish is of no use to anyone as a true sign of identity. What does a Dominican or a Puerto Rican living in New York have to do with a Spaniard, a Colombian, or an Argentine?

BE YOURSELF, UNLESS YOU CAN BE BATMAN. I was completely alone. *Más solo que la una*, to say it the old Spanish way. I was alone in Donald Trump's terrifying country, ruled now by his entourage of wealthy crooks, all of them as heartless, cruel, and rapacious as birds of prey. I would turn on the radio and his name instantly shot forth like a profanity. Each morning brought its gelid weather forecast and its terrifying piece of news. They wanted to destroy everything as quickly as possible: the Environmental Protection Agency, the environment itself. They were visibly impatient to poison the air with the smoke of power plants, to poison the water with toxic spills. The secretary in charge of public schools was a plutocrat whose priority consisted in dismantling them as soon as possible. The highest official responsible for fighting climate change said that climate change was a hoax made up by the Chinese. The housing secretary was a Black man who said that African slaves had come as immigrants hoping that their grandchildren or their great-grandchildren might one day enjoy the American dream. That phrase, "the American dream," made me gag again as it never should have stopped doing. A malignant activism made sure no infamy went unaccomplished: they lifted the ban on lead ammunition for hunters on public lands, eager to pollute the water, the earth, and the bodies of animals once more with a toxic metal. They acted with a ruthless Bolshevik resolve, determined to destroy at any cost and as quickly as possible whatever they came upon, inflicting the maximum possible damage on their class enemies.

ONLY ONE OTHER THING IS MORE DESIRABLE. I now admitted to myself that I had never stopped feeling helpless and afraid in this country.

Deep down, sometimes with a keen awareness, I had always been afraid of the overbearing power of the police and the impersonal cruelty of a vengeful system of punishment capable of crushing the anonymous and innocent lives of the mentally ill or the wrongly convicted. I felt fear and vertigo when the plane, preparing to land, rolled sideways to begin its descent and you saw through the window the huge planetary scale of the ocean shore, the marshes and woods, the sprawl of identical suburbs and of a city that went on forever, spreading like a galaxy toward the edge of total darkness.

REPORTING TOOLS IN CASE OF A CATASTROPHE. I had a closer relationship with statues than with actual people: the beautiful statue of Mnemosyne in Straus Park; the Union general on horseback at the end of my block; the Buddhist master outside a nearby temple on Riverside Drive; the Duke Ellington statue on the other side of the park, where Harlem begins, at Fifth Avenue and 110th. I felt called to the statues and even simply to the names on certain street signs. At Eighty-Sixth and Broadway I saw the name of Isaac Bashevis Singer, who lived there when he was already a wealthy and successful man. Two blocks down, at Eighty-Fourth Street, there was an intersection named in honor of Edgar Allan Poe: Edgar Allan Poe Way. Ranks and distinctions always apply. An Edgar Allan Poe Way is not as important as an Isaac Bashevis Singer Boulevard. My own street, 106th, was named Duke Ellington Boulevard. At Seventy-Seventh and West End there was a Miles Davis Way. Miles Davis lived in a house that now bears a plaque and used to be an old rectory. He lived there for many years like a man buried alive, a vampire shunning the light of day, coming out at night, feeding on cocaine and never sleeping.

EXPERIENCE A TRUE VIRTUAL REALITY. Many years ago, in one of those past lives that only return to us in dreams we instantly forget when we wake up, or fictions we invent, someone told me there was an equestrian statue of Duke Ellington in the neighborhood. Duke Ellington on horseback like a glorious condottiere of Black music, a dandy in an Art Deco tuxedo and a pair of riding boots with spurs, holding a baton in place of a riding whip and standing at the gates of Harlem. Then, in a future life that I never foresaw, I found myself living on this street that bears his name. A boulevard named

Duke Ellington is almost as elegant as an equestrian statue of Duke Ellington or as the glorious glow of a Duke Ellington recording. In time I came to identify the various disparate facts that, coming together and aggregating like organic waste, had given rise to that legend or hoax that someone had once told me or that I only thought I'd heard but really made up myself. At the end of West 106th Street, the one renamed after Ellington, there is indeed an equestrian statue. It honors a Civil War general who was born in Switzerland but emigrated when he was very young. Now he sits upright on his horse looking west atop a marble staircase, eternally facing the river and the vast continent beyond as if prepared to ride across, holding the reins in one gloved hand and his wide-brimmed military hat in the other. Farther north and east, at the corner of Central Park near the small lake with a Dutch name, the Harlem Meer, there is a statue of Duke Ellington. He is not on horseback but rather standing next to a grand piano on top of a wretched contraption that looks like a scaffold and also a monument, not to jazz or to Duke Ellington but to wedding cakes, with Duke Ellington on top of it like a miniature groom, a miserable groom standing alone at the altar and also atop his own useless cake.

LET YOUR JOURNEY BEGIN. My street was very wide, but also quiet, with broad sidewalks and very little traffic. The width of the sidewalks is one of the beauties of New York. Outside a building across the street from mine I would often see splendid drawings done by children in colored chalk, resembling primitive paintings of animals and symbols: a dog, a sun, a row of squares for hopscotch. I would see the drawings but not the children who made them. A ruthless doorman sometimes erased them with a power hose. On that sidewalk, one night in December, Bill Evans came back from playing at the Village Vanguard to find all of his belongings in a pile: what little furniture he owned, his clothes, his records, his piano, his bed. He had been evicted for not paying the rent. Seeing a tall, skinny man go by, gangly, in a trench coat and glasses, with that tired air that is so common here, I would squint or close my eyes and see Bill Evans, the ghost of Bill Evans, a rare fellow man in a city of strangers. Pale-faced, engrossed, moving with the furtive gestures of a junkie, he would have darted out of the building almost always by night. He would have crossed the street at the light on 106th and West End Avenue, where I too have waited so many times to cross. He would have turned on Broadway at the corner now occupied by a KFC that stays open all night, so you see people asleep with their heads on the table among the leftovers and the bags of food and plastic containers. He would have walked to the subway station at 103rd Street and taken the 1 to the Seventh Avenue stop near the Village Vanguard. It was the same stop where I used to get off to go to a different job. The door to the Village Vanguard opens directly onto a narrow staircase leading down to the underground realm where ghosts find shelter.

THEY TURN UP WHERE YOU NEVER IMAGINED. I could have marked each of their addresses with different colors on a neighborhood map, taking advantage of the various pencils I now kept always at hand: one color for musicians, another for writers, one for the dead, another for those who never existed, another for those who so vividly pictured themselves walking or living here that they must somehow have left a trace of their presence, a shadow, fainter than other shadows but perceptible to those who paid close attention or who possessed the right instrument or sensing device. Billie Holiday on 104th, where the post office stands. John Coltrane on 103rd. Hank Jones lived at 108th and Broadway in a single room that served him as a minuscule apartment. He died there at ninety-two. A score of Debussy's Études stood open on an electronic keyboard and the Grammy he had won years earlier was put away in a shoebox. Hank Jones accompanied Marilyn Monroe on the piano when she sang "Happy Birthday" to JFK. He was a gallant old man to the very end, a studious and active musician. I must have crossed paths with him many times on that sidewalk without seeing him or without recognizing him. On the very corner where he lived I once saw the pianist Fred Hersch walk by. No one else may have recognized him. There is probably no other city where people walk alone in such a state of absorption. Fred Hersch is someone who nearly came back from the dead, from a coma that was almost terminal. He and I were walking down Broadway at the same pace, quite close to each other, but I didn't have the courage to say hello, to tell him how much I liked his music.

IT CAN CATCH YOU ANYWHERE. Federico García Lorca would have walked frequently down these same sidewalks during his time at Columbia. Flat-footed, a little clumsy, always hurrying from place to place in the city bustle. Seen and unseen. Six months later he left New York and never came back. Down Broadway, which is nearly unchanged in its architecture after all these years even if people are dressed differently, a stout old man walks slowly in a dark suit, formal, a foreigner, thinking that his murdered son must have stepped on this very sidewalk. His ghostly son, frozen by death in the prime of youth.

WHERE HAVE I HEARD THAT VOICE BEFORE? In a few minutes I could walk from where I lived to the corner of Riverside Drive and 109th. That is where Hannah Arendt lived until the end of her life. When I found out, I thought about the mark I would make on the neighborhood map. Then I realized that if Walter Benjamin had not taken his life in September 1940, if he had reached Lisbon and sailed to New York with the ticket and the visa stamp he had already secured, he would undoubtedly have lived on one of these streets too, perhaps in this very building. Toward the end, his will and his imagination were focused on New York. He had started learning English. He was fond of American films and he read Faulkner, *Light in August*, but found it so hard that he helped himself along with a French translation. It is surely characteristic of Benjamin to begin his study of the English language with a Faulkner novel.

WHEN THERE IS NO PATH, YOU BLAZE YOUR OWN TRAIL. Benjamin pinned a map of New York to the wall of his Paris apartment. He wrote letters to Gretel Karplus, Adorno's wife, with whom he was probably or had once been in love. There are indications that they may have met secretly once or twice. Sometimes his letters were addressed to a PO box. The names of the women in Benjamin's life seem taken from a novel, perhaps a novel enticingly titled with a woman's name: Gretel Karplus, Asja Lācis, Ursel Bud, Olga Parem, Jula Cohn. He eagerly awaited her letters, with their exotic US stamps and the names of New York streets written in the upper corner of the envelope in her own hand. Seeing her handwriting was almost like seeing her walk down the street toward him—short hair, dark eyes, sharp features—back in Berlin. The envelope said "Christopher St.," and he searched for it on his map, putting his face right up to it because he was very shortsighted and lacked the money to buy a stronger pair of glasses. It was the same way he leaned over a scrap of writing in a tiny hand or over a dusty, ancient-smelling book in the Bibliothèque Nationale in Paris. When he was finally able to make out the name of the street on the map, he made a mark with one of his colored pencils. Gretel Karplus mentioned in a letter that she and her husband had gone to see Lotte Lenya at a nightclub. It was like being in Berlin, Gretel said, as if those years had returned, 1925 to 1932. But the Christopher Street address is temporary. A few months later Karplus writes that they are preparing to move into a larger apartment facing the Hudson, on the thirteenth floor. Benjamin instantly searches his map for the blue swath of the river on one side of the island. Another envelope bears her new address: 290 Riverside Drive. From the desk, she says, you can see the river through the window. She is looking at it as she writes. "I wish we could go on a walk together along the Hudson, talking at ease about everything."

NO MATTER WHO YOU ARE, WE ADAPT TO YOU. She pictures the walks they will take together when he finally comes to New York, the places she will show him. She even likes to imagine that she will have the courage to drive so they can see the city by car. Benjamin decides to learn English. He asks her to write him in English and feels pleased to understand her letters when she does. He reads Poe, "The Man of the Crowd," and takes down some notes for his project on Baudelaire and the city. He reads Henry James, *The Turn of the Screw*. He discovers Melville and reads one of his lesser-known novels, *Pierre*, where he finds stimulating descriptions of the streets of New York in the mid-nineteenth century. He reads James M. Cain, *The Postman Always Rings Twice*, which makes a big impression. He watches American films to get used to the sounds of the language. One night he discovers Katharine Hepburn and falls instantly in love with her.

"I recently saw—for the first time!—Katharine Hepburn. She is magnificent. She reminds me very much of you. Has no one ever said that to you?" Increasingly anguished letters arrive at 290 Riverside Drive during the last days, from Paris, from an internment camp, from Lourdes: Benjamin says he has "a terrifying sense of being trapped." The world crumbles all around him in Europe, but their letters keep going back and forth. In one of them, from the summer of 1940, Benjamin tells Karplus he had to leave Paris very quickly, bringing nothing but a toiletry bag and a gas mask. In the penultimate letter to arrive in New York he says to her, "We must make sure to put the best of us in our letters, because nothing suggests we will see each other again soon."

WHAT HOPE FOR THE DEAD? But he could have escaped. He could have postponed for a single day the decision to take a lethal dose of morphine at the Hotel de Francia in Portbou and found the border open, the path clear across a ravaged Spain to Lisbon and then New York, safe at last, stunned, restored by the calm and the fresh air of the ocean crossing. After all the walking he did in Berlin and then in Paris, New York would have been a continual temptation to venture forth. I saw his ghost from the back, the way his friends used to say he was instantly recognizable in a crowd, "stooped like a turtle," Asja Lācis said ironically, as those who aren't in love can always afford to be toward the ones who go on loving them despite their coldness and perhaps because of it. Walter Benjamin is walking down Broadway in the conspicuous suit of a European exile, formal, as always, even down to the moment of his terrible end—the suit, the tie and vest—invariably polite, curious and half blind, experiencing a giddy sense of pleasure in observing everything around him, the signs, the lettering and logos of the brands, sometimes too with a sense of being back in Berlin, something he never felt in Paris, the noise, the rush, the general air of commercial vulgarity, the people speaking German, Yiddish, English with a German accent, the Jewish smells and flavors in the delis, the joy and guilt of having fled the apocalypse in Europe. He would have felt much less foreign and alone than during his years in Paris. Many of his old Berlin friends were in New York, the ones who arrived before the war or at the same time as him, and then the ones who would come later, the survivors, the resurrected, who came back from the land of the dead telling awful stories or keeping an even more terrible silence, wearing long sleeves even in summer to conceal the blue numbers tattooed on their forearm.

ESCAPE IS THE ONLY OPTION. He would walk past Columbia or along Riverside Drive, holding on to his hat and glasses in the wind that blows from the Hudson. He would sit on a bench in the sun in Straus Park. He would finally recover, after the war, all the documents and manuscripts he had left behind in Paris under the care of Georges Bataille, the unruly mass of his book on Baudelaire and the arcades and the world of the nineteenth century. Perhaps he would attain what had proved impossible no matter how hard he tried during his earlier lives in Paris and Berlin, a relatively secure position in life, a job at a university, perhaps the New School, something that would allow him to have a fixed address, a decent income, the necessary calm to write all the books that always had to be deferred because of poverty, political uncertainty, the precariousness and urgency of his newspaper writing. In émigré apartments on Riverside Drive or West End Avenue, in curtained rooms lined with books and cluttered with European furniture and ornaments, he would have plunged for hours into a thick fog of tobacco smoke and German philosophy. With a friend, on the street, he would have come to a sudden stop in order to explain something, oblivious to the irritation of those behind him at seeing their straight and expeditious paths disturbed. He would not have accepted the heat as an excuse to give in, like almost everyone else, to open shirts and light-colored jackets. The dead remain remarkably faithful to the past. No country is more hostile or more foreign to them than the future, that place where those who survived were able to settle so casually once they let go of all their memories.

PREDICT YOUR FUTURE. So I can't say that I was very surprised to see my old acquaintance sitting in Straus Park that day, as I had seen him before in Madrid, perhaps in Granada as well, and now more recently in places that had become such an important part of my life in the city, The Hungarian Pastry Shop, the farmers' market up by Columbia on Thursday and Sunday mornings. He seemed entirely out of place and yet as much a part of the scene as the lost souls who populate the park when there is even a little sun. I was familiar with almost all of them. Lost souls are as faithful to certain places as ghosts to the houses they haunt. There was a fat woman with cropped hair and childish bangs who used to sit with her hands on her big thighs, raising her face slightly to the sun. There was something masculine about her, but with a soft, eunuch-like quality. Around her neck she wore a collection of keys and a wreath of subway cards and loyalty cards from various drugstore chains in the neighborhood. Sometimes she spoke to herself, sometimes to the homeless person or the tired old man sitting on a nearby bench. When she spoke to herself, she seemed to be peremptorily addressing someone else; when she addressed others she seemed to be talking to herself. Some days she was still and quiet, others she was talkative and restless. Then she would smoke, taking quick drags on the cigarette, avidly but with a kind of repressed constraint.

THE OFFICE IS WITHIN YOU. On the next bench over was the crippled Vietnam veteran, red-faced, his hair and beard a dazzling white under the military cap. In decent weather he wore shorts. When he got to the bench, he would unscrew his prosthetic leg and place it upright on the ground next to the good leg, in the same white sock and shoe. He massaged the stump and exposed it to the sun, letting it jut out over the edge of the bench. Two Black women in formal hats and mourning clothes gave out religious pamphlets and copies of the Jehovah's Witnesses magazine. That day the only novelty was a well-dressed, long-haired young man who was scribbling rapidly on a spiral notebook that he held open on his knees. He might be there just that once or he might turn into a regular, attracted by the park's peculiar magnetism, its small triangular garden, the statue of Mnemosyne lying on her pedestal as on a comfortable bed. It was fitting for a neighborhood so rich in names and ghosts to be presided over surreptitiously by the muse of memory, even if she mostly went unnoticed. Over time, some of those who were most faithful to the park would disappear. I always remembered a very tall, very thin old man, extremely pale, with a faint white fuzz of hair on his skull, which protruded beneath the yellow skin. He had no teeth, no flesh on his cheeks or muscle on his arms. Walking was becoming increasingly hard. He moved forward on stiff legs, swaying to keep his balance and dragging his feet. He would sit down and spend hours without doing anything or speaking to anyone, just holding a cup of coffee in one hand. I'm not sure exactly how much time had to pass before I realized he never came anymore.

FIND OUT RIGHT NOW IF YOU'RE A WINNER. I could tell it was him even from across the street, less on account of his face than of his manner, the way he sat, the cap with the earflaps buttoned on top under a kind of pompom, and the perennial satchel on which I noticed a pair of straps that allowed it to be carried like a backpack. He had spread a cloth napkin on his knees and tied another one around his neck as a bib. The canteen and a small plastic bottle stood beside him on the bench. I saw him unwrap a sandwich and offer some to the fat woman with the keys and customer cards around her neck. She looked at him, perhaps not understanding the meaning of his gesture. As soon as the light changed I would cross over and greet him. It was lunchtime, and up until that moment I had not spoken to anyone or used my voice in any way. Now the fat lady was smoking, sucking on the cigarette as if she were spitting, and she was also telling him something, even though she was looking away. He was nodding thoughtfully. I could have crossed now but I preferred to go on watching. He would drink from the canteen or the small bottle and carefully wipe his mouth. Then the light changed again, so I had to wait. I saw him give the fat woman a piece of sandwich and a paper napkin. Then he folded the square of foil in which the sandwich had been wrapped and put it away in his satchel along with the two napkins, the one that had served him as a lap cloth and the one he had used as a bib. He took a map from the satchel and spread it open on his knees. He was looking at a cell phone and jotting things down on the map, which he then folded up neatly and slipped into his coat pocket. He stood up and said goodbye to the fat woman, whose mouth was full of food. For an instant I thought that he had raised his hand to his cap in greeting. That he had seen me. Then he looked away. The light was green, but I didn't cross. I felt suddenly afraid that he wouldn't recognize me when I approached; that I would call out to him and not be heard; that my voice would not come out of my throat, as when you want to speak in a dream and are unable to do it. I saw him walk past the Jehovah's Witnesses and, much to their surprise, take the pamphlet and the magazine they were offering and put them in his satchel. He slipped the straps around his shoulders and crossed Broadway heading east, past the corner with the Duane Reade (though there is a Duane Reade on almost every corner, a Chase, a Bank of America, a Starbucks; they only begin to disappear as you go into Harlem). And that was the last time I ever saw him.

FEEL EVERY FIESTA MOMENT. Every time you wait at a corner for the light to change there is a quick human vignette, a still frame in the continuous sequence of the walk. At Amsterdam and 110th, a Black kid is skipping in place like a runner trying to stay warm, bouncing on his rubber-soled sneakers as if he were climbing. Music can be heard coming out of his headphones so clearly that it must be blasting in his ears. He skips on one foot and then the other, dropping his head to let the hood drape over it more fully, and he begins to cross before the traffic comes to a halt. Farther up, in front of the cathedral, a man and a woman are having an argument, standing very close together and so near the curb that a passing bus has nearly grazed them. Mutual hostility makes their closeness suffocating. The man looks very serious though a little distracted. The woman lifts her eyes to speak to him and her mouth is twisted with weeping. The man is holding two plastic bags full of stuff, one in each hand. The woman, choking back her tears, can no longer speak and merely rests her closed fists without violence on the lapels of his old coat, as if capitulating, while he glances sideways at the light, perhaps waiting for a chance to flee.

STUTTERING THE FIRE THAT BURNS WITHIN ME. Now there is a blind man. They are at Amsterdam and 125th. He would like to ask him what the city is like when you cannot sense it through your eyes. All ears. Nothing else. The noise, the clatter, the rumble of a bulldozer or of subway cars passing beneath your feet. He would like to know the peculiar quality of each person's footsteps: slow, quick, dragging, rhythmic, random, heavy; each as distinctive as a human voice. He imagines the sound of all the different footsteps on a single street, of all the footsteps in the city, moving in polyphonic rhythm. The ones that are drowned by the noise of traffic and construction, the ones that grow distinct again as silence spreads in interludes of calm. Like many times before, and just as he was entering Harlem, he left the phone's recorder on without realizing it. He listens to it later, closing his eyes though he doesn't really need to: a particular acoustic archeology belonging to that day and no other, to the streets of this city, so distinct from any others. He can hear again, on the recording, things that he doesn't remember having heard: sparrows during a lull in traffic; the voices of children at play, laughing loudly; then a long scream that is initially hard to place. It was a Black man, at 125th and St. Nicholas, pacing in circles on the sidewalk. He appeared to be shouting at the mannequins in the window of a store that sold cheap African clothing, accusingly pointing a finger at them as if they were callous witnesses, then launching himself at a stone wall, taking a few steps back to get a running start and kicking it as if he meant to climb it, finally raising a fist as if to strike it though he never did; it was always just that furious gesture, as if he were knocking on a huge door that no one else could see. Perhaps images are fixed more firmly in memory than sounds: he remembered perfectly the man's circular dance on the sidewalk and the way he struck the wall, but he had forgotten his scream, a kind of long wail, really, preserved in the recording, blending with the noise of buses and sirens and the periodic beeping of the crossing signal for the blind.

THE BOX OF TERROR. There are as many different stories as there are different faces, says Svetlana Alexievich. As many voices too. And for every face, for every voice and every story there is a different way of walking, a different gait and rhythm to the steps. The way people walk is as unique as their voice or as their face. It will never be repeated. With the invention of the daguerreotype it became possible to preserve faces. Voices began to be collected just over a century ago. We know Baudelaire's face, but not his voice. We have photographs of Chopin, and the last months of Poe's life are documented in a series of increasingly disturbing pictures. But we have no moving images of any of them. There could have been some of Pessoa or Benjamin. We could have known what their voices were like, but they were never recorded, or if they were, the recordings were lost. Walter Benjamin spoke often on the radio. There could be an early film of Oscar Wilde. Objects in motion remained invisible to photography for a long time. Passersby, carts, horse-drawn carriages, leave behind a faint trace in some of Eugène Atget's pictures, a kind of glowing, foggy exhalation. The streets of Paris are always empty in his photographs, not because he wanted it that way but from technical limitations in how the image was captured. This confers on them an unplanned realism, a poetry of disappearance. People, horses, dogs, busy gentlemen as well as idle ones, workers, seamstresses, bill-stickers with pots of glue, they are all there but they leave no trace. They are there and they are gone, which is the common lot. Then, as the first moving pictures appear, one does begin to see human beings, but they pass very quickly, hastening to vanish as soon as possible, driven by an urge to extinction. What would it be like, a moving picture of De Quincey, a film where for a few seconds you could recognize him, very old, dressed like a beggar, lost in the crowd on Oxford Street with that look about him of a decrepit child.

AUTHENTIC HUMAN HAIR. He can hear his own footsteps on the accidental recording and they seem even stranger to him than the sound of his voice. They are somewhat arrhythmic, heavy, clunky, stubborn like a mechanism made of simple gears and bellows. He wants to close his eyes and hear the footsteps of every person who walked down the same streets as him on that day, up Broadway, Amsterdam, making gradual readjustments as if charting a course at sea, straight north at first for hours, then northeast, then east along 125th Street, north again on Frederick Douglass Boulevard and then northeast, to the very end of the island, the river, the great geological barrier of the Bronx, marked by a belt of highways and bridges. This city, where people seem to walk faster and in a straighter line than anywhere else, is also full of slow, plodding motions, of halting steps and dragging feet. There is a city of the swift and a city of the slow, mixing and flowing together in the Mississippi of Broadway like the many different currents that form a river's seemingly uniform stream. The swift will not allow the slightest interference with their stringent paths, urging those who walk more slowly to step aside lest they be delayed for a single instant. They could step aside themselves, but it would be an abdication of the privilege conferred on them by their health and their physical momentum. They run up or down the steps to the subway at a gallop, angrier and more impatient still because people who walk slowly take even longer to climb a flight of stairs.

NO RATS NO ROACHES NO MICE IN YOUR HOUSE. The swift are impelled by health, money, physical appearance, the pressures of work, the golden substance of time, measured in minutes and seconds. The slow are going nowhere, or if they are, it makes no difference if they get there late or if they never arrive. The slow are old, fat, sick, homeless, deranged, paralyzed, hobbled, missing a limb. Extreme obesity is an unconquerable slowness. Normal bodies suddenly display a kind of excrescence, a giant, shapeless rump hanging to one side like a stuffed bag. A small man limps forward lifting and extending the giant sole of an orthopedic shoe. A very fat woman in a wheelchair with a missing leg. Some wheelchairs are motorized and others must be pushed by hand. Some are highly complex machines that can be guided with the chin or with the tip of one finger. People walk on rounded plastic legs, or legs made of metal bars, or jointed legs that end in an athletic shoe. The slow are wearing busted sneakers without laces, old slippers that can barely hold their swollen feet, or they just wrap their feet in shreds and rags and tattered plastic bags. They are bowed, hunched over, twisted, slumped over the frame of a walker or the handle of a supermarket cart where they carry their groceries or the junk they pick up here and there, anything they can find. There is something exorbitant to almost all of them, a disproportion, an excess, extreme old age, obesity, a hunched back, a stench, a general decay.

WELCOME TO TRINITY CHURCH. They hobble by on light aluminum crutches or old wooden crutches or leaning on canes and sticks like pilgrims and prophets, a broomstick, a piece of plastic tubing. They move like cripples in a diffuse medieval procession to a miraculous shrine. Some are lame, some crawl, some are pushed in wheelchairs or go a little faster on motorized tricycles. Some are bloated with sugars and greasy toxic foods, some had a foot cut off because they could not afford treatment for their diabetes. Some are families that were evicted from their homes, often Black women with several children, carrying or dragging a suitcase. Otherwise they stand on the sidewalk next to their bags with a look of stupor and fatigue outside a subway station, heading who knows where once they begin to move. Nearby, like arrows, the swift go by at the height of their powers, pressed for time, indestructible, with a hard, sinewy youth about them, fresh from the gym, immune to age, with a sports bag slung over their shoulder, the women in tights, their hair pulled back, a bottle of vitaminwater in one hand and a cruel resolve to their upturned chin.

WALK IN BLISSFUL COMFORT. The next stage, for the slow, is to lie huddled in a heap of rags on a street corner or in the gutted entrance to a vacant store or simply in the middle of the sidewalk. Someone suddenly stands still, lacking the strength to push their walker uphill or through a pile of dirty snow left behind after a storm. Someone collapses to the ground and does not move. On a corner outside a Popeyes a Black man in dirty clothes is lying faceup on the sidewalk. His belly is showing, he is missing a shoe, the nail of his big toe is sticking out through the sock. Some walk by without looking, some stop for a moment and then continue on their way. An older woman leans down and touches his face, asking him something. The man's eyes are closed. His chest is heaving irregularly. It is much colder in the shade, you can see his breath condensing. A few customers look out the window of the Popeyes. Others continue eating. A police cruiser arrives. People look from a distance.

AFRICAN HAIR BRAIDING. Big shoe stores and clothing stores on 125th. Bank branches and boarded-up stores, new buildings made of glass and old apartment blocks of redbrick. Men's barber shops with pictures of Black models. Women's beauty parlors offering relaxers and African braids. Bright African robes and headwraps in shop windows: green, yellow, red. Stacks of videotapes in the window of a music store that closed years ago, Blaxsploitation films, grimy sun-bleached posters advertising horror movies and erotic films and thrillers. Street stalls line the sidewalk. They sell African sculpture, necklaces, pendants, cell phone covers and chargers, crude knock-off luxury handbags, scarves blowing in the wind in imitation silk, Christian saints, Buddhas, Virgins, African gods or warriors, fertility goddesses with udder-like wooden breasts. They sell perfume bottles with xeroxed labels, rows of glass vials with dubious glistening oils that smell of sandalwood and patchouli. A fat woman in a bronze-green Statue of Liberty robe is handing out flyers for legal services. Her face is the same shade of green as her rubber crown. Her boots and the bottom of her robe are stained with muddy slush from the puddles of dirty snow along the curb.

PAWNBROKER CASA DE EMPEÑO. He has noticed as well a different type of person who moves slowly, the type that talks or shouts, announcing Christ's imminent coming or whipped into a frenzied tirade against invisible foes. A man in an oversize jacket that reaches below his knees is spinning on the sidewalk, the sleeves of his coat flapping and dangling like rubber arms. He stops and raises an accusing finger at someone. The mannequins in a clothing store. Then he starts spinning again. He begins to kick a wall covered with peeling posters, backing up to get a running start before he strikes. He strikes at the wall as if knocking on a huge door.

JEWELS DIAMONDS GOLD WATCHES. The new prevails over the old; the swift over the slow; steel and glass over brick and stone. Banks and real-estate firms have much larger storefronts than African salons and barbershops. Logos for cell phone brands; young white people laughing on billboards with their mouths wide open. The poor cling as best they can to the punished surface of a city that was once theirs and from which they are being evicted. Names stir the imagination and the urge to walk: Harlem, Dr. Martin Luther King Jr. Boulevard, Malcolm X Boulevard. The two men, who in life were adversaries, are posthumously reconciled in the shared destiny of their assassinations and the coming together of their names at a street crossing.

THE ALHAMBRA BALLROOM. He collects place names like an explorer. Past a certain point, the walk becomes an exercise in sustained hypnosis where he is both the hypnotist and the subject. He crosses worlds and continents. There are no more Starbucks now but there are many churches; modest churches in what used to be old shops, and then the corner stores they call bodegas, using the Spanish word. On the doors of the bodegas there are oversize color photographs of scrumptious food: grilled hamburger meat, fatty bacon strips, melted cheese, thick slices of roast beef or turkey smeared with runny yellow mustard. Now he walks through knots of men speaking African French. They are leaner than American Black men, the way they sit is different, the way they stand and talk in groups. There are new smells that are not the smells of fast food: rice, grilled fish, grilled plantains, unleavened Ethiopian bread.

FIRST EBENEZER BAPTIST CHURCH. As he turns north again it all grows more subdued, the sky expands, the street seems wider because the buildings are no longer tall. A broader prospect opens up before him, a large horizon that makes him breathe more freely and provides new vigor to his tired legs. Later, on the accidental recording, he will notice how the sounds begin to fade or disappear until nearly all that's left is the monotonous rhythm of his steps. The sidewalks, too, are unobstructed, with barely any people. Beauty parlors, bodegas, churches, African or Haitian community centers. Farther north you start to hear voices speaking Spanish, to notice Spanish signs on the bodegas. In front of him a boy with a backpack in a hooded winter coat is walking hand in hand with his father. It's not something you see very often in the city. Here children old enough to walk by their parents' side are pushed along in strollers that are too small for them, scrunched up, staring at an iPad or a phone. Some strollers have extendable arms or supports into which the device is placed so that the child, without needing to hold it, can look at the screen from an adequate distance. The father, mother, or caretaker pushes the stroller while talking or typing on the phone. He slows down so as not to pass the father and child. The boy is saying things, the father leans a little in his direction. The hooded coat, the boots, the satchel on his back make him look like a boy in a fairy tale. Unexpectedly he is seized by a jolt of tenderness that solitude and time turn into sadness. Suddenly nothing and no one is near.

ASSOCIATION DES MALIENS DE NEW YORK. It is even quieter now, a wide street, a broad expanse without traffic, like a square or like one of those American towns with low buildings that gradually give way to the plains. A kind of nearly secret and deserted border zone. What was vertical has become horizontal, clamor has turned into silence. A two-story motel with a wide parking lot reinforces the sense of strangeness. In front of the motel there is a small park enclosed by a railing. Farther still, an auto shop, a garage, a post office, also quite low, with a flag waving against the clear sky. As if the walk had lasted so long that it led him into the interior of the country. He sees a river or a broad canal, the curved crossbeams of an iron bridge that is painted white, a sheaf of highways, the fluvial and geological divide that separates the island from the great continent beyond, Manhattan from the Bronx. A name that rings with the slow, deep sound of a bell or a gong: the Bronx, as powerful as the name of certain Asian capitals on a school map, Samarkand, Ulaanbaatar.

BUILT TO FIT YOUR LIFE. Rivers and bridges are the United States' greatest beauty, the joint wonder of nature and engineering forcing each other into heroic disproportion, an immense river tamed and a human work exalted to the scale of a landform—a canyon, a gorge, a mountain range in profile against the horizon. Each crossbeam and pillar, each rivet and rusted surface of peeling paint is witness to the great drama of matter's resistance to the onslaught of wind, rain, and snow. Worn, bent, expanding with heat and contracting with cold, from one extreme to another, and then the ceaseless violent vibration of cars and trucks on the roadway, the force of rushing water against a pillar, the powerful pull of gravity. Crossing the bridge is like passing beneath the solemn gates one pictured slowly opening in fabled city walls, the gates of Ulaanbaatar, the Great Gate of Kiev. By car, one would barely notice. On foot, you know from the moment you step on the quivering walkway and gaze at the silent river below that you are crossing a border. Whatever lies ahead will be very different from what came before, a new world for your foreign eyes and ears.

HAPPINESS IS HAPPENING. Three guardian-like figures sit at the other end of the bridge. He keeps walking at a steady pace, overcoming without effort the impulse to go back. He can't tell yet if they are facing him or if their backs are turned. They are motionless, positioned at the exit to the bridge, by the side of the road. Two of them walk away toward the highway that rises from the river. As he gets closer, he can see the way they reel and stagger in a kind of strange and stiff Saint Vitus dance. One of them is missing a leg and leans on a crutch. They move among the cars that are waiting at the light, one of them holding up a piece of cardboard with some writing on it, and the other, the one with the crutch, shaking a plastic cup by the drivers' windows. The light changes and they scurry as best they can between the moving cars. The third man has not stirred. He is sitting on a low stone wall, letting his legs dangle. The hood of his parka completely covers his face. Walking past him, he is aware of being watched and he hears the jingle of change in the cup. He is not good at not looking, has not learned to walk past another person as if no one was there. He turns his head and is met by the man's dark gaze. His eyes are bright, the whites around the irises very clear in the shade of the hood. He is a Black man, old, with a grizzled white beard. His gaze is full of dignity. Walking past him and looking away, he hears the sound of the man's voice at his back. "Good morning, sir," it says politely and sarcastically.

BLINK AND FEEL GOOD. Now he is in a different city that is not ruled by the straight line, the grid, the horizontal. In the Bronx there are hills, gullies, stepped streets, curving avenues, steep stone walls, staggered planes that rise in the distance to various heights, like those cities in Yemen built on steep hillsides of dark rock. To arrive at his destination he must now walk steadily uphill. Yankee Stadium stands like a coliseum in one of those fantastical cities that in a thousand years will lie ruined in the middle of a desert, or perhaps be gradually taken over by a tropical jungle as temperatures rise and the ocean reaches the foothills of the Bronx, turning them into coastal cliffs. Dwarfed by the breadth of the esplanade and the height of the building, a man is taking a selfie in front of Yankee Stadium, stretching his arm and the selfie stick as far as he can, smiling, straining every muscle in his face, raising the thumb of his free hand in a gesture of triumph or success.

PUT YOUR MONEY WHERE THE MIRACLES ARE. Today is the day when the sun finally comes out, when it even feels a little warm if you stand out of the shade and the wind dies down. The day when the snow begins to melt, the dirty snow, old and filthy like a pile of wool stained with mud, a kind of pumice stone riddled with grains of soot and burned gasoline, pushed in piles against the sidewalk by the brutal blade of a plow until it turns into an impassable barrier, trampled, puddled into dark lagoons, snow that seems to decompose instead of melting, gradually revealing as it does what lay concealed beneath its lofty shroud, a days-old archeological deposit that emerges now entirely on its own, no one has to dig it up, to classify the things that lie half-buried still, embedded in a substance that no longer corresponds to the word "snow" but is rather a volcanic ash, the burned detritus of a new Vesuvius trapping in its matrix the complete compendium of a civilization's material signs. A stark air of extinction clings especially to things that have only partially emerged: a woolen glove like a hand coming out of the earth, a Dunkin' Donuts plastic coffee cup with a straw still sticking through the lid, the corner of a flip-top box of Marlboros, a ghastly toilet scrubber, the broken skeleton of an umbrella, a bird cage, fortunately empty, a bucket of KFC with a few leftover pieces nibbled by rats, a whole rat, still frozen, emerging from the snow, a pile of dog shit, a woolen cap, a plastic fork, a crushed pigeon, a baby diaper, a sponge covered in hair, a microwave, the black suction cup of a toilet plunger, thousands of cigarette butts. Streams of dirty water flow along the curb as the snow begins to melt, dragging small objects toward the sewer grates. The wind disperses them, lifting plastic bags up in the air, snatching at the tattered shreds of plastic on the branches of a tree, branches that are bare and black but will flower overnight as soon as it gets warmer, when the sun begins to shine a little brighter and everything is toppled and transformed again.

352

OUT OF THE ORDINARY. Just as the space around him is now wider, sounds and images have grown more powerful. The memory of seagulls and the hazy morning light in which the walk began is now so distant that it seems part of a different life, an earlier era, moistness, fog, like sense impressions left behind in someone else's memory. Each step requires greater vigor now because the path goes steadily uphill. You have to look at things more closely because the colors have intensified, the words you read or hear are more vehement: a yellow sign on a red background, a blue sign painted over a brick wall, covering it completely, like a brazen demand. Now you hear people speaking loudly in Mexican or Caribbean Spanish. The city has boosted its colors and multiplied its voices and turned up the volume. Hip-hop beats, bachatas, and reggaeton blast onto the street from auto shops and second-hand tire stores. Cars drive by playing deafening music with the windows down. Over Jerome Avenue run the elevated subway tracks. Each time a train goes by, a rhythmic clatter is unleashed that shakes the earth and drowns out every sound. Beneath the tracks you walk as in a shady portico, the ground is barred with stripes of light. Every few minutes the raging storm of clanging metal returns. Sounds and colors are equally strident. Mexican workers wave their arms outside the auto shops and tire stores, lifting colorful signs above their heads with low-price offers to attract passing cars. The sudden novelty of this new world seems to make the earlier worlds traversed over the past few hours recede in time. At street corners where the subway stops, the stalls of African, Indian, and Caribbean bazaars spread at the foot of the iron stairs. There are no more Starbucks and very few banks. He realizes it has been a long time since he last saw a yellow cab go by. There are more botanicas, hair salons, and ethnic restaurants than cell phone stores. Smells are as excessive and intoxicating as the colors and sounds. Elsa la Reyna del

Chicharrón. El Gran Valle Restaurante Lechonera. Bizcocho Dominicano de 3 Leches. Bizcocho Dominicano para Cada Ocasión. Las 3 Sirenas Ricos Tacos al Carbón. Gordito's Fresh Mex. La Esquina Caribeña.

THE GREATEST VISIONARY MEDIUM AND HEALER. Jerome Avenue smells of roast pig, rotisserie chicken, burned fat, rubber tires, gasoline, melted cheese on a Subway sandwich. It smells of McDonald's, Dunkin' Donuts, Domino's Pizza, baked potatoes, and roast yuca. At the entrance to each restaurant there are big color photographs of dishes gleaming with sauces and melted fat, their inordinate abundance paired in each promotional picture with a two-liter bottle of Pepsi. It smells of fast food and Caribbean food and chicken manure. Live Poultry National Chicken Market. The smell of manure is as dizzying as the deafening cackle. In a shed outside an auto repair shop, red-crested roosters pace arrogantly among stacks of tires. The tire stores are like Egyptian temples, deep halls with colonnades and walls and narrow passageways of piled-up tires of every size, huge trailer-truck tires rising in cyclopean stacks. Moving among them are the tiny figures of the probably undocumented immigrants who work there. They toil in groups, removing tires from a car, installing tires, screwing in a fender, taking apart entire cars for scrap. The hammering, the cackle of birds, the pulse of bachatas and reggaeton, a Julio Iglesias song with backup singers and violins, all is drowned by the crashing cataract of metal coming from above each time the subway passes, on and on.

HELP US FIND YOU. Rooms for rent. Cuachimalco Flowers. Pentecostal Church of Christ of the Antilles. Christ Is Coming. Loco Sam Cógelo Fiao Buy Now Pay Later. Every bit of available space is taken up by a sign. Dominican Hair & Barbershop. Jehanni Hair Salon & Nails. Color Drops. Duck-Feet. Nails, Eyelashes, Eyebrows. Jesus the Way the Truth and the Life. Barbecue Chicken Breakfast Sandwich. Handwritten signs taped to a lamppost, flashy posters with crowded pictures of music bands, a flyer for a Sunday dance. International Charro Show. Los Rayos de Oaxaca Here for the First Time from Beautiful Oaxaquita. Nigeria Express. Send Money Fast to Ecuador Honduras Guatemala. Vivero Bronx Live Poultry. Pague Aquí Todos sus Billes. Rincón Supremo Lechonero. Pay All Your Bills Here. El Original Conjunto Mar Azul. Your Dream Figure Lose Pounds & Inches. Los Preferidos Jorge Rodríguez and his Band.

THE LORD'S VOICE CRIES TO THE CITY. Movers, Junk Removal. Empeños Pawn 24 hours. Be at your ideal weight in just a few hours. La Encantadora Jennifer and her DJ Jhovanny Jhovanny. Zacarías Ferreira and Frank Reyes Together Just One Night for a Historic Concert. Frank Reyes and Zacarías Ferreira are dressed like sea captains, in jackets and caps, spreading their arms wide in front of a Caribbean seascape with a cruise ship in the offing. La Encantadora Jennifer is a woman in a low-cut dress, with wavy hair extensions voluptuously cascading over a large bosom that opens like a balcony beneath her. Best of the Best Bachata, El Grupaso LTP the Cyclone of Bachata. Santiago Cruz Interplanetary Tour. Chiqui Bombón Life Tastes Like Fruit. Sunday Matinée Yiyo Sarante's Official Farewell. Bucket of beer $10. Bottles $80. The Lord of Bachata. But neither the singers nor the bands in their matching hats and outfits nor Chiqui Bombón nor Encantadora Jennifer command as much attention in the posters as the DJs, in all their insolent glory. Haughty looks behind dark glasses or mirrored lenses. Bare chests in silver jackets. Buzz cuts, braids, a sideways hat, fanciful names like Mexican wrestlers. DJ Chulo Jay. DJ Sobrino. DJ Perverso. DJ Krazzy Loco. DJ El Yefry. DJ Lobo.

SAN RAFAEL BOTANICA AND DISPENSARY. The botanicas are bursting with the profuse imagery of baroque chapels, crammed with the assorted junk and tackle of every cult and miracle. The archangels Michael and Raphael brandish their swords and step on Satan's serpent head. Figures made of plaster or plastic look like a mix between calendar saints and Marvel superheroes. Victor Florencio Visionary Child Prodigy of the Bronx. Retail and wholesale distribution of a wide selection of religious articles. Anais Fernández Spiritual Adviser. The Virgin of Guadalupe, the Virgin of Lourdes, the Virgin of Fatima, the elephant god Ganesha, a cheerful Buddha with a bulging belly, Shiva with his wheel of arms, a Black Christ on the cross, an Indian medicine man holding a pipe, St. Martin de Porres, St. John Paul II, a Darth Vader with a saint's halo, a Santa Muerte holding a skeleton Baby Jesus in its arms, a character from *The Lion King*. In the window of the San Rafael Botanica and Dispensary stands a life-size Ecce Homo with sores and lashes and a baroque tangle of rancorously twisted thorns digging into his brow. Instead of being tied to a column, he leans piteously on a pair of golden crutches.

IF YOU SEE SOMETHING, SAY SOMETHING. Everything changes constantly. Plump Hispanic women holding children by the hand, then a moment later beautiful African or Pakistani or Bangladeshi women whose faces are framed and accentuated by veils. He is no longer aware that he's walking. He is nothing but the rhythm of his steps and the tracking shot of his gaze. He has no attachments or memories anymore, no ties, nowhere to go back to, no life left vacant in which to reassume his place. All eyes, all ears. Nothing but eyes and ears. He walks up Jerome Avenue as he walked up Frederick Douglass Boulevard before, and Martin Luther King Boulevard before that, and a shady stretch of lower Broadway, but also Menéndez Pelayo in Madrid, Oxford Street, other streets in Paris and Berlin that were known to Walter Benjamin, the Rue des Beaux-Arts, following the footsteps of Oscar Wilde. A blank space, suddenly, a black hole after the botanicas, the poultry markets, the hair salons, and the auto shops: an entire city block taken up by a low building, a kind of tumulus without any windows or signs, a black hole, gray-walled, as dreary as a prison or a grave, with all the nondescript, distinct inhumanity of the United States' official architecture. A building that conceals itself, refusing to display a window or a narrow slit or so much as a name to the outside world, a perfect bureaucratic barrow, probably correctional, with cameras in every corner, and as impervious to posters or to any visual marks as it is to sound. The walls look like pumice stone, giving back no light, absorbing sound. There's a glass door but it is dark inside and all you can see is a patch of bare linoleum and a withered ficus, the kind of tragic waif of a potted plant that you discover here and there in some corner at an airport. There's a line of people waiting outside the door, each person isolated from the rest by a certain amount of space on the sidewalk and by a particular form of visible affliction. An obese woman in a wheelchair sucks on a straw from a plastic bucket with the Wendy's logo. Her hair is dirty and she wears old-fashioned glasses with thick lenses. Then another woman: miniskirt, fishnet stockings, dyed blond hair, rickety high heels, knees pressed together against the cold. A third woman standing in line in front of her lifts a cigarette to her mouth and half her teeth are missing. There's a man with a shaved head and pale blue eyes, his neck entirely covered in tattoos, his hands as well, a gothic letter on each of his knuckles. Among all the dark-skinned, bronze-skinned foreigners going about their work, only the people waiting in that line are visibly white and native-born. They alone stand motionless, pale as zombies, gaunt as corpses, or buried in the quicksand of their own obesity. They wait and stare into the void. Whatever they are waiting for, as well as the affliction that has brought them here, has some relation to this barren building and the grim radiance of its architecture.

THIS BUILDING IS ONLY FOR TENANTS AND THEIR GUESTS. And here it comes, trudging up the narrow sidewalk, the slow procession of the hooded and the ragged, pushing supermarket carts, men and women who are sometimes hard to tell apart, just as it is hard to tell apart the young ones from the old, the drunk from the merely destitute, dragging their feet, holding their carts as they ease them down the curb to keep the bags of plastic bottles and of empty soda cans from toppling down. At the entrance to a supermarket they will put them into a recycling machine, a penny a piece, or they will sell them at redemption centers where you can see, through a darkened entryway, a high nave with a metal roof and mountains of bottles, cans, plastic containers, pierced by dusty shafts of sunlight that come in through the skylights. They had to come on foot because their cargo prevents them from riding the subway. They arrive from all over the

Bronx, perhaps from Harlem or even farther south. They resemble Inuit, bundled up and hooded in their jackets and their coats, in heavy boots and gloves, their faces burned and blackened by the cold, red with drink, a pair of wet, beady eyes behind a ski mask or a scarf, their bodies bowed by rummaging in garbage cans.

IF YOU SEE SOMETHING. There is a bracing sense of imminent arrival; a nearness that gives objects, faces, voices, and smells a dreamlike precision. There is a sense of faltering fatigue, of dizzying overabundance, relieved only by a parallel sense of nearly complete impersonality. At first, during the walk, the sense of self recedes. Then it seems to lapse. Finally, it disappears. You give yourself so entirely to everything external that you end up, for long stretches of time, for several hours, being practically no one. The riches of the world are better stored in an empty house. The street is not a path he follows but a current carrying him along. He is led by his footsteps, not by his will, his motion governed by the cerebellum with the same automated and primitive efficiency that regulates his heartbeat and his breathing. He has walked for hours at the same steady pace and it has also felt like sitting by a window on a train, watching everything go by without the least effort.

EXPERIENCE THE SPELL. There is a widening of space, a growing brightness as he leaves behind Jerome Avenue and the elevated subway tracks. New Fordham Road is the penultimate stage of his route. Fordham was the name of the village or rather the loose grouping of farms and meadows where Edgar Allan Poe came to live with his wife and mother-in-law. The light of the sun transfigures everything after so many overcast days. Rills of water trickle from the eaves as the snow begins to melt. The sidewalks widen in the sun, making space itself seem larger. At the intersection of Fordham Road and the Grand Concourse of the Bronx, an encampment of vendors spreads as at a crossroads in the ancient world. After the long uphill climb, the Bronx opens into a wide plain, a kind of Central Asian plateau traversed by trade routes stretching away in all directions. In the far distance of the Grand

Concourse there are views of continental solitudes, bluish silhouettes of towers like those deceptive domes and minarets that rose before De Quincey's eyes during an opium trance. Looking closely you can see the pencil profile of the Chrysler Building and the Empire State, which are not as tall or as thin anymore as the new luxury towers of the inconceivably rich, the unseen lords and masters of the Earth.

WE HAVE A LOT TO TELL YOU. Real and imaginary worlds will gradually begin to mingle when you're alone. Under the effects of opium De Quincey glimpsed down a dirty London street the golden domes and spires of a dazzling mosque gleaming in the sun. There is a breadth to the Grand Concourse like that of an urbanized Communist capital, a horizon of tall buildings terraced like Tibetan monasteries. At the top of a huge brick tower there is a broken clock. Every window on every floor is boarded up. Many years ago he saw an identical tower in a dream that he never forgot. It was night in the dream, and the tower was crowned by a glowing red star. Someone's voice said in his ear: "That is the star of the Bronx."

TRAVEL THROUGH SOUND. He has come to a place in a dream, a caravansary somewhere on the Silk Road. Cheap fabrics, multicolored hats and scarves of fake silk flash in the sun and wave in the wind. Foreign tongues mingle under the canopies as do the heavy scents of food and perfumes brought by merchants from distant lands. Women in high Mesopotamian headdresses sit majestically on plastic stools next to their stalls. An immemorial commerce is carried out by brisk gestures and loud, haggling cries. The poor come to this place to look for provisions, for merchants who speak their own language and will sell them things that smell and taste of the worlds they left behind. The same stand sells bead necklaces, seed necklaces, gold hoops and earrings, fake African sculptures, flip-flops, cell phone chargers, cell phone covers. English is just another language in the riotous Babel of tongues efficiently and summarily spoken in heavy accents. Much more common is the luscious Spanish of Santo Domingo, Mexico, Ecuador, and Cuba. *"Le pregunté qué tú quieres y ella me dijo que su mayor prioridad* *en este mundo son las uñas."* On the sidewalk, a group of old Cuban men is playing dominos in the sun, listening to Celia Cruz on a big boombox of the kind that kids with a supple step and a defiant look used to carry on their shoulders at full blast in the eighties. The old men are talking about someone who is a *súper* but wants to *resignar* because the guys in his building put trash down the toilet and make his life hell. They're on a sidewalk in the Bronx but they could just as well be sitting outside a café in Havana. A counterpoint takes place between the dry clicking sounds of the dominos and the high, honeyed voice of Celia Cruz. *"Como era millonario, qué digo, multimillonario, billonario, ese hombre ya lo tenía todo y lo único que le faltaba ganar era la oficina más poderosa del mundo."* *"Fue el papá de él que le dejó una inmensa fortuna."*

TRYING TO FORGET HIS NIGHTMARE. In the Bronx, the worst night-mare of the yellow-haired megalomaniac came true. Still standing on the Grand Concourse are the monumental buildings of a civilization that fell mysteriously into decay and was abandoned by its original inhabitants: banks with columned porticos, large stores with Art Deco towers and fa-cades, movie theaters that look like Roman baths or basilicas. Tribes of strange-speaking, dark-skinned, slant-eyed people of short and rugged build overran the borders, occupying buildings so solidly made that they did not fall into ruin even after centuries of decay. In abandoned movie the-aters they set up their places of worship and celebration; in what had been department stores with tall mirrors, carpeted stairs, and burnished count-ers they crammed their food stands and their stalls of cheap merchandise. They lit bonfires in public gardens to hold their primitive feasts. The wide, solemn sidewalks were filled with their teeming crowds, their cluttered stands of cheap fake goods and their strange music which was often deaf-ening, vulgar, always a little threatening. Where an old, distinguished busi-ness used to stand—a bank, a law firm—there was now a pawnshop, a greasy restaurant, a beauty shop for women who wore flamboyant hairstyles and long artificial nails in garish colors. On the plains of the Bronx, within sight of the city, which is a blue and chimerical island far in the distance, the bar-barian tribes have pitched their camps. Each morning, very early and still in the dark, they descend on the city. They take underground trains that go be-neath the river and elevated trains that shake with metallic fury as they cross a bridge. They go there to serve food, to pick up garbage bags in restaurants, to cook, to scrub dishes in airless basements that turn into ovens in the sum-mer months, to sweep the streets, open car doors, wipe old people's asses and care for their Alzheimer's; they go there to care for people's children, to climb the scaffolding outside a building, raise skyscrapers that reach ever higher, deliver food on bicycles through blizzards, open ditches in the asphalt with pneumatic drills, breathe toxic substances without masks, work twenty stories up without insurance, dump chicken parts into a deep fryer, drive a taxi for twelve or fourteen hours straight, and never once be able to get sick and miss a day of work. The same trains will carry them back at night, exhausted, dozing in their seats or on their feet, holding on to a subway pole so as not to fall asleep and crash to the ground.

REMEMBER YOUR HANDS. He's no more than an observer among them, a camera, an iPhone's audio recorder accidentally left on inside his pocket, tapping rhythmically against a set of keys or some pistachio shells. Since the phone is in his right-hand pocket, the steps on that side can be heard much louder, as in the limping walk of a crippled, stubborn man, the seconds and minutes changing ceaselessly on the cell phone screen in an endless metamorphosis of numbers rising at different speeds. Someone, later, may be able to study this recording. It will be possible to reconstruct much of his path from the footage of police surveillance cameras and of the cameras outside the banks: a face that is hard to distinguish in the shadow of the hat, between the raised lapels of the winter coat he wore on that cold morning, on the long, timeless day of the walk. A figure lost among others as they come and go, swift or slow, pushing baby strollers or supermarket carts with plastic bags full of beverage containers that tremble and seem about to fall, the tinkling of glass bottles and aluminum cans. All of this will be recorded. A timestamp will mark the moment he appeared at each corner: the hour, the minute, the second and tenth of a second. The route traced by the GPS on his phone will be a long diagonal beginning at South Ferry, heading north on Broadway, east at 106th, north again at 125th.

A NEW SPECIES IS BORN. He is a secret agent, not from a distant country but from an earlier time, taking note of everything that for those who live in the present is normal to the point of invisibility. His mission is so urgent and so vast that he can never rest. The training he received allows him to move unnoticed among the natives and to handle their everyday devices with sufficient ease. To preserve a perfect cover, he will allow himself no contact with his superiors or with the command post back in his own time. Carefully and surreptitiously he gathers any information that seems relevant. The future is an inaccessible and probably hostile country about which one must learn as much as possible. Once there, an agent knows the grave danger involved, how difficult it will be to return. The progress of technology will enable us to travel into the future without adequately resolving the problem of getting back. Harder than sending a spaceship to Mars is bringing it back with its crew safe and sound. Perhaps he's trapped now in the present, unable to return to a past that is in fact not even so remote, just twenty or twenty-five years back. He could never have imagined how terrifyingly exotic this new world would be, a place more categorically remote than North Korea, Babylon, Tenochtitlán. One of his tasks would be to study future climates, temperatures, the condition of the oceans and the atmosphere, verifying whether certain forecasts came true and learning possible preemptive lessons. The expedition has been undertaken with the utmost secrecy. But something went wrong, an accident, an oversight, and now he knows there is no going back, all possible escape routes have been blocked, the hidden passageways, the locked door deep down in some dark basement. Banished for life to another time as to a different planet, he perseveres nonetheless out of professional pride or simply because he enjoys the task, living in a calm exile, an inner solitude that will never cease anymore even if he partly begins to adopt the accent and the gestures of this other country, not much more of a foreigner really than any of the men and women he meets among the stalls of Fordham Road and the Grand Concourse. Just one more of them.

INTERACTIVE MAPS AND 3D TOURS OF THE PLANET. When he was living in the white wooden cottage that is now barely visible across the wide avenue, Edgar Allan Poe wrote a short story that took place exactly two hundred years in the future, in 2048. By then there are hot-air balloons that can rise a hundred miles in the air and carry four hundred passengers at speeds of over 150 miles per hour. Poe was captivated by hot-air balloons. One of his most commercially successful stories was a thoroughly documented and perfectly false narrative of a crossing of the Atlantic in just three days in a maneuverable balloon. It was from Poe that Jules Verne learned the literary allure of a balloon flight, as well as that of polar expeditions. He read Poe in Baudelaire's French translations. No one knows where the seed of literature will fall, or along what paths. The photographer Nadar, who was friends with both Verne and Baudelaire, became a balloon pilot and an aerial-show impresario. The balloon was as prodigious an invention as photography. When Baudelaire was living in Brussels, ailing and embittered, Nadar came to town to perform a series of balloon flights. He urged Baudelaire to go up with him, but Baudelaire refused.

TO CREATE SOMETHING THAT WILL LAST IN TIME. The white cottage, the tall, leafless oak trees that surround it, the park spreading to one side impose on the eye a suggestion of space that effaces or suspends everything else around, the neutral void beyond the edges of a photograph. The wide concourse and the big apartment blocks vanish into a landscape of farms and meadows, an open sky stretching to far woods on the horizon, with glimpses of the sea. From this elevated plot of ground you can see the island, tapered like a ship, pointing its prow toward the sea and bound by its two rivers. With a powerful spyglass you could make out the church spires and the ship masts far in the distance. More than half the island is covered in fields, farms, pastures, wooded hills traversed by streams, paths traced over the course of centuries by native tribes that are now vanished or decimated. The house stands in an area of farms and meadows that must have changed little since the time of the Dutch settlers. Being so far from the city, it seems a place of refuge or of strict retirement from the world. A writer who spent his whole life tumbling from one city to the next, fleeing creditors, seeking out newspaper commissions, an editor to publish his books, a rich patron to help him pay his debts and start the journal he never stopped dreaming about; a writer who lost himself occasionally in nights of alcohol-induced delirium and amnesia, wants to live now in the countryside, far from the uproar of the city and the hounding of his enemies, surely also from the lure of drink. Poe lives with his wife Virginia and her mother who is just as much of a mother to him, who lost his own when he was three. Mrs. Clemm calls him Eddy and he calls her Muddy. She is his father's sister. Virginia is his first cousin. She was thirteen when they married. Their life together in the tiny house seems vaguely like a strange confabulation among characters in a tale, defenseless, isolated from the world in a little hut in the woods where now and then a stranger arrives.

TERROR HAS ITS OWN THEATER NOW. They thought the country air and the fresh food and milk would help Virginia's health. For years she has suffered from tuberculosis, coughing to the point of choking and spitting up blood. The immaculate order and cleanliness of the cottage makes the poverty and deprivation of their lives all the more apparent. The reason the fireplace is so clean is that they can't afford to buy wood. Virginia spends her days ailing on a thin straw mattress. She covers herself with a spotless sheet, nearly transparent from being washed and mended so many times, and with her husband's old military overcoat from his days as a West Point cadet. There is little else in the house: a shelf of books, a cage that held a bird or a few birds, a family cat. Virginia places the cat on her lap over the coat for a little more warmth. She has a round, girlish face, flushed pink with constant fever. When Poe and his family lived in the house there were cherry trees all around. In the mornings, if he doesn't take the train into the blue haze of the city to try to earn a little money or see if someone will publish a short story or a poem (things written anyhow, cribbed from others or from his own earlier pieces), Poe works in the garden or goes for a walk down a country path.

THE SEER EDGAR POE. You have to climb a few wooden steps and ring a doorbell next to the closed door. Nothing can be heard inside. Not even the doorbell. Perhaps it is closed today. Who is going to visit this remote miniature house, what tourist, what lover of literature or devotee of Poe? Europeans, probably. People who were drawn to literature as teenagers by reading his stories about hidden treasure, murder, ruined mansions in the fog of a desolate moor, characters who wake up to find themselves trapped in a casket. There were horror films where seeing the name Edgar Allan Poe in the opening credits was already a promise or an invocation. On the shelves of stationery stores deep in provincial Spain you would find editions of Poe's stories with an illustration of a skull and a dripping candle on the cover. Those covers were like lurid movie posters: black as night, red as blood. The stories had not been translated into Spanish directly from the original but rather from the French translations to which Baudelaire, more than a century earlier, had devoted himself as passionately as to his own writing.

HE HAD TO TAKE REFUGE IN MYSTERY. This room on the ground floor of the cottage is where Virginia died. Virginia Clemm Poe. She was too weak by then to climb the steep stairs to the upper bedroom. Although there is now a period bed in the room, it's very likely that Virginia died on a pallet placed directly on the wide planks of this very floor. It is chilling to step across it. You want to make no noise so as not to disturb her in her illness, in her death. Poe had spent his life writing obsessively about very beautiful and very sick young women, about the beauty of dead women who can come back to life when they are already in the grave, or take possession, like vampires, of the soul of any other woman who tries to take their place.

AND TO THE CORDIAL WARMTH OF DRUNKENNESS IN THAT WORLD. A docent shows him around the house with a flurry of gestures and a voice that is better suited to the large halls of a museum. Standing very close to his visitor, in a small room with a low roof, he speaks as if they were at opposite ends of a museum lobby and he needed to raise his voice. It is, of course, an enthusiastic voice, full of possibilities, a baritone, the voice of a guide leading a tour group through a museum or a cathedral. In fact, one must stoop to go through the doors and even more when going up the stairs, which are quite narrow, twisting and turning to make the most of the cramped space. "People say, 'How small they all were,'" the guide explains, "but it's not true, they were just like us. Poe was a tall man, five feet, eight inches. Their roofs were low to save on building materials and for better heating." He is a young man, an enthusiast, whose height and professional ambitions are out of proportion to this tiny place and to the lone visitor who came today, a foreigner no doubt, a little frightened, a little daunted by the legend of the Bronx, though secretly priding himself in being able to refute it.

IF YOU FALL YOU WILL BE TRAMPLED. On the landing there is a cut-out of Poe taken from one of those daguerreotypes in which he seems so deeply wretched. It is actual size, and according to the guide very popular with visitors to the house who pose next to it for pictures, draping an arm over Poe's shoulder with a big smile, best buddies with the poor dead man with the funereal face—that face that is like the face of a prematurely buried man in one of his own short stories or in an English movie from the sixties, shot in lurid Technicolor and featuring Peter Cushing, Christopher Lee, an actress in a low-cut dress who screams in terror, yielding in advance to the vampire's bite.

AND IF YOU SLIP AND FALL IN THE WATER. It is a poorly funded house museum, part of the Bronx Historical Society. Entrance is five dollars and the guide is the only employee. Upstairs, in a room with a pitched roof, there is an oil portrait of Poe. It looks very much like one of those sinister paintings that have such an important role in the horror movies of the Hammer Film production company, portraits that can come to life or reveal a likeness to a ghastly forebear. Only a truly low-budget film would feature a portrait like this one, in its gaudy frame. Movies of that sort were filmed in Spain in the seventies, the star and often the director was an actor named Jacinto Molina whose stage name was Paul Naschy. The guide stands in front of the painting and talks about it as if he were explaining *Las Meninas* or *The Night Watch*, or perhaps describing by dint of a prodigious memory every detail of a cathedral altarpiece to which he keeps his back turned. "This portrait was personally bequeathed to the Edgar Allan Poe House by its author. He lives in the Bronx and is a well-known member of the community, a war veteran. He is currently ninety-three."

THEY WILL TOSS THEIR SANDWICH WRAPPERS AT YOU. Upstairs, in the main bedroom, there is a large flat-screen TV and several rows of plastic chairs. There is a low, narrow window and by bending down you can look outside. With a flourish, the guide reaches for the remote. "It's time for our audiovisual experience." Though he speaks to just one visitor, he keeps his gaze slightly unfocused, as if addressing a large group whose other members are invisible for some reason. The visitor says with cautious politeness that it's not necessary, he only came to see the house, not the audiovisual experience. "But it's included," the guide says, baffled at first, then disappointed or dismayed, with a little pity as well for this man who doesn't know how to get his money's worth or properly value what he's missing. They are both speaking English now though they know their native language is Spanish. The guide's name is Glenn, and he is almost certainly Dominican. Downstairs, in the room with the fireplace, there is an area cordoned off with red rope to keep visitors from entering. But on the other side of the rope there is only a rocking chair and a small writing desk. Glenn says that Poe used to sit on the rocking chair. Perhaps the only thing that is truly genuine about the house is the meagerness of the space and its absolute deprivation, which is unmitigated by the various period details to which Glenn feels such defensive attachment.

NO ONE CAN PICTURE THE LONELINESS. It's overcast now, the light coming in through the windows is a pale gray. A dead light from the past. He would have liked Glenn to leave him alone at some point, to stop explaining things. He never truly sees anything unless he is alone and in silence. He goes over to a window and Glenn stays close to him. He hears him say at his back that this is not where the house originally stood. It used to be nearby, higher up, on the side of a hill. It was moved in 1913, to preserve it when an apartment building went up in its original location. How strange, among all the things that were lost, that something so fragile would survive. Glenn says that from the porch Poe would have been able to see the Long Island Sound.

RETHINK HOW YOU LIVE. After Virginia's death, Poe fell into a state of lethargy, or calm. Perhaps being in mourning was a relief after years of endless anxiety about her health, all those sleepless nights hearing her coughing, struggling to breathe, vomiting blood on the sheets. When people asked how he was doing, he would say, "I am well, very well, better than ever." He wrote and published in journals much less than before. But this decline in his literary fortunes must not have been as bitter as being ceaselessly besieged by poverty. A friend went on a walk with him through the city and saw his patched boots nearly fall apart as he jumped over a puddle on a muddy street. Poe himself had contributed to his own misfortune as effectively as his worst enemy. He had a suicidal talent for falling out with those who could have helped him and turning viciously against his protectors. A cartoonist drew a picture of him preparing to write a scathing book review not with a pen but with a tomahawk. He had offended with equal virulence those who deserved it and those who did not. Perhaps because he was ashamed of his poverty, the generosity of those who helped him gave rise to a gratitude that would soon sour into rancor. Far less talented writers achieved much greater success and earned amounts that were unimaginable for him. Others had stumbled from birth into privileges that he was denied. Others inherited fortunes, houses, high positions. The popularity of some of his stories and poems had enriched the owners of the journals where they were published. Professional reciters could fill theaters by declaiming "The Raven." He had been paid nine dollars for the poem. He was told he had many readers in England, France, even Russia. Sometimes he was sent a clipping from a foreign newspaper and he would keep it and take pride in showing it. Despairing of the hope that justice would ever be done to him, he squandered his strength on sad literary vendettas, ferocious reviews of second-rate books in which his refined taste and critical sense were tainted by resentment.

I KNOW THE HORROR OF THOSE OPEN EYES. The most constant feeling in his life was abandonment: a drunk and absent father, a mother dead of tuberculosis in abject poverty when he was three. Once, toward the end, he wrote in a letter, "I have many occasional dealings with Adversity, but the want of parental affection has been the heaviest of my trials." On the day he walked out of the cottage for the last time, bound on a trip he thought would last several months, he brought with him a miniature portrait of his mother. On the back he wrote the date and a few words in a tiny hand: "My adored mother, E.A.P." The woman in the portrait looks like a teenage heroine from a Jane Austen novel. The wealthy merchant who took him in never adopted him and left him nothing in his will. Poe was a déclassé, like Baudelaire, De Quincey, Melville, and Benjamin: the blows of fortune, along with their own tumultuous characters, left them without a stable place in the social order or in the commercial and property-owning class to which they belonged—to which Poe, too, could have belonged, if his guardian had been more patient or generous with him, or Poe himself more tractable. They all practiced, in addition, a precarious and socially suspect profession associated with a disordered and disreputable life, a useless trade pursued by people of no practical sense, as dubious and extravagant as the circus or the theater, fitting no productive or commercial category and failing to ensure the minimum of security and respectability that even a lowly secretarial position could provide. Black sheep and reprobates, failed heirs, useless slackers, derelict dandies, bankrupt rentiers, proletarians dressed in bourgeois boots and overcoats (patched-up overcoats, boots that were falling apart), skilled in obsolete crafts and lonely, meticulous trades that were wrecked and tossed aside by industrial production and mass commerce.

GIVING HIMSELF AN INJECTION OF LEPROSY. Poe and Virginia's mother stayed in the tiny house like a pair of strange orphans, living as aunt and nephew, son- and mother-in-law, mother and son. Poe was not so much a widower as an orphan, mourning a wife who was only thirteen when they married and also his first cousin, a childish, asexual sister more than a wife, buried in a nearby cemetery that he visited often, sometimes at night, in shirtsleeves, or draping over his shoulders the military overcoat that must have still retained her scent. From her bed, Mrs. Clemm, Muddy, would hear him leave the house and shut the door. Then she would stay up until he returned, always fearing the worst, that he would lose his mind, or vanish like so many times before to reappear several days later in a drunken stupor. Sometimes she would hear instead the sound of his steps as he paced up and down the echoing porch. On clear winter nights the whole sky must have been a dark and blazing dome. There would have been no gaslight this far from the city, no smoke from factories or chimneys to cloud the view.

EXACTLY WHAT YOU WISH FOR. Downstairs, by the entrance, where the kitchen used to be, there is a modest stand with publications and souvenirs: postcards, key chains, prints where the cottage looks like a Gothic mansion on a stormy night. Glenn keeps everything in perfect order. The money he collects for the entrance fee goes into a wooden box with several compartments. Each time he sells a ticket, a postcard, or a souvenir, he draws a little cross in the corresponding box on a form. He accepts credit card payments with a little dismay. It forces him to bring out a rather ancient device and make sure he can get a connection. Poe looks out from the row of postcards on the stand with successive expressions of misery and grief, trapped two centuries ago in the frozen, brutal faithfulness of a daguerreotype.

THE PUNCTUAL HANDKERCHIEF OF PARTING. In the general imagination Poe wears a small black mustache just as Mozart or Bach wears a wig, Dracula a black cape and tailcoat, Superman a pair of blue tights, Marilyn Monroe a platinum-blond hairdo, and Karl Marx a prophet's beard. In fact, Poe only wore a mustache during the last two years of his life. In earlier portraits, whether sketched or painted in oil, he wears long sideburns that reach down nearly to his chin, but no mustache. He is a complete stranger: a dignified young man with a kind, agreeable expression and big eyes that are wide open. Although he looks sensitive, perhaps a little lost in reverie, he could well be someone in a very different walk of life from literature, a lawyer, maybe, or a clerk, someone leading a peaceful life but having no great prospects, perhaps from lack of initiative. There is sadness in his eyes, even abandonment, but not fear, much less a pall of misery.

YOU'LL TAKE INVISIBLE PICTURES. The first photograph is a daguerreotype taken in 1847. It is his first portrait with a mustache. Less than a year had passed since Virginia's death. The mustache is small, clipped neatly at the corners of the mouth, Chaplinesque, with slightly twisted ends. The later pictures form a sequence as gradually dismal as Rembrandt's self-portraits of old age, ruin, and decay. Two of them were taken within days of each other, in November 1848. The third, which is also the last, dates to mid-September 1849, just a few weeks before his death. In November 1848 Poe was in Providence paying a visit to one of those widows with literary inclinations who were drawn to him and whom he occasionally courted in the hope of attaining through marriage a certain social and financial stability in life. They found him irresistible. He recited his poems in a whisper and copied them in his own hand with a special dedication. They were captivated by the lost, magnetic gaze of the widowed poet and by his Southern manners. His dignified elegance was ennobled rather than spoiled for them by his obvious poverty. The rumors of his nights of drink and ruin, which were not unfounded, added an attractively alarming quality to his ceremonious manners. He made promises to abstain from drinking. He behaved charmingly at social gatherings. Then he got savagely drunk, disappeared for a whole week, and everything was ruined.

NOT TO KNOW IF YOU ARE IN THIS WORLD. In the November 9 picture he looks hungover and filled with regret. His mustache, which is thicker now, accentuates the bitter grimace of his lips. His facial muscles seem contracted and collapsed. Around that time he took a large dose of laudanum as he boarded a train to Boston, and when he turned up several days later he remembered nothing except terrifying hallucinations. In the November 13 photograph he seems somewhat recovered, some of his dignity is back, but his general appearance is one of insurmountable despair. He is wearing the military coat with the big lapels, the one that kept Virginia warm. In each picture his forehead seems larger, more swollen, his dirty hair more plastered to his skull.

LONGER HYDRATION FOR YOUR EYES. Glenn sees his visitor to the door. "It's always nice when someone comes," he says. "Weekends are busier, especially in summer, but during the week it can get a little lonely." He admits with some regret that the two other houses where Poe lived, in Richmond and Baltimore, are larger and attract more visitors. He shivers and rubs his hands together at the door like the owner of a house eager to return to his domestic warmth. On June 20, 1849, Poe left the cottage for the last time. An anxious feeling of being confined to a single place for too long must have been as powerful a motive as the need to earn money. He intended to give public talks, to find journals that would accept his work again, to muster up subscribers for a literary journal he had envisaged for years, in chimerical detail: the layout, the type of font, the various sections, the list of contributors who would send pieces from abroad, the immediate success in sales, the money that this time no one would stint or steal from him. He just needed to persevere until he found subscribers and an investing partner to set things in motion. Nothing more.

TO FLEE THROUGH THE STREETS, TO SEEK SHELTER IN THE UPPER FLOORS. He carried a briefcase or a valise with his lecture notes and a trunk filled with books, manuscripts, and a few changes of clothes packed by Mrs. Clemm. He said as he was leaving that he regretted it, and was afraid of not coming back; that he would write daily and send money once he earned some. An outbreak of cholera had just been declared. That summer more than five thousand people died in New York City. When Poe reached Philadelphia by train, the cholera had spread there too. He fell sick. To ease his fever he took calomel, a compound of mercury. It made his gums bleed and it caused confusion and what he called "cerebral congestion." There is no reliable account of what happened in Philadelphia. It seems that he ran into some acquaintances and got abysmally drunk with them. A few days later he was in jail, charged with drunkenness and disorderly conduct. One morning he turned up at the workshop of a printer and engraver known to him from earlier trips, John Sartain. Poe was wearing only one shoe. He said that he had lost the trunk with his books and clothes and the briefcase with his lecture notes. He claimed he was fleeing from enemies who were trying to kill him. He had heard them on the train, carefully plotting his murder, and they had followed him at night through the streets of Philadelphia. He needed to change his appearance so he could elude them. He asked Sartain for a razor to shave his mustache. His hands were trembling so badly that Sartain feared he would hurt himself, cut his own neck. Sartain clipped Poe's mustache with a pair of scissors.

MAKE YOUR ASPIRATIONS A REALITY. Now his face seems strange again and naked. He asked to borrow some shoes but Sartain could only provide him with a pair of slippers. In cloth slippers, without a mustache, a suitcase, a cent, or the least judgment, Poe wanders through Philadelphia like a lost soul. He tells Sartain about some of the hallucinations he experienced in recent days. Standing at the window of his cell, he would see a woman dressed in white calling out to him from the prison tower. Or the door of the cell would open and his enemies would bring in Mrs. Clemm with her hands tied behind her back. Two of the men would restrain him while the others began to mutilate Virginia's mother with hatchets and saws: one foot, then another, then a leg up to the knee, a hand, the other hand. During his brief spells of sanity, he writes letters to Mrs. Clemm begging her to come find him. Just as cruel is a different hallucination where he sees the white cottage and the cherry trees standing clearly before him, and knows the door will never open again to let him in.

BLOOD THAT SLOWLY LOOKS OUT OF THE CORNER OF ITS EYE. Somehow or other, with Sartain's help, he manages to get to Richmond on June 14. He has recovered his trunk, though not his lecture notes. It is not a serious loss since he practically knows them by heart. In Richmond the cholera epidemic has subsided and public slave auctions have recommenced immediately with great success. Richmond is the city of Poe's childhood and early youth. Unexpectedly, he is renewed by being there again. The outcome of his harrowing trip has been a peaceful and pleasant return to the past. In

Richmond, refined people with a taste for books are flattered to know that this old acquaintance of theirs is now a famous writer. He gives a few successful lectures. He recites "The Raven" in a hypnotic, singsong cadence. He reencounters a love of his early youth, Elmira Shelton, now a wealthy and attractive widow. They make plans to get married. Poe abstains entirely from drinking. He also finally manages to find an admirer with deep pockets who is willing to fund his journal. In late September he must return to New York to make arrangements before the wedding can take place, and also to see to the journal and let Mrs. Clemm know about this new life in which naturally there will be a place for her.

THIS IS THE TIME TO LIVE. When Elmira says goodbye to her fiancé he does not look well. She presses his hand and finds it hot with fever. The last daguerreotype is taken around this time. Poe is once again wearing a mustache. But he has more than ever a look of anguish and despair. His eyes are unfocused, his mouth contracted. His necktie, put on anyhow, is too tight around his neck. There is no relation between that face and the external facts of his life during those days in Richmond. He looks like a man in the grip of terror.

ON A SINGLE DAY. We know he was in Baltimore on September 27. There was no reason for that stop. There are different accounts of his reappearance on October 3 after a gap of a few days. One of them says that he was found unconscious in the gutter. According to another, a witness claims to have found him in a tavern during one of those corrupt election days when drunks were rounded up and taken to the ballots. He is carried to a hospital. The doctor in charge of him is an educated, compassionate man who has read his work and recognizes him. His name is Dr. John Moran. Poe does not know where he is, has no idea how he got there or who brought him. Nor does he know where he got the filthy clothes he's wearing. Near dawn his arms and legs begin to shake and he lapses into delirium. He is drenched in sweat. He speaks and points to the wall as if he recognized people walking down the street, people who sometimes fill him with terror and other times with an urgent need to call out and be answered. He makes motions with his legs as if to walk after them. He repeats a name, Reynolds. To calm him down, Dr. Moran says that a good friend of Poe's is coming from Baltimore to keep him company. Suddenly clearheaded, Poe looks him in the eye and says, "My best friend would be the man who gave me a pistol that I might blow out my brains."

THE FACE OF NIGHT. He spent six days in the hospital, going through spells of delirium and extreme exhaustion. On the walls of the room he saw shadows and faces. On the morning of Sunday, October 9, he grew very calm and quiet. Dr. Moran leaned down because he saw his lips move. He heard him say, "Lord help my poor soul."

THEY GROW LIKE MUSHROOMS. He has left the cottage. Evening is coming on. The sun is still high but there is a hint of dampness in the air and the shadows of the trees have lengthened over the gravel walks and the park's ragged winter grass. He sat down to rest on a bench, to reconsider or absorb what he has seen. The satchel lies open on his lap and he is looking for an apple among his various papers, clippings, documents, folded maps. He bought it at the farmers' market on Union Square, who knows how many hours, streets, compressed lifetimes ago. The immediate past widens like the skies and avenues of the Bronx. It is a perfect apple, easy to hold in one hand, red, green, yellow, with a scent that seems like it was preserved in a deep wooden chest where the harvest is stored from year to year. He wipes it with the handkerchief that he always keeps neatly folded in his pocket. Leonard Cohen had a knack for folding his clothes when he packed or unpacked his luggage in a hotel room during a tour. He cleans the apple, or rather gives it a polish to bring out the colors in the cold, blond light of the late-winter sun. He takes a first hungry bite and his mouth fills with its rich juice. On a nearby bench there is a flurry of young Black women with small children talking and laughing loudly, showing each other their cell phones. They have long stick-on nails that in some cases are starred and striped like the American flag. Schools are letting out. Down the paths that crisscross the park come Central American mothers with indigenous faces, holding hands with children bundled up in big hoods, like young Inuit, carrying their satchels on their backs. A homeless man goes by pushing a supermarket cart full of junk and rags, dragging his feet, leaving behind him a smell of alcohol, urine, and shit.

ALONE I WANDER EXHAUSTED BY THE RHYTHM. He never tires of gazing at the far horizon, the wide-open skies of the Bronx. When he gets up he becomes aware of the whole unexpected weight of his fatigue. He wipes his hands and mouth with the handkerchief and puts the apple core into an overflowing garbage can, making sure it won't roll to the ground. All around Poe's cottage there are very tall leafless trees, oaks, or perhaps maples. When Poe was alive they were cherry trees. He has to stuff his hands in his pockets and walk briskly to shake off the cold. As he nears the crossing of the Grand Concourse and Fordham Road again, he begins to come back to the present. The cottage was a time capsule. Now reality returns as a loud, teeming scramble of busy lives and haggling commerce. Vendors yelling over their merchandise, music pouring out of wide-open storefronts and from cars going by with the windows down. People buy and sell, people feed, people scrounge for shelter and sustenance in this hostile environment, improvising a portable version of the life they left behind. They play their music very loud. They open cheap markets that sell bright textiles, women's veils, tight party dresses on wide-hipped, big-bosomed mannequins. They bring with them their hair salons for men and women specializing in African braids, extensions, and relaxers. Their fruit stands. Their food carts. Their street vendors yelling from the back of a van that has been turned into a shop counter, "fresh fish, octopus, shrimp, fresh fish, octopus." An ice cream man goes by pushing a cart painted with the Ecuadorean flag, ringing a little bell. An indigenous woman with braids has placed a large pot of rice and beans in a supermarket cart. Puerto Rico Qué Rico. Another woman sells fried churros dusted with sugar, and a third sells candied peanuts from a pushcart with a tin funnel that sends out puffs of fragrant smoke smelling of burnt caramel. On every corner there's a different Spanish accent. *"Así soy yo, mi amor. Si no te gusta, esta es mi vida. ¿Qué otra cosa podemos hacer?"* Voices and melodies change and blend, and so do smells, the scent of corn, beans, fried chicken, and roast pig. It is Fordham Road and it is also Africa, Santo Domingo, Southeast Asia, the beautiful face of an Indonesian woman framed by a veil. It is rural Mexico, Peru, Ecuador, the Andes. With quick, polite gestures he collects the ads and flyers that are offered at every step and that go into his overflowing pockets. He turns on the audio recorder so as not to miss any sounds. He takes photographs of advertising posters and jots down what he reads on shop signs. In the window of a bakery there are Barbie dolls in bell-shaped dresses that are birthday cakes. In a botanica there is a Christ on a cross made of seashells of all sizes that are painted white, and next to it a Black goddess or priestess in an Egyptian headdress holding in her open hands a gold snake with glass eyes.

QUICK CHEAP DIVORCE AND PAPERWORK ONE HOUR. Chicken, eggplant, pork, okra, chayote. Lula Seafood Fish Stew. Juan Peña Style Barber Shop. Juan Ángel Lezama El Coyote Pride of Oaxaca. Tina African Hair Braiding. Loans Empeños We Buy Gold Compramos Oro. Beauty Salon La Flaca. African Caribbean Market. Tacos Tortas Burritos Quesadillas Sopas Nachos Carnitas Huevos Rancheros Sopa de Marisco Chicken Sandwich Enchiladas Steak and Onions Mexican Soda 2 Liter Bottle. Perfection Hair Salon Straightening Highlights Hair Extensions. Banco Azteca Wire Transfers. La Perla International Latin Food Specialties and Seafood. Tripe Chicken Pork Fresh Goat. Specializing in Mexican Sodas. Send Money Anywhere in the World. Jesus Is the Path the Truth and Life. An Incredible Selection of Meats in One Place. Mango Tamarind Delicious Coconut Ice Cream. La Migra Los Magos del Norte La Banda Sinaloense with Sergio Lizarán The Prodigy Final Farewell Singing All His Hits DJ Cholo Jay.

YOU WILL HAVE A NEW LIFE. He begins to leave it all behind, to walk past it with his satchel and his sportsman's or explorer's cap, unmistakable from the back, anonymous Mr. Nobody, pausing here and there at the window of a botanica or a cell phone store that is blasting electronic Arabic music, a kind of thumping hip-hop blended with the floating chant of a muezzin. He switches sidewalks frequently, though mostly now he tries to stay in the waning sun. He slows down to take pleasure in the warm smell of corn tortillas or in the variety of hairstyles offered on a sign for a Nigerian barbershop. Fordham Road goes gently east, downhill, sustaining in its course the rhythm of his steps despite his great fatigue. No matter how far he walks, the city will always spread farther, without end, past the Bronx and the iron bridges, the swamps and the far, low-lying neighborhoods of Queens. He goes deeper into the crowd and at a certain moment he is suddenly lost from sight, in the blink of an eye, as abruptly as if he had gone down into the subway. Inside his coat pocket the voice recorder is still on. A police or a fire truck siren can be heard far away, and the steady rumble of the subway up above; then it all begins to fade, to grow distant and disappear, all except the stubborn rhythm of his steps.

COME LIVE A FITNESS EXPERIENCE. I came to the city two months ago with a MacBook Air in my backpack and a suitcase full of notebooks—some blank, others already covered in writing—and with binders full of clippings and envelopes stuffed with flyers, and with pencil cases, erasers, pencil sharpeners. I brought a phone to take pictures of shop signs and to record conversations as I walked down the street. Now, as I prepare to go back, every notebook is filled with writing and there are yet more clippings in each binder. A cylindrical cardboard box that once held a fancy flask of cologne is now the little chest where I keep the pencil stubs I have used up. I don't know if the task brought me here seeking its own completion or if it took advantage of this trip and co-opted it, imposing these two months of solitude and withdrawal just as it had earlier imposed on me the habit of writing in pencil and of filling every notebook from the very first to the very last page. The task began as an accidental distraction in my life and ended up taking it over entirely. I don't know, either, if I came here under its influence or following a different impulse that remained initially concealed and has gradually come to light: the need to say goodbye. Consciousness reveals only a small part of what happens in the mind. Our will may be an illusion, and what is truly decisive may occur at depths known to us only through the equivocal evidence of dreams.

VENTURE INTO THE WORLD. You never know how many places you will have to go to, how many you will have to leave behind in order to appease the anxious urge to keep on looking for a new situation in life, an urge that will turn out to be like all the other ones you feel. Some extraordinary thing is waiting that you can't miss, a film, a book, a piece of music, a new love, a new town. You read a review and you want to buy the book immediately; you feel oppressed by the quiet and comfort of your home one morning and are desperate to go out, not knowing where; a newspaper article and some color photographs of a city make you want to visit or to move there. It may not be so different from the urge that others feel for a new car, a cruise, a trip to a Caribbean resort, the urge that makes them stand in line all through a winter night so they can buy the newest cell phone.

UNEXPECTED DREAMS. This room, this desk by the window, has been my office for the past two months. I have looked through this window for who knows how many hours and days over the past eight years. I have seen the bare branches of the gingko tree outside gradually covered in leaves in April and I have seen them turn yellow in November, casting a faint golden glow as dusk began to fall a little earlier with each passing day. March and early April have been unusually cold this year and the leaves on the gingko have yet to sprout, just as the almond and the cherry trees along the river have yet to blossom. I will not be here when they finally emerge, fan-shaped leaves of a tender green fluttering in the breeze, a rush of sap rising from the roots, the chemical prodigy of photosynthesis.

SEE ART EVERYWHERE. For several weeks, during the grayest days of February, a plastic bag was caught in a high branch of the gingko tree. One of those generic bags they give out in every store, always with the same inscription: THANKS FOR SHOPPING WITH US. There was an ominous air about it, like a tattered rag, a flag, a black pennant for the triumphant invasion of plastic trash. Nearly every tree in the neighborhood has one or several plastic bags caught in the branches, some intact and others torn to shreds. Some have been there for so long that they are faded, frayed, shaking in the wind like Tibetan prayer flags. This particular black bag was directly in my line of sight when I looked out the window as I worked. It hung limp and dismal when there was no wind. It shook and fluttered when the wind picked up, swelling and rising like a captive balloon, or lashed by drifts of snow and by those gusts of freezing rain that bite into the skin like needles and peck at the glass like furious birds. One night, the wind roared and whistled so violently that I woke up at dawn and didn't manage to fall back asleep. When I looked out that morning the bag was gone.

THE WAIT IS OVER. I wanted to fill every page of every notebook. I covered them in penciled writing and with clippings that I pasted as contentedly as a child or a craftsman, taking pleasure in my eyes and hands, the sound of scissors slicing paper, the smell of glue, the concentration needed to cut with care around a sign or a silhouette. I have learned, at least, to leave a margin. I have filled my mornings with long and ceaseless walks and I have spent my afternoons at the desk by the window, in my movable office, which for a while was sedentary.

COME EXPERIENCE SOMETHING DIFFERENT. When I arrived two months ago I thought that in this time of solitude and withdrawal I would be able to finish the task. Now I am about to leave and realize it is not done, because the journey back, both in anticipation and once it is accomplished, will be a necessary part of it. I pack my bags but the task continues. I put away the notebooks in the suitcase, then the binders, the pencil cases, the cardboard boxes, until there is little room for anything else, a few books, a few items of clothing perhaps that will mostly serve as cushioning. The bulkiest book is a wonderful biography of Baudelaire that I have read compulsively of late, a book that keeps me up at night, unable to sleep, and that I will finish tonight during the foreseeably sleepless flight to Madrid. I have put away the splendid case of twenty-four colored pencils and also the ink-well, which I never use since I can only write in pencil. Imagination comes to a halt, words run dry when I try to write with a pen.

YOUR BODY WAS MADE TO MOVE. Every object turned into a clock, an urgent stopwatch in these last few days, an hourglass telling time by a visible diminution of its size or of its contents, a shampoo-clock in the shower, a bodywash clock, marking the end of this period of seclusion and of my life in the city. The jar of honey from which I took a spoonful each morning for my coffee is more than half empty. The medicine bottle rings hollower each time I grab it from the cabinet. There are no more calendar pages with numbered boxes to cross off. But it makes no difference, since every object is a clock. The pencil I wrote with during these past few weeks is so short now that I can barely hold it between my fingers. The first thing I've done each morning upon waking, sometimes also in the middle of the night, has been to look at the red numbers on the nightstand clock. In the kitchen there are other clocks, one on the oven, one on the microwave. In the living room there is one on the DVD player and one on the cable box. On my phone there is a clock and a stopwatch, on my wrist there is a watch with numbers and small moving hands. There is another stopwatch in my pulse and in my eye-balls when I rub them with fatigue, and another one is beating like a solemn pendulum inside my rib cage. The light, lingering a little longer each day in the window and on the building opposite, has been a sundial. The shade, rising gradually from the sidewalk to the upper floors and finally extinguishing the last remaining glow on a western cornice, has been a shadow dial. There is a water clock of words spilling onto the paper from my hand and from the tip of the pencil as I write. When I walked alone for many hours through the city my legs were the ticking hands of a clock measuring time in a two-step rhythm. In the afternoon and in the middle of the night, the metal sounds coming from the heating pipes and radiators were another clock embedded in the fabric of things. My breathing was a clock, the air that fills my lungs and is released shortly after with a faint whistle before rushing back in. Writing was another way to measure time. The particles of graphite coming off the pencil were like grains of sand.

WHAT'S YOUR RITUAL. In the past I have left New York with a sense of rupture, as if something that had never managed to become complete was being interrupted once again. Today I am surprised by a neutral mood that is only altered by a slight dizziness. The fatigue of going back and forth so many times suddenly weighs on me. Perhaps there is a temporal instinct inside me, a clock that measures long durations, saying I will not return. I feel no sadness at this premonition, or almost none; I feel relief. As far back as I can recall, no period of my life, or lives, has been without a fracture—between places, loyalties, desires. I did not plan it this way, but I realize now without sorrow that it is all coming to an end.

MY OFFICE ALWAYS TRAVELS WITH ME. I worked so intensely over the past two months that I now feel the need to rest, to return. I purged and cleansed myself internally by spending so much time alone devoted to a single task. This place has been my office and my workshop, my cell, my monastery. I do not know how many miles I walked or how many pages I wrote by hand, in pencil, in these past few months. The laptop can tell the exact number of words that accrued as I made a fair copy of the writing, turning it into something less haphazard. Each blank page appeared before me like a smooth slab of concrete on a city sidewalk, like a storefront, a window display. I clipped, gathered, and recorded so many fragments of conversation, so many newspaper headlines and advertising phrases that I now have a great need for silence. Too many voices—heard, read, imagined, or invented—give rise in combination with intense solitude to an incipient sense of delirium. You have to close and shut down everything before you leave, and then do nothing. Close the laptop, and the suitcase, and the final notebook; close and lock the door to the apartment, your abolished cloister, just as the taxi driver will finally close the trunk to the car.

DRIVE TOWARD THE UNEXPECTED. It is a Sunday afternoon, so there is little traffic on the way to the airport. The loud bustle of the street vendors continues in Harlem. From the window of the taxi you can see the city fall away, recede, catch a glimpse of it across the East River through metal beams and suspension cables. There is a soft, objective clarity to the April afternoon. The edges and the outlines of things are unblurred by distance. Even the worry of having neglected or forgotten some crucial thing at the last moment is not very pronounced. Fatigue acts as a sedative. There is a great relief in being done, in being able to consign a part of life to the archive of concluded things; as if one had finished a task, or were about to. Beneath it all, like a perpetual undercurrent, is the notion that the future is no longer boundless. There is no more time for life experiments, as there still was during the past few years. Ten or fifteen years ago my life was still bordering on youth. Ten or fifteen years ahead lies that strange and inconceivable thing, old age. There will be no new city to indulge in the illusion of beginning a new life.

CURIOSITY WILL BE YOUR COMPANION. Baudelaire travels to Brussels for a few days in 1864 and is trapped in a puzzling paralysis, a strange, self-imposed exile that will be the last episode of his conscious life. During the twenty years prior, though he always stayed in Paris, he changed his address constantly, moving from place to place without forethought or rest, writing poems or essays on art for the newspapers, fleeing from creditors who never ceased to pursue him, sending his mother awful letters filled with desperate pleas and blackmail. In total he lived in thirty different places in Paris, once moving six times in a single month. One night, at eleven o' clock, he gets to Brussels by train and goes directly from the station to a nearby hotel, the Hôtel du Grand Miroir. He will stay there indefinitely, even though he finds it a loathsome place. But then Brussels, too, strikes him as a ghastly city, and Belgium as a revolting country, yet he will do nothing to distance himself from an atmosphere that he finds stifling and a place where he can find no way to make a living. The owner of the hotel torments him with her demands and her acrimony when he is late with the bill. He makes constant plans to go back to Paris and always cancels them at the last minute. In long, convulsive letters to his mother he promises to visit, but then defers the trip for just a day, a day or two, a week, and in the end he always finds an excuse, sickness, poverty, work. In Brussels, where the weather is almost always foul, he doesn't even enjoy walking. Brussels is a town of muddy streets and hostile strangers where it is impossible to take a pleasant walk.

DISCOVERING NEW THINGS IS WHAT KEEPS YOU ALIVE. Sick, forced to stay in one place, confined to his dark room in the hotel of the Great Mirror, Baudelaire writes terrible things against Belgium, the Belgians,

Belgian women—who seem vulgar and fat to him—and against the ugly fashions of Brussels, and the king, and his subjects' bovine deference. His health worsens every day. He is afraid to go out because he suffers from vertigo and fainting spells. He fears that he will lose his mind. One day he writes with clearheaded terror that he felt the flutter of the wing of imbecility brush against him ever so slightly. He plans books that he will never write. Perhaps they seem more real to him when he describes them in detail in his letters to his mother. He wants to write a book of Confessions, like Rousseau, and a long, ferocious pamphlet against Belgium. He wants to finish the volume of his poems in prose, which changes fluidly in form and even in title as it moves through various incarnations, and which, in a conjectural and approximate way, may already exist, scattered across the pages of the various papers and defunct journals that published the poems. Sometimes this future work is called *Paris Spleen*, sometimes not. Baudelaire will never get to hold it in his hands. On the large, densely printed pages of mass newspapers devoted to business, politics, and advertising, it will be hard for anyone to notice those brief, barbed pieces of poetry, with their delirious visions of the city and its monstrous or eccentric denizens. Paris, that underwater realm of strolling opium eaters.

A WHOLE WORLD OF PLEASURES. As a young man he was frugal, drinking almost nothing except the light wines of Burgundy. Now he drinks cognac and laudanum. Opium dissolved in alcohol relieves some of his ailments while causing and magnifying others. Now, in Brussels, in his darkened hotel room, Baudelaire has become a true disciple of De Quincey, a full companion in the brotherhood of addicts. In the course of two years he travels to Paris only once, shortening his stay so that a few days later he is already back in the needless horror of his life in Brussels. On March 31 he suffers a stroke that paralyzes half his body. Friends carry him back to the hotel. A few days later he develops aphasia. When Baudelaire finally boards a train for Paris, leaving Brussels and the Hôtel du Grand Miroir, he is a ghost of himself. His smooth and closely shaven face has never been so pale. With his white hair, his unwrinkled features, and his withered body, he is a zombie staring fixedly ahead in complete silence. The longer the silence lasts, the more piercing his gaze becomes. Sometimes, barely opening his lips, he utters a repeated sound, a kind of croak that his friends finally decipher: *"Crecoeur, Crecoeur."* He is not even able to pronounce the words *Sacré-Coeur.*

I WANT TO CRY CALLING OUT MY NAME. He had once written: "Sometimes I am overcome by a desire to sleep for an infinite time." Baudelaire spends the last year of his life in a room in a sanatorium, by a window overlooking a garden. On the wall there is a painting by his friend Manet and a reproduction of one of Goya's portraits of the Duchess of Alba. Only his eyes and the set of his mouth remain unchanged: his lips are pressed together in the same attitude of concealed stubbornness, arrogance, disdain; his eyes are filled with an impenetrable solitude. Those eyes, that mouth, the outsize forehead and the weak chin, that face that seems so strangely naked can be seen in all of Nadar's photographs and especially in the portrait by Fantin-Latour. Years earlier he had translated a short story by Poe in which a man, hypnotized during his final agony, continues to heed commands and to reply in a hideous muttering voice from the other side of death. What took place in Baudelaire's mind and in his imagination during that last year of his life cannot be known—what dreams he had, what lasting visions in the grip of opium, what poems and what imprecations must have briefly taken shape in him and vanished instantly. When his friends came to visit he would stare at them fixedly, as much of a stranger among them as in Fantin-Latour's group portrait. Occasionally he would grip someone's hand and stare at him without blinking. He would open his mouth and seem about to speak, but in the end the words never formed inside his throat or on his lips. Sometimes he managed to say a few simple things, *"Oui, Monsieur," "Bonjour, Monsieur,"* mimicking an acquiescence that had never been part of his character. Sometimes the photographer Nadar came by and took him to a dinner with friends. Baudelaire remained motionless, docile, impassive, sitting at a corner of the table amid loud laughter, conversation, bottles of wine and clouds of cigar smoke. He became his own wax statue: pale, smooth-skinned, close-shaven, with an old man's scrawny neck rising from an open collar that was now too wide, his eyes as fixed as if they were made of glass.

I DON'T KNOW WHAT IT IS OR HOW YOU SAY IT. One day, when Nadar came looking for him at the sanatorium, he silently refused to leave. He didn't move his head, just pressed his lips together and looked away. Soon after, he stopped getting out of bed. He lay under the sheets that came up to his waxen face. His mouth stayed firmly shut. No words came out of it anymore, and barely any sounds. His eyes stayed fixed on the ceiling. When people visited he turned his face toward them, seemed to heed whatever trivial words of comfort they would say, then turn his face back to the wall. He began to develop sores and ulcers on his back from lying in bed so much. He squirmed in pain and discomfort but never let out a single moan or complaint. When he died, no one realized it in time to close his eyes. They stayed open even in the coffin.

YOU CAN'T IMAGINE WHAT AWAITS YOU. The metal detector goes off as I walk through. But I placed my watch, wallet, cell phone, and keys in the tray. I go through again and the same thing happens. A security guard tells me to stand with my feet apart and raise my arms. The wand beeps when it touches my hips. Then I realize that I was carrying a pencil sharpener in my pocket. The guard holds it between a gloved finger and thumb, inspecting it while keeping an eye on me as well. She says with scornful magnanimity that I can gather the metal objects from the tray, studying the tiny pencil sharpener as if it might contain an explosive device. Just as she drops it in a plastic bag, a different alarm goes off somewhere else. A guard stationed at the X-ray scanner lifts a backpack and asks who the owner is. They have stopped the belt. Another guard is setting a suitcase upright. The backpack and suitcase are mine. When I raise my hand to let them know, the guard who took away the pencil sharpener looks at me no longer disapprovingly but with open contempt. Standing in my socks, holding my belt in one hand and hitching up my pants with the other while I try not to lose sight of my shoes, cell phone, and jacket in their respective plastic trays, I must face the guard who set my backpack aside and the one who lifts my suitcase from the conveyor belt, surprised to find it weigh so much despite its small size.

BECOME A BMW LEGEND. Luggage is beginning to back up, as is the line of tired and impatient travelers. Some look at me accusingly once they realize that I am the reason for the holdup. Yet another guard, stockier and even more serious than the rest, tells me to step aside and go to a separate table. He asks me in a procedural tone if the suitcase and backpack belong to me and if anyone, whether an acquaintance or a stranger, helped me pack them or was in possession of them at any time. I say no, trying to put on my belt and slip my feet into my shoes without bending down while maintaining eye contact with the guard. He asks if I am carrying any liquids or metal objects and I say no and then immediately regret it. He unzips a pocket on the backpack and extracts a pair of scissors and the tiny metal barrel of a pencil sharpener, the kind that stores the shavings in a little compartment. The guard opens the lid inquisitively and the shavings fall and flutter to the ground around him. He looks at me as if expecting an explanation. I stay silent, continuing to slide the belt blindly around my waist, which is quite hard.

FIND EVERYTHING YOU NEED. The guard closes the pencil sharpener and sets it carefully aside. Then he proceeds to the scissors. They are short, blunt scissors with plastic handles, almost like the kind children would use at day care. The guard slides a gloved finger along the edge of the blade and gives me a look that feels somewhat accusing. "Sharp metal objects are forbidden," he says. I feel a little relieved because I have managed to buckle my belt and put on my shoes, though the laces are still untied. I try to pluck up my courage and say that I was allowed to carry the scissors through other security checkpoints before, but I keep quiet. Now he sets the backpack aside, though he does not return it, and he tells me to open the suitcase. He asks again if I am carrying liquids or metal objects and I say no, but he no longer believes anything I say. He feels under the folded clothes and slips his hand into a pocket, taking out the inkwell and giving it a shake before my eyes. He unscrews the lid and sniffs the ink before screwing it back on. Holding the inkwell in a gloved hand, he looks at me sternly and asks me what it is. "An inkwell," I say. I make an effort to speak clearly, to pronounce the English word correctly: *inkwell.*

BE THE FIRST TO OWN IT. He sets it down next to the scissors and the pencil sharpener as carefully as if he were handling incriminating evidence. He proceeds slowly on purpose, to make me nervous, to let me know that he is in charge, and can make me miss my flight if he so wishes.

Luckily I came to the airport quite early. One by one he empties all the notebooks from the suitcase. He opens them as if looking for something hidden between the pages. Clippings, tickets, and loose notes fall out, which are of interest, though for the moment he chooses to disregard all of them except one: a heavily underlined newspaper article about the Islamist attack in Nice. He looks at the various papers and he looks at me. He opens a flat cardboard box that used to hold a cell phone charger, and out come dozens of flyers for erotic services and African fortune-tellers that I collected in Madrid. He looks at the flyers and he looks at me. He puts them back in the box. Now he asks for my passport, my boarding pass, and a document showing proof of residence or stating the motive of my stay in the United States. I show him my green card, to no effect. I show him an ID card from the university where I worked for a time. As a document it is partly false, since I no longer work there, but it expires in two years so it is not entirely improper to produce it. A minor and harmless deception. "Are there any other metal objects in your suitcase?"

RELAX YOUR SENSES. I was going to say no, but I no longer dare. One has seen so many movies that it seems better to remain silent and not say anything that can be used against me. From the bottom of the suitcase, beneath the huge biography of Baudelaire, the guard accusingly removes the splendid case of twenty-four colored pencils, a thin metallic box, more elegant even than the MacBook Air. Holding the case in one hand, standing over the open suitcase and backpack and surrounded by clippings, pencil shavings, erasers, notebooks, and pencils, the guard looks me up and down and asks what I do for a living. I have to make a large mental adjustment: he is not older than I am; he is not an adult invested with authority and facing a defenseless young man. He is the young one, and I am a gray-haired man of sixty-one. "What do you do for a living?" he says, beginning to put everything away carefully and in reverse order, except the scissors and the inkwell.

CONNECT WITH WHAT YOU REALLY LIKE. Now my office is the minimal space of the tray table next to the window, beneath the lonely overhead light in the darkened cabin. I ate almost none of my dinner and I'm not sleepy. I took a sleeping pill, but the space is so tight and the seat so uncomfortable that it will be impossible to rest. My office is the tray table, the pencil, the open notebook. Later on it's the laptop where I read Spanish newspapers with all the expectancy of impending return. I made the mistake of purchasing Wi-Fi. There was a time when you would set off on a transatlantic journey and know that you were isolated from the outside world for many hours, in a state of perfect indolence that you couldn't be faulted for since it was forced on you. Now there is no solitude, no silence, no respite. Online banners, photographs and videos open around the articles or even suddenly inside them without prior notice. I should have sat still with my eyes closed, or continued reading the biography of Baudelaire. Nervous stimulation tires you out and simultaneously makes it impossible to rest. Spanish voices, heard again after two months, seem as intrusive in the restless dark, amid the faint breathing and stirring of bodies, as the loud headlines and the online ads. Now, suddenly, so close to the end, on the eve of return, I feel afraid that they will never fade again, those voices that were so intoxicating in the past few months, after I began to notice them a year ago, like a scientist inoculating himself with an excessive dose of the pathogen whose antidote he was hoping to find. The voices surround me still, as if they came from the sleeping bodies in the cabin.

CONNECT FROM WHEREVER YOU WANT. The man shot dead at the Paris Orly Airport yelled, "I am here to die in the name of Allah." The theft of a Secret Service laptop worries American authorities. Marine Le Pen is the favored candidate for young French people between the ages of eighteen and twenty-four. A woman accuses her ex-boyfriend of pouring glue on her vagina. Two elderly people die when their house burns down in Alicante. Angelina Jolie buys a twenty-five-million-dollar mansion to start a new life. The mystery of the sixty-one infant skeletons found on a beach remains unsolved. Police kill a man who tried to take a soldier's gun at Orly airport. Celebrities reap the gains of their social media following. Astrologer Susan Miller is an internet sensation. The actor who played the Red Power Ranger confesses that he is guilty of murder. A wave of robberies in Los Angeles claims Kendall Jenner's jewelry. Jude Law says the war in Syria must end. Emily Ratajkowski walks the streets of New York in her underwear. A brothel featuring realistic sex dolls opens in Barcelona. An Algerian novelist is charged with blasphemy. Fake-meat scandal reaches Brazilian supermarkets. Torrential rains affect sixty thousand people in Peru. Fifteen bodies found in a ditch inside a jail outside Caracas. Arrested after hitting his wife on the head with a hammer in front of their baby. Victoria Beckham registers her daughter's name Harper as a trademark. The man taken into custody in Antwerp after trying to run down a crowd of pedestrians had a rifle in his car. Police detain a man dressed as Hitler in the German dictator's native town. Scarlett Johansson opens a gourmet popcorn store in Paris. Officers who shot and killed an unarmed Black man in Louisiana are freed without charges. A group of apes kills its former leader, returned from exile, and cannibalizes his body. A segment of the Appian Way is found beneath a McDonald's.

TO MAKE US ENJOY THE GOOD TIMES. And what can you do in the midst of it all? What use are your childish avocations, your love of the task, placing one word after another, drawing or composing a sentence as carefully as possible and then, after placing a period, starting another until a page is filled, and then a notebook, and then another? But not just that; also everything you never used to notice, thinking it was insignificant or unworthy of your work: making the bed in the morning after opening the bedroom window to let in the clean, cold air; appreciating what you would never have discovered on your own, the beauty of immediate and ordinary things; preparing a good meal for your loved ones and cleaning the kitchen as you go, setting everything in order just as you clean your desk or as you clean a sentence of errors and distractions or superfluous adjectives. What can you do? What depends on you? To what degree does it matter or mean anything, what you do, what you have done for so many years? Many of the finest works ever written, painted, or composed received no attention and resulted in no spiritual or moral benefit or reward for their authors. Many more than you think must have disappeared without a trace.

REALITY SURPASSES THE IMAGINATION. What to do, then? What is the impulse that guides you? What justifies you in this task to which you devote your life, often for days on end, without pause, from the moment you wake up to the moment you go to bed, and before that, too, and also after? Terrible things are happening in the world at every moment. For a writer or an artist to be ignored is a laughable misfortune. People are tortured and hanged in underground jails in Syria. Central American immigrants are robbed and murdered on that terrible train they call The Beast. People drown in the Mediterranean trying to cross from Africa to the shores of southern Europe. Walls and barbed-wire fences rise along international borders, lit by searchlights at night, equipped with automatic sensors and patrolled by soldiers and police with attack dogs and automatic weapons. A cement wall can split between two worlds an olive grove in Palestine as small and as carefully tended as the one my father had on the road to Granada. Helicopters and armored ATVs give chase to emigrants who manage to cross the border into the deserts of Texas and California. A girl's face is burned with acid in Afghanistan because she wants to go to school. A gang of five drunken men rapes a girl at a barbaric Spanish feast day, recording it on their cell phones and egging each other on as they take turns, then gloating about their exploit on the internet. Another terrifying gang of men tortures a hippopotamus for an entire night in a filthy tank at the San Salvador zoo, using axes, hammers, even a chainsaw. A sperm whale washes ashore on a beach that looks like a picture in a travel brochure; it has starved to death and they find sixty pounds of plastic bags inside its stomach. In the middle of the Pacific, on the Midway Islands, the most remote from any landmass, the albatross feed their young with plastic cigarette lighters that they find floating in the ocean and mistake for squid, which are their usual food. A demagogue with a head of dyed-blond hair runs as a candidate in the Dutch elections and is enthusiastically supported by ignorant and resentful crowds. Political demagogues crop up and multiply across the world like an epidemic of terrifying clowns. So far they can be identified by the utter shamelessness with which they incite hatred and by their big yellow hair.

NEVER HAVE FISH AND PLANKTON IN THE MEDITERRANEAN FED ON SO MANY HUMAN BEINGS. And what do you do in the meantime? How do you not give up and hide? Where do you find not just the strength but the rationale to devote yourself to this, to be always doing what you're doing even now, in an airplane seat at two in the morning under a reading light, so uncomfortably that it borders on contortionism, surrounded by sleeping bodies in the dark while leaning over an open notebook on a folding tray that shakes with the smallest turbulence? The pencil I was using got so small that it was hard to hold. In the backpack I found another pencil that I bought in Lisbon, with a thick lead. The kind of pencil a carpenter might use. It forces me to write in a larger hand, more loosely, with a more expansive gesture. It makes a thick line and it wears rapidly, so I have to keep the pencil sharpener ready. Luckily I always carry a few. It is a tradesman's or an artist's pencil, tending to make diffuse marks rather than lines; a pencil that pulls me along, carrying me at full speed over the notebook's pages and covering them with writing in an instant, so I have to turn them quickly. The sound it makes on the paper is richer and more nuanced, a sound of crumbling matter. If I knew how to draw I could use this pencil to create shade and volume. What am I doing with this pencil at two in the morning, as far from arriving anywhere as I am from having left, thirty thousand feet above the Atlantic, overexcited by lack of sleep, listening to the scratching sound of a pencil on a piece of paper beneath the giant roar of airplane engines?

JOIN THE MECHANICAL REVOLUTION. How am I able to overcome the insecurity that comes back so often without warning to paralyze and batter me; the fear that the result of my efforts may be well below my aspirations; the general dismay at seeing how little room is left for literature? I live in this world, and not another. In this time. The fact that I am foreign to it, or feel that way, grants me no immunity. An immigration officer can lock me up in an airport cell if I seem suspicious. An inspired fanatic can set off an explosive vest next to me while I have a cup of coffee at a sidewalk table in Paris or Madrid. As I sit writing with my pencil, deaf even to the roar of the plane, Donald Trump and his new accomplices will be plotting at some secret meeting of new ways to despoil the rivers, the earth, and the air. Any creep can defame you with a phrase on Twitter. Nearly everything you love is at risk of disappearing. You can't even enjoy an escape into nostalgia, since you know there never was in fact a better time. You feel nostalgia not for things that happened but for what might have taken place; not for what was, but for what without too much difficulty might have been. While those people destroy the world, increasing their wealth immensely through the destitution of the vast majority of human beings, you want to build something, to see something through. It will not require you to squander resources or to exploit anyone else. Chances are it will also be entirely useless. The most you can aspire to is to provide some stranger with a little company.

A JOURNEY TO THE HEART. On the subway, sitting across from me a few days ago, a young woman was reading a Samuel Beckett novel with evident excitement. An old woman, my mother, slowly and laboriously reads the novel that Elena Fortún was never able to publish, recognizing in its pages the bitter capitulations as well as the secret pride of her own life. In a squalid cell in Birmingham, Alabama, Martin Luther King Jr. strengthens his will to resist by reading Thoreau's "On Civil Disobedience." Those same pages had been read, sixty years earlier and in a different cell in South Africa, by a young lawyer who was not yet known as Mahatma Gandhi. An unknown work can survive like a buried seed to multiply and spread through secret channels, finally bursting into the light after a very long time. In his last days fleeing through France, Walter Benjamin took solace and distracted himself by reading *Le rouge et le noir*. At age seven, Stendhal finds a copy of *Don Quixote* in the gloomy house where his father took him when his mother died. Reading the adventure of the windmills, he finds himself laughing out loud for the first time since her death. You do what you want, or what you can, or what you can't help yourself from doing, and you give it your all. But you can't know what the result will be, nor are there guarantees of any kind. Trendy, mediocre works are usually acclaimed. Truly good ones are overlooked for such a long time that when their qualities are finally recognized the author may be long dead, in which case some rich collector will make even more money by buying and selling what was crafted in obscure poverty. One of Poe's many desperate letters begging for a small loan or pestering editors for his pay can be sold at auction for half a million dollars. A copy of the first edition of *Ulysses* is worth $450,000 because it was kept in a safe for eighty years, suffering no deterioration and losing none of the rich blue tint of the original cover. A Basquiat painting of crowned Black heroes and boxers hangs on a thieving Russian oligarch's bathroom wall.

ALL PATHS THAT LEAD TO MADNESS. Nor should you think that failure and obscurity are proof of talent simply because they frequently go together. You may be neglected and be worse than someone who enjoys great success or a measure of recognition. Your love for literature need not be requited. Your zeal and your devotion to the task do not mean that the end result will be memorable. Perhaps you won a prize because they didn't want to give it to someone else. And if you didn't win a prize you thought you deserved, it doesn't mean you're better than the one who did. You have no certainty. You never will. The one who praises you may be lying or lacking in judgment. The one who makes a painful and negative remark may be right. You do what you can, not what you want, and you do it because you can't help it. Nobody asked you to. Nobody owes you anything. Some will find it laughable, even reprehensible, that at a time of so many urgent social causes and terrible injustice you devote all this effort to something that is primarily justified aesthetically, beginning and ending with itself: a good painting, when there were still generally accepted criteria to judge paintings; a sonnet that meets at least the objective demands of meter and rhyme. As a teenager I was very impressed by some of Gabriel Celaya's verses: "I could write a perfect poem / but it would be indecent in our times." Why indecent? How can it be indecent to do something well? And what are the grounds for such arrogance? Is perfection such a simple thing? Are you so sure of attaining it simply because you decide to pursue it?

WHY GO SOMEWHERE ELSE WHEN EVERYTHING IS RIGHT HERE? But this is all just lack of sleep, the flight, the pleasant Portuguese pencil and the sound it makes, the wide pages of the notebook and the single malt I ordered after dinner, to compensate for the airplane food and to forget I ever ate it. It's just the oceanic darkness in the window and the single light above me, the light of airplane cabins, that so resembles the light in a religious allegory. I am absurdly reminded of Caravaggio's *Saint Matthew*. My right hand and arm ache from so much writing. I have a callus on the first joint of my middle finger like the one I had as a schoolboy. The noise of the engines and the shaking of the tray table have been communicated to my skull. Walter Benjamin, shortly before France fell, wrote in a letter to his friend Scholem that every well-made essay or article one could write and publish in those circumstances was a barrier against the forces of darkness. Sick, and nearly mad, Baudelaire took a final melancholy pride in having devoted his whole life to a single task, the crafting of well-made sentences. You, for your part, will not be hounded by hunger, syphilis, the gestapo, or the NKVD. There is no risk, at least for now, that a tyrant's henchmen will come at midnight to confiscate what you have written, to lock you up in a cell and sentence you to twenty years in a camp above the Arctic Circle, or just shoot you in the back of the head, not without first making it clear that they will also ruin, because of you, the lives of everyone you love. You enjoy a great privilege. A group of religious fanatics in Nicaragua burns a woman alive because they think she's possessed by the devil, but nothing like that can happen to you. No one has a sense of proportion when judging personal misfortunes. In one of his songs, Leonard Cohen sarcastically compares the calamity of the European Jews to the bad reviews his albums occasionally receive. The self-centered friend to whom you just bared your soul, telling him that you were diagnosed with cancer or that the love of your life has left you, may go on to complain about what poor reception he gets on his cell phone. But you will not be arrested or stoned to death because of what you write; in part, of course, because what you write, what anyone like you is capable of writing, is not worth the slightest concern. One of the great misfortunes for dissident writers in the Soviet Union was that Stalin held literature in such respect.

WEAR YOUR BEST SMILE. Meanwhile, here's Marine Le Pen, contending for the French election, and Donald Trump with his gold Lex Luthor hairpiece, misgoverning the world like a megalomaniacal villain out of a cheap novel, a Goldfinger, a Doctor No.

TIME TO DAZZLE. I have closed the notebook. My wrist hurts from writing. I have turned off the reading light. I shut my eyes but I can't fall asleep. The words and voices I gathered for so long—copying, clipping them with scissors, gluing them into seamless mosaics, storing them in cardboard boxes—keep up a steady murmur that I am no longer able to stop. Live authentically. Enjoy a free exclusive experience. Take control. Call us, we can help. I want to focus only on the moment of arrival, the incredible fact that in a few hours I will be in Madrid, in my other life, my real one, my house. The comfort you deserve. The house of your dreams. Where you want to be. Like my friend the scientist who collects bits of ocean trash, I fear I have fallen into an intoxicating compulsion, an obsession from which I can no longer break free. There is a toxic quality to all those voices that seem to whisper only in my ear, to be directed just at me. Hearing voices that no one else can hear is a sure sign of a mental disorder. There may be a form of madness that makes it impossible to forget them, to stop listening to them, and sweep them from your mind and memory. Choose the bundle that suits you. Bring us your old cell phone. The messages disperse and seem to vanish, but their substance, the toxic compounds they contain, persist even more insidiously because they are invisible to the naked eye, like plastic microparticles lodged in the tissues of marine animals or like amphetamines, antibiotics, and antidepressants excreted in human urine to travel through pipes and water-treatment plants to the sea. Verbal trash builds up in the brain like heavy metals on the muddy ocean floor. It's not an intellectual but a physical condition. A kind of nausea or malaise similar to the boundless fatigue that came over me during the last days in New York, something as immediate as the first signs of food poisoning. Deep sleep can flush it out. But it has been a long time since I slept with any real sense of rest, plunging into genuine oblivion. I'm not sure how many hours I have been awake. It is no longer New York time, nor is it six hours later in Madrid. When my eyes close I am in complete temporal darkness. Take charge. Experience control. Only sleep and genuine company will heal me. The truth is that I can only sleep now if I'm with her. Living alone for a long time in the thick closeness of the self is like working in a cellar or a pit. The only antidote to ghosts is a genuine human presence. Only the voice of someone dear, the real voice of friendship and affection, can dispel or push away those other voices that no one else can hear but you.

NOW YOU CAN BE THREE INCHES TALLER WITHOUT ANYONE KNOWING. This is the shortened, interrupted night of return. I open my eyes and look at the phone in total darkness. It says it's two o'clock in the morning. It seems like the trip and the night will last a good while longer. Then suddenly the lights come on, breakfast is hastily served to a bunch of crammed, befuddled passengers like animals in an industrial cattle farm. The window shades go up, a flood of unexpected sunlight fills the cabin as the airplane tips sideways for landing.

FEEL LIFE THROUGH YOUR EARS. I walk very quickly through the vast empty spaces of the terminal, faster still down a moving ramp. Panoramic windows show a landscape of arid hills bathed in a kind of desert light. I overtake the other passengers, who are dazed with sleep or lost in an airport that is so unpleasant the first time you are there. I walk with instinctive assurance, knowing that I am in my country, my world, Europe. I am not afraid of the policemen or the immigration officers. I won't see anywhere the ostentation of American flags or the official portrait of the yellow-haired megalomaniac. I barely have to stop at passport control. The sign that says EUROPEAN UNION CITIZENS always fills me with joy. I am able to go even faster because I didn't check a bag and am not forced to endure, as many times before, a grim wait at early dawn by a baggage belt that will not start. Lack of sleep, and being back, fill me with a light and floating sense of unmoored clarity, as in a dream. Polished floors and gliding ramps assist my progress. Elevators and moving stairways spare me any effort, like obliging porters in the time of the Orient Express. Automatic doors swiftly fly apart when I approach. As soon as you step outside an airport terminal you notice a country's smell: the arrivals hall at JFK smells of fast food, fried grease, hot pizza dough. The first waft of early morning air in Madrid carries a Spanish smell of tobacco and coffee with milk.

LEARN TO READ YOUR BODY. At the taxi stand I barely have to wait. As soon as the driver opens the trunk, I place my bag inside, heavy with all the notebooks. Everything is on a smaller scale. People are not as tall, or muscular, or obese. Cars are smaller and drive faster over an immaculate highway. Everything is quick and simple. The city lies in a lazy calm that makes it seem like Sunday morning. "Everyone's left town for Easter," says the taxi driver in a strong Spanish accent that I always find a little startling when I return from a trip.

TRY ON A NEW IDENTITY. I used to arrive at this same time of day during those first years when I didn't yet live permanently in Madrid. I would spend the whole night on the train and see the sun rise as the taxi drove through the city. If I came by plane, on the first morning flight, I got as little sleep the night before as if I had taken the train, from eagerness and impatience, or worrying that the alarm would not go off or that I would fail to hear it. The moment of arrival and delight was also the moment the countdown to departure began. But during those first hours, that first day, time was an untouched treasure, a bright, safe home, the one she had arranged in every detail with all her care, with all her instinct for beauty and light. It was our shared house, even if I was only there for part of the year. We furnished it together and we split the rent in affirmation of our life together despite the distance or the time we had to be apart. I would set the suitcase on the floor and open the front door with my key, and as I stepped inside I would be met by morning sunlight and a faint perfume of cleanliness that was already like taking in a deep breath of the nearness of her body. Places change over the years, pictures in an album. But the feeling of arrival and of warmth remains the same: the purity of space, the sense that the air itself is tinged by her presence. Sometimes I arrived after a tiring journey or a bad hotel night, discouraged by some problem in my work, some setback, oppressed by some commitment, or by fear or regret. Sometimes I was tired, sleepless, hungry, filled with desire, in need of shelter and reprieve and absolution. The particulars fade, though they are meaningful and do not deserve to be lost. Early on I would write down each time we met or had sex. I should remember how she wore her hair on a certain morning, what perfume she had on, what we said to each other when we met, assuming there was any time to speak; what the house was like, what the view was from the balcony or from the window. Everything is reduced to a few decisive strokes, like a tale whose essence is preserved through very different retellings: the trip, the early morning in Madrid, the house when I arrived, and how I gazed and breathed its calm, and then the passionate encounter, the darkened room, the day outside, the gifts I'd brought with me: a pair of earrings, a cigarette lighter, a tin boat in bright colors, a terracotta horse from China, the silk robe, the one with the red flowers.

REVITALIZE YOUR SKIN. Now the taxi comes to a stop. Two months ago I took a different taxi at this same time of day and in the opposite direction. Everything is the same and everything has changed. It was a colder morning, but the light was just as clear as now. The first time Louis Armstrong went back to his house in Queens after a tour he was so moved that he couldn't get out of the cab. He and his wife had bought the house not long before. For the first time in his life, past the age of fifty, he was about to go into a house that belonged to him. He looked out the window at the fence, the small yard, the brick facade, and could not bring himself to step out of the car. The taxi driver grabs my suitcase from the trunk and is surprised to find it weighs so much despite it being a carry-on. There is a sequence of continuous motions, as at the airport earlier; a fluid, everyday choreography. The doorman helps me carry the suitcase and backpack up the front steps, then he holds open the elevator door and closes it behind me. My heart is beating very fast.

YOU STILL HAVE TIME. It took me a few seconds to find the key. I couldn't remember where I put it in the backpack two months earlier. I opened the door and was met by the clear light of early morning. The sun has just come up over the rooftops across the street. The house still smells like new, the light that comes in through the windows makes the varnished floor gleam. Draw the house you want to live in. Draw a blueprint of your desire. Each object, each book on the shelves by the entrance has been carefully chosen by her. Even the curved Japanese plate for the keys. I take it all in, rapidly and slowly, as if time were standing still. To see the apartment and breathe in the air is already like seeing her, like entering into her life, witnessing beforehand her simple gestures and the way she moves and speaks; like sensing with complete immediacy the peculiar quality of her soul and the cast of her intelligence, seeing her and at the same time seeing everything else through her eyes. Lorca writes in a letter: "Draw a blueprint of your desire, and live there always under a rule of beauty."

TELL US WHAT YOU'RE LOOKING FOR AND WE'LL FIND IT. I looked up and saw in her eyes the same surprise as mine at this unannounced encounter. But if I happened to look up just then, in that particular direction, it was because I was sharply and unconsciously warned by my sense of hearing and perhaps of smell. "I didn't know you'd be here so soon." She stands there in the silk robe with red flowers, sleepy and surprised, her hair a little tousled. The robe has stayed intact through all these years, from the very beginning, the first encounter, across so many cities, countries, different houses and hotels, departures and returns. The colors have not faded, the fabric has not frayed or lost its sheen. It has only grown more supple, more inviting, closer to her skin which has burnished it with its ceaseless touch; warm silk and flushed skin sliding on each other over the years without wilting or fading; silk falling to her feet like a spreading circle of petals when she undoes the belt; when the robe, ebbing from her shoulders, slides with ease along her body to the floor, spilling as she rises, as she puts her hands around my neck and brings her mouth to mine.

AN IDEAL PLACE TO HIDE. I am all ears, in the silent bedroom where the warmth of bodies is preserved after the night is over, in the early Sunday calm. I want to hear her newfound voice in my ear and my own voice whispering into hers. I am all ears, all eyes to look at her, all hands and fingertips, a body clasped to hers. There is a strange sterility to a body that doesn't touch another. Trace the outline of her face with your fingers, trace her chin, her nose and mouth, the shape of her smile as it begins to form across her lips. I am suddenly aware, just as they vanish, of all the anxiety and fatigue of work and travel, the loneliness of those long walks, like an unpleasant and incessant noise that only becomes perceptible when it stops, so that only as silence spreads like a miracle do we notice it is gone. This is my house, my island. Nothing will happen to me here. We are each other's shelter. Memory remembers poorly, or imprecisely, obscurely, without sensory qualities. I had not remembered her face properly, her voice, even less the things we cannot see or hear, the particular feel of her skin, the smell of her hair, the taste of her mouth. When she whispers my name, I am no longer nobody. When I say hers, I am no longer invoking a ghost or a dream.

SINCE AT ANY GIVEN TIME AND PLACE. It was the first summer of my adult life. For the first time I had a job, a paycheck, a place of my own. It was a rental apartment in a bland, recently built and nearly uninhabited development on the outskirts of Granada. The only bus that went there had to drive through empty fields and past the very last of the city's working-class neighborhoods, the Polígono de Cartuja. Part of the area had paved roads and streetlights that turned on at night, but no buildings. There was a single, dreary store. It sold everything and it languished in the general desolation. The few pieces of furniture in my apartment were as blank and featureless as the many identical buildings you could see through the windows. The development had been christened with one of those auspicious names so typical of the time, Nueva Granada Park. The word *Granada* was almost as unreal as the word *Park*. Some of the passageways between buildings resembled strange streets without any front doors. With my first paycheck I made a down payment on a rather large tape deck that sported the novelty of having detachable speakers. Mostly I listened to tapes that my friends made for me. One of these friends, a great music lover, had introduced me to Monteverdi's *Il ritorno d'Ulisse in patria*. I would listen by turns to Monteverdi, Charles Mingus, Lou Reed (*Rock 'n' Roll Animal*), Patti Smith (*Horses*), and a small-time band from Madrid called Leño. I also paid the first installment on the Summa Artis encyclopedia, which I had read avidly as a student at the university library. Each evening after dinner I would read a chapter. During those first few months of my new working life I read the entire volume on prehistoric art and the one on ancient Egypt. For some reason I got bogged down forever in Mesopotamia.

WHERE YOUR MOST SECRET FANTASIES. After fourteen months of military service in the Basque country at the bloodiest height of terrorism, it was not an entirely simple matter to adapt back to reality. Also, to the fact that I was no longer a student, that I had to wake up early each morning and go to an office. I was grateful to have a job, and at the same time I tried to adapt my expectations to the constraints of real life. Earning just enough to live was not discouraging, since I'd never had much before. What did worry me was that the job was precarious; I had been given a one-year contract that was not renewable. Also, that my vocation seemed to be going nowhere.

WITH A NEWFOUND EASE. I wrote short stories set in the countryside and partly inspired by Juan Rulfo, or stories in which the mundane and the fantastic came together in the manner of Julio Cortázar. By the end of my military service I had an unfinished draft of a novel that I rarely thought about anymore, though I kept it in a couple of binders stuffed with typed pages and rough handwritten drafts. Now and then I submitted stories to provincial writing contests that did not seem hard to win, but where I never even made the short list: the City of San Sebastián Prize, the City of Motril, etc. I wrote a few lyrics for a friend who sang flamenco, and for a novice rock band.

YOU WANTED TO COME BACK. That summer I spent the afternoons lying in bed in my rented apartment, listening to tapes or reading, so absorbed in books and so inwardly discouraged by my love of literature that I barely wrote anything. I just read. I read crime novels. I read Baudelaire and Thomas De Quincey: *Paris Spleen*, *Artificial Paradises*, *Confessions of an English Opium-Eater*. I must have learned about De Quincey from Borges. I started reading Baudelaire because Francisco Umbral called himself an admirer and a disciple. Umbral's daily column in *El País*, which I read faithfully, was titled "Madrid Spleen."

416

EVERYTHING FITS IN A POCKETBOOK. Those three books cast such a spell on me that I even stopped reading crime novels. They were like nothing I had seen before. They had great narrative pull, but they were not novels and didn't even seem like works of fiction. They were not books of verse, either, but there was a poetic force in them as ravishing as in Lorca's *Poeta en Nueva York*. There was a testimonial quality to Baudelaire and De Quincey and at the same time a visionary fierceness, as if they were wounded, torn apart, swaying constantly between sharp-edged clarity and delirium. You could take these books with you and read them in spurts, on the bus that took me into town each morning or while having breakfast at a café, even in the office on August mornings when things were slow. As with a book of poems, each reading made them richer and more surprising, disclosing new treasures. And you could read them out of order, as if the chapters were poems falling into new arrangements as random as they were decisive, creating unexpected sequences of inner echoes and connections.

CHOOSE YOUR OWN ADVENTURE. Despite their power, none of the three books awakened in me the spirit of imitation that had been with me since adolescence. I would read a story by Borges and immediately find myself writing something similar, a kind of parody, from the plot to the choice and placement of adjectives. If I read Cortázar, I wrote Cortázar stories. If I read Rulfo, I wrote Rulfo stories. If I read Chandler, I wanted to create a lonely, sarcastic detective with an office on the Gran Vía de Granada. It's a world that has grown distant, the summer of 1981.

BEHIND EVERY DOOR. It was different with Baudelaire and De Quincey. They both affected me deeply even though there was no relation between their writing and my life. But their voices were so unique that they did not allow themselves to be imitated. It was a music too original and deep for anyone to extract a simple melody that might be copied. A true influence is much more than a particular aesthetic teaching or the emulation of a literary form or style; it is a sudden awakening into the world's immediate reality, discovering anew and as if from its deepest sources the worth of words and images, the categorical purity of the original names of things. I had been living in Granada for seven years when one day that summer, steeped in Baudelaire and De Quincey, I saw the city for the first time. I saw what stood before my eyes and I saw myself from the outside. In my pocket there was an envelope with a month's pay. It was cash; not much of it, but still comforting in its concreteness. I had spent the morning in the office, my boss was gone and it was August, so almost no one came. I had eaten at a cheap local place where I was already a regular. I crossed the Gran Vía and went down the Zacatín, shady and cool on that relatively mild afternoon. My head was filled with De Quincey's vexed peregrinations down Oxford Street and Baudelaire's through Paris; with their ecstatic glimpses of urban beauty and noise, their raptures, their visions of opium and hunger. When I came to the Plaza Bib-Rambla, it was as if I had landed in a strange seaside town, exotic and unknown, a dazzling souk somewhere on the Silk Road. The same square I'd crossed so many times before seemed aflame with beauty. The lime trees, the flocks of birds, the flower stands, the sound of water in the fountain, the hulking tower of the cathedral rising high over the rooftops, the bronze angel with his sword above the chapel of the Tabernacle, the clamor of voices blending with the noise of water and the song of birds, young women wearing miniskirts again now that it was summer, the shining pulp of figs that Gypsy women dunked in buckets of cold water before they peeled and sliced them, the big bright billboard for Winston cigarettes with Rita Hayworth in the black dress she wore for *Gilda*.

VOYAGE AU BOUT DE SOI-MÊME. Baudelaire's invitation to a voyage was happening to me in my own city, free of charge and just a few blocks from the office where I worked. I looked and listened to the city until my mind began to dissolve in it as in an opium dream, and I could see myself as well from the outside. I saw the silhouette of a man walking alone in the crowd. A prince in disguise, says Baudelaire, a homeless man, a spy, an opium addict, a photographer, a foreign agent following strangers, a kindly man moving through Dublin with a potato in the pocket of his coat, a man in love, turning every corner with a shudder of anticipation, a man come back from far away, from other lives and regions of time, a castaway shipwrecked in the city's desert island, blinkered with thick glasses like Pessoa or like Benjamin, always carrying a satchel, large, and worn, and dark, from which he will never part.